DARYL J BALL

THE NAME OF THE BEAR

Published 2019 by Daryl J. Ball
Copyright © 2019 Daryl J. Ball

Cover by Ravenborn Cover Designs
Book Design by Lia Rees at Free Your Words
(www.freeyourwords.com)

ISBN: 978-0-9959668-9-5

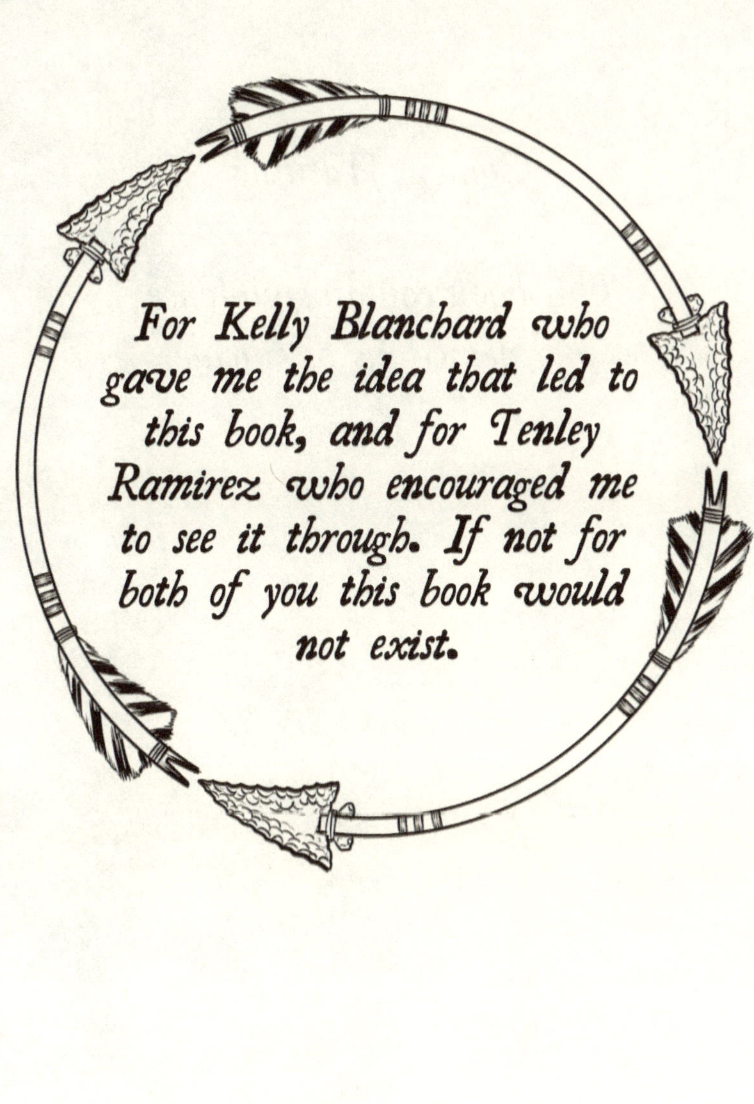

For Kelly Blanchard who gave me the idea that led to this book, and for Tenley Ramirez who encouraged me to see it through. If not for both of you this book would not exist.

THE NAME OF THE BEAR

ONE

Chapter 1
Mochan

The large brown bear padded along the grassy terrain, pausing on occasion to sniff the air. There was little doubt in Mochan's mind that the bear was aware of his presence. It was the first animal that had come along in quite some time. Despite being alone, if Mochan wanted any hope of not being seen as a disgrace to the hunters when he got home, he would have to attempt to kill the creature. How he could even do so, he was not sure, but for the rest of the people of the village of Meadhan, he had to at least try. Mochan adjusted his stance, checking that his hair was still tied back, remaining crouched as he intently watched from behind the outcropping of rocks. Maybe good fortune had befallen him. He was neither the strongest nor the fastest, but he was the closest and knew his way around a knife and spear as well as any of the hunters.

The bear's pace had slowed as it drew closer to Mochan's position. The young hunter's heart raced; the bear was bound to depart at any moment. Mochan's fingers tensed around the hilt of his spear, unclenching enough to keep his grip light. He would need to be able to extend his arm quickly in order to attack and stay out of the bear's reach. His heartbeat not yet rapid enough to drown out the sound of the bear padding along the grassy terrain. *Steady.* He would only get one chance with a bear as big as this one.

Placing his free hand against a rock, Mochan pushed up on his toes, feeling the grass beneath his feet, his arm tensing as it extended. He leapt sideways over the rocky outcropping. He landed—barely—on the bear's back and swiftly drove the point of his spear down into the bear's neck. The bear twisted around shaking Mochan off and moved to swat him. Mochan tightened his grip on the spear and scrambled away. He had to keep out of striking distance at all costs.

Ducking back behind the rocks, Mochan sliced a portion of a small section of rope with his knife. Taking the smallest part, he wrapped the knife at a perpendicular angle tightly to the shaft of the spear below where the spearhead met it. He could hear the bear's approach and dashed around the other side of the rocks. The moment Mochan entered into the bear's view, it reared up on its hind legs. His heart pounding, Mochan planted the butt end of the spear in the ground right before the bear dropped back down. The head of the spear drove into the bear's throat, the knife stopping the bear from reaching him while Mochan scrambled away again. If it had been a stronger, wider spear, the bear would be dying, but Mochan already knew that would take additional work.

Mochan had drawn more than merely first blood, but he would have to finish this battle using his spare

   DARYL J BALL

knife. That was less than ideal: tales of fallen warriors had taught him that, as rival villages had all but wiped out the people of Meadhan within days of his birth. When the bear finally backed up to retreat, the spear still lodged in its throat, Mochan rushed forward, slashing the blade of his spare knife across the bear's front. The bear reared up on its hind legs, but the earlier wound forced it to drop back down, the shaft of the spear snapping in the process. Pressing his luck, Mochan slashed the legs again, while also narrowly avoiding the bear's teeth.

The grassy terrain was stained with blood, most of it the bear's. The bear lumbered, its breathing ragged. Teeth gnashing as it growled, its footsteps growing heavier.

Moving back behind the rocky outcropping, Mochan crouched, his spare knife ready. He had to end this soon. This land was too close to the border for the neighbouring villagers not to hear the wounded roar of the bear. His muscles were aching, but his body had never felt so alive with energy. This was what it truly meant to hunt, to be up against a superior foe. Was this how the warriors felt when they fought to maintain what little territory Meadhan had left? That surge of strength, the clarity of purpose and mind. The bear's breathing drew closer. A few more steps and Mochan would have his triumph. Blood trickled onto his head and he quickly backed up. He sliced upwards, startling the bear with the sudden movement, before rolling back into a crouched posi-tion. When Mochan raced forward, he could feel the breeze over the terrain rushing past him, the coldness of it upon his bare skin. Tuning out everything, he drove the knife downward into the space between the bear's eyes and nose, putting all his strength into it. As the bear tried to shake him free, he gripped one of its ears with his free hand, wrapping his legs around its head. He held on with all he could, wrestling with the bear until the life faded from its eyes and it sank to the ground.

Pulling himself free, along with his knife, Mochan staggered, retrieving the broken pieces of his other weapons. He tossed all of it to the ground in front of the bear's face, last laying his bloodied knife on top, and dropped to his knees. He was fully aware that such a kill went beyond skill and luck. The bear had allowed it and the Priesthood had taught him how to be thankful for that.

"Great Brown Bear, rarest of the land warriors of this great plain, hear me now as your spirit leaves this world," he said, eyes fixed on the bear's lifeless body. "I, who slew you this day, discard my birth name of Mochan. This day, know that I honour your sacrifice to my blade by taking a new name."

After pausing to think for a moment, he continued "Henceforth, I will be known as Mathghamhain, for it means 'bear', and I have been the one to slay you, mighty one. Know that your death is not in vain, that you give life today to many who need it so we may better defend our village and families." Reaching out, he pressed his face to the bear's, feeling the warmth wash over him. His own breathing slowed as the rush of the battle wore off.

Wrapping his arms around its head, he reached

under its chin and soaked his hands in the blood. Painting his face with the bear's blood, he felt the air touch the newly covered skin. It felt odd, but it was what had been taught to do by other hunters, on behalf of the Priesthood, should the occasion ever arise. When he was done, he cast his eyes to the highest reaches of the sky.

"Let this land know that I have taken the bear's being unto myself, that I truly am now Mathghamhain, he who is the bear. Let its mighty spirit know peace in the afterlife." A ritual was not crucial for the everyday creatures they slew. Indeed, they got little more than a thank you for their sacrifice. This bear had been a mighty foe. Rising to his feet slowly, Mathghamhain lay both his hands over the bear's eyes and closed them. Only one of them had need of sight now.

How to get the bear back to Meadhan was the next step. With his current proximity to neighbouring villagers, Mathghamhain could by no means leave it and fetch aid, nor could he drag it the whole way due to the bear's weight and the distance involved, but he could start. The abrupt chill in the air was enough to make his skin prickle without a breeze to cause it. He dropped down, looking around; he had been taught that such changes could mean danger. The air over the bear rippled, and a voice came from out of nowhere and yet from everywhere at the same time.

"Mathghamhain, hear me."

The words were so clear and distinct, yet familiar in a way he could not explain. He looked around wildly for their source. "Show yourself, whoever you be," he responded, reaching for his knife. A voice should not be able to be heard and have no owner, yet there was no one in sight save himself and the lifeless body of the bear.

"Mathghamhain, I am a spirit. Do you not sense that? Do you not know the presence of one when you feel it? Hear me," the disembodied voice came again, no closer than before and yet still so close that it was as if it were right by his ear.

The words troubled him, but it could be a trick. Spirits did not answer, they presented themselves through another's actions, through signs. That was what he had been taught, that was how it had always been. "You know my name, newly taken as it is; if you are truly a spirit, why are you here now? Why speak when no spirit has before?"

"There are things that cannot be told through mere signs. I am Mathghamhain, just as you are, and I bid you beware, for you will be wounded again before you reach your village." How could such a coincidence be possible? Since there was no one else about, there was but one explanation. He had, after all, released the bear's spirit to the afterlife and taken its name for his own.

"Mathghamhain? My name is taken in honour of the bear who died at my hand. Are you the bear's spirit come to bid farewell to this world?" he asked, following the sole line of reasoning that he could.

"My name means 'bear', as yours does, and had you not slain the great bear, I would not have been able to find you and bring you this warning. You will bleed again before you reach Meadhan. Beware," the voice said, becoming faint.

"I thank you for your warning, great bear spirit." Mathghamhain felt the chill in the air fade. He remained crouched a few more minutes but no further words came from the spirit.

Looking sidelong at the lifeless body of the bear, he sighed. He had no intention of saying anything to anyone in Meadhan about this odd conversation. Spirits didn't really linger in the living world simply to warn of a possible wound he might sustain, did they? That seemed ridiculous; of course, he would likely bleed again. He was already wounded and dragging a massive animal all the way to the village by himself, or close enough for others to see and come help him. The odds of someone as lean as he was stumbling while pulling such weight and getting hurt were all too likely. It was scantly a warning, but he did not dismiss it outright.

At the earliest available opportunity, Mathghamhain wanted to talk to the Priesthood about this. The Priesthood was the guild that owed no village allegiance and sought to maintain balance and see to the faith of all the people of the land. They handled questions any villagers might have about how the world worked that the Educators Guild could not. Their visiting was, as such, always a great occasion in the villages but, because of the fact the Priesthoods' members kept themselves isolated, it also meant they had no ready supplies for their own well-being. Tributes were provided by each village that the Priesthood collected on their visit and stored back at home. It was a near-impossible guild to handle being a member of, which was why their members tended to be older. He remembered when he was younger asking Luch, one of his early teachers about them, and the man had explained the Priesthood rarely even considered taking someone on as a member. Anyone who felt compelled to join it needed a level of devotion to it and a studious discipline of an undreamt-of level. Most who considered it oftentimes joined the less rigorous Educators Guild.

Mathghamhain was certain that spirits speaking directly to people the way the bear had was not a thing he could ever recall learning about from any priest.

CHAPTER 2
Mathghamhain

It took Mathghamhain what felt like ages to drag the bear to within sight of the small village of Meadhan. He used branches from trees he passed to act as a surface when laid on the ground upon which the bear's body could lie. To keep them from separating as he rolled and pushed the bear's carcass, he made use of vines. It was certainly better than scraping the body along the ground. So far, he had not bled anymore than expected from scrapes he had picked up fighting the bear earlier, and he had already cleaned those best he could. What had the bear's spirit said? Perhaps he was tougher than it had thought.

"Ah, the last of our wayward hunters returns, I see," one of the warriors scoffed as Mathghamhain came to the village entrance, while others rushed past him to

help bring the bear's body inside. Brennus. Of course, it was him. They had been rivals since childhood and the warrior had increasingly ribbed him since the day the guilds had accepted the applications of both young men at the age of 13: Mathghamhain to be trained as a hunter, but Brennus had shown promise as a potential warrior. That promise and the status it brought with it had been a point of contention between the two in the four years since. "Stole another village's kill, did you? When they wake up, they are going to be wanting to use you for target practice, I would think."

"I killed the bear, Brennus, my two hands, my spear, my knives. I have been reborn in releasing its spirit. Mathghamhain is my new name. My hunter name. My true name," he retorted as the bear's weight was taken from him by others. He watched as the carcass was taken inside the village while other warriors, and those not assisting in moving the bear, observed. His teeth ground in anger from Brennus' joking at his ability. Stumbling, Mathghamhain's knee hit a rock hidden amid the grass, cutting it open; blood trickled down his leg as he recovered his footing. He had bled before reaching the village, just as the spirit of the bear had said. His eyes widened at the realization that the warning had been accurate. It had to be a coincidence.

"You? You would claim a kill by yourself that even the strongest warrior amongst us could not have managed alone? You are nothing but skin and bones. It is why you are a hunter, capable enough to hunt small animals but not for battle. You call yourself Mathghamhain now? You do the name a disservice, that is a name for a warrior!" Brennus came nose to nose with him. Other warriors came forward, moving swiftly to separate them.

"I did battle with it. I bested it through skill and strategy, through cunning and speed, as any warrior would. Its spirit was freed by my hand and I have rightfully taken the name of the bear unto myself." Mathghamhain retorted forcefully pushing his hair away from his face as he glared back at the warrior in defiance.

"And I say you lie! You do not deserve this name, but would pepper Meadhan with your lies, letting the women and children hear your outlandish claims. Stealing from another village will bring their wrath down upon us all—and Meadhan is already on the brink of being wiped out. No, Mochan, you are not welcome here if you bring such danger to us and compare yourself to a warrior. I will be the one to prove that you are a liar and unworthy even of being called a hunter. I challenge you old *friend* to a duel! You bring shame to us all and so I fight for our honour. It will be answered and restored by your death," Brennus seethed as other warriors tried to drag him away.

Mathghamhain shook with anger at the challenge. He knew Brennus to be headstrong, but it was as if his rival had been waiting for the chance to make such a challenge. If the warrior had not been restrained, Mathghamhain was certain they would have fought right then and there. Clenching his fists tightly, he could take a small measure of comfort in the fact that it was unfair for members of different guilds to face each

other in a challenge. He had known Brennus all of his life, and the name he had taken as a successful warrior suited the young man all too well. If the duel happened, it would be against a heavily trained warrior, while Mathghamhain had no experience with the weapons they used outside of the basics; he was not even used to wearing protective armour.

The Chief of the Warriors Guild, Cynwrig, looked from him to Brennus and back, before throwing his arms up in the air. "There will be a battle at dawn. Brennus, the bravest of the brave, against the hunter, Mathghamhain, newly named for his triumph in a personal battle against the brown bear that we will feast upon this night." Cynwrig grinned, instantly dashing Mathghamhain's hopes that being from different guilds would protect him. His heart sunk as he looked at Cynwrig with a mixture of confusion and pleading in his eyes.

In response, the old warrior leaned in close to Mathghamhain's ear and whispered, "If you truly did best that bear by yourself, then I suggest you show Brennus as little ground tomorrow. He will kill you if you give him an opening. If he is right though and you endangered us all? It would be best for us all that he kills you quickly," he warned as he patted Mathghamhain lightly on the shoulder before heading inside the village to catch up with Brennus.

Limping into the village, Mathghamhain finally sat on the nearest bench as soon as he was able, letting Eluned tend to his scrapes, giving her no protest as she did so.

"I find it amusing that they doubt you battled a bear

yourself," Eluned smirked as she cleaned his wounds. Like all of the young women in Meadhan, she was a member of the Caretakers Guild, charged with the general maintenance of the village and tending to the cooking and the injured. She was only slightly older than he was and he was grateful that at least someone believed him so far.

"And why is it that you can tell that which a warrior doubts?" Mathghamhain replied as he looked away from what she was doing in order to gaze about the area in search of any sign of Brennus.

"You are lean like all of the hunters. Your muscles taut so that you can strike effectively when need be but every hurt you take is quickly obvious," Eluned explained. "These wounds were gotten while being extremely active. If you had gained them fighting against another person, they would be deeper. These were obviously picked up while doing your best to avoid greater injury. A bear is a dangerous and fearsome animal to face alone. That you survived is likely why they doubt your story."

"If ever there was any doubt that you were born into a family of hunters, I believe that erases it," Mathghamhain grinned looking back at her as she finished up. "It is a shame that the only guild open to women is the Caretakers. I have complete confidence that you would have been a mighty hunter as well."

"Thank you for that. There is a benefit though, my life is not put at risk by leaving Meadhan. With how many of us were left orphaned by past attacks against this village, knowing that I am in a position to try and help us stay alive is comforting," Eluned replied before

standing up. "You had best be going so you can report where the kill was made and I wish you good luck in your duel Mathghamhain. I will not be there to watch, I know you understand why."

He nodded in response as she walked away. Seeing another hunter die in front of her would be far too harsh a reminder of the loss of family she had endured as a child. She was also right that he still had to make his way to the Hunters Guild hut so he could mark down where exactly he had found the bear. It was important to ensure certain areas were not overly hunted in, especially places which were so close to the edge of their territory. Upsetting a neighbouring village as Brennus had accurately stated would result in trouble that Meadhan was not equipped to handle.

"I am sorry Mochan. My apologies, I mean Math-ghamhain. It is a good name and your parents would have been proud that you found your true name," Loegaire grinned. The old hunter was the Chief of the Hunters Guild but more importantly than that, as far as Mathghamhain was concerned, the man had raised him after his parents' death. Loegaire was the fastest and most experienced hunter in Meadhan and no one would ever dare to accuse him of showing favouritism to Mathghamhain despite their closeness.

"I hope so but would they still be proud if I had found it only to die the next day in a duel? Chief Loegaire, I am a hunter. Brennus is a warrior. How is a duel even allowed? It would be unfair."

"It is because it is about honour. If you decline, you

essentially admit he is right. Mathghamhain, I have watched you and Brennus fight each other for many years. We both knew it was only a matter of time before a formal duel took place," Loegaire sighed. "I will make sure you have a sharpened sword in time for the duel. Enjoy tonight and get rest. You are the reason we have such a feast after all, no matter what Brennus claims. Save tomorrow's worries for morning and then do your best. You may not be our best hunter but you killed a bear and I cannot think of any other hunter that has ever achieved that alone. If you can do that, I know you can win against Brennus."

"Thank you, I certainly hope you are right. I only wish there was a different way," Mathghamhain whispered before clasping hands with his Chief and mentor for perhaps the last time. "I will do my best to make you and this guild proud."

Stepping out of the hut after he had spoken, he made his way to the large building where he lived alongside so many others. It was where his bed was and if he was going to get any practice for the duel in as well as take Loegaire's advice somewhat then he needed to rest a bit before the feast that evening.

After the whole village had feasted, Mathghamhain found his way to the fire where stories were told at night. His fellow hunters had gathered by him wanting stories of how he had single-handedly killed a bear, although a few warriors soon joined them asking for further details.

"You got lucky, but you certainly made the most of

it, young Mathghamhain. You will need to do the same tomorrow. Especially since your opponent is not a big lumbering bear but a trained warrior," Caiside remarked. The warrior had been nodding in appreciation as Mathghamhain described the precision of his strikes against the bear. He was one of the senior warriors, but also could be counted on for advice by all villagers.

"His name is Mochan," Brennus spat as he grabbed a seat nearby. "Do not let his description of alleged attacks fool you into believing his outlandish tale."

"You have already made your challenge," Cynwrig warned as ale was brought out and passed around. At the Warrior Chief's warning, the discussion ended, and talk soon turned to other tales amongst those gathered. Tales by warriors of the latest clash with neighbouring villages dominated but farmers also had their own shorter stories of amusing incidents from the field that day. Those quicker tales and the laughter that accompanied them helped to lighten the mood between stories of battle. The drinking and storytelling would last into the darkest part of the night. Mathghamhain did his best to limit his consumption, although he noted Brennus made no such move. Hopefully, that would lead to an advantage.

CHAPTER 3

When morning came, Mathghamhain woke with a dull headache. Shortly afterward, his fellow hunters showed up,

and escort him to the small hut where he would be waiting until the duel began. They were all too glad to suit him up with something resembling appropriate armour. The Warrior Chief Cynwrig dropped by as well, checking to see how prepared he was.

"While I would not let any of my warriors wear this into battle, it looks to be in decent condition," Cynwrig mused as he checked that there wasn't more than the usual amount of padding. "You will need to stay sequestered here until it's time for the duel. Someone will come to get you. Keep your wits about you, and hopefully, you can give young Brennus a half-decent bout during your final moments."

Mathghamhain knew the Warrior Chief meant well, but he could have done without the reminder that he had little chance of surviving. The only thing he could do now was wait. He could always refuse to duel but that would lead everyone to believe Brennus was right and Mathghamhain would be denied his new name, not to mention the shame it would bring on the entire Hunters Guild. He could not allow that, not after the success he had, even if it meant his death. Now he was faced with having no other strategy besides surviving and taking any opening that presented itself. On the heels of his greatest triumph as a young hunter the day before to his life now being all but over because he had been called a liar. It was humbling, to say the least.

"Mathghamhain, hear me. You doubt yourself but this is a battle you can win exactly as you did yester-day," the voice came in the suddenly chilled air within the hut.

Of course, he thought, now the spirit was back. It had warned him he would be wounded again but that had been a mere coincidence, it was not what could be considered a notable prediction. "I hear you. Why do you come now? Do you think I am not simply heading off to be slaughtered by my peer?"

"Mathghamhain, I did warn you, did I not? To survive you must be aware at all times of your surroundings, whether it be in the air or on the ground, and even the space between. I say again you can win this battle," the spirit said sharply.

"Brennus is a skilled, talented warrior. He was quickly accepted for training by the Warriors when he came of age. He has proven himself repeatedly since then. I am but a hunter, tasked with finding food," Mathghamhain said, standing up. He shook his head lightly and began to pace inside the small hut, his eyes darting to the entrance constantly.

"Mathghamhain, every opponent has a weakness. What is a hunter but a warrior by a different name? Is your opponent not smaller and less mighty than a bear? Are you not named for a bear, mighty and strong?"

He could hear the smile in the spirit's voice, if a spirit could do such a thing.

"He knows weapons, tactics. I have been trained in how to use a knife and a spear neither of which is a weapon in this duel," Mathghamhain responded. He was outclassed by Brennus.

"Is not a knife merely a smaller sword with a greater choice of movement granted to it? You know how to move and fight with a small blade unencumbered by armour. You already know how to fight, without the large blade and protection your opponent requires. Do not try to face him on his terms, do not try to fight like the warrior he is but be the warrior you are trained as already.”

“I have no choice. He has greater reach and is protected. He knows how to move that way, while I do not,” Mathghamhain responded even as the air seemed to gradually resume its normal temperature.

“Hear my words, Mathghamhain…” The voice sounded fainter and further away and he was unsure where it was coming from. Several more minutes passed without another word from it. The spirit had departed once again, the air having warmed. Be a hunter in the duel, not a warrior it had said. How could he do that with what he was up against? It sounded impossible. What did a bear know about combat really? This was a fight between men.

Cynwrig opened the hut door and looked at him before moving to pat him down again. “Come, young man who would go by the name Mathghamhain, the time of your duel for honour has arrived,” he said before leading him out of the hut to the clearing in the centre of the village. A circle had been drawn in the dirt wide enough to allow Mathghamhain and Brennus to fight within. Nearly all of the men in the village had gathered to watch him be humiliated and killed, as well as a small handful of the women finding seats on benches that had been placed there, at a safe distance to watch from. Brennus grinned broadly from the far side of the circle, his short sword already in hand and a shield on his left arm. His armour was as

clean as could be, as if it had been forged made that morning, its metal thick enough to blunt the impact of any weapon and the shield looked to be even thicker and heavier.

Gulping, Mathghamhain left Cynwrig's side as the Chief warrior moved to the centre of the circle. The warrior lifted his arms to the sky after Mathghamhain moved to the side opposite to where Brennus was. Cynwrig furrowed his brow and it took Mathghamhain a moment to realize what the warrior was waiting for. There was the Hunter Chief, Loegaire, striding towards him at a much quicker pace than was his norm. He carried a sword and shield as promised, which he presented to Mathghamhain when he reached him. Now, with the sword in his hand and the shield mounted, he waited.

The weight of the armour the hunters had strapped him into was heavy, made from older, less refined metal, patched and worn, previously belonging to a slain warrior. The short sword felt uncomfortably heavy in his grasp. Its blade sorely needed to be re-forged and showed visible signs of having recently been sharpened. The shield had been punctured numerous times but the straps were still good and the front of it was tightly fitted with a cloth to cover the puncture marks from being easily visible from that side. Cynwrig dropped his arms to his sides and stepped from the circle to join the other spectators.

The rush of footsteps was clearly audible and he barely got his shield up in time. Mathghamhain, arm aching from the reverberation as his opponent's blade slammed furiously against the shield, swung his sword how he had seen the warriors do. The sword was nearly dropped when it struck the shield of Brennus, unprepared for the weight and backlash of the hit. He jumped back as his opponent's sword came at him again, nearly catching him in the centre of his chest. He certainly hoped the crowd was enjoying this.

Gritting his teeth, Mathghamhain lifted his shield high enough to cover his head. Crouching, he moved forward. One stride at a time he moved, keeping the sword at his side. The point facing up and outwards, forcing his rival to step back. Even so, Brennus brought his blade down on Mathghamhain's shield. Mathghamhain's arm stung, the reverberations of the impact travelling all the way to his shoulder.

As the duel moved closer to the centre of the circle, Mathghamhain thrust his sword upwards. He felt the blade hit flesh, and twisted it. Lowering his shield enough to confirm how much damage it felt like he was doing, Mathghamhain was greeted by the downward swing of his rival's sword and a hiss from the warrior. Mathghamhain barely got the shield up in time again to protect his head from the blow, letting out a gasp of pain as the blade cut into his arm. The shield fell broken to the ground.

Jumping back as best he could, Mathghamhain landed solidly on both feet. He rushed forward, swinging his sword. It forced Brennus to go on the defensive. Mathghamhain's breathing was getting heavier, his muscles aching increasingly with each swing. Mathghamhain kept pushing unrelentingly to keep his opponent back. He could feel his own strikes weakening. He dodged the retaliatory swing but stumbled. The weight of his sword was proving too heavy for him.

Digging deep, Mathghamhain found the strength to move the blade finally. It pierced his rival's lower leg. Mathghamhain scrambled to his feet. His opponent's sword caught him hard across the chest, slashing through the armour where it had been patched. The force drove the hunter down into the dirt. Mathghamhain lay on his back, his chest heaving. Against an animal, he could plan and dodge, but this was impossible. Brennus was giving him little opportunity to drive a sword through the armour and draw blood.

Pushing himself to his knees, Mathghamhain lashed out again, thrusting his sword away from his body. It barely connected with the warrior's armour. With that act, Mathghamhain fell forward face first, the exertion too much for him to remain conscious any longer.

Mathghamhain gripped his head, and opened his eyes gradually, alarmed he was still alive. Casting his gaze about the small enclosure, he recognized it instantly. His own home. Had the duel not happened yet and it had all been a dream? No, he could see someone, hear them speaking but not loud enough for him to make out the words yet. Sitting up, he honed in on the voice, the ache in his head returning as his eyes settled on the two men sitting across from him.

"Ah, young Mathghamhain has awakened finally. Right, let us get on with it then," Cynwrig's voice rang out as the man moved towards Mathghamhain, laying a hand on his right shoulder gently. "It was by no means an elegant duel, but a duel it was, even if the outcome was not one anyone had prepared for. You have proven yourself. The charges laid against you have been dropped. As soon as you are recovered enough to walk, you will be joining us. Congratulations, young Mathghamhain, you are one of Meadhan's warriors now. We will hold a formal ceremony soon," the Chief said, nodding at Mathghamhain before walking away and glancing at the other man. "As much as it might pain you, Brennus, you saw his heart as much as we all did, we expect to see it nurtured and honed by our next battle. Remember, you are the one who insisted on waiving a rematch despite our suggestions."

"Aye Cynwrig, after all, he faced me as a man and that alone showed he had honour in him…and he fought valiantly for it as well. He is after all the reason I am still alive. We could have either both lived or both been killed. A rematch was unnecessary as it was my challenge that had to be settled and it was," Brennus said leaning forward. That sounded strange when it was not accompanied by words ridiculing him. How could he and Brennus both be alive despite the clear rules of the duel?

Standing slowly Mathghamhain watched as Cynwrig left through the door and fixed his eyes on Brennus."We both yet live, and you are in my enclosure. You, who have done nothing but cast doubt on me since we were children."

"We both live because the duel was ruled a draw, Mathghamhain. I had to argue long and hard for that to be the end of it. A fitting name, indeed, it would seem. You are a mighty and fierce combatant and

clearly would sacrifice all to protect what is precious to you. You are in my charge now to train as a true warrior, a hunter no longer, for you have proven yourself wasted in such pursuits as that," Brennus said without a hint of condescension about it as he rose from his seat. With the amount of disdain the warrior had for him the past several years, it was an odd thing not to hear.

"A draw? How? I was wounded. I remember falling, then darkness. I barely grazed you," Mathghamhain protested.

"Your attack. You drove me back along the length of the circle, from one end to the other scoring occasional small hits with your blade. That final thrust only nicked my armour because I stepped back. You had me on the defence at the end." Brennus explained. As he did so, Mathghamhain noticed that the warrior was watching him intently, looking for a reaction, the hint of a smirk on the warrior's lips.

"You stepped outside the circle! That's how it was a draw," he said, putting it together.

"Indeed, I intended to take you out quickly. It ended up being ruled an even contest: I had inflicted greater wounds but you showed heart and great strength in driving me out of the circle, which should have granted you the win but you were also unconscious. A draw seemed the fair ruling," Brennus shrugged unbothered but Mathghamhain had known him too long to believe that was, indeed, the case.

"So I see. And of all the people to train me as a warrior, they assigned you?" he chided, still trying to wrap his head around it and get the warrior's real thoughts on the matter.

"Watch your tongue, Mathghamhain. Yes, Cynwrig and the other Chiefs agreed that if you are to be a warrior then you need training by someone who will bring out your best and greatest effort. They felt that meant me. Also, I have little doubt it was their way of punishing me for failing to beat you, but also refusing a rematch in order to determine a clear winner," Brennus snapped back before calming down quickly. "Besides, outside of possibly Hunter Chief Loegaire, who knows you better?"

As if to drive home the point that he had calmed down again, Brennus, with a broad grin, walked over and touched his forehead to Mathghamhain's. "Do not take too long to heal. The moment you can walk again we will begin your training in earnest. Think of it: this is truly what was meant to be. We as orphans fighting to find our place, to prove ourselves, and now we will do so side by side—this time truly as warriors."

Smirking, Brennus clasped both of Mathghamhain's shoulders tightly. The pressure applied brought tears to Mathghamhain's eyes and he let out a cry of pain. Brennus immediately let go, laughing as he did so.

"You be mad Brennus, we have never worked side by side on anything, and I have no doubt your way of training me will be far more enjoyable for you than for me," he glared at the warrior. Despite the ache throughout his body, Mathghamhain was confident he was rested enough to walk competently. That did not mean he was in a hurry to train.

"Mad I might be, but I am still your better. Rest up, eat up, I will let the nearest member of the Caretakers

Guild know you are awake enough to eat finally and then…" Brennus halted mid-sentence and casually gestured to Mathghamhain as if he had suddenly remembered what he had been about to say. "Oh, then you will show me how you slew the bear so that we can begin there. Use it to teach you how to wield a sword properly and keep your head up at the same time," Brennus said cheerfully before laughing again as he strode from the room.

A warrior. He had not only survived the duel but was now considered a warrior to be trained by Brennus of all people? Mathghamhain knew now that he had survived the duel on a technicality. What had the spirit said? Fight as a hunter in order to win? That a hunter was a warrior as well? He had faced Brennus and nearly lost his life. Swung wildly, using strength and determination, but a hunter planned each move and executed attacks with precision. Had he done that, might the win have been decisive? Yet he had ignored the spirit a second time. He would have to do better to honour the spirit of the bear from which he had taken his name.

CHAPTER 4
Caisíde

"When Mochan was small and barely more than arms and legs, I would never have imagined he would have grown up and trained as a hunter, let alone achieve the near-impossible and change Guilds to become a warrior,"

Caiside observed, watching as Brennus and Mathghamhain fought another practice duel. It had been over a month since the young warrior had taken on the task of re-training the former hunter and it continued to be an entertaining spectacle.

"Brennus will have him trained in time. Thankfully, he's still keeping Mathghamhain limited to the wooden practice swords or our newest recruit would likely have gotten himself killed by now." Cynwrig responded from next to Caiside. The Chief was younger than him but was far better suited to leadership than he could ever have been.

The sound of running footsteps caused both men to turn and see what the commotion was. There were few possibilities if Caiside thought about it. Sure enough, it was one of the younger women, Agrona. It was fitting that she would be the one to deliver a message, given her late father had been Cynwrig's predecessor as Chief.

"Warrior Chief Cynwrig, it is time. The Guild has made its decision," the young woman beamed. "Even now everyone is beginning to gather in the middle of Meadhan so the announcement can be made."

"Ah, at last! I will gather those warriors here with me and we will be there as quickly as we can," Cynwrig grinned, bowing at the young woman. "Thank you, brave Agrona, we shall not delay you further."

Caiside watched amused as Agrona hesitated for a moment, staring at the two young warriors who were sparring. With the exact way her head tilted in doing so, he was positive it was Brennus who had her eye.

Before Caiside could say anything Agrona had abruptly turned on her heel and sped back to the village entrance.

"Caiside, I suppose we should let Brennus know to wrap up the training for now," Cynwrig smirked, already heading over to talk to the young warrior and Mathghamhain. As dedicated to his craft as Brennus was, Caiside had little doubt the warrior would not want to miss an opportunity for a celebration in honour of the election of a new Guild Chief.

Watching as Cynwrig spoke to Brennus, he frowned. While news of this nature was certainly one way to end a practice session quickly, it looked to Caiside as though Brennus was not at all pleased. When it came to the Caretakers Guild, the rule was such that its Chief could not be wed, and the Chiefs tended to be of marriageable age. Normally, this posed no issue, but Caiside could understand the frustration for Brennus amongst his age group. They were limited in number of both men and women thanks to the war that had seen so many of their parents' generation killed. The upside in the case of Brennus was that the young warrior did not seem interested in any one woman over the other at this point, although Caiside did have to wonder if he was aware of Agrona's seeming interest.

As Brennus and Cynwrig passed him heading for the village's gates, Caiside found himself walking next to a weary and bruised Mathghamhain. Offering the young warrior a hearty slap on the back as they followed behind their Chief, Caiside grinned.

"Despite how it must feel, young Mathghamhain,

you are improving. Slowly, but still improving. It does not help that you are being trained at a slightly older age, even if it is accelerated. Our Chief is of the hope that Brennus can bring you up to a competent level within six months rather than the usual full year," Caiside offered reassuringly.

"That is not much comfort Caiside. He seems to have taken the request to accelerate my training to mean hit harder and faster than he normally might. I fall asleep within seconds of laying down now, and wake up sore, having to force myself to move."

"It will pass, especially as your strength increases. It was not any innate skill as a warrior that brought you this far but rather your heart and determination as a hunter. Meanwhile, try to remember that Brennus gains nothing if he fails to train you but gains an ally if he succeeds. This is as much about testing him as it is about training you!"

The centre of Meadhan was bustling with activity when the Warriors finally arrived. Parts of conversation could be overheard as people spoke rapidly about who could possibly have been chosen. It had been over a week since Boudica, the previous Chief of the Caretakers Guild, had passed away suddenly in her sleep and it was generally assumed her second-in-command, Andraste, would be elected. Still, a formal election within the Guild had to take place. Despite that, Caiside could not help but notice Mathghamhain was not paying attention. No, the young warrior-in-training's focus seemed set solely on one young woman in particular. Thankfully, it was not Agrona as

that could presumably cause new issues between the young warrior and Brennus.

"Close your mouth Mathghamhain before anyone else realizes you are staring. Especially, since the young woman in question is my cousin," Caiside said with a smirk. He would need to have a word with Brennus and his Chief about teaching the young man how to not be so distracted, but that could wait until another time.

"Cacht ingen Luch is your cousin?" Mathghamhain asked incredulously, shaken out of his distracted state by the older warrior's words.

"Yes. It is not like you have never seen her before, so do not stare. It is impolite. Now then, let us go see who our poor Chief gets to work alongside," Caiside retorted as they made their way into the crowd. Mathghamhain's eyes never seemed to fully leave where Cacht was. Well, right up until she was called forward and announced as the new second-in-command to the Chief of the Caretakers Guild. Even he had to take pause at that. She was the same age as Mathghamhain and Brennus, certainly, but the thought that she was old enough to be in a position of leadership surprised him. He knew it should not have but it was easy to forget she was a young woman now. It was a shame her late father Luch wasn't around to bear witness to this moment.

The thoughtful look on Mathghamhain's face made Caiside wonder what exactly the young warrior in training was thinking.

The blow against his shield caused Caiside to grunt. It had been unexpected in its swiftness. Stepping to one side, he pivoted to get past Mathghamhain's defence only to have his sword miss. The younger warrior had ducked far lower than most warriors ever dared to and was even now rising back up in even closer quarters. What was the boy thinking?

"Caiside, watch out! He's going to…. Never mind," Brennus shouted as Mathghamhain's shield arm came crashing down on Caiside's elbow. The sudden shot of pain caused him to loosen his grip on his sword, nearly dropping it.

The young warrior was now showing off. Mathghamhain had come far in the past five months but he was still in training. Caiside seized Mathghamhain by his belt and tugged back sharply, hooking the young man's leg with his as he did so. Mathghamhain fell flat on his back, staring up at him.

"You have made impressive progress Mathghamhain but that was a major risk you took getting that close." Cynwrig smiled as Caiside helped the young warrior back up. A sparring session like that one would most assuredly mean there would need to be far more in the next few weeks in order to properly keep a constant eye on Mathghamhain's growing skill.

"I warned you Caiside that he does that with his shield," Brennus smirked. There was clearly a bit of pride in his voice, and why would there not be. As his trainer, Brennus had achieved a lot with Mathghamhain in the past few months.

"Yes, you did, I simply did not think that was what you meant. Going for the joint was smart on his part. Although it does strike me as a thing you would have taught him instead of something he would have thought of on his own," Caiside answered, casting a watchful eye over to where Cynwrig and Mathghamhain were conferring.

"You know me so well Caiside! I taught him something similar but that was his adaptation of it. He has been quite creative the past month, I am having to remind myself that he is not an actual threat when we train with how often he has nearly struck me. That is not something I ever thought anyone would say about him, especially not myself."

If he was getting the better of a young, strong warrior like Brennus already, how dangerous was Mathghamhain going to be once he was finally up against an actual enemy, Caiside wondered? When he had been named Mochan, the young warrior-in-training had been mostly an afterthought in nearly everyone's mind. Now, ever since the duel with Brennus, he was causing many in Meadhan to take notice. Caiside was fairly certain he had even caught his cousin, Cacht, looking thoughtfully in the young man's direction on several occasions as of late. It was a fascinating change the past two seasons had brought.

CHAPTER 5
Mathghamhain

For over six months now, Brennus had been relentless in making sure his lessons were practiced until every facet of a move was perfected and could be done even when half awake. Even with the colder season having begun, the only day's rest from training he had gotten had been when Brennus was out with the other warriors, patrolling the lands Meadhan held. Sometimes they battled neighbouring villagers who ventured too close and at times there were casualties. When the number of warriors in Meadhan accounted for nearly a fifth of its population, any losses they suffered had a major impact. It was one of the reasons Cynwrig was adamant about him being trained as quickly as possible. Today, he thought was to be different. He had been decreed in a test two days before, executed by several of the warriors, as fit to join them. It would be his first day as a fully trained warrior. For its part, the spirit of the bear had finally seemed to have moved on to the afterlife. There had been no visits from it since the morning of the duel for honour against Brennus. For that Mathghamhain was thankful.

He clasped hands firmly with the Hunter Chief, offering Loegaire a hint of a smile and a promise he would survive his first real test.

"You may be trained as one of them now Mathghamhain, but never forget you were a hunter first. Do us proud out there."

"My heart is that of a hunter, and as I was once told, all hunters are warriors. I will unlikely be the last hunter to join them, especially if we keep suffering losses. Perhaps we should think of ourselves as one group," Mathghamhain grinned, checking that his equipment was set as he did so. Taking one last look at Loegaire and other hunters who had not departed for their daily hunt yet, Mathghamhain turned and followed the warriors.

It was an uneventful patrol he thought after they had been out for a while. He wondered if theirs was an average-sized number of warriors compared to the other villages. Sure theirs was a fairly small one but it was hard to accept the idea of a larger group of warriors being able to stay busy. He was sandwiched between them all, nineteen in total—Cynwrig's way of protecting their least trained warrior until he had some real experience. It dragged, walking in a group, as a hunter he had gotten used to listening and observing every little sound and movement. The sound of the armour as they walked made hearing anything difficult. The first indication he had that anything was amiss was when everybody suddenly halted. He knew what that meant from his days as a hunter and likely it meant much the same now. There was something nearby. They broke apart slightly from the ranks they had been walking in. Only two of the warriors stayed close to him, Cynwrig's hand signals directing the rest to their positions. Now Mathghamhain could also readily hear it, the faint crunching of leaves not far ahead.

The warriors who had been directed further ahead

advanced slowly along the smooth grassy terrain and then suddenly it was as if a strong wind had struck up causing a flurry of activity. Enemy warriors appeared from all sides, wearing armour that looked recently made and brandishing slightly longer and more imposing swords. Steel. He had seen it before in the village—the sole steel blade in Meadhan had been claimed in battle ages ago and now was brandished by Cynwrig. The rest of them used iron.

The enemy struck quickly, making their attacks before stepping back into a defence position before he and his fellow warriors could retaliate. With each attack they were losing ground to this enemy, being slowly driven back. Mathghamhain was shocked to see how easily they were being bested, these warriors he had sparred against, heard tales from, and who seemed so dangerous. There was but one conclusion, he thought, as he did his best not to lose his footing in the melee: The enemy did not seem to be any larger in number, but they were winning to such a degree that it was obvious that the Meadhan warriors were simply outclassed. The ease with which the enemy was attacking and driving them back spoke to that. Then he had Cynwrig at his back, "Sword out, keep your back to mine. We need to get to cover and regroup or we will all be slaughtered. We have fought these men before."

Mathghamhain kept his eyes sharp, moving when Cynwrig did. The Chief moved rapidly but steadily making sure of each footfall before taking it. Others of their village moved like he and Cynwrig were. Back to back and heading to the sole place nearby where they could have cover. The woods, they were not much to speak of but he knew they were rife with wildlife. Now, what usually provided food, would buy them time to live.

It was several minutes before Cynwrig spoke again. They lay flat on their stomachs in the disturbed ground of the woods. The surrounding vegetation and leaves barely hid them. They could not fight like this, but they were together and could be given instructions.

"Did anyone manage to kill one of those bloody bastards?" the Chief Warrior's voice hissed. It was odd to hear him rattled.

"Not that I saw but we have three dead on our side based on a quick count, I think we may have wounded one of theirs. One of them was limping when I looked back," Brennus offered. His sounding unsure was as bizarre as Cynwrig sounding unnerved. How different they were when they weren't in the village. Out here in the field of battle was the reality: They were as human as the rest of them. A quick glance upward as the men were speaking, confirmed Mathghamhain's suspicions: Caiside was keeping watch while they deliberated.

"They stand between us and Meadhan. If we do not find a way to drive them back, we lose everything. We wait, we breathe, we rush them from behind and we strike them down without mercy. Make every strike count," Cynwrig said, his voice growing in strength as he spoke, making eye contact with each warrior one at a time. "No being fancy, no merely wounding, or trying to drive them off. We kill. This day we kill as it may be our last stand. Our final battle with them."

Mathghamhain had heard from Brennus that Cynwrig could motivate a seed into a tree but he had dismissed that as hyperbole. Hearing for himself what the warrior meant was impressive. It was a good speech, even if the plan sounded disastrous. It could work but they would all likely die in the attempt. The sacrifice of a handful to save their village? There had to be a better way to win.

"There is always a way to win, Mathghamhain. I have told you before have I not, a hunter is another name for a warrior. Forget the swords and the shields. It is pretty dressing to instil confidence, think as a hunter, think of the enemy as another beast to be slain. How would you do so?" the familiar spirit's voice came at his ear. He hadn't even noticed the change in the temperature of the air this time. The other two times it had spoken to him no one else had been around, but now? Could the others hear it?

"I thought you had departed this world," Mathghamhain whispered. "We are outclassed and outnumbered. They have better armour and that fancy dressing as you called it is powerful."

"The reality of battle has gotten to Mathghamhain, Cynwrig. He speaks to the air; his mind has broken when faced with our enemy," the hushed words of Brennus came.

"Hunters are trained to hear and sense things others cannot. They talk to the spirits of the animals they kill and thank them for dying so we might live. Does it truly surprise you—any of you—that he talks to a thing

that is not there?" Cynwrig hissed before glancing at Mathghamhain. "If you are, indeed, talking to the spirits, what do they suggest we do to survive?"

Was Cynwrig really asking for his advice? Surely then they were in trouble. What did he know of this type of situation? Lifting his shield above his head he noticed the other warriors watching him in earnest, not that they could hear the spirit, but were looking to him, the least experienced among them, for a plan?

"It would explain much," Brennus said now watching just as earnestly.

"They see in you what you can be Mathghamhain. Think of them as hunters, direct them as you would hunters in a battle against a herd of animals. You have hunted animals with antlers and with claws before. The enemy you face this day is no different. The antlers are stronger and the claws sharper and longer," the voice of the spirit came again.

"It says we can win if we stop being warriors and become hunters instead, if we see the enemy as animals with extra-long sharp claws, if we act as hunters would against a herd of wild deer," Mathghamhain offered.

Looking to the treetops and then to the warriors as they came forward, Mathghamhain rose to his feet and continued.

"We lure the enemy into an environment we control. Everything around us can be a weapon, a trap to be sprung, we simply need to lure them in," he said even as the air resumed its normal temperature again. Of course it was already gone. It had said what it had come to say and departed. *Typical, offering advice but no specifics.* "The spirit has left, it clearly believes we are now informed enough to succeed."

"Then show us, Mathghamhain. We do not have much time," Cynwrig answered directing the other warriors to follow his lead. Mathghamhain squirmed, unsure how to respond. He kept his eyes averted while he tried to think of what he could possibly say. To be in this position, everyone turning to him and with how much trouble they were in, was this any different from risking everything on an all or nothing attempt to win?

Mathghamhain looked around getting a better idea of what they had to work with. Brennus was one of their strongest warriors and also amongst the youngest: He could move to lure the enemy in. The enemy would likely suspect a trap but Brennus could surely get them close enough for the rest of them to strike. They could use the lower branches by pulling them back to throw balls of packed dirt as projectiles. Those would distract the enemy and if they got a few lucky shots in, blind a few of them. What else, he wondered still perusing their surroundings. Those who could climb could attack from above, dropping down on the enemy. With most of a plan figured out, he looked at the group to make sure he had not lost their attention while he was thinking.

"We may not be able to lure them in but perhaps we can drive them in by catching them off guard," Mathghamhain said after relaying the plan. As he spoke, he thought of an additional approach they could take. "If anyone sees animals around, try driving them out into the open where the enemy is. Make them unsure if it is us or not."

Having explained everything, he proceeded to demonstrate the curled up stance he wanted those in the trees to use. It had been the most he had ever spoken to another human being let alone a warrior. Giving commands felt oddly comforting. This had to work. They had to disorient the enemy as much as possible and then strike them down before they could regroup.

"A risky plan if ever I heard one, but it might work," Cynwrig said nodding his approval, moving to scout for branches they could use as makeshift sling-shots. The Chief signalled to Brennus who moved out of the woods slightly to scout out where the enemy currently was, allowing Caiside to rejoin the rest of the warriors. Once the preparations were made, Mathghamhain watched as Brennus, sword drawn, headed fully into the clearing they had fought in. Hopefully, he did not get it into his head to try and prove himself by fighting the enemy yet.

It was several minutes later when the footfalls of armoured warriors could be heard approaching. One of Mathghamhain's fellow warriors had been thoughtful enough to scatter fallen branches out as far as they could from the woods, in the hopes that the approaching enemy would step on them and provide extra noise to warn of their approach and direction. It was time. This would either work and they would survive, or they would fail to carry out a half-planned risky scheme, a reckless gambit inspired by a spirit.

Mathghamhain threw his arms up as he had seen Cynwrig do previously to give a command without speaking and threw them down immediately, listening as several remarkably solid balls of mud, leaves, and feces whizzed past him, hitting the ground outside the woods and some hitting a target decidedly higher off the ground.

Brennus rushed past him holding up three fingers, while flashing a grin, before grabbing a low branch and moving to scale the tree behind Mathghamhain. Good, they had hit three of the enemy, and even if they had not hit them in the eyes it would anger them. That would throw them off enough. Mathghamhain moved to lay against the ground, sword out in front of him, listening to the cautious footfalls of the enemy. He waited patiently until one set was close enough, then sharply lifted his sword as he moved to his feet, driving the blade through the warrior's leg and then bashing him in the face with the flat of his shield. It staggered them enough that he could pull his sword back and move in to slash the enemy's throat, killing them. One. That was one.

The sound of bodies hitting the ground told him all he needed to know as he glanced about at the success of his fellow warriors, those who had climbed high into the trees to attack from above. Precision hits, that was crucial, make every hit count. The woods were ringing with the occasional sound of metal clanging against metal and the crashing thuds of falling bodies. The damage and noise they were causing proven by the speed at which he saw several red squirrels race past deeper into the woods. All around him was the sound of humans traipsing about, killing each other. He knew they were bound to lose at least another of

their number but they needed to beat back enough of the enemy to drive them away and claim victory without everyone dying. What had seemed impossible earlier now might be possible.

He instinctively grabbed the arm of the warrior behind him, so that he could twist and snap it, but caught himself in time. One of the enemy warriors had already gotten close enough for there to be direct combat and he had barely won against them through sheer luck and the fact Brennus had drilled into him how to counter every possible move, if one paid attention.

"At ease Mathghamhain. Our warrior bear. The battle has drawn to a close. You led us to victory this day. Our village will write songs of this victory, snatching it from the jaws of certain defeat and death," Cynwrig chided him when Mathghamhain released his arm. The Warrior Chief moved to face him as he spoke while lifting his hands to the air in a signal of triumph. The others of their group emerged from their positions within the woods and into a clearing again. Cynwrig all but forced him to do so as well.

"We have won this day my friends!" the Warrior Chief shouted while looking around. Where there had been nineteen of them that morning now there were fourteen. The number of dead enemy warriors was greater, the woods hiding how many there were. Mathghamhain found himself watching at Cynwrig's direction as those amongst them still capable of it dragged the fallen enemy into the clearing and laid them out, gathering them all in one place as others stripped them of their armour and weapons.

"You led us to victory Mathghamhain," Cynwrig whispered. "It was a grand day when fate decided you should be a warrior instead of a hunter. I see it now was to help us this day. You will get the first choice of the bounty for yourself. This is your victory more than it is mine after all. Would that the spirit who advised you had a body, they would have the second pick."

"It was a victory, but we lost too many. A true victory would have seen us win without any loss," Mathghamhain mumbled at his Chief even though he was smiling. He had not only proven himself but had also shown Brennus to be an effective trainer of warriors. That elevated his former rival, as well. "Brennus was the one who trained me as a warrior, he should get first pick after you and Judoc."

"Ah, and I know what a fierce rival he was for you, young Mathghamhain. It is a sign of a leader to recognize those who helped you to victory. He will choose, after you and I, then, as my second, Judoc will choose, followed by everyone else," Cynwrig nodded thoughtfully as they watched a commotion break out where the bodies were being gathered. "What is the problem?"

"One of them yet lives," Brennus shouted back over to them, his sword raised as others held the enemy warrior still. "He was merely unconscious but has now awakened. We were about to grant him death."

"We lost men today Cynwrig," Mathghamhain said softly to his Chief. "Yet we destroyed the enemy. He has fallen and lost, his village will have no ready warriors now, a small force at most, a weaker force. We

could claim it, grow our holdings, truly turn this into a triumph for Meadhan on a day upon which we faced certain doom. Bring this enemy warrior into our guild. Keep a steady eye on him; if he is a warrior, grant him the choice to give us his allegiance or to fall on his sword." *They needed the numbers, did they not?*

"You grow greedy: take a victory we barely claimed and try to turn it into a greater triumph and come home with more than we left? That is the hunter in you," Cynwrig responded, walking with him as they approached Brennus and the others. "You cannot resist the idea of being in battle and not coming home with something to offer everyone. Well then. Let us see what the warrior chooses."

"Hold your blade brave Brennus. We would grant this fallen warrior a choice. What is your name warrior?" Cynwrig asked, looking to the badly beaten warrior whose armour was stained with blood, shield shattered and their sword arm slightly bent the wrong way.

"I am Nuallan from the village of Nabaidh. Your men are absolute brutes. You were ours to kill! We have faced you before, this was a new tactic today by you. We should have won," the warrior answered sternly fixing Cynwrig with a hard glare.

"We had a new warrior with us to give us direction, Nuallan. The rest of your forces have either fallen or fled. We offer you the choice of life under our command or to choose death, either by your own hand or by the blade of the warrior Brennus," Cynwrig said holding up a hand to have the others let Nuallan go so he could stand.

"A fine new commander you have then this day," Nuallan said drawing himself up to his full height, sticking his chest out defiantly. "I would choose life but not fully under your command. I would prefer to pledge myself to follow the man who led you today, wherever he might command me."

"That was not one of the options," Brennus spat, touching the tip of his sword to Nuallan's chest. Anger flashing in the young warrior's eyes as he looked to Cynwrig for approval to run the enemy warrior through.

"Mathghamhain," Cynwrig said slowly motioning to him to step forward. "Nuallan, this is the young warrior who gave the commands today that led us to victory over you and your fellow warriors. As brave Brennus said, I offered you life under my command. I will, however, direct him to spare you his blade if Mathghamhain accepts your offer, but if he does, if I sense for even a second you are working against the will of our village, you will both die by my hand. Mathghamhain, it is your call to make."

"I accept. You took me as a hunter and made me a warrior and this day trusted me to lead a battle we were losing and we triumphed. I will take Nuallan under my wing as Brennus did me," Mathghamhain answered walking forward and holding his hand out to Nuallan. If this discussion was not being had in front of Nuallan, he was certain every warrior present would explain why it was a bad idea. Cynwrig had taken a chance on him, now was his opportunity to take one as well.

Mathghamhain locked eyes with Nuallan, his body feeling like it was on fire, the aftermath of battle leaving him fuelled by nervous energy.

"My Chief will not get the chance to kill you if you betray us," he said choosing each word carefully, speaking them slowly, "I will see you dead myself. Know that your life is now mine to command."

The enemy warrior reached out with his good hand, "I accept this condition, Mathghamhain, my liege, my commander," Nuallan said with a small smile. They clasped hands, their future forever intertwined.

Finally, after the bounties had been claimed and the dead burned to ash, the warriors of Meadhan began their journey home. It was now that Mathghamhain had time to reflect on the troublesome truth that Nuallan had readily turned on the village of Nabaidh. In truth, Cynwrig's allowance that Nuallan identify each of the dead and his knowledge of their weapons may have simply been an exercise in survival for the former enemy warrior, for the prisoner completed the task without any obvious signs of distress for his fallen brethren. Mathghamhain could not help but be suspicious still, and if the looks he had received throughout the bounty collection were to be believed, his concern was shared, widely. He would need to keep an extremely close eye on the warrior. Mathghamhain would not allow his risk to cost the people of Meadhan, the village he had grown up in—his people—of everything they had.

CHAPTER 6
Nuallan

The celebration in Meadhan lasted well into the wee parts of the morning. Nuallan was not surprised since their warriors had taken a near devastating loss and turned it into a triumphant win. He was grateful that despite that fact, one of the first things to take place upon arriving in the village had been one of the women, named Eluned, checking his arm to be sure it would heal properly after setting it. After that, no matter how relaxed any of the warriors found themselves, they made sure there were always two of them keeping a constant eye on him. That was in addition to the young warrior, Mathghamhain, who he had pledged himself to in order to save his life. Watching that particular warrior was interesting. Their Chief, Cynwrig, and the others had all finally retired but Mathghamhain? His new liege was still far too awake.

Even now, after he had been confined and secured to a seat inside a locked hut, Nuallan could still hear Mathghamhain outside, restlessly pacing. Nuallan was not sure if he had truly thought this through beyond not being killed. Meadhan's warriors taking him inside their village was a risk. After all, they had no proof he did not intend to help the remaining warriors of Nabaidh wipe out Meadhan by having him aid them from within the village.

Back home in Nabaidh, truth be told, he was used to being considered an outsider due to the height and slightly fairer hair he had inherited from his father, a northerner. Trying to make a new home here in Meadhan where they seemed more open to taking risks? That sounded to him like a village he wanted to be part of. If these warriors fought Nabaidh again, he would have to hope that either he was not present or, if he was, that he could prove that Meadhan indeed had his loyalty now. As it was at the moment, he certainly was not going to get any sleep tied up as he was. With enough time he could likely get himself free but that would risk undoing the work Eluned had done on his arm, and also show that he could not be trusted when what he wanted the most was a chance to finally find acceptance.

Nuallan glanced around at the interior of the hut. It was small and barren save for a bed, another chair, and a chest. Overall, it did not look to be the sturdiest structure and other than the furniture, he found it hard to believe it was meant to be a regular dwelling. There had been nothing so small in Nabaidh, so was it simply meant to be a temporary holding room? There were questions he wanted to ask but until they trusted him, Nuallan doubted they would tell him anything that might be used against them.

Wriggling in the chair, Nuallan tried to get it to move along the floor so he could get closer to the door. Maybe then he could get his new liege to come inside and they could talk. His efforts proved futile as the chair fell over and he hit the ground.

Mathghamhain

Mathghamhain paced outside the locked hut even after the sun had come up. He had barely even had time to enjoy the feast the night before. He had been focussed solely on making sure no one had any doubts that he was serious about keeping an eye on the enemy warrior he had taken as a servant. Thoughts also plagued him regarding the nature of the win. The bear's spirit coming to him right then when they needed it most, while welcome, did not quite match what he would expect for advice from a creature such as a bear.

It had properly warned him of a wound soon to come which could have been simple foresight if it had been granted in the moment of its death. Appearing the next morning to advise him how to fight Brennus? That had seemed reasonable as well. The bear had fallen to a hunter, why would it not suggest fighting a more well-armed foe the same way Mathghamhain had it? Advising a whole group of outmatched warriors to use hunter tactics against a superior foe? That did not add up quite as well, and there was the fact that it was the first advice the spirit had given him in half a year. The spirit's absence until now had led him to forget to bring it up when the priest Drust had visited Meadhan not long ago, and it would be nearly another year before he got the opportunity again.

Watching from where he paced as the last remnants of the fire they had all been sitting around earlier finally went out, Mathghamhain sighed. That was when he had heard the soft thud inside the hut.

Grabbing his sword and shield, Mathghamhain armed himself before moving the heavy block that held the door shut, peeking inside. Noting that Nuallan was still secured but on the ground, he chuckled before closing the door and securing the block again. Shaking his head, Mathghamhain watched wearily until Caiside and Judoc finally came by. Turning the duty of watching the hut over to them, he finally was able to step away. Still ruminating over his questions about the spirit, Mathghamhain passed through the entrance to Meadhan but not going much further than that.

Looking in the dim darkness, Mathghamhain sought out the stone he had tripped over several months earlier. It was the closest he could get to finding a spot connected with the spirit that was not the hut he had been in before the duel, the one now occupied by Nuallan, since the bear's carcass was now long gone and he was unsure of exactly who in the village the hide had been used for. Finding the stone after several minutes of careful searching, Mathghamhain moved to sit cautiously on the ground with his legs around it. He recalled that one needed a touchstone to reach a spirit but he had never known anyone but Drust to do so. He needed answers and right now the only ones who knew he was being guided were Mathghamhain's fellow warriors and he could scarcely ask their advice on this matter. It made him wish the Priesthood kept a representative in the village at all times. The fact that they did not, made it significantly harder to consult with them when the spirit of the great bear he had slain granted life advice sporadically.

Right now, he could have certainly used it.

"Spirit of the same name as mine, I ask that you grant me an audience this night. I, who you have seen fit to guide in the past even when I was too stubborn to follow your wisdom," Mathghamhain intonated carefully, his eyes looking straight ahead. Being able to tell if the spirit showed up was going to be difficult given it was already fairly cold.

He waited patiently for several moments but nothing came. That had been attempt number one. Maybe he needed to be more insistent. Surely there had to be a way to get its attention other than being about to be injured or saved.

"Mathghamhain, the spirit of the bear I did slay many moons ago, I request an audience that I might know your wisdom and reasons for your guidance so far," he said hoping it helped a bit even if it was less formal and word heavy. He let out a soft sigh of relief as he felt the air chill around him enough to cause his bare skin to prickle at its touch. "Thank you, spirit."

"You would ask me to come to you? To command me? You who has proven to not be capable of obeying commands? Why should I do as you wish when you have not shown yourself to be one worth listening to?" the voice of the spirit growled.

"I do ask your forgiveness for that, but would also counter with the fact that yesterday the warriors looked upon me, their least trained for guidance in how to win and followed my commands as though I were the Warrior Chief," Mathghamhain countered hoping it did not offend the spirit. The whole conversation so far had him on edge, and it was partly

because to anyone else it would look as if he was talking to himself, loudly.

"True, true, and it was my guidance that gave you reason and the knowledge that I was giving you guidance that made them listen. What is it you would ask of me, gentle Mathghamhain," the spirit said, its voice genial now.

"I would ask that you properly identify yourself, spirit. You, who claims the same name as I, named for the bear, Mathghamhain. I had believed you to be the bear's spirit but never have I heard of such a spirit lingering so long in the world nor of providing advice. Am I meant to be a member of the Priesthood now as well, not just a hunter turned warrior?" he asked moving to stand before his legs cramped with how sore he was from both the battle the day before and then standing most of the night. The cold air, despite the sun having risen, was not helping matters.

"Ah, a question much overdue, young Mathgham-hain. Well then, hear now a tale that you might struggle to understand. Yet, to answer the question asked, you must wrap your mind about my words," the spirit said before the air warmed ever so slightly. Despite the mild change in temperature, the spirit lingered still. "I am precisely who I said I was that first day we spoke. I, like yourself, am Mathghamhain. You thought I meant I was the bear you had slain when in truth I am much closer to you than that, for I am you and you are me. More accurately, you are who I once was. Your own self trapped in my own past, con-demned to linger here so that I might prevent my fate."

That, Mathghamhain thought, beginning to pace, truly boggled the mind. The spirit was talking of a time not yet come, of being his own spirit but from many years in the future. It was somehow here and now guiding him? It was, indeed, as the spirit had warned, hard to wrap one's mind around.

"Wait, so twenty years from now I die, or rather you die, but then why is your…my…spirit not lingering there but, instead, here? Why linger at all?" he stammered.

"It has much to do with the nature of our death, it would seem. I was faced with a great enemy and they wielded a mystic item, an artifact if you will, that when they used it, as they thought to slay me where I did stand, it did instead drive our spirit from our body and send it back here to this time and place, to where you did slay the bear. I suspect it was at that time for that is when we became Mathghamhain, a singular moment of great importance to our past and so I was drawn to it. There and then, when I realized what had happened upon seeing you—ourselves much younger and knowing the event so well from our past—did apply my knowledge of smaller events yet to come to guide you," the spirit answered, but its tone seemed to waver in warmth the longer it spoke.

"So I see, or do try to, but what good does guiding me now do when we do not die, as it were, for another twenty years? That is a long time from now and few of the village ever live to see such an age as that would make me…us…then," Mathghamhain said his mind whirling with additional questions as he continued to pace. More than ever before he wished

he had been in the Educators Guild or the Priesthood. Maybe then he might have a chance of making sense of it all.

"Yes, well, I intend to change history, that I might guide you through events so that you do not suffer pitfalls unnecessarily but become stronger and better prepared. That way, should the day come twenty years hence that you are faced with my killer, you will be ready to triumph and we will yet live," the spirit of Mathghamhain said.

"I see but that would…no, I do not wish to think of it right now. So you intend to guide me in ways you feel will lead me to victories in life where you did not have them. That changes history does it not, and you would not be…no, never mind my ramblings, you already said there was magic involved. To question such forces is to give way to madness," Mathghamhain responded, casting a glance over his shoulder towards Meadhan as he did so.

"So we are in agreement then. Live as you feel you must but accept my advice when I give it: after all, it is your own and who better to offer you advice in matters than one who understands you more perfectly than any other by virtue of being you as well?" the spirit of Mathghamhain from the future offered.

"Yes, we are in agreement. Advice from the future to change the present and so undo your past that is yet to be. I thank you my spirit of the future, for being here to guide me. Together we will avert the troubles that did cause us to fall so many years hence," Mathghamhain said growing in confidence but still weary from the long day and night. The concept of talking to his own future self while in such a state made him wonder if any of it was really happening. Maybe he had passed out and was dreaming this whole conversation. It would make greater sense. He had sought answers this morning and now he had further questions.

Waiting for additional word from the spirit, Mathghamhain's pacing grew increasingly frantic. There was no response coming though and the air had resumed its previous temperature. Finally, Mathghamhain stopped and stood still. After a long moment of reflection on the conversation that had happened, he picked up the rock he had sat around. The one that had caused the first of his future spirit's warnings to be shown to be true, and hurled it away from Meadhan as far as his weary arm would allow. That accomplished, he strode back into the village, barely giving the warriors guarding Nuallan a nod while on his way to his home. Stepping inside, he had barely removed his armour before falling face-first onto the wooden pallets of his bed, fast asleep.

CHAPTER 7

"Ah, you are risen now my liege" Nuallan's voice cut through the silence of the room as Mathghamhain sat up. Tall and robust and of the lightest-coloured hair he had ever seen, Nuallan was something to behold now that he was cleaned up and bereft of armour and weapons. For obvious reasons, his new servant was still tied up, but no longer confined to a chair. Judoc, with his gaze fixated on Nuallan while standing next to him, was clearly there to keep an eye on the former enemy.

"Yes, thank you, Nuallan. I could use food but I know it would not yet have been cooked with how early it is. Are enough members of the Caretakers Guild awake that I can put in an early morning request?" Mathghamhain asked before setting his feet on the floor. The pounding in his head starting as soon as he did so. A consequence, he realized, of too little sleep, not a thing he could recall ever having been a victim of before.

"There may be one or two. I did hear rustling outside not that long ago but you started to stir before I could confirm who it was. Would you like me to check now, my liege?" Nuallan's response came promptly. The response caused Judoc to chuckle, much as it did the same for Mathghamhain. Nuallan, all tied up, had, indeed, volunteered to go request food, as if it was the most natural thing in the world to do so.

"Yes, please do so. Judoc, can you escort him, please? I can already feel my stomach grumbling its displeasure at being unfed. And, also see what can be done about reducing a headache I have acquired. Perhaps a warm broth would help," Mathghamhain added, watching as Judoc untied the former enemy's feet. As soon as he had done so, Nuallan simply nodded his head and then sharply turned on his heel and strode from the room with the second-in-command of the Warriors Guild following swiftly behind him, purely because Nuallan could not be un-supervised.

Disciplined, Mathghamhain thought. What kind of training had Nuallan been subjected to in Nabaidh that he was that precise and easily commanded? Was he truly the last of the warriors they had fought two days past? How many got away?

Moving while Nuallan was out of the room Math-ghamhain found something more substantial than the basic protective leather attire that he could wear. He was about to depart the room when both men ap-peared at its entrance, with Judoc brandishing a cup with steam emanating from within its confines on behalf of the tied-up warrior.

"Your drink as requested, my liege, and I must say you look already a great deal sharper than you did a few moments ago when last I saw you. There were many women preparing food already, my liege, and you have been put down as a priority to be fed in any case," Nuallan offered with a wry smile. Mathgham-hain stole a quick glance at Judoc who confirmed Nuallan's words with a nod.

"My thanks. Nuallan. You are already proving yourself a well-disciplined servant," he said, taking the cup and sipping from it, letting the warmth of it waft over him and down his throat to quench his thirst and beginning to subdue his sleep-deprived induced headache. It was likely to be an issue for a few hours yet but the drink and a good solid meal would help as would the fresh air and anything that took his mind off of it.

It was not long afterward that he was seated around

the first fire of the day and was brought a plate by Agrona. It was heaped with freshly cooked meat and numerous fruits, even an egg from the birds they kept in Meadhan had been sacrificed. Usually, only the Chiefs enjoyed that luxury. Mathghamhain had little doubt that the status being granted him right now would not last beyond this day. Not unless he kept proving himself indispensable.

That, Mathghamhain thought to himself, with a smile, would not be overly difficult if his future self continued to offer helpful advice. Nuallan had been taken back to the hut where he could be re-confined for his own meal. He would need to check on Nuallan again soon in order to help the warrior assimilate with this village.

With his meal completed, Mathghamhain returned his empty plate to the nearest woman, offering her a warm smile as he did so. Normally, he was overlooked in favour of those in charge or who excelled in their guild, but when she smiled back he was positive his recent successes had altered how he was viewed by others. For now.

It was another while yet before his headache had subsided enough that he felt up to seeing what his fellow warriors were doing, but first, he wanted to check in with the hunters or at least his former Chief, lest they think he had forgotten them. Locating the man was never easy. If he was not in his room, often he was outside the village itself watching for the first signs of returning members of the Hunters Guild and directing them as need be.

"Brave Loegaire, how are you this morning, how

goes the hunting the past few days?" Mathghamhain asked as he clasped hands with the man. His long-time mentor was easily the tallest of the entire village but too lanky to have ever been considered for the Warriors Guild. Loegaire knew it and had embraced it. However, the Chief did have the strongest legs out of all the hunters and warriors combined—a testament to the fact he was the fastest. It was strange, Mathghamhain thought, to address more than one person in Meadhan as Chief. Usually, you only ever had to talk to the Chief of your own guild. Would it be simpler, he wondered, if the guilds all used a different title for their leaders?

"Ah, the bear himself is finally awake to offer greetings to his former Chief. Good morning, brave Mathghamhain. No fresh kills yet save for what was gathered in the early hours of dawn's first light for breakfast," Loegaire grinned. "You are looking well-rested and I see now that you are up and around your new servant, Nuallan, has been allowed to move around somewhat. Escorted of course, but it is greater freedom than he has had since you brought him here. He seems incredibly focussed on you at all times. I hope, for your sake, you can successfully convert him into a member of this village that we can all trust."

"He has pledged himself to my service. I suppose he takes it more seriously than any of us expected. He will, indeed, need to learn to be at ease more if he is to win any friends here. Still, there is something commendable in how devoted he is," Mathghamhain responded. Even as he said it aloud, he could not help but wonder why Nuallan would be so devoted—from his attentiveness, to his eagerness to fetch him breakfast—especially given how easily he turned his back on his own village of Nabaidh. It might even be worth asking the spirit about the man, next time it chose to speak to him.

"Ah, the good news is he, at the least, is indeed loyal to you. In fact, he has not made any indication of even attempting to run, although Cynwrig has made sure there is always a warrior keeping a tentative watch over him to be safe. I suspect whoever was on duty last night before you woke is an extremely tired warrior this morning. It will make it easy to determine who it was I suspect as well. Greetings, Nuallan. You do your liege well to be so attentive in your servitude to him," Loegaire said holding his hand up in salute to the man.

The enemy warrior was being accompanied back over to where Mathghamhain was, still tied up of course. Mathghamhain gave Caiside, who accompanied him, a questioning look only to get a shrug in response. It would seem that now that he was fully awake, he was in charge of looking after Nuallan himself.

Nuallan, not truly considered a member of this village, did not warrant a handshake as greeting nor the proper affection of the term "brave" that the hunters and warriors all greeted each other with unless another term of similar respect was substituted. Not that Nuallan had a hand free right now that he could have shaken hands with, but that was beside the point.

"Loyal Nuallan, I present you formally to the Hunters Guild Chief, Loegaire. He trained me well when I was younger and even if he was not a Chief, I would expect you to grant him the utmost respect if you would be loyal to me," Mathghamhain said standing to one side as Nuallan returned Loegaire's salute with a sharp nod.

"I am slowly learning who is important here, not that all are not important in their own way. I can but hope that one day, my liege, that I will have earned their respect as well," Nuallan offered, practically bowing at Loegaire.

"Loegaire, I am afraid I must go now to see what Chief Cynwrig would have of me this day. I hope the hunters continue to be successful in all their hunts," Mathghamhain said, shaking his former Chief's hand once again before turning to head in search of where Cynwrig was. He had a fairly good idea it would be the training grounds. He wanted to head there anyway to test Nuallan's skills when not in a life or death scenario. It would also be a good opportunity to check how recovered the former enemy warrior's arm was.

Listening to Loegaire's response in return as he turned, he only stopped to look over his shoulder once to confirm that Nuallan was following. The man moved far too silently to simply trust that he was present. It took little time to reach the training grounds which lay to the west, within its own enclosure, just outside the village. Waving to Brennus as he did so, Mathghamhain set foot into the enclosed area. A warrior was always on duty there to defend it, considering the items within its walls, that and the area was in high demand.

"Ah, brave Mathghamhain, you are looking much

better than when you were last seen around the fire before I retired for the eve," Cynwrig greeted clasping his hand tightly and pulling Mathghamhain in close for a hug of sorts. It was half-hug and half-shoulder block to check one's strength against each other. That was really the best way Mathghamhain could describe it. It had thrown him off the first time he had been pulled into one upon joining the Warriors Guild but now it was all too familiar.

"Indeed, it was a most restful sleep, I find more so now that my head is cleared enough to recognize that fact. Perchance is there any space upcoming on the field to test loyal Nuallan in sparring? I would gauge my new servant's skills in safe surroundings lest their lack cost us upon the field of battle," he asked even as Nuallan came in close to his side. Mathghamhain had little doubt that everyone present understood that he meant for that sparring session to be heavily supervised and with wooden weapons.

"You will need to wait on Brennus for he is currently practicing his parrying alone on the field, believing that no one else is yet awake enough to need it. Your mentor is many things Mathghamhain but aware of others needs he rarely is," Cynwrig's response came as they walked towards the training ground in question.

"I do understand, after all, brave Cynwrig, I did train under him extensively. He is a perfectionist and if he is practicing his parrying, it is because he feels it is lacking in a way that none but he can notice," Mathghamhain grinned realizing how well he had come to better understand Brennus these past months.

As he walked away from his Chief and towards Brennus in the middle of the circle that comprised the training ground, Mathghamhain wondered if there were enough warriors present to form a ring to prevent Nuallan from potentially attempting anything once untied. Holding up his hand in salute to his mentor and comrade at arms, Mathghamhain was barely able to get his shield up before the man's sword came crashing towards him. The grin Brennus wore showed the warrior had fully anticipated he would block it in time. People never changed, Mathgham- hain thought.

"Greetings brave Mathghamhain, you used to be quicker in your defence. Perhaps it is a remnant of your overzealousness in sleeping following your tri- umphant victory over the enemy," the warrior chided. "An enemy that even now you clasp to your breast, even if it is because he has offered his allegiance to you and you alone. A viper in disguise if ever there might be one."

"You do Nuallan a disservice Brennus. He has so far given no reason for us to doubt his loyalty as a servant. Perhaps you might be willing to spar with him so that I might gauge his skills in a safe combat setting. Would you be willing or will you give up the field of training that I might use it myself for such a test?" Mathghamhain asked returning the warrior's' grin with his own.

"A fitting idea as I would gladly welcome a living sparring partner but at the same time I do not wish to kill him should he forget it is mere practice. Nor do I wish to run the risk of him getting lucky and ending

my life. It is not my place to die in training but rather on the field of battle—the last to fall after a glorious bloody battle in which we are the victors," Brennus replied as he stepped to one side, gesturing to Mathghamhain to take his place. Mathghamhain could not help but shake his head at the response. Surely, Brennus understood they would be using wooden weapons. "I am certain this will allow you not only to gauge his skills but for me to gauge your own so that I can see what areas you need to improve upon."

"Brennus, you speak as though you can determine your own fate when you know that no one but the spirits can know that of ourselves," Mathghamhain responded with a sigh. "You also presume to suggest that you would fail to find something I need to improve no matter what. You would find fault in brave Chief Cynwrig's skill despite his position and experience."

As Mathghamhain spoke, he retrieved two sets of wooden weaponry and gestured at newly arrived warriors to surround the circle while he finished his discussion with his mentor. Brennus was good and observant but his childhood rival never ceased to amaze him in terms of how much of a perfectionist he could be.

"Of course I would. You are, after all, despite your recent triumph, still but a novice as a warrior. You are barely tested in true combat, your triumphant leadership two days past was but your first real experience," Brennus smirked as he moved outside the circle. Pausing for a moment, the warrior studied Nuallan before untying him and shoving him into the circle.

Brennus proceeded to only wait long enough for Mathghamhain to hand a set over to Nuallan before sheathing his sword, tossing his shield around his back, and throwing his arms up. "The sparring between Mathghamhain and Nuallan begins now," Brennus intonated before throwing his arms down rapidly.

Nuallan's wooden blade came in fast towards Mathghamhain in a flurry. Mathghamhain threw his shield up blocking every blow with ease, finding that he constantly had to quickly move his feet and adjust his stance. There seemed to be no pattern as to where Nuallan's sword would land next. It made it harder to get his shield up in time. Mathghamhain was taking particular note of how Nuallan moved to change his attacks, how he danced back upon his feet and lunged forward each time. Finally, as soon as the chance came, Mathghamhain caught the underside of Nuallan's shield. The action allowed him to drive his servant's shield arm up skyward.

Hoping to limit Nuallan's ability to reposition his shield, Mathghamhain withdrew half a stride then lunged to disarm his opponent. The plan failed at the last second. He was unable to stop his lunge in time. If Nuallan's sword had not been wooden, it would have impaled him easily. It was clear that the former enemy warrior's arm had definitely recovered.

Moving to regain his footing, Mathghamhain shook his head as he stared hard at Nuallan, puzzling it out. Nuallan was able to use both his hands equally. It explained the speed and why his servant was able to strike from so many positions. He had heard rumours of such a thing but had never seen it. Getting his first

glimpse of it while in combat with one who possessed such a skill was not the ideal time to do so. It did serve to emphasize how deadly such a skill could be. Nuallan would be indispensable as a warrior if he was ever trusted enough to be armed while out with them.

Staring upon his new servant, Mathghamhain suddenly dropped into a crouch much as he had in the past when facing large beasts and once again got behind Nuallan's shield to push it away. This time, he pressed against Nuallan's arm until it was driven as far back away from the centre of the warrior's chest as could be possible without breaking the man's arm to do so. Bringing his foot in to trap Nuallan in that stance, Mathghamhain brought his shield arm up rapidly, using it much like a knife in battle and caught Nuallan hard on the chin, staggering the man, forcing him to take a step back. He had learned a useful fact about his new servant and the other warriors present would be aware of it now, too, should Nuallan try to betray them. Grinning at Nuallan, he set the wooden weaponry down and held his hand out to help him up.

"You are cross-dominant when it comes to using your hands. Too bad you have now lost that skill as a surprise in combat but it would have been good for us to know before sparring. We are allies, all of us now, such a secret should not be kept," Mathghamhain grinned as Nuallan got to his feet.

"Indeed, my liege, but you did prove to be a capable and quick thinker the other day as a foe, to let you know something I could use as an advantage would scarcely have suited one who is less skilled and adept at tactics," Nuallan said before tensing suddenly.

Looking over his shoulder, Mathghamhain spotted Brennus approaching closer to talk and waved at Nuallan to relax.

"It is simply Brennus, my mentor, offering his own words of advice on how the sparring did go," Mathghamhain reassured his servant. "What words do you have to offer Brennus? I am certain you have many."

"Mathghamhain, far be it from me to advise on the use of your foot to control a battle by trapping your opponent but it is always a good idea to do so if one can do it without being struck. It was a great risk you took in doing so especially since you clearly were aware by then of Nuallan's advantage in using both arms equally against you and his adeptness at switching his shield and sword with little effort between hands. That ability to switch so quickly is a greater skill than the equal dominance of his arms," Brennus said before looking to Nuallan, nodding at him.

"Was this a true battle and there were more of us, you might have wounded your own fellow warrior with that stunt you pulled," the warrior continued before proceeding to offer advice. "Always drop your arms back if possible when switching so you avoid damaging an ally. However, if you are surrounded by the enemy and with no ally next to you, then switch the way you did in sparring. You also need to work on anticipating why they might be moving how they are. Mathghamhain is a former hunter and will not hesitate to drop into his former preferred stance when fighting a beast; beasts move on four legs for the most part so he must drop to their level to properly face them. Take note of your opponents choice of move-

ment. Recognize why they might use it and deduce from that how they might move the rest of the time. Everyone has a preferred way of fighting. No one can change from one to the other without difficulty or showing themselves to not function naturally that way."

"It is helpful advice, Brennus. I am thankful for your observations and hope to one day soon be trusted to join you and your fellow warriors, that I might call you an ally and not simply ally to my liege, Mathghamhain," Nuallan responded nodding at the warrior. "I had not before seen a warrior who moves like a hunter nor do I recall the last time I observed a hunter in action enough to note that is what my liege was doing. Now that I know, I will be certain to study that method of fighting so that I might add it to my own range of fighting techniques."

Moving to retrieve the wooden sparring weaponry, Nuallan bowed low to Mathghamhain "Would my liege care for a second round?"

"Actually, Nuallan, I would test my skill against one such as yourself now that I see you have a unique skill set with your own arms," Brennus interjected, a broad grin crossing his lips. "Mathghamhain can observe this time but let us summon Chief Cynwrig over to call the session as I suspect he, too, will want to observe this battle."

Mathghamhain did his best not to wince at his mentor's words. It meant Nuallan had done a danger-ous thing—he had caused Brennus to view the man as a challenge.

CHAPTER 8
Nuallan

It was two additional sparring sessions later that Nuallan finally moved to sit with Mathghamhain and consider what to do next.

"I am afraid I do not understand, my liege. If you are the gifted tactician you have proven yourself as, why then are you considered the least amongst the warriors of this village, one who is trained as both a hunter and a warrior?" Nuallan asked. The line of questioning was risky, but since he had not been tied up again yet, it was a good opportunity to learn about the warrior specifically. Who was this man to have been offered the chance to change guilds? It was not a thing he had ever seen done in Nabaidh.

"You speak out of turn, Nuallan. I am only newly trained and have only recently earned my place. It was not all that long ago that I was one of the lowliest thought of young men in Meadhan," Mathghamhain returned, his voice barely louder than a strangled whisper. "It was naught but luck that led to my transition from hunter to warrior. Luck, the patience of Brennus, and the wisdom of Chief Cynwrig. It was desperation that led to them asking my advice on how we might find triumph in the jaws of defeat."

"Indeed, so you are a natural at it and should be angling to prove that it was not a fluke, that you are qualified to be in a higher position of authority," Nuallan suggested, seeing a possible opening to help the conversation proceed.

"You speak heresy and forget yourself loyal, Nuallan. Do not let the others hear you or you will never earn their trust. They will see you as seeking to destroy us from within when you failed to do so from without," his liege responded growling in anger. "You have not even earned a place of safety here and you speak of treason."

"Not of treason, my liege, but of taking your seeming rightful place in a role of leadership, not questioning the effectiveness of the current," Nuallan countered.

"It is a minor difference," Mathghamhain began to say as Cynwrig was spotted approaching, looking fairly angry in demeanour. That worried Nuallan. Had someone overheard and gotten word to the Warrior Chief already?

"Alas, it would seem, brave Mathghamhain, that even so soon recovered from your rest, we have received word of an encroachment of warriors to the south. There seems no rest these days from enemy villages," Cynwrig said glaring at Nuallan as he spoke despite the fact that Nabaidh was further west of them than it was south.

"So soon. It would seem we are to be sorely tested while they feel us to be weak," the young warrior responded.

"What we must do is strike before they get too close to being able to harm our growing fields and catch our best beasts. We may be a small village but we are not weak," Cynwrig countered watching as Nuallan rose swiftly, offering his hand to help Mathghamhain to his feet.

"My brave liege, and Chief Cynwrig: to the south, where you indicated, is an enemy that, while great in number, lacks easy access to metal and proper weaponry," Nuallan spoke hoping his advice would be accepted. "They are foragers by nature and will scavenge and strike with fires if they feel they will lose. You will need to move swiftly to face an enemy that torches the land."

"Ah, you do well to aid us by providing us with this knowledge. Mathghamhain, can you think of how we might best utilize this knowledge? After all, you are the one with the familiarity of hunter techniques. Are scavengers not much similar, in so far as your knowing how to counter such acts?" Cynwrig asked.

"We must douse ourselves with water prior to attacking if possible, keep the metal armour to a minimum as it will grow quite hot by the flame even if hide as the alternative burns much easier it does not hold heat. We can move to encircle them if we know the edges of their attack and work our way inwards to cut them off," Mathghamhain suggested.

Nuallan was impressed. Despite his new liege's words to the contrary, he did, indeed, have a mind for such things and clearly, the Warrior Chief Cynwrig recognized that. Spotting the other warriors coming to join them at the entrance of the village, he cleared his throat.

"Nuallan, is everything okay?" Mathghamhain began but then nodded. "We will need someone to stay and guard you in the hut."

The nature of the response bothered him. It suggested Meadhan sent all of its warriors out, leaving

none behind to protect it. It was foolish but did explain why they had fought so fiercely even in the face of certain defeat.

"I do not know if we can afford to spare anyone, Mathghamhain, we may need to have him bound and brought with us," Cynwrig began. "Plus, he may have further knowledge about our foe he can share."

"That would still require a warrior being needed to guard him, it would simply be out in the open rather than within the village. Brave and wise Chief Cynwrig, we are already greatly reduced in number, we should allow Nuallan to be armed again provided he stays with me. We could use the extra set of hands, risky as it may be," Mathghamhain countered.

Nuallan watched, listening fascinated at how easily the warriors seemed to naturally accept looking to his liege for advice on how to proceed. Could Mathghamhain truly not recognize it?

"I am thinking a multi-pronged attack might be best even with our small numbers. Leave two to guard the village. The rest of us and Nuallan can split into three groups. Two to take the extreme sides and one to come up the middle to attack them at their centre as we herd them together," Mathghamhain finished.

"It is as much the same plan as I would suggest brave Mathghamhain. Again you do, indeed, have a mind for tactics even without a guide. There be hope for you yet," Cynwrig grinned, smacking the warrior across the back.

"My liege did lead you all to victory for a reason, did he not?" Nuallan said quietly. Were they really considering trusting him to be armed? The idea was madness. He gulped after he had spoken, taking a step back as the warriors crowded around to further discuss his liege's proposed strategy.

He was positive that Mathghamhain's plan to take him with them into combat would be overruled. It was asking too much of these warriors to trust him that much already. He had only been there a couple of days, most of that time tied up.

Nuallan was so certain of what would happen that he looked up in shock when the warrior named Caiside came over directing him to walk with him. They were going to arm him.

CHAPTER 9
Mathghamhain

The first real sign of the encroaching enemy came a good while later, at which point two of their guild broke off in a charge, at Mathghamhain's direction, and sliced through the enemy cutting into them mercilessly. The rest of their group was already peeling off in two directions, save for Nuallan and himself who advanced forward in the direction they had all been heading initially, Cynwrig hanging back with one of the others to hold the line and defend against anything that got near Meadhan.

"You need not try and explain my strengths to them. You can be loyal without trying to talk me up to them. Cynwrig already seems determined to curry my favour and my own mentor has been oddly deferent to me today. I suspect our victory over your former village has much to do with it and they are slowly wrapping their minds around how decisive a victory we did snatch from so certain a defeat," Mathghamhain said to Nuallan before pausing. "And you are still technically a prisoner…you should not be doing anything to potentially anger them, no matter how well-meaning it is."

"You were all quite done for. The balls of dirt were a thing of brilliance. They caught us unawares," Nuallan responded, eyes focussed on the enemy ahead."We knew not to enter the woods to engage you and were content to flush you all out but that attack caused us to be enraged and pursue you where we should not have. Disrupting an opposing force's well-laid plans and discipline is not an easy feat, my liege. You should be impressed and honoured for managing it, to say nothing of the final victory."

"Even so..," Mathghamhain responded, halting and gesturing to hang back behind him. "Crouch."

As soon as he had spoken, Mathghamhain charged full speed forward, sword pointed outwards. Leaping at the last possible second, he flipped his sword downwards. As he did so, he brought his shield around to protect his face on the downward fall. The move gutted the opponent who had flattened himself in the tall grass. Beckoning to Nuallan, he watched as more of their foes rose from hiding. The enemy had set an ambush and now he and Nuallan had to face a greater number of them than intended.

"To my back, my liege," Nuallan shouted as he reached his back. His sword drawn, they greeted all attackers head-on with simultaneously selected slices of their swords. The field quickly ran red with the blood of the enemy who still advanced. They could not hold the line this way for much longer. He could already hear Nuallan labouring to breathe.

"Be ready," he called out knowing neither Nuallan nor the enemy would understand what was meant, not even his fellow warriors would nor would the hunters he had once run with. It was essentially a way to say he was going to change tactics. Lunging on the next hit, he kept moving forward keeping his sword steady as he ran through that foe and the next one after him before pulling it free. He could not feel Nuallan directly behind him at present but knew he would in due course. He had to trust his servant would remain true to his pledge of allegiance. The alternative was certain death for both of them.

Diving face-first to the ground, he rolled over onto his back and lifted his sword as he was jumping back to his feet. That was when he saw Nuallan close enough for his plan to work.

"Drop," Mathghamhain yelled at the last possible moment, watching as Nuallan did so just as he reached his feet, and used the warrior as a springboard to get additional height and crash down on the approaching enemy. The move cleaved the enemy's head with a blade right through the centre of the man's face. Keep doing the unexpected until help came was the plan at this point. An ambush could not work if they stayed unpredictable in their movements.

Slicing through them as Nuallan turned to take the line of attack that he had previously faced, Mathghamhain could feel his servant's grin now that they had resumed hacking through the enemy. Their countering not stopping in the constant motion until he could see an end to it coming. A relief delayed by the sighting of additional movement, coming from both directions as his fellow warriors and more of the enemy came onto the scene. Now was the time for the actual plan to work. When Nuallan had said this enemy had great numbers he had not been jesting. It had felt like a never-ending field of them and that was even with the rest of the warriors facing their own waves of them.

Mathghamhain was shocked they had lasted for as long as they had but this was ridiculous. The sun could already be seen to be lower in the sky than when they had set out. Had they really been out here that long, he wondered as the battle finally ended in a field of blood and weaponry? He looked wearily at the others as they all realized around the same time that they had run out of people to kill.

He disliked that, despite how much Nuallan had aided them all, Mathghamhain's fellow warriors were looking a bit too eagerly at his servant with blood-thirst in their eyes. Outmatched in experience as Mathghamhain was, he had to do something quickly to protect his servant.

"Nuallan was the sole warrior with me. We held our position amidst an ambush while we waited on you all to herd your opponents this way and join us," Mathghamhain said moving to stand in front of Nuallan, to shield him if necessary. "The enemy did wait for us laying there in the fields to hide until we were nearly on top of them. He is not an enemy but a good, faithful, loyal servant, and warrior. A warrior like all of you."

"There are, indeed, a far greater number of bodies strewn about, and in most creative ways of dying. I would say I am inclined to believe you, brave Mathghamhain," Brennus said coming to join him in shielding Nuallan. That was odd, of all the people to defend him, it was his former rival. Then again, Brennus was also the one who had trained and mentored him.

It did not help that Brennus was also a fairly young member of their guild. Despite that, the warrior remained one of the fiercest and most studious when it came to the art of combat. His presence in defending Nuallan and himself would speak volumes toward quieting the others for that fact alone. There was also the fact that Brennus had quite the temper if angered.

"If you all feel it is death I deserve, know that I have served my new liege with nothing but loyalty and honour but I do understand your hesitation in trusting me still," Nuallan said stepping out from behind them both, his sword now sheathed and raising his arms in a sign of surrender to fate.

Watching the reaction of the rest, Mathghamhain noticed that there was grumbling before they stopped advancing and all of them slowly sheathed their swords. A cheer went up not in victory but in toasting Mathghamhain. It took him a moment to realize even that Brennus beside him was also cheering.

"Mathghamhain, you are brave, indeed, and a masterful leader. They will once again sing your praises back at Meadhan when they hear of our bloody and glorious victory this day," Brennus grinned as the warriors headed back towards Meadhan, carrying their fallen second-in-command. Other warriors were rushing towards Cynwrig and speaking hurriedly as they reached the Chief's position, telling fantastic tales of the victory they had won and how Mathghamhain's plan had worked, even in the face of the greater enemy number than expected, and the brutality with which the enemy was faced and defeated with no foe left unfelled.

"You continue to honour us with your insights Mathghamhain. Judoc's death is a terrible one but I have a feeling there will be an easy decision to be made soon enough," Cynwrig said, despair in his voice even while clasping Mathghamhain's arm and raising it once again in victory. The equally triumphant and sombre group of warriors could easily be heard entering the village. Despite the cheers, Mathghamhain worried what Cynwrig had meant.

CHAPTER 10

When the feast following their victory had concluded, Mathghamhain glanced up from talking to Nuallan to see Brennus approaching and then clasping him more firmly on the shoulder of his shield arm than he liked.

"Brennus, you seem quite angered despite our recent victory…come…relax…sit with us…" Mathghamhain suggested looking at his mentor worriedly. Even more so when the warrior's grip tightened to the point he could feel the man's thumb starting to drive itself into his shoulder muscle.

"Chief Cynwrig held a vote. Brave Judoc's replacement needed to be named. You were left out of the vote because of another matter being voted upon since your view might have skewed things, brave Mathghamhain. I know you to be relentless in combat and as a hunter. Even so, I did not vote for you, not because I do not feel you are incapable of the position but because I feel you need additional experience before being elected to such a role of authority. Even if you have found yourself in such a position the last two battles you've been in. You will still have my allegiance," Brennus said loosening his grip before reaching out and bodily hauling him to his feet grasping him in a tight hug to his chest as if trying to squeeze the life from his body. "Chief Cynwrig will be along shortly to tell you himself, but you are now the second-in-command and Nuallan, you have been instated as a provisional member of our Guild. You have proven yourself on the field of battle in protecting your brethren in the face of overwhelming odds, but I will still be watching you—as will we all."

"I thank you for the trust, Brennus," Nuallan said rising to grip the man's hand while turning eyes on Mathghamhain. "Congratulations, my liege. I did say you were destined for such a role, did I not? It would seem that the spirits are not the only ones to know what is to come even if the lowliest creature of the ground could see the inevitable."

"Second-in-command, you say, and my brave servant is now a warrior of the Guild, provisionally anyway, after only two days. It is a lot at once, Brennus," Mathghamhain responded looking from Brennus to Nuallan, then to the approaching Cynwrig who was flanked by the rest of the Warriors Guild. From the look of things, Loegaire was also with them. This was unusual ground but had he not previously seen such an acceleration in standing less than a year prior with Caiside's cousin in the Caretakers Guild? Strange as it was, he had led them in tactics twice successfully had he not? He deserved this even if he did understand why Brennus and others might think otherwise. That he had been voted into the position told Mathghamhain that enough of his fellow warriors, all of whom had been doing this for much longer and were arguably more deserving, had chosen him for the role. That was a lot to wrap the mind around. Released from the tight embrace Brennus had him in, Mathghamhain clasped Chief Cynwrig's hand and then Loegaire's, bowing to each in turn. "Brave Cynwrig, Brave Loegaire. You both honour me with your dual presence this evening."

"Indeed, it is fitting that your former Chief is here to recognize this glorious appointment. Know this evening, brave Mathghamhain, that you have been voted by your peers to be the second-in-command of the Warriors Guild. That you will be entrusted to prepare and execute strategies when we are called upon to defend these lands and should the means be made possible, to claim new lands as we expand for our growing populace." Cynwrig began, his tone and formality causing Mathghamhain to stand perfectly still. He did not dare flinch and give the impression he was not up to the role being thrust upon him. "Know that you will be expected to be in attendance to my person for many a meeting and strategy session as we choose each day's agenda. Know that you have been entrusted with the responsibility of commanding the guild should I be absent or incapacitated. That should I perish on the field of battle or in illness or from injuries accrued, that you will be required to lead until such time as a vote can be taken for a new Chief to be chosen to lead our number. That despite being the second-in-command, you will not have full command in such an event unless so voted as you will share command with brave Loegaire or his successor if he has perished by such a time."

Mathghamhain wanted to respond immediately, as everyone present was staring at him as if he was supposed to say something. What could he say? Even the spirit was being silent, yet would this moment not be considered major enough that it would speak?

Cynwrig rescued him as the Chief bowed to him and held out his hand palm up. In it was a small piece of metal. "Do you accept this decision Mathghamhain?" he asked.

Looking at all their faces watching him intently, Mathghamhain specifically searched Loegaire's before nodding his agreement. "I do accept this great honour and thank you all for entrusting me with such a responsibility. I, who was the least of you not long ago," Mathghamhain answered before kneeing carefully while Cynwrig slammed the metal piece against his breastplate, permanently affixing it to indicate his new position. The sudden thrust against his chest nearly threw Mathghamhain off balance.

"Excellent! There will be a formal announcement tomorrow for the benefit of the rest of Meadhan," Cynwrig responded. Before Mathghamhain could reply, he saw that the Chief's attention had turned to Nuallan.

Despite what Brennus had said not much earlier, he was still concerned. Yes, Nuallan had been helpful today but he had only been out there in battle with them because they could not risk leaving him in Meadhan unguarded. Now that they were back in the village, Nuallan should have been tied up again. Cynwrig could, indeed, well be about to order such a thing be done and chastise him for not doing so already.

"Brave Nuallan, newly come to Meadhan and loyal servant to brave Mathghamhain, know that you have proven yourself a faithful and valiant warrior of strength, speed, and unwavering courage in the face of overwhelming odds both from ally and foe alike," Cynwrig spoke, causing Mathghamhain to breathe a quiet sigh of relief. "You have been elected to be a provisional member of our Warriors Guild. No longer must you rely on Mathghamhain to be at your side for protection. We shall treat you as a fellow warrior and it is my hope that soon enough you will become a full member."

Nodding his affirmation, Nuallan bowed deeply and kneeled, his head lowered. "I accept your decision and am honoured to be part of such a Guild. My allegiance will ever be first to my liege, though," Nuallan said in a firm voice, while Cynwrig nodded and drew his sword touching both the warrior's shoulders with the flat of the blade.

"Rise then, Nuallan, strong and brave warrior. Welcome to our Guild," Cynwrig added before re-sheathing his sword. "I will leave you to your celebration, brave Mathghamhain, but would ask that you join me first thing in the morning alone ahead of the announcement, that we might discuss plans for the days to come. I am most anxious to pick your mind while it is still so strong of thought in tactical nature."

"Of course, brave Cynwrig," Mathghamhain nodded watching the warriors scatter to their own celebrations. Those had clearly been delayed by the vote he had not been a part of. Only Loegaire lingered, moving close to him and placing an arm around his shoulders.

Looking questioningly at his former Chief, Mathghamhain followed the man's gaze to Meadhan's entrance. Nodding his understanding, he gave a quick whisper to Nuallan to make haste to catch up with the other warriors. Immediately afterward, Mathghamhain followed Loegaire in order to see what needed to be discussed so urgently in private.

Outside the village gates, he watched as Loegaire looked at him sternly. "Mathghamhain, I knew you to be a valiant and capable hunter. To see your skill put on display in the area of warrior combat and tactics is quite thrilling and a sight to behold. It is a testament that we had been holding you back for far too long making you naught but a lowly hunter. I would ask that you accept this apology."

Mathghamhain looked shocked at his former chief

before holding his hand out to clasp it. "Loegaire, hunters are warriors who fight beasts, not men. They are simply a different type of warrior. We are all warriors at heart. You never held me back for we are all equal. Do not think of hunters as being lower than warriors. Never think that, and now that I am second-in-command to Chief Cynwrig, know that I will work hard to see that hunters are given the proper recognition they are due. Meadhan could not be managed or have ever survived these past years without you or the Hunters Guild, nor could it without Cynwrig and the Warriors Guild or any of the other Guilds."

Despite his words, Mathghamhain still felt the need to further reassure Loegaire that nothing had really changed. To see the man feel the need to apologize made him uncomfortable and he wanted to put a stop to it quickly. "We all must work together and are better as a whole united force. It is in recognizing each other's strengths that we have our greatest strength. United we must be if we are to continue to face such continued opposition from the neighbouring villages."

Even as he finished, Mathghamhain was surprised when he realized how oratorical his choice of words had been. The shock was not his alone, he noted, since Loegaire looked like he was desperately trying to keep his jaw from hanging open.

"You speak with greater wisdom than your years, Mathghamhain. Be proud of that, and thank you for your belief in us. I fear such equal recognition will never happen. Too often we are all steeped in how we are raised, in tradition, and the needs of the many.

Hunters provide food, warriors keep us all alive, even if the food does as well. Hunters, if we were gone, the village would survive thanks to the farmers. If the warriors were gone, it would fall to those less skilled to keep us protected. It is hardly balanced," Loegaire said even as he gripped Mathghamhain's hand tightly and smiled. "That does not mean to say that times cannot change, only that as things are currently in our time and world that equality is not a thing to be striven for."

"One day, perhaps, then we will get the chance to make it possible for such equality, brave Loegaire. I thank you for your continued candour, loyalty, and friendship. I will try to make time to visit with you more often. You have been a good friend, even back when I was a child and you were first named Hunters Guild Chief," Mathghamhain replied.

With a nod and another clasping of hands, Mathghamhain turned to head back into the village. As much as he wanted to hang around Loegaire longer, they both had responsibilities elsewhere. That and with his long-time connection to him, Mathghamhain still struggled with the fact that Loegaire was not his chief any longer. He was doing his best to not let it show but if he hung around the man much longer, it would be impossible to hide.

TWO

CHAPTER 11

Knocking an enemy warrior off their feet as he moved forward, Mathghamhain put extra emphasis into it. Stepping on the man's foot with his full weight, he felt it break. In the few years since he had become a warrior, it felt like there was fighting constantly. At times they were short skirmishes, but increasingly the warriors of Meadhan were in full battles, like today. He was not sure if the warriors from other villages were getting too eager to expand, or if it was something else driving their need for violence. Back when he had been a hunter, the Warriors Guild primarily patrolled the land, with only the occasional skirmish.

Things had clearly changed.

Shaking his head, Mathghamhain surveyed the field of battle. Cynwrig and he had planned thoroughly for this battle. They had gone over every aspect of it in painstaking detail from the day they had laid claim to a portion of the village's land. They needed to be ready for the retaliation. Now a few months later, that day had come.

Mathghamhain nodded to himself as he continued past the wounded enemy warrior. No sense taking the time to kill the enemy if he could simply incapacitate them and end the confrontation quicker as a result. When the battle was done, they could decide what to do.

He took no pleasure in such an act, yet, as it had for the majority of the time since he had been named the second-in-command, the spirit did not speak. Its continued silence in the matters of battle was reassuring to him. It suggested he was doing the right thing so the spirit was not needed to steer him. With each successful fight, his reputation for tactics and ferocity had grown. The other warriors had taken a chance by voting for him as Cynwrig's second-in-command and he felt he had grown quite well into that role. It had certainly helped that the number of warriors in the guild had increased steadily as more boys upon coming of age had been accepted into the guild. The Hunters Guild could not say the same. None were found to be better suited to hunting, nor did any of the boys seem to really consider applying to Loegaire's guild. That was despite the best efforts of that Chief, along with his second, and Cynwrig, and himself to make it sound rewarding.

Getting closer to the centre of the fray, Mathghamhain's eyes widened. A single word escaping his lips. "No!"

Only Caiside was close enough to turn and see the cause for the exclamation. Chief Cynwrig had fallen. Mathghamhain's legs felt heavy as he desperately tried to get closer. It was as if the earth itself was trying to slow him down. As he continued to press forward, it became clear the rest of the guild had seen what had occurred, the carefully constructed plan began to

show signs of falling apart. Mathghamhain wanted to be by Cynwrig's side as quickly as possible but he also had to take charge before all was lost.

Rallying the warriors with shouts, Mathghamhain gestured to them what he needed them to do. As soon as he was certain they understood, he began to move once again, leading by example. As much as he wished to reach Cynwrig, it would have to wait until the battlefield was cleared. Around him, his fellow warriors did as instructed and stopped working to incapacitate the enemy but instead to either kill them immediately or give them plenty of reason to retreat.

It was after what remained of the enemy had been pushed back far enough to retreat that Mathghamhain sheathed his sword and dropped to his knees in despair beside Cynwrig's still form.

Despite all their thorough planning, it simply was not enough. They had missed something in their strategy meetings. And now, brave Chief Cynwrig, for so long the leader of the Warriors Guild, was dead.

Crouched over him, Mathghamhain could not tear his eyes away. They had become friends these past three years. Everyone in Meadhan looked up to Cynwrig. His death, it was too much; it could not be real. Cynwrig had been chief for fifteen years now, longer than any chief before him had been, and had always, always recognized the skills and talents of his guild's members, utilizing them as best he could to the utmost effectiveness. It took Mathghamhain a few moments to realize he was crying. He had not cried since he was a child. What would the guild do now? What would the village do? His thoughts were interrupted by a sudden chill in the air.

"Brave Mathghamhain, you do the guild a disservice by lingering too close to the fallen chief. Now is the time to rise and command. Now is the time to give them a reason to believe that you can lead them when the vote does come and in the days ahead. It is clearly what Cynwrig was grooming you for. If you do not act quickly, Brennus will try to position himself as a better candidate due to his strength and speed. Others as well for their experience. Rise, show your strength for action and will in these darkest of times," the spirit whispered.

Mathghamhain's lips drew tight. He did not have time for this.

Scowling, he wanted to yell at the spirit for speaking right now and about such things. This was neither the time nor the place and the spirit should have known better, *his* spirit should have known better! He hated it even further given how much truth there was in its words. The fact that the air was still chilled told him that the sprit was not quite done speaking. He had to brace himself for what was said next before he reacted aloud. It was as the spirit had said, he did have to show strength now and show he still deserved to command with Cynwrig's death. They needed a warrior who was familiar with commanding and he had been in that role for two years now. It should be his to claim by right, not one he had to win by vote, but if nothing else, the village of Meadhan for all of its struggles found solace and clarity in abiding by tradition. Mathghamhain was still not okay with the spirit bringing it up now.

"I know what you are thinking, Mathghamhain. Tradition is only tradition until you are able to change it and you cannot change it until you are Chief and able to convince the other Guild Chiefs. In the meantime, you must do as it dictates and show your resolve and command with power and understanding," the spirit's voice came again.

Nodding at Cynwrig's fallen body, he reached out carefully and mouthed goodbye to the Warrior Chief, moving the deceased's eyelids closed before slowly getting to his feet. By now the rest of the guild had returned from dispatching the enemy. Watching each of the other warrior's eyes one by one, his face steady and calm, Mathghamhain fought back the emotion he wanted to show. He stood slowly and let the words of the spirit guide his actions right now more than he might have wished to under the circumstances.

"Fellow warriors. We carry brave Cynwrig to Meadhan that he might be afforded proper burial rites as is befitting his long-held position, so that not only might we mourn, but all that benefited from his years of service to the village might be able to as well. It is the least we can do in memory of him," he said carefully, watching as Nuallan bowed and slowly stepped forward, a full member of the guild for over a year now, sword sheathed and shield on his back, to help lift the fallen chief as soon as others joined him. One by one each warrior fought their own impulses and stooped, surrounding the body of Cynwrig.

As they did so, Brennus moved in close to Mathghamhain, going nose to nose with him for a brief moment of defiance before he, too, moved towards

Cynwrig's head to lift it, leaving the feet to be carried by Mathghamhain. That defiance was a message and it caused a shiver to run through him. He had fought side by side with Brennus closely now for years. The thought of facing him as a rival once more filled him with dread. He would have to figure out how to deal with it back at the village. For now, duty and friendship took precedent. Lifting Cynwrig's feet, he knew this was a tradition but had never seen it executed. That the one in command must be at the rear and show his strength in humility by taking the lowest end of his predecessor on the long road back to the village.

The walk was slow but it was by no means silent as a long slow unified chant was spoken by them all crying out to help Cynwrig's spirit ascend to the afterlife. This was not a loss mixed with a celebration like when Judoc had fallen. There was nothing to celebrate this day. Unwavering in how aloft they held their fallen leader, Cynwrig's shield and sword laid across his chest to keep it with him as he had served using them in life. It was while doing so that Mathghamhain realized the air had never warmed: the spirit was still present enough to speak.

"You see even when they do not wish to, they bow to your rank but that will only last for so long as you give them cause before they resist. You will need to win their hearts, not simply their swords in the days ahead. They will not let many days go past without a true chief of the Warriors Guild," the spirit said so close to his ear it felt unsettling.

He said nothing. He was trying to mentally command the spirit to be silent right now. Years upon end without being heard from and it was choosing now to make its presence known and offer advice in the most irritating way possible. Mathghamhain was starting to dislike his future self's sense of decorum.

Loegaire was the first to see them marching towards the village and immediately dropped to one knee as he moved to one side so they could freely enter through the gates, others doing the same as they saw the march coming, the women folding their hands in front of them and bowing their heads. Mathghamhain could not even take any joy at seeing Cacht again in a large gathering. Too often as of late, she was nowhere to be found, a result of how busy she had become the past year when she unexpectedly rose from second-in-command of the Caretakers Guild to Chief.

Words about Cynwrig's bravery and leadership qualities lasted the rest of the week as the hunters went to great lengths to hunt down the most magnificent beast they could find by any means necessary so that the celebration could be done with the finest of prepared food.

Four days into the feasting, one of the senior warriors, Bradan, tapped Mathghamhain on the shoulder. Stepping away with them to speak in private, Mathghamhain did his best not to let his emotions show as the warrior explained to him that, while he had proven a capable second-in-command to Cynwrig, he would not have his vote for Chief. Bradan even proceeded to elaborate that it was in part due to Mathghamhain's lack of overall experience compared to almost everyone else in the guild but that it could not be definitively proven that his tactics were not in some small part responsible for the Chief's death. Suppressing his anger at the suggestion, Mathgham-hain nodded his understanding. It bothered him but the spirit didn't show up to suggest anything to change this warrior's mind. Before the warrior could turn to leave, Mathghamhain extended his hand outward to clasp Bradan's.

"Thank you for taking the time to let me know. It is greatly appreciated," he said nodding firmly. It was, after all, a strong sign of respect that he had been told in advance at all. Watching as the warrior left, Math-ghamhain headed back to rejoin the feasting. As it turned out, that warrior would not be the only one to show him such respect.

Over the course of the next day, over half of the Warriors Guild took him aside, telling him much the same thing. Keeping mental track of their numbers, Mathghamhain was positive now that with a vote he would surely lose but it raised the question of whether he would remain second-in-command under a new chief. Heading out of Meadhan early the final morning of feasting, he made sure Nuallan had not followed and stared out across the fields. Frowning, he slowly walked until he reached the sight of where he had killed the bear so long ago.

Setting foot by the rocky outcropping he had used for shielding in that fight, he ran his fingers deftly over their surface, feeling the rough edges as his thoughts spun as to how things would proceed now. He had proven himself countless times the past two years, had he not? Had not Cynwrig praised his decisions repeatedly and many times deferred to his decisions when it came to strategies? Was he not, in fact, responsible for the victories that had afforded their village new land to watch over, farm, and hunt upon? Why would they not choose him?

"They will not choose you because they are too full of drink. When they sober up before the vote, they will see and remember why they have as much as they do. It will not be easy but you should perhaps prepare a reminder before the vote is taken. You know not who else might be chosen. Loegaire has long been the Chief of the Hunters Guild and is supposed to be co-leading the Warriors Guild with you once the feasting is over," the voice of the spirit came, hitting Mathghamhain like a ton of logs. He had not even felt the temperature of the air change this time.

"What then would you suggest as a reminder? I am not going to try and stage a battle to prove my success in tactics. I cannot best them in experience or speed or strength. I am but a hunter who was made a warrior," Mathghamhain protested at the words of the spirit even as his thoughts began to spin as he recalled a constant thing he reminded others about. Perhaps there was a way to change things.

"You already know what you have to do. Is there truly another way? Yes, it is a painful choice to make but think about the changes you can bring about? The way things would become possible," the spirit intoned eagerly. Could a spirit be said to be eager sounding?

"It would mean a grave betrayal of trust and friendship. I cannot. It is unfathomable to even contemplate such a thing, no matter the results,"

Mathghamhain growled.

"The thought already crossed your mind. You cannot deny it now…it will ruminate in your thoughts until it is no longer a viable option," the spirit said before there was again silence.

Rising gradually, Mathghamhain scowled at the rocky outcropping. He could not do what the spirit was suggesting. It was too much, no matter how good its advice had been so far. How could his own future self even suggest such a thing? There had to be another way. He did not truly want to be the Chief of the Warriors Guild that bad, surely.

Striding back at a much slower pace than was his norm, he paused when he saw the hunters departing for the day. Greeting them as he passed with a salute, he stopped in his tracks only when he saw Loegaire at the gates. No, this was not the way to become Chief, Mathghamhain thought, as he offered the man his hand. Clasping Mathghamhain's hand, the Hunter Chief looked at him worriedly.

"It is a bit early for you to be out so far from Meadhan, is it not? I would think with as much drink as you and your fellow warriors are ingesting these past few days that such a stroll might be a bad idea for you. Clearing your head before the work begins of leading the Warriors Guild until a new chief is elected?" Loegaire asked as he let go of Mathgham-hain's hand.

"It is, indeed, early Loegaire but, as you so well deduced, it was wholly necessary if I am to clear my head and prepare myself for the difficult days ahead," Mathghamhain began before diving into the subject of

combining the Guilds in lieu of the alternative way of going about things. "We are to lead the Warriors Guild jointly until such time as the election of a new chief can be performed. Perhaps now would be the time to broach the idea that since this is the case—you being chosen to offer guidance while I temporarily lead the Guild—that it is due to not simply your experience but, as you are the Chief of the Hunters Guild specifically, that qualifies you. That is, in part, because as has been discussed before by us, that hunters are a different form of warrior. One fights beasts, the other their fellow man, and what are men but beasts who have become civilized and work together?"

"It is a possibility that only you might consider, Mathghamhain. What is it you are getting at by bringing this up? Do you doubt, truly, that they will not hold an election to the role of the chief as soon as the feasting is over, rather than give you a chance to lead at all with my guidance?" Loegaire asked, sounding somewhat thrown by what had been said.

"What I am getting at, Loegaire, is if that is, indeed, part of why you as Chief of the Hunters Guild are the designated guide whenever a Chief of the Warriors Guild dies and the second-in-command must temporarily take command, perhaps it is in part due to old laws of our people that recognize that hunters and warriors should, in fact, be one Guild separated only by a thin definition of beast and man. Why should the Hunters Guild then not have a say in the election of a new Chief if, as we know, they are in fact warriors?" he responded with a wry smile now. This had to be a viable alternative surely.

"You speak madness, Mathghamhain. You suggest the guilds be merged with one chief. You wish to position me as chief over the warriors?" Loegaire asked even more worried than before.

"Not you, nor necessarily even myself. Instead, I would suggest, before an election be held, that the guilds be told they are merging and for a chief to be chosen from amongst them and a new second-in-command. Put both roles up for consideration. After all, you have a second-in-command as well, do you not?" Mathghamhain responded while wondering if he could recall who that currently was.

"That is even more preposterous! The other guilds would not go for it either if they learned it was even being considered as it would make one guild far larger than the others. It would wield twice as much power, as if…" Loegaire began before stopping mid-sentence. A look of realization dawning on his face.

"As if the Warriors Guild was, in fact, made into two initially because of the balance of power needing to be equally distributed. The lands we have are growing. We need more farmers. We need more of everything, but no one can direct each portion or recognize the needs of another guild because each has a chief and each one is equal in power to the others," Mathghamhain rambled as he warmed further to the idea even though it was a far cry from what he had initially wanted to suggest. "What if, instead, there was one central chief overseeing all the guild chiefs. That way the guilds could all be coordinated in their efforts so that no one gets overlooked or seen as less important. Farmers for crops, hunters for food, the caretakers for the village's upkeep, the warriors for defence, we might even have need of new guilds if the numbers grow. We already know from Nuallan that Nabaidh has a Metal Workers Guild, for example. As it is, our numbers all remain stagnant as each guild tries not to grow too large in order to maintain balance so nothing gets expanded. The Warriors Guild has acquired new land many times, but most of the time it is not used other than to be defended, making the warriors have to work even harder to patrol it all when the whole village could be using it if the farmers grew in number. The warriors hold back their numbers in order not to be seen as too powerful, yet they need to because of all the lands we have now. Think about it, Loegaire. Think of the differences that could be made for Meadhan if we let the guilds grow as they needed to. Rather than simply striving to acquire land from others, we directly seek to add the villages and gather them. It would allow population growth. We could flourish."

"It is as I already stated, Mathghamhain, madness to suggest such things. You know I think well of your ideas and support you often enough but this talk—you ask too much of the village. Do you not see that?" Loegaire asked concernedly now and backing away slightly.

"You shall see. I will pitch the idea to the chiefs besides yourself. I care not for myself in any such role but it is worth considering, is it not? A way to grow as a village, to be powerful, to stop the encroachments?" Mathghamhain offered.

"It is never going to happen, brave Mathghamhain. We may need to change your name to Mad Mathghamhain if you do not understand the insanity of which you speak," Loegaire said hesitatingly, unwilling to meet his eyes.

"Loegaire, you seem to clearly be apprehensive about this. What is it you are trying so hard not to say. We have known each other for years, we should be able to speak candidly," Mathghamhain offered reassuringly, trying to get to the root of the problem.

"I will support you if you talk reason. We can jointly lead the Hunters and Warriors Guilds until a new chief is chosen. Do not seek to reach for more than that much. It will meet with too much apprehension," Loegaire grumbled before he turned on his heel and departed, leaving Mathghamhain there to wonder if he should be concerned and think about things a bit longer. That was when the air chilled around him. He was suddenly quite grateful Loegaire had left if the spirit was about to be a nuisance.

"He does have a point, does he not? Yet he holds you back. You speak of wisdom and a future for Meadhan, yet you spoke to but one person. To speak to others might yield better results or it might result in even further distrust and apprehension," the spirit's voice came.

"He does but it is viable. There is no other way save for actions I dare not take nor can I even consider with true thought to perform," Mathghamhain responded before pausing. "Be gone this morning, future Mathghamhain. I need the solitude of my own present-day thoughts if I am to manage through the coming hours."

The sudden silence and lack of any further words from the spirit told him it had heeded his request or at the least chosen to remain silent. He was as yet uncertain how it worked.

CHAPTER 12
Caiside

Caiside stood in front of the gathered Warriors Guild in the centre of the training grounds waiting until he had their attention. As the most senior warrior left in the guild, he had been selected to conduct the election. For the purposes of making sure it followed proper protocols, the Chief of the Hunters Guild, Loegaire had been brought in to assist. The fact that part of today's vote also involved the Hunters Guild had played a small part in that decision as well.

"We have the results of our most recent vote. Mathghamhain and Brennus are the two leading candidates to become the new chief. Both of them will be required to leave while we hold a final vote, one that will determine who is to be chief and who is to be their second-in-command," Caiside said gesturing to both men as he did so.

He noticed the look the two men in question exchanged with each other. The fact was, both men had, for years, alternated between being rivals and trusted allies in battle. No matter how this vote went, the results were guaranteed to make that situation volatile. It was no surprise it had come down to the two of them. They were the most experienced of the younger warriors. No one wanted to choose a Chief who was older, for it increased the odds they would need to choose yet another one that much sooner.

As soon as the two candidates had left, Caiside sighed. Now they would have to go through the formality of a vote, again. Mathghamhain was less experienced than Brennus but had served the past two years as second-in-command. Brennus had the experience and had even been the one to train Mathghamhain, and strived for everyone to be the best they could be, but could on occasion let his anger get the better of him. Given those two options, Caiside knew his own choice.

"Before we vote, is there any discussion?" he asked of the warriors. Most would have already made up their minds but the opportunity to have anyone who was less certain be swayed one way or the other could make a difference.

"Mathghamhain is better at group strategy."

"Brennus is tougher, and will push for us to be at our best."

"Mathghamhain may not be of sound mind—he talks to spirits, yet is not in the Priesthood."

"Brennus is reckless once a battle begins, he wants a fight."

Caiside continued letting the varying opinions be shouted out, glancing over at Loegaire. He hoped the man would give him an indication of when to cut the discussion off. Loegaire, however, looked more amused than bothered by the various opinions. Caiside was about to formally ask the man out loud when he noticed the shouting had died down. Finally.

"I think that is enough to work with. Everyone line up and as before, when it is your turn, pick a pebble and drop it in the bucket that represents your choice. The left is Brennus, the right is Mathghamhain," Caiside explained while Loegaire moved to gesture to the respective buckets. "If you are unsure which is which when it is your turn, please ask and one of us will remind you."

It had been slow going, but the warriors had now not only all cast their votes, but the results had been tallied. With both Brennus and Mathghamhain back in the room, he could reveal the final result.

"Thank you, everyone, for your continued patience the past few days as we set about choosing a new chief for the first time since most of us joined the guild. Brennus, Mathghamhain, if you could both join Loegaire and I up here at the front," Caiside began. The murmur amongst the collected warriors was one of anxiousness and he could not say he blamed them. It had to have been as nerve-wracking for all of them as it had been for him, and Caiside was happy that this marked the end.

Loegaire suddenly holding a hand up to silence them was something he would not have thought to do. Caiside appreciated the man's experience right now. He could merely hope the other item they had to vote on did not take nearly as long. One that Cynwrig and he, at Mathghamhain's suggestion, had discussed holding before the fateful battle that had taken the late chief's life.

"It has been decided that our new chief shall be…" Caiside began, looking meaningfully at both candidates. "Mathghamhain, with brave Brennus as his second-in-command."

As soon as he had announced it, Caiside noted the flickering of a grimace cross the lips of Brennus even as the man moved to steady Mathghamhain who looked ready to faint from shock. Although the warriors had all cheered the announcement, it was not nearly as loud as he had expected it to be, despite knowing full well how many had voted for each candidate.

"Now, we will take a break, and tomorrow we will meet again to vote on the motion put forward previously by our new Chief, that the Hunters Guild and ours be combined. This would allow us to bolster our ranks, with the Farmers Guild being requested to expand into assisting in the gathering of additional food," Caiside added hurriedly before everyone dispersed.

"Wise Caiside," Brennus said stepping forward and speaking loud enough that everyone could hear him. "You need to lead with why we need to bolster our ranks. This vote tomorrow, fellow warriors, is because we need the numbers so that we may maintain the lands that we have won these past years. Wins we achieved under the sound tactical advice of brave Mathghamhain and the dear departed brave Cynwrig, may his spirit know peace."

"Yes, thank you, Brennus, for that reminder," Mathghamhain added, stepping forward now as well, and looking much steadier on his feet Caiside noted

thankfully. "I thank all of you for this trust afforded me. Brennus and I will soon meet and find ways to continue to see this guild prosper."

Caiside took advantage of the fact that Mathghamhain and Brennus had the attention of the guild enough that the warriors had not dispersed yet. Stepping in front of the two men, he affixed the brooch and stripe signifying the rank of chief to the front of Mathghamhain's vest. The one for the armour could be added later. Having affixed it, Caiside moved on to present Brennus with his pin as second-in-command. Stepping to one side as soon as that was done, he gestured to both men once again and the Warriors Guild cheered. That seemed to mark the end of it as they began dispersing immediately afterward.

Moving to tidy up, Caiside had little doubt there would be quite a bit of talk once word reached the rest of Meadhan, even before a formal announcement was made regarding the result. That, and he would surely find time to have a celebratory drink with both men sooner than later.

CHAPTER 13
Mathghamhain

"I am most grateful and personally gladdened you did not see fit to delve into your earlier words when the vote was being determined, brave Mathghamhain," Loegaire whispered in his ear as they walked back into Meadhan to celebrate.

Beaming, Mathghamhain slapped Loegaire across the back. "Yes, well it did not seem the place. You and I can discuss it again soon. I still feel the idea has merit," Mathghamhain began before noticing Brennus. Despite the warrior's earlier words, he was fixing him with a stern gaze. Whatever it was about, he wanted to deal with it immediately."I will catch up with you soon, Loegaire. I wish to talk to Brennus for a moment."

Taking note of Loegaire's nod of understanding, he walked briskly over to where Brennus was. Extending his hand outward to clasp his new second-in-command's, Mathghamhain noted that despite the stern gaze, Brennus did not seem to be angry, fortunately. Mathghamhain was still certain the warrior would have words for him later when it was the two of them in private. He was certainly not looking forward to the initial strategy discussion with him.

"Brennus, what troubles you?" Mathghamhain asked. "You know that I feel honoured to have you as my second-in-command." The warrior seemed to noticeably tense at the words which gave him concern for the future. Still, Brennus was staying calm.

"I thank you, brave Mathghamhain, for that. You have been both a valued comrade in arms and a devout warrior under my training. It is a privilege to take up the mantle of second-in-command from you. It is your rightful place to be Chief," Brennus responded, the tenseness dissipating. If there was any resentment in Brennus at how the vote had gone, he was doing his best to try and hide it.

"You do honour me with your words, Brennus," Mathghamhain smiled before bringing his hand in for a firm clasp with the warrior. "Come, we should join the celebration. I have not had the chance to relax with our guild much the last couple of years and you can show me how it is done."

"Socializing has never been your strong suit, Mathghamhain. I am not sure it is possible to teach you how," Brennus chuckled, the tenseness having faded completely now.

"You trained me as a warrior, did you not? And look how well that turned out. Clearly, you excel at teaching. Are you saying you are not up to the task?" Mathghamhain teased.

"I never said any such thing. If I can train you, of all people, into being not simply a warrior but one who becomes Chief, you know full well I can teach you how to socialize better. Come! Today we celebrate!" Brennus smirked, grabbing Mathghamhain by the arm and dragging him towards where the rest of the people had been gathering.

The cheer that greeted them both was louder than he had prepared himself for. It was an odd feeling, especially with what Mathghamhain knew more than ever had to be done but it would have to wait a while longer. He was now chief of the Warriors Guild, but it would take time to see his ultimate goal achieved of a central chief overseeing all of the guilds. For the moment, he would let Brennus lead him in celebration with the rest of Meadhan.

Nuallan

"Brave Brennus. My liege," Nuallan spoke as he approached the two leaders. He had waited until both had had plenty of time to celebrate. He did want to have a moment to discuss his concern with Mathghamhain before the vote tomorrow. Unfortunately, that meant interrupting his liege's celebration temporarily. He also had to do so in a way that he would not be accused of seeking favouritism, especially as he was still technically Mathghamhain's servant. For the past two years, he knew his liege had done his best to make sure he was not afforded any preferential treatment when drawing up battle plans. He certainly did not want to undo that hard work.

"Ah, loyal and brave Nuallan. What would you speak to me of?" Mathghamhain asked turning his attention to him. He was going to regret this, Nuallan quickly realized. Mathghamhain looked more relaxed than he had in months and he was about to ruin that.

"It is nothing of great import my liege and Chief. I merely wished to discuss your intention to make a hard push to unite the Hunters and Warriors Guilds. While it would seem on the surface a fine idea, I must suggest caution as you are so newly elected you do not want to have too much change too soon," Nuallan suggested. There was no real danger in saying it aloud. The only ones within easy listening distance were their fellow warriors and they already knew about the idea. He did not like that, despite this fact, Mathghamhain was rising to his feet, gesturing for Nuallan to follow him so they could speak in private.

He had definitely ruined the mood.

"I thank you for your advice, loyal Nuallan," Mathghamhain said reassuringly once they were sufficiently away from the crowd. "However, there is much that needs doing if we are to thrive, and unity is but perhaps the only way we can do so. We must show we can present a strong and united village. To solidify our hold over lands, we need more warriors. We do not need to be always out looking for a battle or all patrolling together. We can be like the hunters are and go our own ways covering greater ground. Some can hunt and others can patrol. If we are a united group, we can patrol and show strength before we break apart. More hunters will also bring greater amounts of food. It works both ways, does it not?"

Nuallan sighed. He had encouraged this thinking initially. He had seen in Mathghamhain a man destined to lead and sought to push him to seek that out. What that man wanted now? It sought more than anyone ever did, whether it be in this village or Nabaidh.

"Perhaps yes, perhaps not my liege and chief, but you should still wait until you have been chief for a brief period to allow the others to adjust to your position before you try to wield its power in such a heavy manner," Nuallan added before clasping his liege's hand briefly and nodding to leave since Mathghamhain's fellow chief, Loegaire, was quickly approaching.

"Brave Chief Mathghamhain," Loegaire said, reaching both of them. "You know I trust you, old friend. Do not think my suggestions the other morning about you being mad were anything but concern for your well-being and to avoid you saying the wrong thing to anyone before the vote that might have put your life in grave danger for your words.”

Nuallan frowned at this. He knew Mathghamhain and Loegaire were old friends but as much as he had wanted to caution his liege, now Loegaire was piling onto it. On a night where Mathghamhain was supposed to be celebrating.

“He and I discussed this exact thing, brave Loegaire. We should let him get back to the celebration,” Nuallan offered, trying to prevent Mathghamhain’s mood from souring too much. Surely, Loegaire understood that.

“It is quite alright, Nuallan. Loegaire, you are my oldest friend and I am grateful for your continued counsel,” Mathghamhain replied clasping Loegaire’s hand. “Even so long after I ceased to be a hunter under your command, you have never stopped offering advice, no matter my actions or our separate ranks. We are equals now, but we have always been able to speak with candour and I hope that never changes. I do have goals, ones that will benefit everyone. If you think I need to have further patience, well, who am I to argue? Come, Nuallan has the right of it. We should all be celebrating. This is the beginning of a new era!”

Keeping a step behind both chiefs as they headed back to the celebration, Nuallan was not so sure Mathghamhain truly understood that Loegaire had been asking him to have more than a bit of patience. His liege was ambitious, and even if Mathghamhain was right about his goals ultimately benefiting every-

one, Nuallan had a feeling that he was not sharing exactly how lofty his goals were. He would have to try and counsel Mathghamhain into slowing down, frequently it sounded like. A new era, indeed.

CHAPTER 14
Mathghamhain

It was another year following the failed vote on the matter of merging the Hunters and Warriors Guilds before Mathghamhain even broached the subject again. In that time he had pushed hard alongside Loegaire to have their respective guilds work alongside each other as often as possible.

Initially, the thought had been to allow both guilds to gain a greater respect for each other, but it had grown beyond that. On more than one occasion, the chiefs of the other guilds had expressed their concerns over the growing strength demonstrated by the Hunters and Warriors Guilds working so closely with each other. Loegaire's long tenure as the Chief of the Hunters Guild had helped in reassuring them somewhat, but only barely. Unfortunately, it also meant Mathghamhain had to, against his better wishes, slow down pushing for his goals even further.

The combined approach had already shown how much greater Meadhan could be when guilds worked together. The hunters had served as advance scouts, freeing up warriors to patrol. Their ability to move stealthily and quickly allowed the warriors greater time for formal plans to be made if there was a problem. The consequence of that had been much quicker battles against encroaching forces and had allowed even more land to be gained. The increased effectiveness in the eyes of the enemy came across as a heightened degree of ferocity, and word spread quickly of it. It was so effective in Mathghamhain's mind he wondered why it had not been done before.

For their part, the warriors would accompany the hunters in hunts, serving to allow large beasts to be taken down with fewer hunters needed. The hunters flushed creatures out into the open and served as point men in distance attacks. It drove animals towards the warriors who would then rapidly kill them. The new approach had the benefit of not only taking down larger beasts, but of doing so with fewer wounds needing to be inflicted to do so.

Today was the next step. Squaring his shoulders, Mathghamhain stepped towards the log building where he was to meet with the other guild chiefs. Loegaire was already inside. It was time to use their unity as an example.

There had been much initial rumbling at the idea when it was broached, but the results could not be argued with. Shorter battles had meant the warriors were home from patrols quicker and less injured, which had led to an increase in the amount of time they could spend in relaxation with their wives. The results of *that* were now beginning to show. He smiled at that, though it was unfortunate that the only woman he had eyes for was completely unavailable. The sole way would be if she stepped aside as the Chief of the Caretakers Guild. She was also going to be at this meeting. He could do this. He was not about to let Cacht ingen Luch's presence distract him.

Taking a seat at the table, he glanced at the others present. Great, Mathghamhain thought, he was the last one to arrive.

"Excellent, now that we are all here, we can get on with today's discussion," Donnchad, Chief of the Educators Guild, beamed. It had been agreed on ages ago, long before Mathghamhain had been born, that any meeting of all the guild chiefs would be led by whoever was in charge of the Educators Guild at the time. It was a tradition that he understood all too well because, while it was the smallest guild, it had the most learned chief.

Loegaire rose first. "It was my hope that Priest Drust would also be here today to represent the Priesthood, given they have shown us how to live our lives and helped establish the traditions of this village. I cannot see them having a problem with what we seek to accomplish. It will benefit all of Meadhan, and that is what they have always led us to believe is most important—the village as a whole and how we treat the land. I would say look to the fact that everyone is generally in better health as of late. That we are putting less demand on the crops and livestock. The success of the unity between the Hunters and Warriors Guilds has meant greater land available for crops, and that we have the resources to defend them better."

Mathghamhain smiled at that comment. He and Loegaire had spent quite a bit of time going over precisely what approach they were going to take with this meeting and in Mathghamhain's opinion, his friend was doing admirably. He knew that in a few years' time the real payoff would come when there were more mouths to feed, when their numbers began to truly grow as the number of deaths decreased and more children were born.

"Yes, it has had its benefits, and I and the rest of the Farmers Guild thank you for that. The real question still remains: What will the Priesthood think of the idea?" Nechtan, the Chief of the Farmers Guild, said rising to his feet once Loegaire had sat back down. "We can sit around trying to guess how they would feel about it, but the fact is we do not know. The guild concept was introduced by them to all villages back when such settlements were created. We have long maintained those laws they introduced. Your unity with the Warriors Guild has truly yielded great results for all of us here, but that has merely meant we can flourish as the other villages have always been able to do. Meadhan had been in decline for many years. A few of you here present are perhaps too young to re-member those days clearly, but it was all we could do to hold on and not be wiped out. Mathghamhain, it was under your predecessor's first years of leadership of the Warriors Guild that we were even able to halt the downward decline and establish a holding level. Now, through these last few years, first with you seconding brave Cynwrig and then as his successor, we have begun to grow in number again. How long before the other villages decide to disallow this and come to drive us back to the point of extinction again?"

"We keep growing and properly. We strengthen

our defences and we keep showing them we will not back down. That is the way we have done so this past year. It has proven quite an effective deterrent," Loegaire said, offering an answer before Mathghamhain could.

"The Priesthood will speak up if they have trouble with it, they have never hesitated before in making their thoughts known," Mathghamhain added, seeking to address the other half of the question. "Their living apart from any of the villages is meant to reduce the risk of any perceived favouritism, a situation made even further necessary by their low numbers. It does mean, however, that we must make decisions without their immediate input. We know their stance on most things, do we not? Is it not in their teachings?"

Hesitating before he continued further with his answer, Mathghamhain made sure to make eye contact with all of them first. "We can argue our case. The Priesthood wish for all the people to flourish. Why would they balk at one village doing what is necessary to grow and flourish after facing so much adversity from the other villages? They should be proud, should they not, that we have triumphed when the others should have been rebuked for trying to wipe us out?"

"The Priesthood are a scattered lot," Cacht added. "They owe no one village allegiance, remaining aloof from us all and rarely venturing from their temples. The closest we get to seeing them is when they come for their tribute. Why should they have a say? So long as we are not breaking any of their rules, we should be free to make choices that pertain to Meadhan."

Her words made Mathghamhain grin although he tried to hide it. She seemed to side with his way of thinking and that made him like her all the greater.

"Perhaps, but they are bound to have a thought on the subject when Priest Drust comes in a few months time for that tribute. Can this vote not be delayed until such a time as we can consult with them?" Nechtan spoke up again.

"The Priesthood is not who we need to worry about. It is our own people we must see to the lives of. That is our charge, is it not? To do what is best for Meadhan?" Mathghamhain countered. "We go ahead with the vote and if we are in favour, we present the options to the entire village to make sure we alone are not choosing an entire people's future. We speak now merely of whether we want to proceed with this idea or not. It is not our place to choose everything."

This outdated reliance on the Priesthood sparked his anger. Drust, the member of the Priesthood that came every year, was old and wizened and barely stuck around each year other than to bless any new-borns and then leave with the tribute. The man had little time for anything else. A man of such an age would surely not take time to consider a new idea that went against traditions. In a few months there would be several newborns ready to receive the blessing, though. The blessings were integral to their beliefs, so Mathghamhain did want the Priesthood to still come. There were traditions he was willing to push against to achieve better things for Meadhan, but its beliefs were not one of them. Suddenly, he felt the air chill and inwardly groaned.

"Now you are thinking as you will need to in the days ahead, my younger self. The Priesthood has put themselves outside the laws of the villages and, as such, why should we subject ourselves to their laws fully when they do not subject themselves to any of ours?" the spirit hissed in his ear. Mathghamhain did not like to admit it, but the spirit had not been wrong yet, had it? It was responsible for the initial ideas he had floated to Loegaire a year ago as to how the hunters and warriors could best work with each other.

"Indeed, indeed. Well, if we take a vote now then it is settled in time enough before the Priesthood comes in a few months, is it not? We should vote and settle the matter. For weeks now we have discussed it at length but today is meant to be when we finally decide," Cacht interjected.

She really was an ideal partner, smart and brave, Mathghamhain thought. He had thought so for years and yet he had never felt brave enough to say any-thing. Now, with her current role, it was too late. Would not a child of theirs have been perfect to be a future chief of the whole village, one born of two young chiefs? A true sign of unity. He had been busy with his own visions of the future and the steps towards this vote the past year, but once a decision was reached, perhaps he would finally attempt for the first time to see if he might be the man she accepted. Was he willing to do that? If she said yes, it would mean giving up her title. No, he would never ask anyone to do such a thing. He could not.

"We should, indeed, take a vote," Loegaire said in-terrupting Mathghamhain's thoughts, thoughts he could not believe he had let his mind wander to. Not when he had to be absolutely focused on the vote he had pushed so hard for. Especially, with the spirit obviously having an interest in how it went, considering its presence.

"Yes, let us vote, then, if we are through with any further discussion on the matter. I know what I will vote if the rest of you do," Nechtan said as the rest of them all nodded in agreement. "I move that since we are all equals and we should, as chiefs, be able to trust the vote of others, dispense with the idea of keeping our vote secret from each other and instead go forward with a show of hands."

"Agreed, let us raise our hands then if we are in agreement. The motion before us this historic day is whether we, the chosen Chiefs of the Guilds of Meadhan, do wish to go forward with becoming a unified village by having a singular individual chosen by all of its people to oversee the guilds with all of us acting as advisors on behalf of our respective guilds," Loegaire said speaking up. "Further, I would ask that, even though our numbers would allow a simple majority to decide the result, and because of its historic nature, nothing short of a unanimous decision will decide this vote, and, should the motion be defeated, we do not revisit it again for another year's time."

Mathghamhain was shocked but also gladdened when he noticed that not only did Loegaire's hand go up in support but of greater significance, Cacht and Nechtan's hands also went up. Finally, the usually reserved Donnchad had his hand up as well surprised him. Having his vote was crucial in a sense, Math-

ghamhain thought. The Educators Guild was the smallest because they were so rarely needed, but their input was indispensable to the future as they, in a sense, served in lieu of the Priesthood's continued presence. They saw to it that all members of the village could read and understand why things worked the way they did. For the chiefs and any who were interested, they also took on the teaching of the ability to write.

"It is unanimous then. This day let it be known that we will be approaching the entire village to vote on choosing a chief for all of us," Donnchad said, standing and taking on the task of drawing this meeting to a close. As he did so, the rest of the chiefs also stood up and congratulated each other in a shaking of hands all around.

Mathghamhain waited until the other chiefs had left the hut to return to guild business, holding back after gesturing to Cacht to wait a moment. Emboldened by the result of the vote, there seemed to be no time like the present to put aside his reservations and take a chance. He really hoped the spirit stayed out of this particular discussion.

"With what can I possibly help you that has not already been discussed, brave Mathghamhain? Did you truly believe the vote would go any other way? You have spearheaded great changes in a short time as chief. Never did I think the Hunters and Warriors Guilds would work so harmoniously together, but is that not the case? Why would there not be even greater unity and benefit if all of our guilds worked in such harmony?" Cacht asked, watching him cautiously as she stood there in the doorway, her amber hair past her shoulders these days, and it likely was a decent amount longer than it appeared with the way it curled at the end into ringlets.

No, Mathghamhain thought, he was getting distracted again. When had he become so easily distracted by a woman? Yet perhaps it was the specific woman she was.

"Brave and courageous Cacht ingen Luch, it was not guild business I wished to discuss but more of a matter of the heart. I know you are unable to be with a man lest you be accused of letting men interfere in your role as chief. I would implore you to consider that as a fellow chief and of…" Mathghamhain began before watching as she held her hand up to indicate he should stop talking.

"Brave Mathghamhain. While you see us as equals, we are not. I would have to give up everything. I need to be extremely selective if I am ever to take a husband because of that. How could I possibly consider you when you are clearly angling for the role you have campaigned so hard to have created. That would put yourself above my current station and where would that leave myself? Even if the rules were changed because you would be of higher standing? Still, I would have to endure others believing you shower favouritism on the needs of my guild instead of being a fair chief should you be elevated to the role," Cacht said before smiling disdainfully at him."Your ambition, while making you my equal, leads you on a path above mine. Can you truly say that it would not change things? That you would still see me as an equal

if I were to give up my title?"

"What is best for Meadhan, our village is what I seek. It may break from tradition, but it has already proven it is a good way, as you have so elegantly stated, Cacht ingen Luch," Mathghamhain responded, grateful she was even entertaining the notion with seriousness.

"Then we shall see in the morning, shall we not Mathghamhain? You have a vision where others do not. A plan where others see only one day to the next. They see a woman and desire them and woe betide that woman if she spurns him in a way that bruises the ego. You? I see it in how you have looked at me for quite some time now: you want to be sure you are my equal, as if you are beneath me and must work for it. It makes you better. It makes you a man worth knowing, a man who could be a husband. You will have my vote tomorrow, Mathghamhain, but that is all," Cacht said straight-faced as she was turning to leave. Mathghamhain was still watching her depart when she looked back over her shoulder from the building's doorway. "That is provided, of course, that you can bring yourself to call me by my name alone and not mention my father's every time we talk. I am my own person."

Mathghamhain let out a long, hard exhalation of breath when she had gone. That had gone remarkably far better than he could have even imagined it would. She believed in his vision of the future, not in the way Loegaire did who had needed convincing, but by judging him purely on what she had herself observed and heard, not needing him to work to convince her.

She believed in *him*. It was a hard thing to digest. Everyone else had to be convinced or pushed down the path he needed them to.

Letting go of calling her by her full name? That would be tricky. After all, had he not known her father much better than he knew her? They had grown up in the same village certainly but every child had known who brave Luch was. Her father had been an educator, and a fine man when it came to teaching the basics of hunting. Luch had been meant to be a hunter but had then displayed a greater talent for educating others, and so had been cast into the Educators Guild upon reaching of age. That was all history, and Luch had told him and other boys that tale many times, wanting them to keep their minds open when they came of age.

Cacht had worked rapidly when her father had died, pushing herself hard, quickly getting noticed for her determination and ability to handle the pressure. It really should not have surprised Mathghamhain a few years ago as much as it did when she had been elected as second-in-command of the Caretakers Guild, and then later to the role of chief. It was a demanding role given the scope of what that guild was responsible for. Without them, the day-to-day functions and upkeep of Meadhan would fall apart. Did it really surprise him, now that Mathghamhain thought about it, that she supported him? After all, they were both young and ambitious and had both accelerated to the role of chief.

As Mathghamhain walked out of the building, he considered tracking down Loegaire to review how things had gone. Now that this day was finally here,

he realized there were many questions he had to better prepare answers for. That was a thing he would have to do from home.

If he was elected to lead Meadhan, and he had to believe he was one possible candidate for it, he would need to do two things quickly. The first one being to determine how the succession would work in the Warriors Guild since usually, the previous Chief died before a new one was chosen. If he was elected, he was effectively being promoted. Should he not then, Mathghamhain wondered, make Brennus the chief at least until they elected one? Who would Brennus choose as a second-in-command, even if only until a vote could be held? Who else was a viable contender as chief? Loyal Nuallan's role would also need to be figured out if Mathghamhain was chief over the entire village for certain or else the favouritism Cacht had spoken of would rear its head there as well. That was another issue then. The actual second one he had thought of was getting the Educators Guild to work with the Farmers Guild to see about making as many improvements to techniques as possible so they could further increase yields.

These were the thoughts that would be keeping him awake this night long after everyone retired to sleep, save for those who kept watch. None of it would truly matter until the election was held and the result was tallied. Mathghamhain had a thought that he should, in fact, wait until Drust was there. That would provide as close to an impartial person as they were likely to find who could tally the results. Meadhan could scarcely afford that if he wanted to get this change implemented immediately though. How, then, could they do a vote and have the results be tallied in an impartial manner? Figuring that out was going to take some thought before he would be satisfied enough to be able to sleep.

CHAPTER 15

One at a time, each villager came forward and cast their vote. Getting everyone to do so in an orderly fashion, as it turned out, had been the quickest part. Donnchad should have come up with a quicker way to tabulate the votes, Mathghamhain thought, stifling a yawn. It had been three hours since all the votes had been cast but they were no closer to knowing a result.

Donnchad's plan that morning had been that once nominations were closed and all the votes had been cast, each Chief would take a turn pulling a ballot from the box, reading it aloud and a mark would be made on the large wooden board that had been set up by the Educators Guild. The ballots had been made from old pieces of parchment, gathered from around the village—no one had wanted to use anything newly-made. From there, after each ballot was read, a villager would be selected at random to verify what it said to make sure everything was kept as honest as possible. It was no real surprise that considering they were only now halfway through the counting that the people were growing restless. Especially as there seemed to be no clear front-runner.

Hopefully, that changed soon, Mathghamhain thought, as people did need to eat and no one was going to break away until the tallying was over. The hunters had worked hard that morning to get all the hunting done before the vote but everything else was at a halt. The vote after another hour and a half had determined that of the nominees, there were three front runners—Donnchad, Nechtan, and himself.

"The hardest part of change can be getting others to accept it. You know this is the role you were born to take. It puts you in a position that we might avoid the fate that awaits you and has already claimed my own self. What will you do when you fail to win? Kill who does in secret, and force another vote? Can you truly accept anyone else in the role but yourself after how hard you worked for this?" the voice of the spirit came at Mathghamhain's ear.

He did not need it talking to him right now, its words were bothersome and full of suggestions Mathghamhain did not care for. He was on edge enough as it was watching the vote unfold. Especially since they were getting towards the end as, with each new ballot drawn from the bowl, it was decidedly emptier and, on one of Mathghamhain's most recent turns announcing a ballot's content, he was fairly certain there were only a handful of votes left, but he was not allowed to look down now, was he? It had been several minutes and two votes had been announced since that moment.

"That is all the ballots," Donnchad suddenly announced, shaking Mathghamhain from his thoughts. Good, it was over. Now, to the result which would be evident to all from the board but still necessitated an announcement. "We have an eventuality we were not prepared for. We have a tie between Chiefs Mathghamhain and Loegaire."

A groan went up from the crowd as the limitations of such a result slowly set in. A surge in votes for Loegaire and Cacht during the latter half of the proceedings had brought that result about.

"Brave Mathghamhain. A gentle word if you will," Cacht said, as Mathghamhain felt her gown brush against him, her voice a hushed whisper. When had she drawn so close, he wondered even as he tried to stop his thoughts from wandering.

"We have more pressing business at the time do we not Cacht ingen Lu…" Mathghamhain said catching himself. Could whatever she wanted to discuss not wait? He was watching what he had worked toward for the past year hit a massive boulder of opposition in the form of a non-result. What if they lowered the voting age and had those who would be of age within the next year cast theirs as well? Would that break the tie? Would that require a vote for it to be allowed? Mathghamhain had to speak to Donnchad about the possibility before the crowd grew increasingly agitated. Since they were all still gathered they could quickly meet and announce the decision, could they not?

"It is the business currently at hand I wish to discuss. Mathghamhain, if we were to unite our votes it would break the tie. To do so and not anger the crowd, though they would need reassurances that my leadership was not overlooked," Cacht whispered quickly in response.

"It would, indeed, break the tie but there is no way to unite the vote without causing trouble. I would be Chief and you would be as you have always been these past years," Mathghamhain began, feeling her press even closer as she moved from behind him to his side. Donnchad had taken notice of their discussion and was looking in their direction questioningly. Loegaire, for his part, tried to keep the crowd under control, telling them they were open to ideas as to how to break the.

"Foolish Mathghamhain, you told me yesterday, did you not, that you desired me as a partner and as a wife? Why not give them that, and in return for me doing this thing, instead of me giving up my role as Chief of the Caretakers Guild and losing all standing, have me be recognized as your true partner in overseeing the entire village?" she said, a smile playing across her lips as she suggested it. Now was that not a fine foundation for a marriage, one that was entirely political, but still, it solved the problem, and if they were wed, she would have to be his partner in more than name, would she not?

"Agreed, but we need to act swiftly if they accept the decision, to solidify the rule. Give them greater than I already have, are you prepared for that? To pursue the unknown and give up your leadership of the Caretakers Guild for a role that has not existed before in this village, or in any village as far as we know?" Mathghamhain asked warming to the idea as Donnchad moved over to whisper at the two of them as well.

"Do I dare ask what you two are so frantically discussing while we are facing a crisis in the Great Vote, one, that I might add, you wanted most out of all of us, brave Mathghamhain?" Donnchad hissed. The Educators Guild Chief had been the last chief to be overtaken in the votes which had resulted in the current tie.

"Indeed, we are discussing a solution you might find handles it readily," Cacht said facing the man. "I have asked brave Mathghamhain to be my husband in exchange for turning the votes for myself over to him and being granted an equal share of the leadership of Meadhan in return."

Well, that answered the question of how Cacht felt about the last thing he had said, now did it not? Mathghamhain had hoped to win her heart, and then her hand, but this would do in the meantime. Had she not said she had noticed he was always working hard to try and be her equal?

"Brave Mathghamhain, is this true? If so, then my congratulations to the two of you but we must quickly tell the other chiefs and then the populace," the Educator Chief grinned.

"It is indeed true, wise Donnchad. I would prefer it have been because of love but in time I am hoping she will come to regard me with it, and that this will ultimately not simply be a political arrangement," Mathghamhain said sighing.

With a nod at both of them, Donnchad moved away from them to approach Nechtan, whispering to him.

"Idiot," Cacht hissed elbowing him gently in the side. "Do you really think I would be so shallow that I

would give up the role of chief for a thing so untested as this if I did not care about you? I should thank you. I used to wait for you to say how you felt and you never did, which made it easier for me to turn suitors away and pursue being chief."

"You mean that if I had said something sooner…," Mathghamhain began, taken aback by her revelation. He was not sure how to respond to her now.

"Yes, now hush, we can talk about it later. Look, Donnchad has finished talking to Loegaire about our plan."

Turning his head to where Cacht had indicated, Mathghamhain watched Loegaire's face. There was a brief look of confusion before the older man finally smiled, turning to face the crowd.

"We have a way to break the tie this day. To appoint a chief over us all, to unite our guilds under one leader who will oversee them, that we will grow and prosper. I concede now with the permission of this crowd to the man who would be your new head chief - Mathghamhain. He will not be in his rule alone. He will have the chiefs of all our guilds to advise him and he will have his fellow chief, to whom he is newly betrothed, and will be his equal in power, the now former Chief of the Caretakers Guild, Cacht ingen Luch," Loegaire shouted as the noise from the crowd began to grow steadily in volume at the an-nouncement. Some in shock and others in joy but it was an acceptable solution. Mathghamhain was grateful no one had objected to all of the votes for Cacht being added to the ones for him.

"Ah, an elegant solution," the spirit hissed, its

renewed presence bringing an all too familiar chill. "Not one I had considered as an outcome for you to gain the chiefdom by. Is it any wonder, then, that it took her suggesting it and not I? Trust her, but do so cautiously, brave Mathghamhain. You do this for the betterment of all, whereas she has managed to parlay her role and beauty into a greater one than she would have had simply by agreeing to wed you. If anything were to befall you, she would have sole rule."

Mathghamhain did his best not to let the spirit's warning tone and attitude towards Cacht get to him. Moving his hand to indicate to the spirit it was dismissed, he hoped no one else noticed or questioned the movement as he rose and walked with his betrothed to where Loegaire had been speaking. The spirit was agitated by news it had not seen coming. Was it possible he had averted the future that the spirit was from by accepting her proposal?

"Brave and courageous people. My people. The people of Meadhan," Mathghamhain began. "I was once a boy amongst you and then I was a hunter but I strove for more. I became a warrior, I became the Chief of that Guild and still, I knew that as I strove to be better, that Meadhan could also be better than it was, that we could finally rebound from our past defeats. That we could be greater. The greatest village in all the lands that the sun shines on when at its zenith. I want to lead us to that greatness and I thank all of you for your votes of confidence to do so. I ask

that, even though there will be trials ahead, you trust me to see us through it all. That my betrothed, Cacht ingen Luch, will hold me steadfast and ensure that everyone's needs are seen to as we grow, as we prosper, as we work towards a brighter future."

The words had come far easier than he could have ever imagined they would even with a bit of it prepared beforehand.

The roar that went up at those last words turned into applause although some were clearly applauding louder than others. In the crowd, he could see the hands of Brennus moving much slower than the other warriors' hands were. He hoped that acceptance from Brennus would come soon, when his former rival turned mentor became temporary Chief of the Warriors Guild. He did not wish for trouble so early on.

"That was a nice speech," Loegaire whispered beside him. "How much of that did you prepare in advance?"

"Only the first couple of lines," Mathghamhain whispered back as he turned his attention back to the crowd. He was trying to take note of who specifically seemed to be reacting more quietly than others, storing it away for future reference as best he could. Those were the people he had to win over now, the ones that Cacht might perhaps have insights into how he might do so. A discussion he could have with her later—after they talked about this revelation of hers about her feelings towards him.

Chapter 16

And I am but saying we should wait until the Priesthood comes so that the marriage can be blessed right then, not several weeks afterwards, even though it will delay the ceremony," Cacht said, following Mathghamhain as he trudged back towards Meadhan. It had been a curious morning but, by and large, not much different than the past few had been since he had been chosen partly by Cacht's goodwill to the role of chief over the whole village. He could not really wield much authority in a position no one knew how to defer to yet, and part of that problem was that both he and Cacht were still technically chiefs of their own guilds. As such, with favouritism was still how everyone thought those guilds would be treated. That would change somewhat fairly soon as Cacht would be stepping down as Chief of the Caretakers Guild. She was staying in the role right now while they elected a successor, which would likely be her second-in-command, Eluned. Given that young woman's history, Mathghamhain was glad to see Eluned achieve such success. As for titles in general, things were bound to get fairly confusing. He would have to figure out a title other than chief for the roles he and Cacht would have. Perhaps Donnchad would have a few ideas. Regardless, he needed to show there was no favouritism at work. His word was as good as it had always been.

"I do understand you, Cacht, I truly do, and I agree

on any other grounds but the ones we face. The people do not listen yet. The final result of the election was based on the idea that we would wed. Until then neither of us has enough votes truly to be chief of the village. The Priesthood is always so busy. We can have a wedding to solidify the rule before Priest Drust arrives. Then when he does and blesses it, we make sure he does so ornately and with greater pomp than usual. It will be a reason for the people to celebrate a second time for their chosen leaders, and by which time perhaps we can already be on the road to unity," Mathghamhain rebutted with a smile. Cacht had done naught but make him smile since the election result. She was still a chief in every way, one who was re-spected to the point of receiving a fair amount of votes for Chief of Meadhan, but when it was simply the two of them? Mathghamhain was enjoying getting to know Cacht his betrothed in a more relaxed manner.

"Perhaps the two new Chiefs, or whichever term we are to be calling you both by, would care to sep-arate for a moment so that I might have a private word with the man who, at this point, is still my Chief in the Warriors Guild, " Brennus said striding towards them, brows furrowed. Caiside and the other warriors, minus Nuallan, were right behind him. All of them armoured.

This did not bode well, Mathghamhain thought, but still, he was their chief and, in truth, he ever would be.

"Cacht, my love, if you would give me a bit of space, brave Brennus it would seem has need of my ear," Mathghamhain intoned as he let go of her hand, having indeed forgotten he had been holding it. Watching her step away but not too far, clearly she did not see a need to travel too far from whatever this was about to be. Braver than any woman he had known in the village, Mathghamhain thought with admiration.

"You should send her home, Mathghamhain. My words are for you alone. They do not involve her in any way save that for the fact that she is your be-trothed," Brennus growled.

"That seems a mighty good reason to me, Brennus. You would disagree. She is, after all, a chief and my equal and soon will be in more than name, and, as such, your superior, no matter what position you hold at the time," he spat, not liking the man's tone. Brennus always seemed so quick to anger and fuelled by a determination to be the best warrior there could be. It was one of the key reasons Mathghamhain had discovered over the past two years that his fellow warriors had not previously chosen Brennus as chief.

"You were taken in as a warrior due to luck as a hunter and you have continued to survive on luck because a spirit guides you at every turn. How can any of us truly compete against that? Fortune has favoured you too long brave, Mathghamhain. I trained you. It is I who should be regarded as fit to be chief, " Brennus seethed drawing his sword while the others quickly drew theirs and moved to encircle the two of them.

Mathghamhain's eyes darted to locate how far away Cacht had gotten. She was near enough and watching, concerned regarding the current situation. He could scarcely afford to fight Brennus. That would be greater trouble than it was worth and yet he could not allow this challenge to authority. Why did the man insist on handling things so physically when he had a complaint? Everyone else talked to him in private. Brennus surely had to know that with a word to the gathered warriors, Mathghamhain could have him re-strained. Unfortunately, that would simply serve to make things worse. It was best to see if he could diffuse the situation instead, and considering the sudden chill in the air, Mathghamhain had a sinking feeling the spirit disagreed with that idea.

"Indeed, indeed, he rises up against you. He is jealous of your power. Of your authority. He gives credit to myself for more than I have, in truth, helped you with. Much of what you have now you did earn on your own without any such guidance from myself. Strike him down for treason. Warriors respect power, do they not? Show them you fear nothing," the spirit said at his ear. The troublesome thing as expected, Mathghamhain thought, always suggesting that he solve problems by killing. He was definitely going to have a talk soon with it. If death was all it was ever going to advise, well, the spirit could move on and leave him be.

"Brennus, take it not as you do. You trained me to be all I could be as a warrior," Mathghamhain began as a reply to the warrior's challenge. "I was a hunter first. I combined the two and have taken those lessons to move toward where we are now in unifying all of our guilds. You are a warrior born and a strong and mighty one at that. You were my second-in-command and there is no reason why you would not be a viable candidate when a new chief for the guild is chosen."

Mathghamhain was determined not to draw his sword but watched, keeping a close eye on the movements Brennus made as the warrior advanced. He knew his childhood rival far better than he would have liked to. They had clashed often enough in mock combat. Fortunately, that meant he was fully on guard when, with a growl, Brennus rushed him. Sidestepping the warrior at the last possible moment, Mathghamhain brought his arm up stiffly, causing it to collide with the warrior's chest. The sudden impact with the man's armour hurt tremendously, and Mathghamhain winced noticeably in pain, but had succeeded in knocking Brennus off his feet.

The fallen warrior snarled as he fell onto his back. Staying down for a moment, Brennus spat at the ground as he rose up again. He attempted to, at least, as Mathghamhain knocked him back down with a foot to the chest. As soon as Brennus had fallen again, Mathghamhain planted his foot on the warrior's chest to make sure he knew to stay down. There was little doubt in his mind that Brennus was not trying as hard as he could have, which made his behaviour slightly puzzling, especially considering the potential ramifications. Drawing his sword after thinking for a moment, Mathghamhain pointed the tip at the man's throat.

"You were my second-in-command, Brennus," he said slowly. "A childhood rival and one who tormented me with disrespect at every turn when I was a hunter. You worked hard when I was entrusted to you

to train as a warrior. A mentor, the best a young warrior could hope for when needing to learn at an accelerated pace. A warrior I was all too glad to have at my side when unfortunate events took brave Cynwrig from us. Still, you have let quiet ambition and resentment eat at you. Today, today you finally sought to act upon it. Was I anyone else, I might truly think you wished my head and were committing treason against a superior and your Chief. I would like to believe I know you better than that and that you were merely looking to test my skill. You have one chance, Brennus. If you prove me wrong and come at me again, I will have no choice but to separate your head from your shoulders and parade your body through Meadhan, before casting it out to be pecked at by the birds—a traitor unfit for proper burial or remembrance."

Having paused in his words, Mathghamhain stepped back and sheathed his sword. Sighing, he looked at his former second-in-command who remained on his back. Considering how obvious it was that Brennus had not put his full effort into the duel, it was clearer than ever that the warrior had not truly been trying to hurt him with this stunt. "The choice is yours, brave Brennus. I hope you choose to put this foolishness aside for good finally so that we might work together toward a glorious future."

"I concede. I taught you too well I think, brave Mathghamhain, my Chief," Brennus began, slowly rising to his feet, head bowed. "This day know that I choose to, much as Nuallan has done in pledging his allegiance to you above all others, I now do the same before these warriors. We do need to move forward to the future. So, from this day onward, you have my eternal allegiance my Chief, my Liege, my Chieftain," the warrior's words coming gradually as if Brennus was struggling to find them now that he had been once again, as Mathghamhain interpreted it, inexplicably defeated in battle by one he viewed as beneath him.

"Then I offer you the hand of your chief in helping you to your feet," Mathghamhain responded. Yes, he was still on guard just in case, but the situation had been diffused and not by the way the spirit of his future self had suggested. This time it felt different, Brennus truly seemed to mean his words. No blood had needed to be shed for this understanding between himself and Brennus to be reached. Helping the warrior to his feet and clasping hands with him, Mathghamhain noted how the other warriors sheathed their swords as well. "All of you, I suggest this day you hold your election. I cannot be chief of our guild and lead Meadhan and have it be fair to all. A new chief needs to be chosen so that the brooches of authority are once again properly understood."

Even when he had clasped hands with Brennus, the warrior's head remained bowed. Was this how the proud warrior was when he was fully humbled? There was no meeting of the eyes, no proud words. Mathghamhain would have to keep an eye on him. The last thing he had wanted was for Brennus to lose any drive to succeed. Perhaps he could offer him reassurance about the future.

"Linger a moment longer please, mighty Brennus,"

Mathghamhain requested while the rest of the warriors had already begun to walk away.

"My liege?" Brennus replied, worry in his tone. Yes, thought Mathghamhain, he definitely had to do something. Seeing his former rival like this was much too strange.

"Worry not. I merely wished to express how certain I am that your time as my second-in-command has taught you what is necessary to lead," Mathghamhain began, offering the warrior a wry smile. "I am sure the rest of the guild feels the same way and that you will surely be elected as chief."

"My thanks, I am fortunate you are able to look past today's incident so soon," the warrior said slowly, head still bowed. "You are a better person than I am, Mathghamhain. I do hope I am chosen to lead the guild and it will allow us to continue to work together. Our lives seem destined to be intertwined."

Giving Brennus a firm handshake after their brief talk, Mathghamhain watched him leave to catch up with the other warriors, the air chilling again as he watched. He had not even noticed the spirit had departed until it returned.

"It is a wise ploy to express your support, it helps cement his newly-stated loyalty to you," the spirit hissed. "And if mighty Brennus proves unworthy of the role, you will have the power to simply kill him."

"You did far better at that than I would have in a similar situation, dear Mathghamhain, proof you are a leader in thought, not only in strength. You know your warriors well," Cacht said to Mathghamhain softly, drawing his attention away from the spirit's comments. Internally, he seethed at the suggestion the spirit had made and was grateful for his betrothed's interruption.

Nuallan had not been there but despite Cacht's words, the spirit's words made Mathghamhain wonder as well if his servant had known that this confrontation was going to occur and said nothing, or if he had been purposely left out so that he did not interfere. Caiside, on the other hand, had been present and had served in the guild longer than any of the current warriors had. The senior warrior should have advised Brennus against this course of action, yet had gone along with it. If Brennus had actually looked to get the best of him, would Caiside have intervened? What did he have to gain by letting Brennus act this way?

Mathghamhain had a theory that Caiside was hoping Brennus would fail in order to prove he was not up to being Chief of the Warriors Guild. No, he had to stop thinking along those lines. If his easy defeat of Brennus today caused problems in the election, there was nothing Mathghamhain could do. After the election, it would not be his problem save for making sure the guild did not tear itself apart in disagreement. Their matters would be for guild members to sort out amongst themselves unless things happened that required his and Cacht's interference.

He and his betrothed had more important things to deal with, Mathghamhain thought, taking Cacht's hand and finally responding to her words. "Yes, but please, stop thinking of them as my warriors. The guild is part of the village, so they are our warriors."

Chapter 17

Mathghamhain stared out across the grassland that began at the edge of Meadhan, his eyes fixed on the small dot in the distance that was slowly becoming closer with each step he took. His armour had never before been polished so gleamingly. It had been claimed by Cynwrig back when they had defeated the warriors of Nabaidh and taken Nuallan to their village. Since then the armour had been improved upon greatly, but still remained one of the only fully-armoured chest plates they had. Brennus had oddly not given him any trouble over keeping it when Mathghamhain had ascended to the role of ruling over Meadhan. The warrior wanted to have his own armour, not one that got passed down, and Mathghamhain had need of it still.

A new designation had needed to be brought up to elevate the insignia to show Mathghamhain was above the rank of Guild Chief. From there, each guild had offered their own input into how to make it as ornate as possible, yet still functional. That had finally brought about the much-needed discussion with Donnchad over titles and it had failed to produce any options Mathghamhain liked. When Drust, the long-serving representative of the Priesthood, had visited, the three of them had discussed it, revealing the Priesthood so far endorsed what Mathghamhain was attempting. It had also solved the question of titles He and Cacht would be Chieftains, with the leaders of each guild now being known as reeves.

Mathghamhain mentally kicked himself as he went over his thoughts. It was no longer even just one village they oversaw, was it? They had recently by force of arms added Nuallan's previous village, Nabaidh. It had been critical to add it first when solidifying his rule. In addition to being their closest neighbour, the village of Nabaidh had a Metal Workers Guild. Nuallan had helped greatly in the aftermath of that battle which had been a case of overrunning what meagre forces they had put together in the past few years. His loyal servant had identified who the Guild Chiefs were and that had led to a choice being presented to them.

That battle had been fought without him. Brennus, as expected, had been elected Chief, now Reeve, of the Warriors Guild, with Caiside as his second-in-command. Mathghamhain was glad for that, for as mighty as Brennus was, he was more warrior than tactician but Caiside had a steady hand and a great deal of experience. There was a reason he had lasted so long and was often turned to by his fellow warriors when it came to matters of trust. The meagre forces that day had been spared as it had been a massive route. Mathghamhain himself had strode into Nabaidh once Brennus and the warriors had cleared the way. He had then presented the Guild Chiefs there with the choice of surrendering willingly or die along with anyone who resisted.

To help them make their choice, he had outlined how beneficial it would be to come under his leadership—greater protection, greater availability of crops, and a fully trained regiment of warriors. It also meant the chance to intermingle more. That was an aspect that would not yield dividends for many years but the men and women of both villages being able to freely do so would grant both villages strength. It was a thing that Cacht had pointed out to him. Mathghamhain's offer had been accepted completely without incident and only a handful of the villagers had resisted and been killed as a result.

It had not been Mathghamhain's wish to simply kill them but between his future self's spirit urging and the fact that Nuallan himself had stepped forward to perform the deed made it a self-contained situation. It also served to elevate Nuallan substantially in the eyes of Brennus as a show of allegiance, greater than any words ever could have. Guilds had been merged with those in Meadhan although how each newly expanded guild operated across two villages was different for each. Brennus and Caiside had opted to trust the newly acquired warriors only lightly until they proved themselves. If Mathghamhain was going to succeed, he would need the Warriors Guild to be cautious and so was grateful for their approach.

That had brought Mathghamhain's thoughts back to this day. The dot in the distance had now become a great many dots, which now resembled people. The Priest Drust, when he had come and learned what they were asking of him as a priest, had met privately with Mathghamhain and Cacht to discuss plans. The priest had made a bigger deal of the ceremony than either of them had expected. The ceremony would be held far out from both villages at a point that was equal distance from them—a sign of unity and a sign that their duty would ever be to the land. Mathgham-hain was unsure how onboard the priest was with everything specifically but when they had talked about their vision for the future in unifying people and being of greater service to them, Drust had seemed pleased. After that, the priest had proceeded to consult deeply with them on how to make the ceremony extra special. That had brought them to today.

As much as Mathghamhain had been pushing for a wedding before Drust had arrived on behalf of the Priesthood, Cacht had firmly held her ground at every turn. His future self's spirit had grown increasingly insistent that if she could not see the advantage in having it done sooner than later, then perhaps Math-ghamhain should cast her aside, that she was not truly worthy of the position and did not properly under-stand what was needed. It was simply one further rift between Mathghamhain and the spirit. The spirit for months had seemed increasingly determined to solve everything by suggesting he kill, so much so that Mathghamhain was determined to talk to the priest about it finally. He had tried bringing it up a few times, but every time he had, Drust had interjected and changed the subject back to Mathghamhain's goals or to the plans for the wedding. After that Mathghamhain had stopped trying. Perhaps once the wedding was over, he would be able to discuss it with the priest. The worry now was that moment would not come until after the spirit's solution to a problem aligned with what Mathghamhain recognized as ne-cessary. So far, that had been avoided but he knew it was likely inevitable.

Mathghamhain's hair had been pulled back and braided tight against the side of his head; some of the women had commented that it made him look noble and showed off the sharp angles of his face. He was simply glad the hair would not get in the way, today of all days. Loegaire and Nuallan dressed him to appear both presentable and warrior-like. The fur that trimmed his boots and hung down his back was from a bear hunted specifically for this dress and the day's feast. It sat affixed to his shoulders and cascaded down his back to right below his waist. His boots had been lined with additional fur where they ended, giving them a snug fit. It all felt awkward and unnatural to him. Another rank, another layer of weight. Mathghamhain hoped he could shoulder it all.

He continued walking, getting closer to everyone, doing his best to not fidget as he did so, or to put his hand on his sword for comfort. His sword had been taken by one of the metal workers in Nabaidh who had adorned the hilt, reworking it to make it more stunning and ornate and strengthening its connection to the blade. The blade had even been re-forged with an additional folding of the metal to make it stronger. Mathghamhain could not recall hearing of a warrior or chief as armoured or as intimidating as he felt right now. What really caught him off guard was the sincere knowledge that for all the work everyone had done to make him look like a great chief for his wedding today, that even more would have been done to make Cacht look as stunning as was possible.

Turning as he finally reached the spot he was to stand, Mathghamhain glanced at where the old priest was waiting, barely smiling at him. After strolling through everyone from both villages who had gathered, he could not help but notice how dapper Loegaire looked. The man was charged today with keeping him steady and also to defend both him and Cacht if anyone tried to attack. The old hunter was his oldest and most trusted friend. Who else would he have chosen? Mathghamhain's eyes became absolutely transfixed when he looked back down the way he had come, prompted to do so by a tilt of the head and smile from Priest Drust. He knew what was going on but it was still interesting to note how everyone had known to look before he had.

Cacht must have begun walking not long after he had, he thought, as she quickly came into view. She was accompanied by her cousin Caiside in lieu of the absence of her late father, Luch.

Caiside was not who held his gaze, though. Mathghamhain stared transfixed as he watched Cacht walk, wondering if anyone else saw more than the beauty walking towards them all. Her hair had been piled up on top of her head between the wreath of flowers, many of which he was not sure he had ever seen before, held together by the meticulous dedication of many women and a bit of assistance from the Metal Workers Guild of Nabaidh. Having such a guild was certainly making things interesting. Some of the hair had fallen either deliberately or by design so that her ringlets perfectly framed her face which Mathghamhain suspected was partly what drew out the ferocity in her eyes. He wished he could freeze that moment so he could always see her this way. It was perfect. It took

some doing but he was finally able to look at the rest of her.

The dress' striking red wine colour affixed in various ways with intricate needlework to give it highlights of rare gold fabric made her stand out in a way no else ever could on the field. Both colours to her dress were the best colours they had available in both villages and he was not sure if they had been used at her insistence or everyone else's. The way the dress clung to her chest and draped to the flared skirt at her knees made it easy to see why so many of the men had tried to win her hand over the years. But they were not worthy of her; they were not her equal. Mathghamhain was humbled that she had chosen him. He was a very lucky man, and to think she had liked him even before he had a title, he simply had not known it. Mathghamhain inhaled sharply as he took in her appearance in its entirety. Cacht had always cast a striking figure, both fierce and beautiful in equal measure, but the way she was dressed this day heightened both in equal measure.

"As much as it may pain you Mathghamhain, do try to close your mouth. It is hanging open right now enough for others to notice and it most certainly takes away from the image," Loegaire hissed from beside him. Had he really been gaping there slack-jawed as if he had only recently learned what it was to desire a woman? He nodded in indication that he had heard Loegaire's suggestion and clenched his jaw enough to be sure it was closed. The rest of Cacht's dress was stunning, staying firmly against her body all the way down until it flared out at her knees. The look created the image that she was one with the land around her as if she was in fact gliding over it. Her smile was clearly visible now and it was absolutely infectious, making him smile back just as brightly at her. Mathghamhain grinned internally to himself when he realized that despite its appearance a degree of armour had been fit into the dress. As form-fitting as it had looked before it was because the fabric had been stretched tightly around a piece of armour that had been perfectly modelled and cast to fit her figure. He did not want to think about how that had been managed without other men seeing her in a way that was meant for his eyes alone. He would not dismiss that they had done that much work to ensure her protection even at a ceremony.

Now that she had reached the front he gratefully accepted Cacht's hand as Caiside placed it in his own before stepping back to join the rest of the gathered crowd. He had not even thought of it before, but he could not hear the chatter of both villages talking or making any noise despite them clearly being present.

"We gather here this day to recognize now a great union, the joining together of the future of a man and a woman, that their lives be now forever entwined," the Priest Drust began before spreading his arms wide. The priest was older than anyone else Mathghamhain had ever met, grey-haired and with evident signs of hair loss on top of his head. It was distracting to see someone so old and yet clean-shaven, although he knew that was due to the man being a member of the Priesthood.

The old priest's foot nudging him shocked Math-

ghamhain out of his thoughts again and he did his best to offer an apologetic smile to Cacht who was staring at him, smiling. Her eyes told him though that she was not thrilled he had gotten lost in thought when he was supposed to be focusing on the ceremony at hand. He would have to apologize repeatedly afterwards to her for that and he had every intention of doing so. Listening, he nodded lightly at her, while Drust intoned that theirs was a union that no one should tear asunder and then the question came. The only part for which Mathghamhain had been able to rehearse.

Mathghamhain was surprised when he managed to get through saying the vows he had prepared to say to her. His promise to always treat her as his equal, that she had made him feel whole, and that together he knew they could accomplish anything life brought their way. Her vows, in turn, were similar although she took the time to mention as well a thing that sounded odd, considering how everyone tended to see her, when she promised to raise any children they had the best she could with a full heart because their hearts were united and greater than any others with how full of love they would be.

Within moments of Cacht finishing, the Priest Drust had blessed the union, wrapping the cord intricately around their wrists to show they were now bound together, and directing them to face the crowd. Everything was happening so quickly, for Mathghamhain it felt like a blur, as he did his best to get through it all.

This part now was the extra part of the ceremony, a part that the Priest had not had to do before either, where Mathghamhain and Cacht jointly pledged to be good chieftains to all of those gathered and lead them in the ways of their people to the best of their ability always, with Drust, in turn, asking the crowd if they would support their chieftains and the roaring approval that was their response.

It was then that the priest said something that Mathghamhain did not quite catch. He hated that his thoughts were swirling so much that he could not focus on what was said, but figured it out quickly when Cacht wrapped her hands around his neck, bringing her lips to his in a kiss Mathghamhain could not ever have fathomed possible. His arms matched her action as he drew her in close, kissing her back as deeply as he could ever imagine kissing any woman. It was how he had always dreamed of doing so with her since he had first taken notice of her as a woman. Their kiss greeted with approval, laughter, and applause from the crowd, only stopping when Loegaire and Eluned, the woman that was serving to steady Cacht during the ceremony, pried them apart with a bit of delicate prompting at their respective shoulders.

"A lovely event, Mathghamhain, but hard times await you," the spirit's unwelcome words came at his ear. Not letting his annoyance show with everyone watching was difficult but Mathghamhain hoped he was doing well enough. "She aspires higher, you two are equals but for how long will that last? The Priesthood now knows of the changes you have wrought. How long until they mention it in other villages? You must strike quickly before your rule is endangered both from within your villages and from without."

Mathghamhain was not in the mood to deal with it right now, he could be yelled at and advised by it later. Right now, he wanted nothing greater than to ignore the spirit and celebrate alongside Cacht with everyone. He was not going to let the spirit's words ruin this day. Escorting Cacht back through the crowd, he did his best to smile for everyone but the damage had been done. The spirit had ruined the mood. Hopefully, by the time he and Cacht left the celebrations for home, his mood would be greatly improved. His future self really should have been wise enough to know not to speak today of all days.

THREE

CHAPTER 18

The span of the lands he and Cacht reigned over these days never ceased to amaze Mathghamhain. They had set out a few days earlier to head to Marcairt, the nearest village in their territory to their destination. Now he stood on the hilltop looking down at the field below where Brennus had summoned them. Certainly, it had been a long trek, but if history was any indication they had wanted to be nearby when word came of victory. It was the latest one achieved in the past year by Brennus as Reeve of the Warriors Guild. No, he thought silently, as he looked down at the field. Not a victory—a slaughter. The grass below was stained with so much blood he could see the change in the colour from where he was, the glint of the setting sun reflecting off the armour of the fallen warriors.

With each new victory, Brennus had led his warriors to, the ruthlessness of their victories became increasingly pronounced. This was the fourth such victory since the wedding and primary duties had kept Mathghamhain confined to the villages. A great deal of change had taken place in that time, with Meadhan having undergone a few transformations to mark it as the seat of government for the lands under his and

Cacht's reign. Other than the two of them, that village was now home to merely a few warriors, the majority of the Educators Guild, and a handful of women, farmers, and hunters. Although each village still maintained its own branch of that guild, they were all led by the same reeve, and those desiring the highest of education came to Meadhan to learn. Similarly, the majority of the Metal Workers Guild stayed in Nabaidh. Surveying the scene below, Mathghamhain wondered what further changes this newest addition would bring.

"He needs to be reined in," Cacht's voice came from beside him, having observed the scene as he had. "Brennus seems determined to increasingly prove his worth and might. At some point, it is going to cost us in numbers if he kills them all before they can surrender. His forces are nearly triple what they were when we wed last year; we are no longer a village being pushed back. We are the ones doing the pushing—we have become conquerors."

"He is proving a point, and yes, he needs to be reined in. I cannot say that I am surprised. After all, if death had claimed you before we could wed as it took Agrona from him, I would take to battle with as much ferocity as Brennus. I hope that when the Priest Drust comes this year, he can soothe the man's spirit. Now, I think perhaps we have observed enough and must see what he left alive for us to add to our rule. The fact that Brennus sent a messenger to check how close we were to reaching them suggests something significant, I would think," Mathghamhain responded as they began their descent towards the field below where the warriors, his vast Warriors Guild, awaited. He knew only a few of their names now but Brennus and Caiside had done a remarkable job handling the increased numbers so far.

As Mathghamhain walked beside Cacht down the centre aisle between two perfectly aligned rows of warriors, he marvelled at how it was not all that much unlike the aisle the crowd had given he and Cacht on their wedding day. That two drastically different occasions could seem so similar. He shook his head, not wanting to dwell on that thought. There was Brennus at the other end with Caiside off to one side. Both seemed poised and relaxed, not the sight of two men who had been through a battle. Indeed, they were having to exert themselves less and less in battle, a by-product likely of having forces that outnumbered any foes they faced now by a fair margin.

"My Chieftains—brave Mathghamhain and courageous Cacht—it does gladden my warrior's heart to see you both this day, even as the sun is setting," Brennus greeted them both, first clasping Mathghamhain's hand and then kissing the back of Cacht's. "We encountered a harder battle than we would have thought but our advance scouts had helped us to be prepared, as you taught in your days as second-in-command of this Warriors Guild, Mathghamhain, my liege. Nuallan, if you would show them what we encountered."

An actual fight despite the appearance of a slaughter? That piqued Mathghamhain's curiosity, a wonder of whether there was something he was missing or if Brennus was simply trying to justify needing so many warriors still, rather than leaving a few at each village to defend it. An idea Mathghamhain suspected he would once again have to suggest. He watched as Nuallan, who he had not even seen, Mathghamhain realized, appeared from nearby leading by rope two magnificent fully armoured four-legged creatures. His eyes widening as he looked from them, to Cacht, then to Brennus, and back to the creatures again. Horses. They were actual horses. Here and armoured, meaning they had been used with the intention of aiding in combat. Brennus had been deadly serious about the battle being tough. It was a miracle they had survived, let alone won. After all, if they had a need to face warriors on foot as well as those who were on armoured horseback, the implications were chilling to wrap one's mind around.

Mathghamhain tore his gaze from the horses and looked at the gathered warriors again. Had they lost many? He could no longer tell. He strongly suspected they had and that despite their poise, every warrior present was badly in need of care and rest. Horses were barely even thought of. Members of the Educators Guild had mentioned them on occasion, having heard tales of them from the mainland. The Priest Drust had also previously verified they existed. Everything that had ever been said about horses suggested a group of warriors using them in combat should have decimated their forces. What had been done to win against such power?

"They are magnificent, brave Brennus. To see them armoured, would they truly bring such magnificent creatures into the field of battle?" Cacht asked the

Guild Reeve as she moved to touch her hand to one of the horses where it was not armoured. The creature responding by stomping its hoof heavily and snapping at her hand, only stopped by Nuallan pulling the horse back.

"There were only these two, used by the leaders," Brennus replied. "I suspect our vanquished foes were not that much more familiar with how to utilize them than we would have been. There are a few others, although un-armoured, in the building they house them in, which they have referred to as a stable. We were told armouring them is quite difficult and involves a great deal more work. We, therefore, on behalf of this village of Crioch, now yours, present these two horses to our Chieftains that they might be used by true leaders. May their strength and speed help protect you, that your reign be long."

"My thanks, Brennus, as per usual you do your position great honour," Mathghamhain said nodding as he turned like Cacht had to regard the horses in greater depth.

They looked strong, and blacker than the night had ever proven to be in his memory. Strong legs that looked like they were built to handle the weight of the armour and the rider. Armoured riders even. They would have to learn how to convince the horses to accept them, as well as learn how to ride them. It would mean further training for Cacht especially as she was already spending part of each day being trained by Nuallan and other warriors in combat. Both would take time but he was looking forward to learning alongside her. The air chilling around him caused

Mathghamhain to wonder what exactly the spirit wanted to say about this development, although knowing it, it was likely to suggest killing the horses.

"First marriage and now armoured horses. Truly the changes we wrought with my guidance have yielded greater rewards than I could have hoped for us," the spirit hissed in his ear before it went silent again. Good, it was keeping things short this time, so far anyway. It was the last party Mathghamhain wanted to hear from right now with so many people around.

"Brave Nuallan, if you would assist us by escorting these horses to the stable you mentioned. Once at Crioch, we can properly welcome its people into our rule," Mathghamhain said moving to grasp the side of the saddle, staying as clear of the horse's head as he could. If he kept his hand there long enough, it was his hope the horse would adjust to his presence. Cacht seemed reluctant to try the same approach with the other horse and for that, he could not blame her. Hopefully, the people in Crioch could offer advice on how to win the horses over.

The slow walk into Crioch with Mathghamhain and Cacht at the horse's sides and Nuallan leading them was a formal affair. The full contingent of warriors marched with them, shields out and heads held high. It was about the presentation, and he and Cacht had gotten practice at it, thanks to past victories. The villagers, for their part, were acting grateful to see them and as if they accepted them fully. It would be a hard addition considering how far out it was from Meadhan, though, and how many of their warriors had been slaughtered, which meant fewer to add to the guild's ranks. Expanding any further from here would have to be avoided. It would need to represent their border.

Brennus, whether the reeve liked it or not, was going to need to station warriors here permanently. To not do so left them at far too much risk. The victories were great but too much expansion too quickly would bring their downfall if they did not act now to stop it. They needed time to consolidate and re-build with what they already had.

He was not looking forward to explaining the reality of that to Brennus.

CHAPTER 19

There are rumblings on the edges of our lands, brave Mathghamhain, and courageous Cacht. Of other villages, particularly to the north, seeking to prepare themselves better should we march further afield," Brennus spoke calmly. It had been nearly two full seasons since Crioch had been added, followed by a stern talk between Mathghamhain and the reeve. Ultimately, Brennus had bowed to the order not to expand further for the foreseeable future. Since then, defences had been the priority for the warriors to deal with. Until the population increased more to handle the amount of land they had available to them, they needed to focus on keeping hold of the lands they had already captured.

The stone building they were currently in had been originally one of several that housed villagers. With fewer people making their home in Meadhan now, one of those buildings had been renovated to serve as Mathghamhain and Cacht's home as well as a large meeting space that could accommodate numerous villagers at once. It was in that room where Mathghamhain and Cacht currently sat, with Brennus standing before them.

"They have every right to worry but have we not already proven our might? Are we not already protecting ourselves by shifting our focus these past months? Growing the crops and finding ways to store them long-term, initiating routes that they can safely travel to share the bounty between all the villages within our lands?" Cacht asked, a quick glance given his way. Mathghamhain knew well what it meant by now. She wanted him to press Brennus for what he was really there to tell them, not an item that could be left until the next time he was there for a normal meeting and briefing. This one was extra, a special audience the Warrior Reeve had requested.

His wife was right indeed, Brennus had to want to meet with them about something specific. The reeve was no coward and too proud to worry about a possible enemy attack, not with how ruthlessly he had taken the lands already and trained the rest of the guild to be. Not for the first time, Mathghamhain wished the old Priest Drust had come for a visit. Brennus being forced to hold back would likely go much better if the priest could put the man at ease over the loss of Agrona nearly a year ago.

"Indeed, wise and courageous Cacht, my Chieftain. We must be prepared but not simply by boosting our defences. Our warriors are as strong as ever but with the switch in focus several have become too complacent, I find. Even our alliance with the Hunters Guild suffers, they do what they can but hunting is growing increasingly scarce as they have reached a point where they can fell even the mightiest beast with relative ease. I seek direction, my Chieftains," Brennus responded as he took to one knee and looked at them from that position, hope in his eyes. It continued to be a strange adjustment, having Brennus be so co-operative. That thought was ended abruptly by the sudden change in temperature.

"I have a solution for you, my brave past-self," the spirit hissed in his ear. Despite his preference to ignore it as much as possible, advice at this point was a thing Mathghamhain could use. He mumbled softly to it in response in order to avoid drawing attention to the fact he was talking to his spirit guide. Hopefully, it had an actual useful piece of advice and not the usual solution to kill. He needed an excuse to leave so he could speak aloud with it.

"Brennus, let us confer, my wife and I, so that we may best advise you. Then we can gather with all the reeves in the days to come to seek the best solution to help manage this situation you have alerted us to," Mathghamhain said as an excuse to leave, and also give himself time to seek a solution that would work for all. He watched gratefully as Brennus nodded and rose to leave, waiting until the warrior had exited fully before he turned to Cacht.

"What is it, brave husband? You are not usually so quick to dismiss a reeve, let alone brave Brennus himself. Something troubles you?" she asked looking at him worriedly. They had long ago established a system of always appearing in complete confidence in each other's words when anyone else was present, only ever raising concerns when alone with each other and it had worked for months.

"The spirit which does, at times, offer advice unsolicited claims to have a solution to the problem Brennus has presented to us but I am wary of inquiring of it as to what that solution is based on past experience," Mathghamhain replied watching as she nodded in understanding.

"Perhaps then before you consider what that advice might be, you should seek another option. You have told me before what this spirit guide of yours tends to advise and while it has led to gains…" she suggested offering him a smile.

"That is a possibility but to whom would you suggest I seek such counsel where one does not favour one side or one guild," Mathghamhain asked, thinking he already had a good idea of the answer she was going to give. It was, after all, the logical choice, was it not? Despite not wishing to ask the spirit yet, he was certain it was waiting anxiously to speak again, especially since the air was still slightly chilled.

"Do not! You need no counsel save your own. Have I not led you to where you are? You were a mere hunter who by luck felled a bear. Now you are chieftain over many villages and adored by all," the spirit hissed, clearly bothered by the idea of him con-

sulting anyone else for advice.

"Who would be that impartial do you think, brave husband? We are due soon enough for a visit from the Priesthood, are we not? Go to wise Drust in advance, seek his counsel, see what he advises. The Priesthood would not see violence as an answer or lead us astray. Your leadership, our leadership, has united so many together," she responded.

"I must counsel against this, young Mathghamhain. It will merely lead to trouble you are not prepared to handle," the spirit hissed insistently. Mathghamhain waved his hand absently knowing it was a futile gesture. The spirit was there permanently and simply kept quiet most of the time. He was overdue to talk to the priest about how it was even possible for his future self to be present in the first place or how common-place it was. This time he would not allow Drust to change the subject. Especially since, more than ever, Mathghamhain was certain that it was a rare thing. That begged the question of what exactly this so-called mystic artifact was that had been used to kill him in the future and send the spirit back in time.

"It is a wise suggestion, gentle wife. It bears looking into. The difficult part will be locating him, as the Priesthood do keep themselves secluded," Mathgham-hain answered as he ignored his future self as best he could. "With as much land as we now have I would wager that, unless they actively moved, we have the priest's temple within our borders. Perhaps by con-sulting the various villages, I can locate the likely area."

"Set out in the morning then, dear husband, and

gather the intelligence. We are jointly the chieftains of these lands. I can manage the business here for a few days," Cacht counselled as she moved to kiss his cheek. "Take your mighty steed and seek out the priest, learn his thoughts on this grave matter with which Brennus has approached us this day. Bring the advice back and you and I will go over it. If it is sound, we can find a way to implement it much as we do all things. If it is lacking, then we can seek your spirit guide's advice and consider both as well as the thoughts of our reeves. Even if both the spirit and the priest give advice that is lacking, then the entire assemblage of the guild reeves can surely be counted on for further advice."

Sighing to himself, Mathghamhain realized the spirit had taken the hint and left them alone. How the spirit affected the temperature he was not quite sure, especially since no one else ever seemed to notice. Something else he could ask the priest about. Maybe if he approached the subject by talking about sudden changes in temperature, he could trap the old man into talking about the spirit. Smiling to himself now that he had a plan for how to broach the subject successfully this time, Mathghamhain noticed his wife had left her seat.

"We shall see how it goes. I am doubtful the priest will be much in favour of anything that gives us an even greater advantage and power than we have already gained but it will not hurt to seek his counsel. I have been meaning to consult him on other matters but never anything so pressing that it could not wait until the yearly visit. A visit which now we are host to

for longer as he goes from village to village," Mathghamhain said stepping away from his seat as well and returning her affection with his own. Brennus had been a special case this day, extending how long they had been in the room, and that audience had since come to an end. Now the time to see about dinner. Perhaps a brief stop at the stable to visit their respective steeds and make sure they were content as well before they retired for the night.

"The priest has indicated at least twice that he had no problems with our goals, Mathghamhain. Why are you certain he will be against us furthering them? The Priesthood benefits. Not to mention having so many villages united leaves greater tracts of land safe for him to travel through without worry of entering an area where a battle could occur," Cacht replied as they headed for the door.

"It benefits him but the Priesthood is larger than one man," Mathghamhain said softly, stopping in his tracks. "Other members of it are currently outside our territory. If they think we may end up overlapping territory covered by more than one member of the Priesthood, it could cause them organizational problems in how they travel. We may already have unknowingly done so. I honestly do not know, Cacht, I worry still that something is going to stop us from achieving everything we have set out to do."

How could he explain the general worry that he was still reaching higher than he should? No one else had ever tried and if they had done so and failed, what had brought it about? There was also the worry that the spirit had not yet presented any specific information regarding where he might eventually face the one who would kill them.

"I understand Mathghamhain," Cacht said reassuringly as she looped her arm with his. "The concerns Brennus brought forward have you shaken. The spirit's ongoing presence in your life has you shaken. I have never asked you to try and explain how it is here, only that it is your burden and I will help you shoulder it best that I can. A good hot meal will help, as will sleep, and ultimately I hope Drust as a priest can offer reassurance for you."

Smiling at her response Mathghamhain closed his eyes for a brief moment. "You are right, of course. Let us go see what can be prepared for our dinner and then perhaps when we are back home again, we can do more than rest before I head out in the morning."

CHAPTER 20

Mathghamhain sat within the Educators Guild building and waited best he could while Donnchad went over the findings he had brought him. It had taken weeks of travel, even with the horse, but he had eventually made the rounds of all the villages. At each one, Mathghamhain had consulted its residents to find out from which direction the priest arrived and to which direction he departed. Fortunately, nothing had seemed to indicate that there was a representative other than Drust within the borders. After that, Mathghamhain had returned home to check that Cacht had business well in hand.

Now he needed Donnchad's help to make sense of the gathered information.

It was fascinating to watch the reeve, as it looked not unlike how Cynwrig had once calculated strategic attacks when he had time for advance preparation. Watching Donnchad do a thing the man referred to as triangulation was confusing but still held his full attention. Finally, the Educators Guild Reeve put his quill down and looked in his direction with a smile.

"I have found the likeliest area but can only narrow it down so much for you, my wise Chieftain," Donnchad said before pointing with his forefinger at the centre of the star he had drawn. It was, if Mathghamhain squinted at it long enough, several triangles which had resulted in a curious design but one that clearly created a specific point where they all intersected.

"There is a reason, wise Donnchad, that I did come to you for such a calculation. It is well beyond my ability to understand and perform. I suspect that even in all his wisdom that my predecessor as Warriors Guild Chief, Cynwrig, may his spirit rest in peace, would be hard-pressed to make such a map," Mathghamhain said smiling at the man.

The Reeve of the Educators Guild had taken well to overseeing a greater number of people, delegating well amongst members of the Educators Guild from the other villages. The eventual goal had been expressed more than once to Mathghamhain that Donnchad wished to allow each village's Educators Guild members to specialize in a different area of education and knowledge while providing the basics to the residents. This, the reeve had argued, would better utilize those who had a penchant for higher learning to go where they could pursue their preferred area of study. Those who came to Meadhan would be those who were taking their first steps as members of the Educators Guild itself. Mathghamhain and Cacht had been thrilled to endorse the idea. The Educators Guild was the most difficult guild to find members for, with only the Priesthood being more difficult. To his understanding from talks the previous year when Drust, the old priest had visited, one did not join the Priesthood of their own volition but instead were called by the land itself to do so.

"Yes, wise and brave Mathghamhain, I suspect you are right. I doubt it would surprise you much to learn that the late Cynwrig had shown interest as a boy in joining this guild before he ultimately settled on and was accepted into the Warriors Guild. Even so, I do know that although he was good with such numbers, making a calculated map such as this one proved to be, would be no easy feat for him. Indeed, it is due to the thoroughness you exercised in gathering information these past weeks from across the lands that I was able to make these calculations so precisely," Donnchad said before moving from the map to sit down across from the chieftain.

"No, that truly does not surprise me in the least. As for the information I gathered, I simply did what seemed to make the most sense if I wanted to locate the priest's likeliest location," Mathghamhain replied averting his eyes. Being commended by a person he knew to be much wiser than himself always felt strange.

"Yes, well, you have always been a smart one, my

Chieftain," Donnchad replied with a slight smile. "Based on what I know of the lands and the origin points of the numbers you did provide, I have narrowed the area you must search to that of a small clearing. One that is not much bigger than the training grounds that adjoin this village. Nor is it too far from here. It would seem that even before any expansion occurred, the Priesthood's temple was located within Meadhan's lands."

"That is, indeed, a small area to comb and on horseback should take no time at all," Mathghamhain said looking up at the older man, beaming as he did so. "Although it would help if we did have some notion of what form the temple might take. That we have never stumbled upon it in these many years does suggest they keep it hidden. That may make for trouble. I thank you for your continued and diligent service, Donnchad. I must leave you though and head out. I miss my own bed and do wish to sleep in it before I head out once again."

Rising from his seat as he spoke, Mathghamhain clasped the man's hand tightly, shaking it. Looking at the map, he sighed, realizing precisely where he had to search.

"I know the area I have to go to all too well, it would seem. Thank you again, loyal Donnchad," Mathghamhain said nodding his head sharply. Taking one last look at the parchment, he waited as the reeve detached it from the large wooden board and rolled it up. Accepting it graciously when it was handed to him, Mathghamhain secured the parchment with a strap before he slung it over his shoulder and exited the room.

As soon as Mathghamhain set foot outside of the building, he took in a breath of fresh air. He had missed this village. Tomorrow he would resume his search for the Priest Drust. Considering the location Donnchad had given him to look in, he had additional questions for the old priest as well. In the meantime, he had not been lying when he had told the reeve he was looking forward to sleeping in his own bed. As soon as he had dinner with Cacht, he planned to get as much sleep as possible before morning came.

His horse was back at the stable so he would have to walk but, despite all the many changes they had wrought in Meadhan the past year, it remained a short brisk walk from the Educators Guild's building to where Mathghamhain and his wife did rule from.

"Faithful husband you have returned. Was wise Donnchad able to help you already? You are back much faster than I had expected from seeing him." Cacht greeted him as she left her seat to come forward and embrace him. Nechtan, the Farmers Guild Reeve, politely excused himself from the room. For that, Mathghamhain was grateful, but hopefully the business the man had been here on was not pressing and could be dealt with the next day.

"He was indeed! He seemed quite impressed with all the information I had gathered on directions the priest has taken and what days he tended to arrive each year. He took that information and has provided an excellent map. I need now merely ride forth to find the Priest Drust and seek his counsel as you did

     DARYL J BALL

suggest in your great wisdom and counsel many days now past," Mathghamhain grinned kissing her cheek lightly before pausing half-tempted to sit for a bit but also knowing time was of the essence if he wanted to get sufficient rest before heading out in the morning. He wanted to leave early if he was going to find the priest and be home before nightfall.

"Then I wish you good luck when you depart to-morrow and trust you will wake me before you head out—that you return to me whole and hearty and we can then go about the business of advising Brennus before he does lose his temper and seek to try and threaten us into action," she said, her smile turning into a slight frown. It was not a look Mathghamhain liked on her and Brennus would pay dearly one day for causing it to ever cross her lips but currently, the Warriors Guild Reeve was as loyal as they came, next to Nuallan. Brennus had to be trusted to have the best needs of the people of all of the villages in mind no matter how much he ached for combat.

"But of course! Just as I trust that you will continue to govern our people wisely. I shall return as swiftly as my steed can ride over the fields," he said kissing her again, this time embracing her as he did so, the feel of her skin against his own making him want to linger rather than head out with her to eat dinner but he knew the sooner he ate the more sleep he would get, and he desperately needed it.

Smiling at her, Mathghamhain closed his hand around Cacht's and exited the building. They could talk about anything less pressing while they ate.

Chapter 21

It had taken hours and much searching on his hands and knees combing through any tall areas of grass to look for where there might be a secret entrance in the ground itself overrun by long grass. It was the only thing that could be the case. The area was nothing but grassland and mostly open field and he had already tried the boulder outcropping that disrupted the flow of it all. It was ironic that this, of all the places there were, was the best place to look. Unfortunately, there was simply nowhere in this area that it could be and he was growing frustrated after a good period of time spent searching. The map could be wrong, yes, but there had been no real other way to try and figure it out and simply waiting for the priest to come out to visit them was a month or so away and that was at the village of Crioch, the place furthest out from where he and Cacht ruled.

"Is there an item I might help you find, brave Chieftain Mathghamhain? It is a thing to see, a chief of chiefs on his hands and knees scrambling in the dirt with his hands and fingers clawing at the long blades of grass in desperation," the oddly accented voice of a female came reaching Mathghamhain's ears. It reminded him ever so slightly of the accent Nuallan developed when he had too much to drink.

She was a good several feet away, too far for him to reach in a single movement. Turning his head sideways slightly, Mathghamhain prepared to rise to his feet while striving to place the accent. It was not one

he knew from any of the villages in his and Cacht's lands. Nuallan had until now been the only one he could recall having anything resembling it. She was young, only a bit older than the age Cacht had been when she became Chief of the Caretakers Guild, and adorned in robes that should have given her away when she moved, and yet had not. Her hair was even brighter than Nuallan's was, and with a shine to it that gave him a good idea of the origin of her peculiar accent. She was a northerner, how far north he was unsure, but she was definitely from further north than Crioch. That she had gotten as close as she had without him hearing her suggested she had come from nearby. With nothing remotely nearby for her to have come from that quickly and silently, that told him something important. She was from wherever the Priest Drust was hiding.

"And does it please your eyes to see me scramble so? Does it please the priest I have come seeking that he hides the entrance to his home so thoroughly that it demeans those who seek it out in such a lowly manner?" Mathghamhain responded gruffly as he moved gradually to his feet looking in her direction and trying to process it.

"You speak as though I and the one you seek are two different people, Mathghamhain, when I am but the priest you seek. Come let us find a better mooring for your noble steed before we retire to speak about what has brought you here to these lands, breaking ages of tradition where we come to you and not the other way around. For if we did want visitors, do you not think we would build where you can see?" she said frowning at him as he moved towards his horse. It was the best thing he could think of to do right now to avoid saying anything regrettable.

"Priest Drust is an older gentleman, wise and known to me and others. You, I know not and I have little reason to believe the veracity of your claims to be the priest of these lands," Mathghamhain finally retorted watching as she walked towards him doing little to mask her steps as she did so. With how she was walking, he could scarcely believe he had not heard her approach, as she was heavier footed than he would have believed possible for someone so slim.

"No, the Priesthood as you know is comprised of many members. That you have had dealings with only the one is due to how long he served this area. Others of our guild are located in other lands and you, in fact, have another residing within the borders of your current land holdings but just barely. Drust did pass away a scant few months ago. If you must know, members of the Priesthood study together but few are chosen to be representatives. Upon Drust's passing, I was the nearest, most eligible one available to take up his mantle in these lands and before you do ask, I am a full member of the Priesthood. You may address me as the Priestess Fedelmid so that we both are on a first-name basis. It is good grounds for any conversation I am told. It promotes trust, understanding, and openness," she said, her gaze narrowing.

Her familiarity with his and Cacht's actions, the way she answered him before he could ask, all of it spoke to her being, indeed, associated with the Priesthood. How had he not known the old priest had died?

　　　　DARYL J BALL

Why did these people insist on maintaining a life so far removed from everyone else? It had not bothered him when he was younger, but now that he had seen those in his lands waiting on any ceremonies until the Priesthood visited, it had begun to. Not that he had ever felt the courage to speak against them. That a person as young as this priestess would be offered such command over the lives of so many was disturbing.

"I see you have one of the steeds. Those horses come from further east but a trade resulted in them slowly making their way inland and to where you were eventually gifted them as part of your new holdings. I do hope you and your wife will consider granting your lands a single unifying name soon," she continued, her words interrupting his thoughts. "Come, brave and wise Mathghamhain, let me show you the grave of the priest you once knew and who gave his blessing to unify and expand, where once people kept to their own villages."

"He has passed on and I am to believe you, so young a woman, is to be the new priest of these lands. Tell me, Priestess Fedelmid, where might I find the other priest within my lands as I would prefer to seek him out and talk to one who has the experience of more than a handful of months," Mathghamhain said watching as anger flashed in her green eyes.

It was such a different appearance—bright eyes and hair—that it certainly would make her stand out when she journeyed, even if the robes of her office of Priestess were not to give her away otherwise. There was little doubt who she was associated with. That did cause concern of a different nature. That this northerner, who was more obviously so than his servant Nuallan, was so far south and living in his land meant others could have slipped in as well. Perhaps there was merit to the concerns Brennus had.

"You would insult me on this, the first day we meet? I who am to be Priestess over the lands you govern with your wife? It is a bad way to begin a working relationship, Mathghamhain. I had called you wise but you are quickly proving to have little of the wisdom and common sense my predecessor did note you to possess. That you would back away from the truth I have told you suggests you are also not as brave as I was led to believe. The truth shall set you free, Mathghamhain. Let us travel. You need not ride your steed, we are close by," she said although her last words were a lot softer and lacked any of the anger he had seen in her eyes or heard in her choice of words so recently. It was an odd thing to hear such words but in so gentle a tone.

"Very well then, show me this proof, this grave of the fallen Priest that I might also know how the Priesthood honours its own," Mathghamhain muttered reluctantly as he took the reins of his steed and moved to follow her. Noting carefully as he did so how she seemed to be taking a fairly circuitous route to get to the boulder outcropping that she could have reached directly in a few steps than by the several dozen she had taken. Was that part of it? He knew the Priesthood to have a greater connection to the land than most but that how one approached something in the land despite it not being alive could reveal truths that the naked eye could not see?

"Behold," she said quietly as she stopped and knelt in front of the boulder outcropping, wiping her hand across the surface, lightly removing the moss that had grown over it and yet, he thought, the moss left no mark on her hand from what he could see. Was the moss even really there Mathghamhain wondered. It had to be, after all, he had even looked at this exact boulder. Moving to kneel beside her, he gasped. It was no mere boulder at all, as it had been clearly carved into, to mark it as a burial spot. There was likely significance to it being here but it was an outlandish notion and so he dismissed it.

"I see not how I could have missed such an obvious thing. Forgive me, fair Priestess, clearly, there are secrets the land does hold that my eyes cannot see despite travelling them for many a year as a hunter," he said quietly looking to her for a moment, her appearance still being a difficult one to shake.

"There is much one who is not learned in the ways of the land might miss, Mathghamhain. Priests are buried close to whichever temple they primarily operated from. They do return to the land which they served instead of as you and others do when you seek to bury your dead where they are from. That is when you bother to bury them at all. I am led to believe at times that only those who gain a degree of notability in the villages ever get a proper burial. The rest are left to burn away, sending smoke wafting across the lands scattering the last of their physical bodies as so much dust to fertilize the earth below it," she said rising to her feet and walking somewhat to the north.

"So am I learning, Priestess Fedelmid. As for your

suggestion, it is a good one, and a name will be considered. It would, indeed, give our lands a unified feel," Mathghamhain said nodding as he followed, the steed's reins in hand, to see where she went now.

Given she was walking away from the boulders and into the open clearing, he was a bit confused regarding how large a secret the land could hold. He watched in awe as she suddenly knelt down and ran her hand below the grasses blades dusting the dirt itself before she rose to her feet and stomped hard on where she had dusted with her hand. Without a sound, the ground dropped out of view in front of her and she began to descend into the opening.

"Excellent, I look forward to learning what name is decided upon. Come! There are stairs, you will not fall. You will need to leave your steed behind. Fear not, the land will see to it that no passerby takes him," she said, only her head now visible from where he stood. He stared after her before securing his horse's reins to the nearest thing he could find and cautiously walking to where he had last seen her, looking down at the opening. It was not that big but the steps looked incredibly well-formed, solid, and bordered by carved wood to define the edges.

"I do not recall ever seeing actual carved steps, let alone an opening in the ground. We descend into the land itself…" he said cautiously, afraid, before a familiar feeling pricked at his brain as he set his first foot down on them. The spirit was trying to say something.

"Do not go down there, Mathghamhain. She is no priest but an instrument of the vilest and evil kind, a

spirit given physical form to lure a brave chieftain as yourself to your doom. Do not go down there. I will be unable to…" it said before its voice was abruptly cut off as Mathghamhain took a few cautious steps.

The opening proved to be larger once one got their head below the surface level. It was a massive cavern. What the spirit had been trying to say bothered him especially since it had stopped talking mid-sentence. Not a thing he recalled happening before even when he had explicitly wished it would have. Exactly how much was there to the Priesthood's abilities that he had never learned about? The spirit's warning took root in his thoughts, leaving him unsure if he should continue. If she was not really a priestess, this could be a trap, but he had to know, and the spirit being so thoroughly silenced honestly intrigued him.

"You halted in your steps, Mathghamhain. Did you truly journey all this way to find the Priesthood simply to halt now as you set foot in our temple and home?" Fedelmid asked looking up at him from the bottom of the steps.

The cavern as he had first thought of it was proving to be much grander. Its walls were not ground itself but intricately carved pillars closely placed together to create a massive room that they were now entering and from what he could see there was still more cavern beyond the pillars. The floor of the cavern was highly decorated and polished to the point he could not even tell if any of it was actual dirt. How long had this place been here to have been so meticulously designed? It would have taken untold generations to achieve such work and he knew not of any villagers or any guilds who could yield such craftsmanship. He was in complete and utter awe.

"I apologize, this place is a great deal to accept as existing, and I was…I halted to consider the idea that I was descending into the earth, not unlike how we bury our dead as you mentioned. That I was not entering a temple but the home of the dead itself and that you are not a priest at all but an evil spirit given physical form to lead me to my doom," Mathghamhain said realizing he was already voicing his concerns the spirit's warning had prompted in him. How accurate was it with that warning, especially considering its history so far on matters and its abrupt silence? What else could cut off such a spirit but another spirit?

"You are suddenly troubled when you were not before. The wisdom and certainty of your venture deserting you when you come across that which you cannot explain. A poor quality in a man who must lead but I assure you, I am not a malevolent spirit. I was a baby once, then a child, and now am grown and have pledged my service to the Priesthood, forgoing any chance at a normal village life. The land did call out to me, having need of me to serve it and this I have done for many a year. Open your mind, Mathghamhain, you who more than anybody else in these lands should understand that things can change and be created where before it was not. Did you not change your own destiny and then the destiny of an entire village? Or do you purport to believe that you are merely a vessel through which the will of the land acted to bring about what was needed? What makes you believe that I wish you ill in any way?" she said

staring at him still without any anger in her voice, but it was clear from her tone his words had hurt her in some way.

"I am sorry for offending, Priestess Fedelmid. All I ever got to speak to your predecessor about was preparing for ceremonies and explaining why tributes are as they are. That or answering questions about why there are an increased number of dead one year to the next, or more births, or offering suggestions as to who should be sent to which guild," he said cautiously.

"That is how the relationship is when we visit. It is part of our calling in which we help guide the next year. You seeking us out? That is new. That is different and you have come to our home rather than the other way around and that means something is of deep concern. That such has occurred does not truly surprise me nor would it any of the Priesthood who know who you are. You walk uncharted territory with your new rule. There is nowhere to look to for guidance regarding how it should be done and yet you have managed in a few years to achieve what many would never even dare to dream of attempting even a tenth of. That suggests a level of focus and dedication not often seen. The kind the Priesthood relishes and you would have been a fine priest with that mindset had that been your destiny, which I realize is an odd thing to say since you have already defied it once. Come," the Priestess Fedelmid said gesturing, before heading behind one of the pillars and down a lit hallway.

Following Fedelmid deeper into the cavern, the further he walked the less carved and ornate Mathghamhain noticed the walls were. There were signs they once had been as well-carved but it had been worn down and broken but still, it all seemed to hold. It was also less brightly lit and seemed to grow darker the further they walked until it ended at a significantly smaller cavern with a much lower ceiling, with little in it save items he recognized all too well. A fire pit and stones to sit on.

"This place looks significantly older," Mathghamhain said cautiously. Watching the priestess, she moved to start a fire in the pit with what looked initially like a simple gesture from her hands, but he saw afterwards (now that the room was better lit) that she had been holding something very small that she had clearly used to start it with. It made him smirk despite not knowing what it was. Of all that was purported to be a priest's grand powers that defied explanation, there seemed to be a bit of the normal approach to things with a flash of the theatrical on their part to hide that fact. Moving to sit so that the fire blazed between them, he watched as she carefully moved to sit and how cautiously she did so. The way her robes flowed was likely, he thought, that she did so to avoid them getting too close to the flame.

"It is indeed. This is where we move to sit in reflection when an idea must be carefully considered. So we seek out a darker area, one with less ornate decor. Considering you sought out the Priesthood, I thought it an appropriate spot to discuss your matter. Now, what is it that troubles you so, brave and wise Mathghamhain?" she said watching him over the flickering of the fire, the smoke drifting upwards. Mathgham

hain was not sure where it left the temple but it looked clear to him that somehow it did so.

"It is the lands I govern, priestess. As you know, we have expanded greatly and added many villages to our own initial one from which we did spring. That requires a greater degree of defence now if we are to maintain it and we have worked tirelessly to make that and providing for everyone the focus now of our rule and less about expansion and conquest. To do right by the people we now govern. We have learned, Priestess Fedelmid, that other villages care not for the actions we have undertaken and are beginning to talk of gathering to invade us, to take away from us what we have achieved," he said watching her face for a sign of understanding. He dared not mention that they were specifically from the north. He had already offended her once, and in her home, he did not dare risk doing so again.

"Indeed, this outcome is inevitable. People often fear change, especially when that change means the potential loss of their own life. Making defences and seeing to your own people, your current course is good and should, as the other villages notice that you no longer are expanding, grant you time to do so, seeing that you no longer pose a threat. As is more likely, they will take the time they are granted by your pause in expansion to strengthen their forces and prepare best they can for when they must inevitably face the change you bring. Drust spoke highly of what you seek to achieve, and as you have no doubt surmised, the land is content with your changes or else we would have opposed you ourselves. We do wish you had found other ways to achieve them than with so much bloodshed but still the results of your actions continue to serve the land and you are considered a friend to the Priesthood," she said nodding at him to continue.

"Perhaps but I know what solution my Warriors Guild Reeve does wish," Mathghamhain began. "It is in his eyes and his stance…long have I had the chance to know how he thinks and feels on matters of combat…he was a childhood rival and later served under me when I was but Chief of the Warriors Guild…now he has sworn personal allegiance to me, putting the past aside but he hungers for combat and more of the bloodshed you wish me to avoid."

"Ah, the warrior who knows the art of combat but not so much the art of patience. The mightiest warrior, which likely granted them their position of Guild Chief, or as Drust indicated, you refer to the leaders of the guilds as reeves now. People such as this warrior, do indeed, make for a difficult situation as they are more likely to make poor choices when matters of anything but combat are required. I trust that he is also the reason why we heard of so much death and bloodshed these past years, more than when it was you who led that guild. Numbers that became staggering and would have been considered as such, if you were but the size of one village. You would have been considered warmongers and barbarians, I am afraid. Instead, your greater number and needs showed it was tactical in nature for expansion and overcoming resistance to change," she said, pausing as she narrowed her eyes at him, something he could barely

make out in the dim light of the fire. "What is this other matter which you are clearly not so eager to discuss?"

Chapter 22

The priestess' words had startled Mathghamhain at first. Was he so transparent that it was obvious there were things amiss besides the situation with Brennus? The time had finally come to discuss the spirit with the Priesthood. A talk that was long overdue.

"The wise Priestess did pick up on that aspect, I see. It has long been primarily my own burden. You spoke of my focus and as bringing about change sometimes with a clear focus and other times without. Several years ago, when I was but a hunter…" he began to answer before she held her hand up for him to be silent.

"Before we proceed, I would but ask that you not denigrate yourself by suggesting you are or were ever a mere anything. Everyone is, and whoever was, served a purpose and had reason. You may continue now," she said smiling lightly as she lowered her hand.

"As I was saying then, when I was a hunter, I was out alone when I came across a great brown bear and, although for such beasts we would work with other hunters to fell it, there were none about and I was able to kill it alone. It was in giving thanks to its spirit that I took my new name, the one I now go by," Mathghamhain added watching as she, to his annoyance, put her hand up again.

"You talk as if you besting a bear alone should ever have been considered outside your abilities. You doubted yourself then. That is always what holds people back in such work, they doubt themselves. Backed into a corner you let go of self-doubt and focused on the job at hand because the bear's death was needed for you to become who you now are. You may continue. I am simply sorting it out as you speak," she said nodding at him.

"Yes, well, having never felled such a beast by myself before I was thrown off when immediately afterwards a spirit did speak to me and advise me…warning that I would find myself wounded before I was home with my kill. I had never heard of a spirit directly conferring in such a manner but I believed at the time it was simply that those who do simply do not talk about it," he said sighing as she made him pause again.

"Directly speaking to you is, indeed, not an aspect even as a priestess that I have heard of although that is not to say it does not happen but animal spirits are not known to linger so long. Then again, you are a unique agent of change the land has," she mused.

"That was my understanding as well, that it was unusual. So, I questioned it and it identified itself as Mathghamhain just as I now was. That led me to believe even more so that it was the bear's spirit. Looking back I should have questioned it more thoroughly. Please let me finish this part," he continued, asking her to wait purely because he wanted to get through this part with minimal interruption. "I thought, I am already bleeding and wounded and

DARYL J BALL

would now be dragging the body of a bear, a creature that weighs much more than I, across the fields for who knows how long before other hunters saw me and helped. Of course, I would get more hurt before I reached the village. I even made it all the way there without help, only to trip over a hidden rock in the ground and cut myself causing anew wound, as had been predicted."

"Your unfamiliarity with spirits led to you doubting again, although I am curious about it giving a verbal prediction. That is not usually the nature of the land. I have a suspicion where this is going so please do continue," the Priestess Fedelmid said as she rose to her feet and went to stoke the fire, causing it to burn brighter.

"I put it out of my mind other than it being accurate, finding it odd that a spirit's last act on this plane would be to warn me of a rock I would trip over, but went back to my own affairs. It was that kill that led to my being challenged on my honour as one warrior believed I lied about felling the beast myself and soon in one-on-one combat we fought under the rules of such duels, wherein the one who loses is killed, but we both lost. I fell unconscious and he had stepped outside the duelling area by accident. When I awoke, I found that the unique case had meant we both lived and that I was offered a position in the Warriors Guild instead of the Hunters as I had proven myself an adept fighter," Mathghamhain said as she walked around to his side and held out her hand.

"Your sword, please, if you will, wise Mathghamhain, I wish to have a look at it while we talk, as it seems to me you are now getting to the true concern you have," she said as he looked at her curious why as a member of the Priesthood she wanted his sword but obliged her nonetheless, standing to unsheathe it and offering the hilt to her.

She grasped it as though born to it which fit rumours Mathghamhain had heard about northerners being born with a sword in hand. Holding his breath until she had moved back to her side of the fire with it, he sat down again and resumed speaking. He had come this far and trusting her as a member of the Priesthood came naturally, but there was still some fear within him of what she would do with it given the warning from the spirit had held him fast while she had moved out of striking range.

"Well over the course of the months and years since then, that same spirit has on occasion spoken to me at odd times, giving advice I had not asked for. I regret that this conversation has not been had before now. Something always happened to prevent it. Early on, I think after the third accurate prediction by the spirit, I questioned it further, finally demanding an explanation. It did identify itself as, in fact, my own self. My spirit cast back in time to now from a time many years from now upon the death of my body, and it wished to advise me so that I would be stronger and prepared to face the foe that had killed my future self," he said realizing how odd that sounded, proven by her setting the point of his blade in the ground and rising to her feet, her fingers perched at the end of its hilt, suspending the blade in a vertical position without it being held.

"I was going to say the land was acting quite a lot to guide you but this is something else entirely and worrisome. Tell me, Mathghamhain, when did you last speak to this spirit?" her voice sounding remarkably angrier than he would have believed possible, her ability to hide her emotions from her voice fading away in full.

"It is not like I asked it to do this, priestess. It started speaking to me right before we descended into this place, warning me not to come down here. That it was a trap, " he said watching her anger start to noticeably dissipate.

"Mathghamhain, you are wiser than you give yourself credit for. I underestimated you, it would seem. Your recent doubts are steeped in a hard truth, your subconscious mind. Do you know what that is? It is seeking desperately to aid you, offering resistance against what you are dealing with. This spirit, it is no friendly spirit, Mathghamhain, despite its claim to be you from a point in the future. No spirit can linger that long without a source of energy from the land. It is a malevolent spirit, Mathghamhain. It may have once been you, as it claimed, but it is now using you, feeding off your doubts to allow it to continue to linger. It is not in this place with you because these places are sacred, there are spirits all around us at all times but a malevolent one cannot enter sacred ground. What else has it told you that you only now question it? I am curious how deep this problem goes," she said her voice having lost all trace of anger, replaced with what sounded like genuine worry and concern for his well-being.

"Malevolent …but I do not…it is why I have achieved all that I have. It guided me in tactics that helped us win many a battle, which led to my being Chief of the Warriors Guild. It suggested how to organize things, to unite the guilds in electing a chief," he began watching as she lifted his blade and this time held it with the tip facing down as high as she could dangling it over the fire. It was fascinating to watch and somewhat worrisome. He knew fire at the right temperature could melt the metal and that was the tip of the blade she was holding so close to it. "Priestess, what is it you are doing exactly?"

"So when you seemed so historically focused, it was a malevolent spirit's guiding hand. In what matters did you act that have been rewarding that it did not advise you on, brave Mathghamhain?" she said smiling. "I am performing an enchantment as you might think of it. I had a reason early on to be suspicious as you gave your explanation that something did not quite seem right with this situation so wanted to see your sword. At the time, so I could see its form and see how I might use it to aid you. Do please continue and answer the question."

"Oh, of course, an enchantment," Mathghamhain said twitching at the word. He had seen her use movement to mask what she was doing already but could the priests, in fact, perform genuine magic as believed? "Yes, well, let's see. It advised against my marriage. It has repeatedly claimed the solution to many of my problems is to kill. Now I face a grave concern, sustaining my people, and I am sure that the spirit's advice will yield, again, that blood be shed."

"So, the act that brought you actual happiness on a personal level is the one it advised against. Do you not find that suspicious? Or that it warned you about talking to me? The things that give you the strength of heart and spirit are what malevolent spirits despise, Mathghamhain. As stated, they flourish in your doubts. I have no lack of belief it wishes to make you stronger than it was in its time but that is to its benefit, not yours. It would seem it is becoming parasitic now, with an increased need to see you shed blood. Unnecessary bloodshed is precisely that, and it will eat at a strong heart and leave traces of it, when you know it was unnecessary and avoidable. You are fighting this. It is right you sought out the Priesthood, I merely wish it had been sooner so that this might be avoided and also because my predecessor had much greater experience, as you can imagine. I am skilled enough to help you but you will still need to be the instrument itself," she said withdrawing the sword finally to his relief and turning it so that it faced upward sitting with it like that in her hands.

"That is…I suppose a fairly accurate assessment but that still leaves me with two situations. First, how to handle the original problem my Warriors Guild Reeve brought up and second, what then do I do about this spirit? It is my own self after all," Mathghamhain said increasingly worried now following her words.

"That you see your main problem as the potential war that is coming, when a greater war is already being waged for your future between the spirit of yourself in the present day and a malevolent parasitic one, speaks to how highly you value your people over your own being. You are, even without its influence, an agent of change, Mathghamhain. If you were not, then the bear would not have fallen as you noted," she said turning his sword to him to take, letting it cut her hand ever so slightly as he took it from her, smiling at him when it did so, not letting any pain it caused show or calling attention to it yet.

"So many people in your home village would not have supported you, so many would not have followed your commands. A woman of your wife's calibre, from what I am told by my predecessor, would not have chosen you, no matter your strength. Men and women across the land respond to you. Not to the spirit influencing you to kill. Killing problems simply puts fear into them. Do they fear you or do they sing your praises?" Fedelmid continued. "Reflect on that before you doubt that you were always meant to be what you are. You will find a way through the dilemma of war that your Reeve brings to your attention. If you do want a suggestion, I would state there are wars that can be won without bloodshed or combat although it may take work to convince Brennus of that idea and yes, I know his name. My predecessor kept excellent records. As for your spiritual problem, that is much more so my realm of advice and expertise."

"To win against gathered forces through diplomacy as my Educators Guild Reeve would call it, I may need to have him with me for that, and Brennus will need to be sated somehow. His blade is far too restless not to be used," he said, taking the sword from her, giving it a cursory look and, not noticing anything different

     DARYL J BALL

about it, he sheathed it. "What exactly did you do to my blade?"

"You are your reeve's commander. Brennus is obligated and pledged to listen to you or else he is an enemy, is he not? That is how it works. As for your blade, as I did say, I cast an enchantment upon it. More specifically, I attached one to it. When it is drawn, the grip of the spirit that torments you is weakened. Should the spirit ever gain too much hold over you, feeding enough on you that it is able to manifest more physically, the blade will be capable of cutting it despite it being naught but mostly material spirit energy. This is due to being charmed to harm creatures of truly malevolent nature. It will still function as a regular blade, as it always has, without weakening this spell," she said moving to put out the fire. "Shall we return you to your steed now that we have seen to your need for visiting here?"

"Oh, that is a powerful enchantment you have weaved then. I was not aware such magic was truly possible," he said, as he followed her back through the hallway.

"There are a great deal many things, Mathghamhain, that people do not truly ever understand. It is one reason why guilds prosper, they allow one to pursue a focused attention into the realm of knowledge, and yes, that includes combat and hunting. All things require some degree of knowledge. When you have passed through these coming days against your personal demon, Mathghamhain, then I hope we can talk again. There are many things you will need to know in the future that will allow you to become a greater agent, and will be needed to help you regain your footing when the malevolent has been removed from you" she added. Gesturing upward, the opening above them once again appeared. He was determined to one day question her about that. Everything else had required her direct touch or been trickery with her hands. Turning to head up the steps he paused, looking back.

"Thank you, Priestess Fedelmid. You are, indeed, a priest and I was wrong to doubt you," he apologized.

"Be well, Mathghamhain. I fear we will not meet again until great change has once again occurred. I may be delayed in visiting the villages. Despite all appearances, casting so much in one day is incredibly draining, and it will take me time to regain the necessary energy for those trips—especially since it will be my first visit. I can but hope you have dealt with this foe of yours by then," the priestess said as Mathghamhain reached the surface, the ground quickly closing up behind him. It occurred so suddenly that he had barely brought both of his feet on the ground.

"You fool. Why did you go in there? Did you not hear my warning?" the spirit's voice immediately was in Mathghamhain's ear now that he was once again on the surface. He had to be careful how he answered with how it tended to respond as much to his thoughts at times as it did to what he spoke and given what the priestess had told him.

"It is a sacred place and is warded against spirits such as yourself. Also, you waited until I was about to descend to attempt to say anything, instead of letting me know in advance. If you know what is to come, then how was it this surprised you?" he asked.

"There is much you do these days, Mathghamhain, that surprises me. You swore to follow my advice and yet you have at many a turn as of late ignored it. Would you truly seek the counsel of the Priesthood above myself…your own self?" the spirit asked growing angry.

"I have to do what is best for all, and your advice as of late has called for blood where it is unneeded. I had a situation as chieftain to deal with, that to ask for your advice alone, knowing your advice lately, would surely have been to engage in slaughter. I cannot serve my people if I were to do that, so I sought the Priesthood's advice," Mathghamhain responded smiling to himself as he mounted his steed. If he hurried he might make it home before Cacht had dinner.

"There are many situations that are solved by killing, Mathghamhain. You sought a second opinion without getting a first and from the worst person in these lands you could have sought out," the spirit sounded vehemently angry now. Why her specifically, Mathghamhain wondered as he prepared to command his steed to break out into a light canter.

"I sought the advice of one who knows the land better than I, better than anyone in them. We all live on them and tend them, the Priesthood is one with them though and knows their will," Mathghamhain responded before pausing. "What do you mean spirit? Why is she specifically a problem or did you mean priests in general?"

"She…that one…the fair-haired one with whom you spoke—she is no priestess, Mathghamhain. What proof did you have of her position, save that she was here when you sought out a priest? The one you know happens to be dead. Did she not engage in actions that you have never before seen a representative of the Priesthood perform? Mathghamhain, you are a fool and are deceived. That woman, if a woman is what she could be called, she is the one who in about fifteen years' time does slay us! She is no priestess. She is deadly: a pox on the land. She engages in magic that defies explanation and this is whom you took advice from?" the spirit hissed angrily.

"Wait, she is our killer? Could you not have led with that when warning me of descending into the temple, spirit?" he said growing angry. The Priestess Fedelmid had told him a great number of things but she had also been adamant about how evil his future self's spirit was and yet was it not his own self? Could he really trust her over that? He had seen her weave unexplained magic, had he not? Been in a place that could not possibly truly exist? He needed to talk to her to get to the centre of this, to hear them both speak at the same time to root out the truth. Turning his steed around suddenly Mathghamhain galloped back to where he had come out of the ground. Sweeping the ground as he had seen her do. Stomping his foot. "Priestess Fedelmid! I need to speak with you! It is about the future and you wishing me harm. We must speak urgently!"

Wavering between pleading and demanding she show herself for nearly an hour, Mathghamhain

decided to go so far as heading for the boulder out-cropping. Looking for the engraving in the stone covered by moss of the Priest Drust, whom he had known for years, who she had claimed had died, he was growing desperate. Unable to make the moss move to uncover it, Mathghamhain finally re-mounted his steed and commanded it to gallop towards Meadhan. He was seething with anger. The priestess was refusing to speak with him now that the spirit had told him her nature. She hid while the spirit of his future self kept itself known. That told him precisely who was more trustworthy. Angry at the woman who called herself a priestess, and spurred on by the spirit's words, he headed for home. Perhaps he would, indeed, be better off trusting the spirit's solu-tion instead of that of one as unknown to him as Fedelmid was. That thought rooting itself in the fore-front of his mind as the horse galloped onwards.

CHAPTER 23

"Brave and wise Mathghamhain! My husband and fellow Chieftain, what is it? You look more troubled than I can ever recall you being," Cacht said greeting him as Mathghamhain stormed in angrily. The ride from his discussion with the priestess or possible evil sorceress, and the babbling of his future spirit in his ear warning him of the grave danger he had put them in, rang through his thoughts still.

"I am…fine! Where is brave Brennus? I would have

words with him immediately. I do possess a solution, if I am right, that can be implemented with a minimum of bloodshed and he must know it before he gets even more restless than he already is," Mathghamhain growled finding his seat, his features softening long enough to kiss Cacht in greeting. The constant urging of the spirit in his ear had left him increasingly resolved to handle this in the most expedient way possible. The guard at the door quickly took off to alert Brennus that he was needed.

"Are you certain that is wise so late? The sun has already begun to set and the moon is rising, our people are preparing to retire for the night. Can it not wait until morning? Are we not to discuss what you have learned?" Cacht asked concerned.

"I have learned that it is as we feared. The spirit craves blood as does Brennus and yet we still must strengthen our forces," he explained. "The priest we once knew, he who wed us, has passed on to the other world, and a young one has taken his place. A priestess who openly exercises magic, and who it seems is responsible one day for the spirit that afflicts my person in the here and now. I will be free of these dangers, Cacht, the sooner we act, the sooner we can heal."

"Mathghamhain, that is a great deal to take in. You have a solution. Do you care to share it before Brennus arrives to answer your summons?" she asked him, sounding concerned.

"It is a solution that will buy us much needed time and end a threat. As ever when I am given advice by the spirit of my future self, there is another way," Mathghamhain said rising to greet Brennus as he

entered the room. Holding out his hand, Mathghamhain clasped his reeve's hand tight and locked eyes
with him.

"Brave and wise Mathghamhain, I see you have returned from your journey across the lands. I trust by
this late summons here that you and courageous
Cacht, my Chieftains and lieges, have at last an answer
to the gathering forces outside our territories,"
Brennus said, looking downward briefly as Mathghamhain had not broken his grip yet and was, in fact,
tightening it.

"I have. It is with this solution in mind, brave, loyal,
and mighty Brennus, childhood rival, mentor, trainer
in the Warriors Guild, later my second-in-command,
now Reeve, I assure you it is with the needs of all our
people and the lands on which they reside that I do
this now," Mathghamhain said drawing his sword
quietly as he spoke and thrusting the tip of his sword
through the armour bindings and deep into Brennus'
body. "It is not personal but blood must be drawn it
seems and yet kept to a minimum."

Cacht gasped at what Mathghamhain was doing
while he stood firm in his action tilting the blade
upright inside the torso of Brennus while the warrior's
eyes bulged out slightly. Brennus gasped, struggling
to speak, blood falling from his mouth. Mathghamhain
maintained eye contact with him throughout until
finally withdrawing his sword, causing the warrior to
fall backwards.

The reeve's dying words as he hit the floor being
short ones that made Mathghamhain feel regret and
guilt, but there had been no other way and Brennus,

on some level, seemed to have accepted that. "I lived…to do…only as…you asked…my liege."

"You killed him? Mathghamhain have you gone mad? He was a reeve! The greatest warrior we have. He trained you. Yes, he could be bloodthirsty and difficult at times but he was loyal, even beyond the calling of his role as reeve. He swore personal allegiance to us both after his failed challenge to your authority!" Cacht yelled, her tone one of disbelief.

"His death, Cacht, stills his blade. He thirsted for blood with alarmingly increased need. We must be focused on defence and strengthening our position, not as he was seeking, to attack an enemy that gathers against us," Mathghamhain answered her, stone-faced, as he moved to wipe his blade clean. "We will face them when the time comes, but to strike before we are secured will harm us all. It is the land we serve, not the needs of our warriors to shed blood, and as you so thoughtfully did point out he challenged us. He only swore allegiance after challenging our right to lead. He had drawn a sword on me that day to harm, to threaten, to coerce. The spirit of my future self did advise me then to kill him for his actions but I did not and perhaps, if I had, this could have been avoided, but now we live with what had to be done."

It had by no means been an easy decision but it had been what the spirit had urged and even fit what Fedelmid had suggested somewhat. Pinching the bridge of his nose, Mathghamhain closed his eyes tightly. He had known Brennus better than he knew anyone else in Meadhan with the possible exception of Cacht. Accepting what he had done would not be easy, but

he would deal with that in solitude, push it deep down inside of himself. It had been the only way. Opening his eyes slowly he straightened up and looked firmly at his wife. "Brennus will be afforded a proper burial for he does not die a traitor like he would have when he challenged our authority. He died in service to us, loyal even in his final breaths."

"You should have told me what you had planned first Mathghamhain. This? This is not how we govern. This is not how we reward victory or loyal service. Yes, he challenged you once, but look at all he did for you both before and since then?" Cacht said following Mathghamhain into their bedroom. The body of Brennus had been taken care of by both of them for the night, to be buried in the morning as their first act.

"No one will know the manner of his death. He did die in service to us. It was on a personal mission at our behest. He will be buried before that can be confirmed. His armour does hide the wounds. We will reassure our people. They will mourn his passing and we will return to the work that must be done," Mathghamhain said, trying to further reassure himself that he had done the right thing. As he spoke, he set the parchment map to one side as well, having still had it with him from earlier. It was a relic really, Mathghamhain was certain he could locate the temple again. It was accessing it that would be the problem. He could deal with that later once he figured out how exactly he wanted to deal with Fedelmid.

Looking to Cacht, Mathghamhain's features

softened as he approached her. Wrapping his arms around her waist as soon as she had removed her armour, he pulled her in tight against his body to whisper to her. "I have missed you, my love. Let me show you," he said putting the business with Brennus behind him for the moment as he ran his fingers up Cacht's back to help her finish undressing. She looked him in the eye questioningly at first and then kissing him for all too brief a moment.

"Do not think, brave Mathghamhain, that such words put the situation behind us but I have missed you, too," Cacht began, staring him straight in the eyes as she pulled away. "But now is not the time. Not after what you have done. It affects far too much to put aside even for a moment. If we are to move forward, to lead, than you and I need to have a long talk about what happened and how to proceed."

Frowning at her having pulled back from him and her words that followed, Mathghamhain's shoulders slumped. Closing his eyes tightly for a moment before looking back at her, he did his best to offer her a reassuring smile. "You are right…of course. We need to talk."

CHAPTER 24

The morning came far too quick for Mathghamhain's liking as it meant questions he was only partially prepared to handle. Thankfully, no doubt in part due to their talk the night before, Cacht seemed to have things well in

hand, as she had sent out at the first sign of wakefulness to gather food and prepare a fire and send word that a funeral would be held later in the morning. Not specifying whom it would be for but that the very act it was a proper funeral was enough to drive everyone within Meadhan quickly to action.

It was a solid three hours later when those who were nearby enough to attend gathered outside Meadhan next to where all Chiefs were buried. The warriors were in full armoured regalia and lined up on one side of the grave that the wrapped body of Brennus now occupied. Mathghamhain stood to one side with Cacht to greet each villager as they passed the grave to comfort them with a word of gratefulness for being there this day after they had deposited dirt on the body. After everyone had done so, the warriors moved from where they had been, to stand with those gathered as Mathghamhain and Cacht took up the spot the warriors had previously occupied in order to speak a few words in honour of the fallen Warriors Guild Reeve.

"Brave and mighty Brennus was a warrior born. Like the northerners we hear tales of, one could say he was born with a sword in his hand. He did serve Meadhan from childhood, always at the heels of warriors when they returned from battle. From the time he was old enough to learn how to spar, he would do so...often at my own expense," Mathghamhain said, trying to lighten the mood, as sombre as it was, by poking fun at himself.

"Brennus always put the needs of the people first," Cacht added offering Mathghamhain a smile, although it looked a bit forced, he thought. "He would be the last warrior standing because no one was getting past him in a battle. No one in Meadhan would have a hair on their head harmed if he could prevent it, and remember that. He was always looking to improve, to be the best warrior that a guild could ever produce, and he has ever been such."

"Brennus always dreamed of one day being the Chief of the Warriors Guild, and for a time, he had to live vicariously through me. First, when he trained me as a warrior and then again as he watched as I became Chief Cynwrig's second-in-command. Upon that brave man's passing, I was chosen to replace him as Guild Chief and Brennus was a natural choice to be my own second-in-command," Mathghamhain said looking at the warriors in particular as he spoke. Caiside was the current second-in-command and would need to lead temporarily. The older warrior was a much calmer hand in combat than Brennus had been, but how at bay the warriors stayed and focused on defence would depend on what their next election decided. Mathghamhain hoped after this was over that he might be able to coax a good choice in that regard.

"Mighty Brennus would achieve his greatest triumphs and establish a legacy when, upon Mathghamhain's election to the position that he does share with me, the role of Chief of the Warriors Guild was vacated and Brennus handily was elected to the role," Cacht added. "A role in which he thrived, even as it was re-titled to Reeve, and did serve our villages with a fervour unimagined by those who would oppose us. Brennus established a reputation as perhaps one of the greatest warriors to ever pick up a sword. It was a reputation that would precede him when battle did come as we expanded our lands. When enemy warriors were defeated, they were eager to join his guilds ranks and serve under him."

"Brennus did spearhead growth. He did forge a mighty Warriors Guild," Mathghamhain continued, catching Cacht's gesture to him to conclude the speech. "A guild that was much expanded so that there were sufficient warriors to defend all of our lands. As you all know, these past months the focus has been on fortifying those defences. Although Brennus did buckle under having to sheath his sword in order to do so, he loyally and graciously put his leadership and might into beginning the great work of securing our borders, particularly to the north. Now, on a mission of personal import to myself and my wife, Cacht, he was killed. Now we lay his body to rest and commend his spirit to the afterlife that, perhaps at long last, it might rest and know peace, not combat, without it bothering him to do so. We thank you, brave and mighty Brennus, for your years of dedicated and loyal service. Your strength of arm and your sense of humour will be missed by all who did know you."

Bowing his head as he finished, Mathghamhain stepped hand-in-hand with Cacht to toss one last pile of dirt on the grave. The words had come far easier than he had thought. He and Cacht then proceeded down the aisle that those gathered had made, leading a procession back into Meadhan for the feast that had been prepared in honour of the fallen reeve. For all that Mathghamhain still felt his actions of the night before justified, he was not entirely convinced that the spirit of Brennus would not also begin tormenting him.

After Mathghamhain had washed his hands more thoroughly than he had in ages, he joined those who had gathered for the feast. It was a mighty one, indeed, and the hunters had clearly outdone themselves on short notice. Gathered and stored crops had been used to add to the feast. The caretakers and educators present had done a marvellous job of setting up a proper feast using sets of tables and getting enough drinks ready. Drinks were always a necessity but even more so when it came to warriors who had lost a reeve.

"I seem to be outlasting far too many Reeves these past years, brave and wise Mathghamhain. I want to try and walk away from my role as Reeve of the Hunters Guild before it kills me," Loegaire said, taking a seat next to him.

"That is nonsense, Loegaire, my oldest friend. Your years of experience and a steady hand will be sorely needed in the days ahead. Losing Brennus is devastating, and there was word from him shortly before his untimely passing that those villages beyond our borders, particularly to the north, are gathering their forces together to fight us at some point in the future. We will need to see our efforts redoubled for defences but also our warriors to be increasingly strengthened. That will require a strong hand to lead them, and I have no doubt that, as we did a few years ago, the Hunters and Warriors Guilds will need to work hand-in-hand to provide enough work for defence,

hunting, and strengthening of arms," Mathghamhain answered, looking at Loegaire for a moment before taking a sip of his drink, his other hand clasping Cacht's hand firmly beneath the table's cloth returning the squeeze she had given it. Despite their disagreement the night before, she was ever his rock and greatest supporter.

"Perhaps it is but an idle wish, but if what you say is true, we will need to revisit things as it is, I suspect. Caiside is the natural choice I think at this point on the warriors part to become their reeve, even if he is much older than tends to be elected. For as much as the guilds have been expanded these past years by the conquest of other villages and lands, we do have our core village here of Meadhan to think of. That does suggest someone from the guild members who would be most loyal to you of all as the best choices to lead any guild. I will discuss the possibilities with my own second-in-command, Corraidhin, and with Caiside about how to proceed and present them to you both as soon as we are able to come up with a few ideas," Loegaire replied before frowning slightly at him, his eyes narrowing. "This personal mission you had sent Brennus on, was it a success before he died or should we fear whatever killed him being within our borders? People will be wondering."

"Fortunately, Loegaire, my oldest friend and mentor, the only one I have left, save for perhaps Nuallan, with mighty Brennus now gone to the afterlife, he was successful. We need not fear his killer as they were dealt with. Brennus simply could not survive the wounds that had been inflicted," Mathghamhain said by way of providing enough of a grain of truth to make it palatable.

"That is good to know, although he did look fine when last I saw him yesterday. Perhaps his wounds had not yet become noticeable even to himself or perhaps I spoke to him before he did incur them. It will be interesting to see how the election goes," Loegaire said in response before patting Mathghamhain on the shoulder and returning his attention to his drink and meal.

"He knows. He has known us so long, has he not, Mathghamhain?" the spirit hissed at Mathghamhain's ear as he waved his hand absently for it to go away without saying it aloud.

"He knows how you react, how you move, how you think, only Brennus knew you better. He will be suspicious. That was no idle comment, was it? It was a warning you see. He is watching you."

"It was late when I arrived back, Loegaire. I did arrive to let my beloved wife, Cacht, know what I had learned. When that was concluded, we did send for brave Brennus to update him as well and to present our decision. He was then dispatched on a quick mission on our behalf. He fell in pursuing it late into the night from what I understand of it. This morning when I arose he was already dead. None mourns his loss greater than I," he said clasping Loegaire's shoulder tightly as he responded to him. Mostly truth again but with a hint of a warning to Loegaire as well. The spirit could have a point. He would need to confer with Cacht in private later over how worried he should be.

CHAPTER 25

Loegaire is, as you pointed out, your longest lasting friend. He is your former Chief in the Hunters Guild and has long been your friend and mentor. He practically raised you. Mathghamhain, I cannot believe you are even considering the idea that he would say something against you. He has nothing to gain from it. You are the person people believe in and flock to. I was lucky enough that you saw me as an equal and were willing to work together to unite as chieftains to see your vision through, he knows this about our people. To speak out against you in any way on his part would be to cause chaos," Cacht said pacing as she watched him. He had been ordered to sit ever since they had retired to their home for the night and Mathghamhain had mentioned his concerns following the discussion with Loegaire. She was now trying to get through to him with the same arguments he had already given himself. The air being slightly chilled did not help either.

"He seeks to take your role for himself. He can claim it as he helped you from day one to build to this, the power behind the throne of the chieftains as it were," the spirit hissed in his ear angering Mathghamhain to the point that he violently jumped from his seat to slap at the air. "Do you think others do not see how he uses his long-standing ties to you? Does he not always get the best seat next to you and Cacht? Did you not supplant him in a sense as the guilds' greatest hunter when you were made a warrior or that you became chief of it so quickly? Let us not forget or that he has long been in the same role while others have grown and thrived in new roles, passing him by. Perhaps a new reeve is needed for the Hunters Guild, but then again, why would he leave the role voluntarily? Where would he go? The only option is death to replace you…perhaps he will even introduce a rule by which he automatically marries your widow if he kills you and replaces you? Words to think about, Mathghamhain. Loegaire is not as much a friend as you insist on seeing him as. You let history cloud your mind."

"May I take it from your sudden leap into action, dear husband, that your future self is telling you to kill Loegaire again? Even more bloodthirsty than the departed Brennus was? No wonder the priestess, or whatever she was that the spirit claims, wanted to convince you it is malevolent in nature. It seems to increasingly be true what with it now trying more than ever to push you towards killing those closest to you. Next, will you have to fight its words when it tells you I must be killed as well?" Cacht said sounding angrier than she normally might. It was one thing for him to speak out against the spirit but for her to do so, it bothered him at times, as if she were criticizing him as well. Everybody close to him seemed to be against him but he had to cling to the belief that Cacht was not one of them.

"I told you before you wed that she agreed to marry you because she sought power. With you out of the way and Loegaire so elderly, the villages would be hers alone to rule over," the spirit hissed this time, eliciting Mathghamhain to draw his sword in anger. The spirit immediately fell silent and he was certain with how it did not say anything about the sword not being able to harm it, that the Priestess Fedelmid, or whatever she truly was, she had been right about one thing. She had done something to his blade, enough to quiet this spirit of his future self. That was comforting in a way. It also made him wonder if perhaps, despite her not answering him, the rest of what she had said was true. The thought caused him to shudder.

"Yes, it was, in fact, trying as soon as you mentioned it to do precisely that, to give me an absurd reason why I should not continue to trust you with all my heart, dear wife. The sword, the priestess or whoever she truly was, did claim that she cast an enchantment around it that would weaken the spirit whenever I drew it forth," Mathghamhain replied keeping his sword out, but lowered as much as possible so he was not at much risk of harming her. "It seems to have done the trick of forcing it into silence as well, although I cannot exactly draw it every time it gets in my ear, now can I? That would make our people talk, but it is for another day to figure out. The question remains about Loegaire, and then I suspect we should be ready to give our blessing to the newly elected Reeve of the Warriors Guild. They will no doubt have chosen by morning, considering the last couple of elections they have had for the role."

"Mathghamhain. My brave and wise husband, do you forget that in the past few elections it was still but the guild of one village? That with guilds, all members do vote? It will take time to gather them all, considering some are stationed as a defence at each village and others are on permanent patrol, low though their numbers may be in those cases, they still have a vote that must be accounted for. I doubt you will hear of an election result before another night has passed," Cacht said, eyeing the sword as she approached him. "We will figure out what to do about Loegaire's words another time, in the meantime, we keep a watchful eye on him. We keep our ears open to any rumblings of dissent, and we address them as we always should, with thought and a fair sense of judgement."

"You are right, of course. Still, it troubles me. I heard the sincerity in the spirit's voice about the Priestess Fedelmid. Enough that I wanted to hear them both talk so that I could carry on a conversation between the two sides even if they cannot hear each other, but I could not get her attention again. It was as if the entrance was no longer there, and yet her words about how to drive the spirit away were precise so far. All of her words have been sound so far and yet the spirit did, indeed, fear her as his killer—as my killer. I cannot leave that unresolved, and now with Loegaire's words, and a gathering army on our borders?"

"You feel surrounded both from within our borders and without. We must be sure to strengthen our defences then as planned but also not let our guard down within our own lands…yet still, be fair leaders. You know that you will ever have my support and I will help you in ruling as we have always done," she said moving her hand to caress his cheek softly. "I would never betray you. You are my heart, Mathghamhain."

"And you are ever my heart as well, Cacht. From

the moment I did first lay eyes upon you when we were but children, I did know," Mathghamhain said softly still holding his blade. His free hand tilted her chin upwards so that he could press his lips to hers. If he could not trust the spirit, Nuallan too wrapped up in Warriors Guild business, and the priestess' support suspect along with Loegaire's, that truly left only Cacht to be his true support and she was easily the best of all of those people.

"This from a man who had to struggle to tell me how he felt, and to whom I had to propose. Although, it was a rather sudden moment since we had not even been courting," she said smiling at him after their kiss broke, her hands running over his chest plate lightly. "I watched you grow and thrive and put your best foot forward as a young man, and become the man you are now. Why would I ever want to lose the love and support of such a man? Is the spirit still, even when given orders by you, under the agreement not to enter our bedroom?"

"Indeed, to my knowledge, it is still under personal oath to me in that regard. Let us test it to be sure, shall we?" he said grinning at her, mischievously pushing her towards the bedroom, not sheathing his sword until they were inside of the room before removing it and his armour. She was all the support he needed and he dared not give her any reason to ever doubt him. Waiting until she had sat down on the edge of the bed to caress her cheeks before taking her to bed, and without pause, until they both were satisfied. Before drifting off to sleep, an all too brief light conversation had been held as to the idea of a name for their united lands.

CHAPTER 26

Nuallan

"You are certain, faithful and brave Caiside?" Mathghamhain said after the Reeve of the Warriors Guild had spoken.

"Indeed, we came to see you directly, our Chieftains, the moment we reached Meadhan," Caiside responded looking back over to him as Nuallan stood there waiting to be called on to speak.

It had been merely a few weeks earlier that Caiside had been elected to take on the role left vacant by the demise of Brennus, with Nuallan chosen to be his second-in-command. During that time they had made sure to scout along the northern border looking for any chance they might have to possibly stop the growing army on the other side. The Warriors Guild had also used the time to spread the news of a name having been chosen for the combined villages and lands under their chieftains' rule.

"I am quite certain my Chieftains, even now we are making sure we have additional proof by sending a few additional scouts and keeping an eye out for their return. If everything we have learned the past few days on our border north of Crioch is to be believed, then our enemies can be whittled down with a minimum loss of life to our side before the enemy can gather too many villages' warriors together into an army to invade us with," Nuallan said on bended knee. It was not strictly necessary for him to do so, Caiside was already standing, but with the additional personal pledge of loyalty he had given to Mathghamhain and Cacht, he would remain down until one of them gave him permission to stand. He had stayed away from being directly involved in their lives for far too long, his duties to the Warriors Guild having kept him busy. He feared that absence was why Mathghamhain looked so on edge and worried. It was a hard thing to see.

"I would say and I suspect my brave and wise husband would agree, Caiside and Nuallan, that if the reports prove true, you should gather every warrior available. The hunters too, so that we can ensure the quickest defeat possible. It would minimize our losses, I do think. The extra show of strength on our part would also send a strong message to those who would gather against us," Cacht spoke firmly. Nuallan cast a quick glance her way at her suggestion to include the Hunters Guild for extra power. Even she had an additional edge to her now. Had the death of Brennus truly had such a deep impact on them both? He could see it explaining part of it but not all. He had to find a way to be less absent from now on. He owed them everything.

"Indeed, mobilize your forces, Caiside, but do not merely fight to route our foes and deliver unto them a defeat. Instead, make it as decisive a defeat as possible, one that will serve to tell other foes that we will not waver. It shall also serve to lessen as much of the enemy's future numbers as possible. Go now. Let us test the mettle of those who would oppose us. We shall come to survey your victory as soon as we receive word that it has been done," Mathghamhain said rising from his seat at the same time as Cacht did to go and clasp hands with Caiside, and after gesturing to Nuallan to stand, clasped hands with him as well afterward.

Nuallan looked at both Chieftains worriedly. They were acting as if they were already under attack and felt threatened, yet so far all evidence suggested the gathering forces in the north would not be striking for quite some time yet, nor were they organized enough. He could understand it if Brennus had been killed well within their borders but otherwise this seemed a rash decision. He did not dare voice his concern, not until he was certain this was an unnecessary act of aggression, one he hoped the scouts he and Caiside had dispatched could prove.

"As ever, my Chieftains, you have my word your will shall be done and victory will soon be yours," Caiside spoke while giving a firm nod of the head.

"You do our family proud, my cousin and Reeve. Swing your blade and lead but also do not underestimate the enemy no matter how much larger our forces be," Cacht said, prompting Nuallan to give her a sudden confused look. It was not a thing that had come up before in his presence to his knowledge nor could he recall hearing her or Caiside refer to each other as cousins before or even as family.

"I would ask you my brave Chieftains to indulge my presence another moment if possible," Nuallan said as Caiside turned to leave. "I was unaware that my Reeve is family to you."

Neither Chieftain answered until they had both returned to their seats, although he did take note of

Cacht's slight frown at the question before she seemed to brighten again.

"Has it not? I do apologize loyal Nuallan. Caiside is the firstborn son to my late aunt, she who was my father's older sister and so he is family but not by a name that makes it obvious. A cousin but one I scarcely know beyond his relation to my family. It was for that reason that I chose him to escort me down the aisle at my wedding. Were you never told the reason? I will admit that had you fallen on the field of battle these past few years, our faithful although often absent servant, that brave Caiside would have been one of those I blamed most for not looking out for you," Cacht said before continuing. "We know well that your loyalty is to us and that your absence is merely because you are serving us in a greater capacity in the protection of all of Cridhe Aonaichte."

Nuallan nodded his agreement at her explanation, smiling at how causally the new name for everything the chieftains ruled over had been used, but was surprised when Mathghamhain seemed to stay silent. It was not hard to figure out why either: he looked distracted by a thing no one else could see, which no doubt meant the spirit was advising his chieftain in some capacity. It was a state he had seen Mathghamhain in enough times over the years that he recognized it quickly. What could it possibly be offering advice about, he wondered? Nuallan's eyes widened when Mathghamhain quickly rose drawing his sword as he did so.

"Fear not, my courageous wife, you whom are ever my heart, nor you, faithful and loyal Nuallan. My blade has merely been drawn to quiet the spirit," Mathghamhain offered as an explanation, although clearly, his liege had noted the confused look Nuallan had on his face as a result of it. "My apologies, Nuallan, at times I grow weary of listening to it when my attention is needed on other matters. The sword being drawn forces it into silence. I am still looking into determining precisely why. Once I fully understand it, I will explain it as best I can. Quickly now, meet up with brave Caiside that together you may lead our forces to victory and put an end to this northern threat."

It was an opening to discuss the risk such an unnecessary attack brought, but his liege had stated it as an order and a way of dismissing him from the room. Nuallan would have to hope the scouts brought news he could use in time to bring to the chieftains soon. Bowing to them both, he turned and exited the room to catch up with Caiside, noting that Mathghamhain had already seated himself again, but with the blade still drawn and laying across his lap.

The next person waiting to enter the room to talk to the chieftains cautiously brushed past Nuallan. If the spirit was offering advice that his liege did not wish to hear right now, then no doubt it was a good thing it remained silenced. Whatever the story with the blade keeping it quiet was really about, it had to be a new development. Nuallan could clearly recall several times when Mathghamhain had been talking with the spirit while the chieftain's sword was drawn. What had changed since then, and had he missed anything else significant while busy with the Warriors Guild?

CHAPTER 27
Caiside

““Your warriors are a fearsome lot. Know that, although we have been defeated this day in the field of battle, you sorely do underestimate the forces that do rally against you. The people are meant to stay in one village, perhaps grow the village itself, not have rule over many. You do seek too much,” Dubhthach said while on his knees surrounded by many a dead warrior. The others of the gathered warriors that the man commanded had either been killed or in a few rare cases had been merely bloodied and disarmed of their weapons. It had been far too brief a battle.

Caiside could not help but shake his head at the man’s words. With how big Cridhe Aonaichte, the territory Mathghamhain and Cacht ruled over, was now, it was nigh impossible for villages to the north of their borders to reach those that were still independent to the east and west. If they could, then perhaps Dubhthach and his forces might have had enough to route the near army Caiside currently commanded on behalf of his chieftains. Instead, Dubhthach and those warriors he had brought with him that were still alive were extremely few in number and surrounded. What bothered Caiside the most about the man’s words was that he had remained entirely silent following his defeat earlier; it was Mathghamhain and Cacht’s arrival that had led to him speaking.

“We underestimate nothing. Long have we

watched as our neighbours have gathered forces against us, waiting and strengthening our numbers so that we might properly put a stop to these machinations. Your numbers at our border grew too large for us to ignore and so a decisive strike was decided on before additional warriors could join you. I would prefer to minimize the odds of my own warriors falling in combat with you," Mathghamhain spoke having left the reins of his steed and Cacht's with Nuallan. Caiside knew that if need be it would be a matter of seconds before Nuallan found another warrior that could be fully entrusted to do so, and hand the reins to them so that he might move to their side just as he would. "What is your name, you who would lead forces against us who would unite all people so that the lands might be better served? My wife and I would wish to know with whom we deal."

"So she is your wife then. I suspected as such. That will be your undoing, bringing a woman to a battlefield, it is no place for such a person. You even call her your fellow Chieftain," Dubhthach said shaking his head best he could despite the tip of a blade at his throat.

"You misunderstand. Proof I suspect that your lands do have need of what we will one day bring to them. My brave husband and I are as one and that you would imply I could not handle myself on the field of battle is to display your ignorance. Do you think he would choose a woman who was not his equal in all things?" Cacht said growing angry in tone. It made Caiside smile, for even though he had never seen his cousin in a battle, he along with other warriors had helped train her at Mathghamhain's insistence and he was positive she could support her words. Still, he could not let the slight of Dubhthach's words stand.

"You shall watch your tongue and show the Chieftains the respect owed them! Your warriors have lost, your life is in their hands," he growled. His fellow warriors were also growing tense, with many of them putting their hands to their blades ready to draw them if necessary, to drive the point home that it was unwise to insult either Cacht or Mathghamhain.

"She does have quite the bark Mathghamhain…" Dubhthach spat before focusing sharply on both chieftains. "I am Dubhthach, Chief of my Warriors Guild, and have been for many a year. You do not scare me, and never would I leave an enemy alive. A further sign of the weakness that will eventually cost you."

"Who did ever say anything about them keeping you alive? They did simply wish to see who would lead warriors against them. To see what sort of foe we are dealing with. No, Dubhthach, your words prove you are a coward and one who does not know what strength or honour is, for you have none it would seem, and a base and vile tongue," Caiside spat back at the fallen Chief, only to feel Mathghamhain's hand on his shoulder, pulling him away before he acted on his anger further.

"As my brave Reeve has stated, Dubhthach, you and your remaining warriors will deliver a message to those who would oppose us when they learn of this defeat you have suffered," Mathghamhain said drawing his sword with one hand and moving to hold back his wife with his other. Cacht was angrier than Caiside had ever seen her. Her eyes ablaze following the insult from Dubhthach. Looking back to his other Chieftain, there was no mistaking the glimmer of an idea in Mathghamhain's eyes.

"You think I will tell them anything that will make them do naught but laugh at the idea of ever having feared you? You are weak and have been lucky so far is all that you have been. Your villages will fall and you will be left as but dust on the wind, so much so that not even the Priesthood will have anything left of you to say a blessing over in order to release your spirit to the afterlife," Dubhthach growled back.

"Oh, you do misunderstand me, foul creature, to call you a warrior would be an insult to every warrior I have ever fought alongside. The message you will deliver is not one you will be able to speak," Mathghamhain growled back before turning, twisting his sword carefully in his hand so that the hilt was extended towards Cacht. It was done so smoothly, Caiside barely even noticed it. It was the kind of thing Nuallan occasionally did and he wondered if his second-in-command had at some point taught Mathghamhain the art.

"I do believe it is right that you do the honours, my love," Mathghamhain continued with a gesture to Caiside with the other hand. It was a signal he knew and noted how his Chieftain stepped back once Cacht had taken the sword. "I wish that I could truthfully say it has been an honour to meet you but it would be a lie."

What followed was sudden and swift as Caiside

motioned to his warriors. The remainder of Dubhthach's men, already on their knees, quickly had their
throats sliced open wide enough that death was nearly
instantaneous. A mix of pride and fear crossed
Caiside's lips as he took note of the look of shock on
Dubhthach's face when Cacht plunged Mathghamhain's blade deep into the man's chest and then just as
quickly withdrew it and slashed the throat, Dubhthach's lifeless body falling in what seemed like slow
motion back to the ground.

Caiside had never had any doubt what would
happen to Dubhthach or the warriors who had accompanied him. From the moment the scouts had
come back and confirmed this was the best time to
strike, something he knew Nuallan had not been fully
in favour of, he had known his chieftains would insist
on this battle. The final execution of Dubhthach and
his men was meant as a message to any who opposed
the Chieftains as to what would happen if they continued to conspire against them.

"Does this bother you, Loegaire?"Mathghamhain
asked once the deed had been done and the sword
wiped clean and returned. The chieftain had kept it
drawn despite there no longer being any threat
present. Turning to see why his chieftain had asked
such a question of his fellow reeve, Caiside noted the
look of mild shock on the old hunter's face."I know
you are fully aware that, as with hunters, warriors are
not exactly known for leaving their foe alive."

"They were on their knees with so few left, they
would not have been a threat. You could easily have
set them free to send back to our neighbours," Loe-

gaire responded shaking his head.

Caiside frowned, there was nothing he could add to this conversation really. He could let his chieftain and the reeve sort it out on their own. He had a battlefield to finish cleaning up. Nuallan still had the horses which left him unavailable. Looking at the warriors he commanded and the hunters who had accompanied them, Caiside instructed them to commence cleaning up. The bodies of the dead enemy warriors were bound to thick logs that had been sharpened at one end and then raised up slowly so they could be planted in the ground. It was not a thing they traditionally did but it was something Mathghamhain had called for, to send a message to the north.

Cacht, for her part, continued to scare Caiside as she had taken the horses reins from his second-in-command and instructed Nuallan to further slice Dubhthach's body up to make sure his was the grimmest, her anger at a level he could not have imagined a woman ever having achieved before. Adding to that, he could still hear part of Loegaire and Mathghamhain's conversation.

"They are being strung up. They are butchered to show what we think of their efforts against us, what we think of their views of us. A warning that a similar fate will befall anyone else, and it serves as a much clearer and believable message than simply setting them free to return home to gather additional forces. An enemy we kill today is one we will not have to face tomorrow, Loegaire. You would be best served to remember that," Mathghamhain was saying.

"It was cold-blooded and unnecessarily bloody, my

Chieftain. You did not used to be so ruthless and full of aggression," Loegaire responded.

Sighing, Caiside went back to focussing on what his warriors needed to be doing, while keeping an ear open in case the argument got heated enough that he might be needed to step in. The heap of confiscated armour, weapons, and shields of the deceased was being organized for transport to Crioch. There the items would either be dispersed amongst the warriors or be sent onward to the Metal Workers Guild in Nabaidh to be re-worked. He was positive that guild would be quite busy for the next while.

"I did not use to have so many people whose needs must be seen to. We cannot afford to take chances, old friend, the enemy will continue to gather against us. What we can do to reduce their numbers, to make them think twice about attacking, for that I would have brave Caiside and yourself lead the hunters and warriors in slaughter. The welfare of the people of Cridhe Aonaichte is ever on my mind, Loegaire. If it is no longer your priority perhaps you should best consider if it might not be time for another to lead the Hunters Guild and we can find you a place to which you can retire. Perhaps in a guild that better suits your new mindset," Mathghamhain could be heard heatedly saying.

Caiside was disappointed slightly in Loegaire. He had known his fellow reeve even longer than Mathghamhain had known Cacht and the late Brennus. Surely the old hunter could understand that, at times, in order to protect so many, you had to take drastic measures. It was still troubling to hear the two men arguing to this degree. Loegaire had served as a father-figure to Mathghamhain since the chieftain was a child.

"I will concede the point, Mathghamhain, if only because you are my Chieftain but I would ask that, if there is a better way, you do find it before such another act of barbarity is performed," Loegaire said nodding reluctantly as he moved to join the others of his guild so they could head out as soon as the battle-field was finished being attended to. Caiside did his best to let his sigh of relief that the argument was over go unnoticed. Perhaps he could find time to talk to Loegaire in private one day soon so that any further arguing could be avoided. Right now, he wanted to check on his chieftain.

"Was there a problem, brave Mathghamhain?" Caiside asked as he approached him after Loegaire had walked away. The anger in his chieftain's eyes was still plainly visible.

"Loegaire was simply doing little other than questioning why such ruthlessness was required. I do understand his concerns. For all the similarities there are between the two, he is not a warrior but a hunter. He may often serve with his guild alongside yours but that does not mean he fully understands how such situations work when we do face an enemy. He will come around, I am certain, he has ever been a supporter even when he does not fully understand or agree with the views of my wife and I," Mathghamhain responded as Cacht came over to join them both. He smiled lightly when he saw how quickly they slipped their arms around each other's waists. "You

took greater satisfaction in ending poor, vile Dubhthach's life than I could have ever expected. Should we be seeing about training you as an active warrior, my courageous wife?"

"You seek to flatter me and with Caiside witness to it. As for Dubhthach, I hope his spirit knows endless torment in the afterlife. One as foul and uneducated as his drove him to be deserves every suffering he receives in it. I am all too glad that you did allow me to silence his foul mouth and end his life," Cacht said as a smattering of her earlier anger began to creep back into her voice before slowly dissipating again. "Perhaps it would not hurt to have me, under the strictest supervision, be trained further in the sparring grounds that adjoin Meadhan. I should suggest to the Caretakers Guilds to have all women trained in the basics as well. That way they protect themselves should the warriors not be available."

"Oh, but I do believe your fellow Chieftain is suggesting that, with mounting opposition on our borders, it might be best to more formally train you further. You will most surely be a primary target should they ever overrun our borders enough. From what I saw, you have a handle on the basics that we already taught you," Caiside said before pausing. "It does look like we are ready now to depart. I do think that you should be allowed to choose from the pillaged armaments later a blade for yourself. Do you not agree, brave Mathghamhain?"

"They may balk that a non-warrior would get such a pick when I might full well choose the best one after my husband has looked them over. Brave Caiside, you and Nuallan do deserve such reaping more than I do, as do all our warriors who did serve this day," she responded although her smile did suggest she would be quite happy if Mathghamhain agreed with the suggestion.

"It is sound thinking Caiside. I am certain, dear Cacht, they will agree that, as you are Chieftain, just as I am, you do deserve a choice. You did slay a Chief of a Warrior Guild of an enemy village, did you not? Are you not my equal? You have earned the opportunity many times over to be allowed such a pick and it is long overdue," Mathghamhain replied, his tone such that it was clear that he was fully behind the decision now.

"I will let my Chieftains continue this discussion between themselves," Caiside said bowing to each of them. Taking his leave, he surveyed the battlefield again. He had intended to be less brutal than Brennus had been but, until this threat from the north was dealt with sufficiently, he might not be able to. The days of simply patrolling were well behind him now but if everything went well, those days might return. Giving the signal to his warriors to begin heading out, Caiside gave a curt nod to Loegaire so that his fellow reeve could signal the hunters to do the same. That would be enough of a signal. He was not sure he was up to talking to the old hunter yet without risking an argument similar to the one Loegaire had just had with his chieftain.

Chapter 28
Mathghamhain

The delegation, led by Donnchad, stood in front of Mathghamhain and Cacht in the log building they ruled from in Meadhan over all of Cridhe Aonaichte. They were a diverse looking bunch, Mathghamhain thought, consisting primarily of people from further out in the lands. It was good that Donnchad led them, Mathghamhain thought, that way it would be easier for him and his wife to fully understand what the delegation was here about.

It had shown up in the late afternoon, no doubt having travelled from Nabaidh early that morning. As much as he had adjusted to having a horse to carry him across the vast lands they controlled these days, he had not forgotten how long it took to travel between the various villages on foot. If Mathghamhain could, once this enemy that was gathering to the north was dealt with, he would work to locate and bring additional horses to Cridhe Aonaichte so travel could be easier, but in the meantime, it had to remain by foot.

"Wise counsel, Donnchad, he who is Educators Guild Reeve, what can you add to what the others have been presented to us this day? Is it true? Can it be addressed and solved and, if so, how?" Cacht said interrupting Mathghamhain's thoughts, watching then as the man who had been addressed stepped forth and opened his arms wide. Well, this should be enlightening, he thought, although it would have saved time if the delegation had let Donnchad explain from the beginning.

"If what I understand is true, my brave and wise Chieftains, what we are hearing today is a consequence of the focus you both did place on boosting defences and our Warriors Guild in order to make us more secure. While you are not held at fault for the priority placed on the well-being of all that you have greatly impressed upon even the most reluctant of people living in these lands, the truth remains that those actions have pulled too much at our resources and those who work the land for both crops and metal. In short, we are stretched far too thin," Donnchad said while also doing his best to avoid eye contact. The murmurs of the delegation as the man spoke confirmed what the Educator Reeve had said as, indeed, what they were driving at. The air chilling caused Mathghamhain's heart to sink.

"They do not appreciate you, Mathghamhain. They take and take when they should be content to have one such as you who is so great over them. You do not need to look out for them, that is not your responsibility. You rose to rule through might and now they want you to be weakened, to be less than what made you chieftain in the first place. They should be taught a lesson," the spirit hissed. With so many in the room, Mathghamhain dared not draw his blade to make the spirit leave. It would definitely send the wrong message. Mathghamhain was certain, as if something registered on a subconscious level, that the spirit knew his gut reaction would be to draw his blade, making the delegation afraid and be a show of might. It was the exact thing the spirit insisted he should rule entirely by.

"This is, indeed, a grave matter, Donnchad. We shall consider how best to remedy this situation for we cannot be weak in our efforts to defend and protect, but if we do not see to the welfare of the people that we are seeking to protect, who then will there be left to defend?" Mathghamhain said rising to his feet after looking to Cacht for confirmation she was on board with what he was saying so far.

He really did not want to commit to anything without talking in private with her about this matter. He also wanted to talk to Nechtan to get a better assessment about how bad the situation was, perhaps Loegaire as well, as the Hunters Guild was responsible for any food the farmers could not grow. That, of course, meant also risking another argument with his old mentor.

"We thank you all for bringing this matter to our attention. We will find a solution. This we do promise you all for there is nothing of greater import than the welfare of the people of Cridhe Aonaichte. Meanwhile, we would ask that you return to your respective homes and try your best to get through. Rest, knowing that we will do our utmost to aid you in these difficult times of change," he finished.

It took a moment for his words to sink in but finally, he watched as heads began to nod slowly, at first one or two here and there, then the rest.

"It will be our utmost priority, we assure you, we shall not know peace until we have solved this situation. We thank you for your time," Cacht added as she rose to join him as they together thanked each member of the delegation in person. It was not necessary to do so but it was hoped that, by establishing such connections, it would be clear to everyone they were, indeed, heard and were valued. It would be far too easy to lose that with how spread out the villages were.

"By your leave then, my brave and courageous Chieftains, as the delegation is now departing, I will return as well to my duties," Donnchad said bowing to him and Cacht both and turning on his heel to depart behind the delegation as it slowly filed out.

"We would ask that you linger a bit longer, wise counsellor. This is a matter that will call for your knowledge, it is suspected," Mathghamhain said moving to press a gentle hand on the man's shoulder.

"Of course, my Chieftains, I will do what I can to assist in this matter," Donnchad responded turning to face them both and wait as he and Cacht resumed their seats.

"We can scarcely afford to lower our defences even after the defeat we did hand our enemies not long ago. They still gather and we cannot be certain how soon they will strike anew. How then can we solve this situation without asking our people to work themselves into the dying hours of the night?" Mathghamhain asked, concerned.

"Until our population increases, you have already done truly what you can, I am afraid to say, my Chieftains. Our gathered warriors have overwhelmed any enemy so far and thus we are no longer losing each battle. Casualties have been kept to a minimum allowing others not to need to leave their guilds to help replenish the ranks," the Reeve began. "We have

the population and the land required to look after everyone and then some, but it is the short term demand while defences are boosted that is causing this current situation. I would suggest we trade with a neighbour who does not wish to kill us to make up the difference in the shortfall for the time being. However, that would require us having items we can trade and we are short on everything right now."

"A trade could yet work, my brave and wise husband, we simply need to figure out what we have that can be traded. In the beginning days of our rule, we did encourage the flow of people between Meadhan and Nabaidh to foster unity and allow variety for people to choose from, and now we have a generation of children who are already taking their first steps. Perhaps if we make a different kind of trade," Cacht suggested. "Instead of simply resources, kind for kind, they provide enough resources steadily to help us through these times and rather than us compensating with a different resource, we provide something we do have. The other villages have much smaller lands, ours have become vaster but only a portion is as yet used for farming."

Considering that the air was still chilled, Mathghamhain feared what possible reasoning the spirit was waiting to use to verbally strike at him with.

"She is needling you, Mathghamhain, cloaking anger at you for not giving her a child yet that can be your heir. An attack on your manhood if ever there was one. She cloaks this anger in the form of a friendly sounding suggestion. Do you not see she wishes to rid herself of you and be married off to a chief of a neighbouring land to gain the trade, and also solidify her rule as she would then be greater in power than her husband?" the spirit hissed and this time Mathghamhain could not ignore it so easily. Moving to his feet, he drew his blade, driving the spirit of his future self away, as he looked apologetically at Donnchad.

"Fear not, wise counsellor. This blade is not drawn with you in mind but a need to feel its weight in my hand. It does arise at times now that I am not a warrior any longer and do not get to practice as much with its swing. One never knows when I might need to and so, at times, I must answer the need, to be sure its weight remains familiar," Mathghamhain gave by way of a quick explanation, to hide the truth, knowing Cacht was well aware of the true reason. It was, indeed, a need to hold the sword, but not for the reason he said.

"Oh, but of course, Mathghamhain. As your fellow Chieftain has noted, we do have an abundance of land not being used for anything but hunting. Perhaps if you were to consult with my fellow reeve, Loegaire, he might be able to disclose if we have sufficient animals about at present. If so, perhaps we can offer a neighbouring village the chance to hunt freely for their price of kills. Supervised, of course, by our own hunters, and a warrior or three as well, to be safe for certain," Donnchad suggested.

"It is a possible part of a solution but not, I suspect, a full one. We should check to see if it is, indeed, an option as it would allow a resource. We will also still need to meet with Nechtan to see what changes can be brought about to provide more efficient means of

 DARYL J BALL

farming and yielding greater numbers of crops with fewer workers. You may be needed to help with that as well, wise counsellor, due to your familiarity with how such things might be done," Mathghamhain mused. "In the meantime, we shall send a messenger to a neighbour who we know not to be currently organizing against us, to open up talks so we know what the options are and if these are even possible solutions. Donnchad, if you could draw up a message that we can send, you can bring it to us when it is ready."

Dismissed finally, Donnchad bowed before turning on his heel and exiting the building.

Staring sullenly out across the open terrain outside the village, Mathghamhain sighed inwardly. At least the spirit was staying quiet. Considering how Loegaire was currently griping about the suggestion that had been brought to him, he had honestly expected the spirit to be calling for the man's head.

"So, yes, Mathghamhain, with the increase in the amount of unsettled land, we do have enough wildlife for what you are suggesting, but it is a horrible idea. You are inviting outsiders in and you are going to try and keep them from not going overboard?" Loegaire ranted. "Yes, it is great to see you trying to accomplish things without engaging in outright butchery, and I appreciate that, but this does not feel like the right solution."

"What would you have me do instead, Loegaire? If we do not act quickly, the current situation could become a crisis. We have sent out a message to see if this village south of us would be interested in such an arrangement. There is no guarantee they will be but if they are and you are against it, then what can we offer instead?” he retorted as he did his best to stay calm and avoid this discussion becoming another heated argument.

“I do not know, this does not feel right though. We should find a way to hold on until the Priesthood visits. The will of the land and how we serve it is their area of expertise. As much as they seem on board with the expansions you and Cacht have brought about, they are overdue to visit. Perhaps the unnecessary attack to the north has caused them to rethink their acceptance, and so have delayed coming to bless us,” Loegaire countered, “and that is not even getting into the fact you already sent a message south, before you even consulted me!”

“That is exactly the issue, Loegaire. These are not the type of decisions you need to contemplate. You merely need to worry about your guild fulfilling their responsibilities so that we thrive. Cacht and I must think over everything. I cannot wait around before sending such messages. Not with how long it will take to reach there and for a response to come or for anything to be arranged. Do you understand how much bigger this is than what you have to deal with?” Mathghamhain snarled back. This was already igniting into a dangerous argument with Loegaire. Again, despite his desire not to have that occur. Why could the man not just understand how important this was? “As for the Priesthood, delays happen. Assuming that it is their way of punishing us is absurd, considering

how many people are impacted. Dismiss that idea from your mind, Loegaire."

There was a brief moment of silence after he spoke in which Loegaire appeared to stare straight out across the landscape before he finally answered, subdued.

"I understand, my Chieftain. Arrange your hunt and let us hope this trade that comes with it does, indeed, help. You are much in need of less to worry about, it would seem. I want to be on hand during it."

Before he could respond to Loegaire's words, his old mentor was already turning on his heel and heading to meet up with local members of the Hunters Guild. It could have gone better, Mathghamhain thought, but Loegaire had answered him on the viability of the idea no matter how much he seemed to disagree with the idea. Yet another reason to keep a close eye on him: it could cause even more trouble than he and Cacht were already worried about from him.

FOUR

CHAPTER 29

It had taken longer than Mathghamhain had intended to set up a trade, forcing them to survive through the colder months best they could, but with promised relief coming. The village he had intended to trade with had not been interested but a village only a bit further south was. That village, Caidreach, had recently secured a small patch of land that linked them now with Cridhe Aonaichte. Mathghamhain was not entirely sure about trading with them as they were unknown to him but they did have interest and so a meeting had been arranged at the shared border. After a small handful of these meetings, terms had finally been agreed upon. Loegaire was still not fond of the whole idea but with everyone else involved being in favour of it, especially after how rough the past few months had been, the reeve had been overruled.

That final negotiating meeting had been two weeks ago, just as the warmer weather had begun to return, and now Mathghamhain watched on horseback. Caidreach's Warriors Guild Chief stood next to him, while a small number of the warriors that the man had brought with him steadfastly watched out for their hunters. The event, dubbed as the Great Hunt, had been underway for a few hours now. It was a sign of co-operation between Cridhe Aonaichte and Caid-reach for mutual benefit. Their new trading partner would gain the bounty of this hunt, as well as any men or women who wished the one-time opportunity to move south. His and Cacht's lands would gain the crops they desperately needed as well as additional farmers.

One of the things that had appealed to Mathgham-hain most about this deal was that they would not only be gaining crops but that the farmers coming to their lands were bringing with them the secret of how they were able to produce such a bountiful yield. They had referred to it as 'irrigation,' and he had been told he would have to be patient if he wanted to see what it meant and see its benefits. If it meant they could depend on the farmlands more and have to hunt less, he was anxious to see how it worked, but he was willing to be patient for it. Even now those new farmers were being escorted to their southernmost village by Nuallan and two other warriors. Caiside was busy further to the north working steadily on de-fences and strengthening the skills of each warrior at his disposal.

For her own protection since a rival village was technically within their lands, Cacht was back at Meadhan to oversee governing while he supervised the Great Hunt. He was fairly certain it was already starting to wind up. He was looking forward to seeing the results but not so much hearing Loegaire's thoughts on it. The old hunter had, as insisted, ac-companied the visiting hunters in order to help

supervise it. At least Donnchad was present as well. Mathghamhain had insisted upon the Educators Guild Reeve's presence today. After all, the man understood the specifics of the trade deal better than he did.

"This has been a wonderful break from the usual pattern, brave Mathghamhain, I would commend you on providing this wonderful afternoon," Caderyn, the visiting Warriors Guild Chief, spoke from next to him. "I know this was meant to be a one-time trade agreement but I myself see no reason why we, with the success this one has wrought so far, cannot become an annual event. A symbol of ongoing co-operation between our lands."

It was no surprise, Mathghamhain thought, that this man had become the Warriors Guild Chief. Caderyn was incredibly broad of shoulder and his armour did little to mask how muscular he was. It was obvious, Mathghamhain thought, as to why they might have been short on animals to hunt. Indeed, even though the hunters were slightly lean, they were all broad of shoulder, and come to think of it so were the farmers that had come. A few generations and children born to such parents would be the pick for any additions to the Warriors Guild in Cridhe Aonaichte, he was certain.

"Indeed, mighty Caderyn. I have no problem taking such a suggestion under advisement. We have spent much of the last few years having to fight to gain ground from which to farm and hunt upon. Having a neighbour we can simply trade with is much preferred," Mathghamhain responded, watching as the visiting hunters could be seen racing towards their general direction, a bear, bigger than any he had ever seen running in front of them.

With the speed the bear was going at, the hunters had obviously not wounded it enough to slow it down but had certainly given it cause to run. Not an ideal way to handle a bear but this was not his hunt. Looking further out, Mathghamhain saw his own people bringing up the rear. The ones who were meant to supervise and yet stay uninvolved. In particular, the one who broke off and headed directly towards him. Loegaire.

"Look at the size of that beast! If that is not a portent of how fruitful our alliance can be, then I am unsure what else one can ask for," Caderyn said triumphantly clapping his hands together."However, I do believe they could use a hand. To me, warriors! Let us help slay the great beast!"

Within seconds, the chief had drawn his sword and along with his fellow warriors headed out to aid their hunters. Wonderful, Mathghamhain thought. Warriors who were eager to help with hunting. What a difference than with how it had been in Meadhan in the early days, and to a lesser extent even now after years of pairing the two guilds together to help each other out. These southern neighbours certainly had much for him to be envious of at the moment. Still, it was a rather large bear. How had all of his hunters missed it? True, they had picked a less hunted area of the lands for this day but even so, such a creature would not have kept itself confined would it?

"Ah good, they left your side, my Chieftain," Loegaire began, out of breath as he approached him. "Those hunters are a wild lot. They have less care for

the land they are hunting on than we do. We try to leave it as undisturbed as possible. They are all too willing to run roughshod over anything in their way, driving any animals nearby out of hiding and then have others on hand to watch for such flight and lead pursuit to bring them down."

"Hardly the same tactics as we use, is it, wise Loegaire? Our hunters flush the creatures out by luring them to where they want them. They do not try to overtake them in speed but then again this could be an isolated example after all. How often do hunters go about such a thing in these numbers? Working together, it can be a strategy that works for them. When we hunt alone we must use stealth. Still, I doubt you simply rushed to my side to complain that their methods differ from ours. They have until recently been two lands removed from our own, we can scarcely expect them to do things the same way as us," he responded. As Mathghamhain did so, he was watching as the bear was surrounded and took a swing at one of the hunters sending their body flying back to hit the ground hard. "I do hope they realize we are not to be held responsible if they get themselves killed."

"I do understand why this had to be set up, Mathghamhain, but this could be the last such bear in any of our lands. We will have to work with smaller animals from here on out. How can you so idly watch as the creature you are named for is struck down by people who are not even your own?" Loegaire hissed at him.

"Patience, Loegaire. We chose these tracts of land because your hunters had not yet really ventured into them. I could not exactly bring them to land that you have deprived of most beasts. We want them to be successful, to feel they got enough out of this trade to justify it. You do forget that they are only getting what they kill here today, whereas we got many crops already gathered and more men to work the land. We would look to have the superior side of a trade which is meant to be balanced. I will not begrudge them such a magnificent kill. That, and it allows me to observe how they function should we ever need to fight them one day," Mathghamhain responded watching as the fallen hunter was quickly carried off a short distance before those who had carried him returned to trying to fell the surrounded bear.

The bear's greater bulk and size were definitely proving difficult for these visitors even with the warriors' swords helping to wound it. Had he really taken down such a creature by himself several years earlier, even if it was a bit smaller? How could he not believe that his defeat of it was not destined when he saw how much these men struggled today.

"You are hearing me but are you listening, Mathghamhain? These are not lands we have really scouted. We could be doing harm here today, destroying a species in these lands that will lead to us starving in the future by its disappearance," Loegaire said watching him concerned.

"It is possible, but we must see to the survival of our people first and foremost, Loegaire. I have explained this before. We must survive the current situation and this trade costs us the least and gives us the most gain. If necessary, we will arrange in future trade with

another neighbour to have animals brought in to breed. The land knows, Loegaire. It knows this is what is needed for us to survive. Why else would it provide such a magnificent kill for our visiting neighbours? It allows them to kill fewer creatures this day while we still reap the benefits of the trade. It is all well and good. Look to the future Loegaire, my old friend," Mathghamhain said tersely before steering his steed to move closer. He wanted to watch as the great bear was finally felled. The hunters who had come looked like they had taken a few wounds but nothing immediately life-threatening if treated. For their part, Caderyn's warriors had been protected by their armour but their blades had surely drawn a fair amount of blood from the beast.

"That is precisely what I am worried about, Mathghamhain. That the land knows and we will pay the price one day soon," Loegaire mumbled. Sighing to himself, Mathghamhain left the post to check on the visiting hunters and warriors.

"I do believe we have never seen such a kill in our own lands, and if I recall what you were telling me before, you felled a bear singlehandedly in your youth to gain your name. One can easily see on a day such as today why such an act would lead to your being made not just a Chief but a Chieftain over Chiefs. It is a rare thing that a beast is able to lay low one of our hunters with a single blow," Caderyn said to Mathghamhain as he approached while the bear was moved to be hoisted with great effort onto one of the carts they had bought with them to transport their kills home. "Look, it fills the cart all on its own, both in size and weight! I do believe that, with the earlier kills, brings us to a full day's hunt already!"

"Indeed, mighty Caderyn, I do believe it does, as your carts are all quite full. The bear I did fell was smaller but they are, indeed, not an easy kill. I do assure you it did take more than that to get to where I am today. It merely provided the opportunity from which I made the transition from being a hunter to warrior. It was still a climb from there. Brave Loegaire over there—who did lead the accompanying group to supervise your hunters—he has long been the Reeve of the Hunters Guild here and did, in fact, train me himself. I would say he is owed your admiration as well since he did clearly train me well," Mathgham-hain smiled looking back over his shoulder to Loegaire not far off. Send some praise his old friend's way and perhaps it would quiet the sting of the day's events that Loegaire seemed so slighted by.

"A mighty hunter he must be, indeed. If we do ne-gotiate this as a yearly event, I will certainly need to try and convince our own Hunters Guild Chief to consider negotiating to have Loegaire teach us his obviously quite effective ways. Also, do not think I did not notice your casual reminder that you refer to your Chiefs as Reeves," Caderyn smirked as Loegaire ap-proached. The warrior moved to quickly clasp hands with Loegaire before the old hunter could protest. "You trained a mighty hunter in your Chieftain. It has been an honour this day to meet you but we must be heading back to our own lands if we are to make it far enough to within our own lands to be considered safe in a reasonable amount of time."

As the Warriors Guild Chief finished speaking, Mathghamhain noticed that he had made a gesture, one the visiting hunters and warriors understood obviously. They immediately, those who still had enough strength of arm he thought, began to start pulling the carts.

"Indeed, mighty Caderyn, let us ride south to our shared border. Loegaire, you can see yourself safely back to Meadhan to let them know of today's success. Take a warrior with you to be safe and the others will accompany me," Mathghamhain said reaching down to clasp Loegaire's hand tightly. His voice whispering for his reeve's ear alone. "You did magnificently today, my old friend. You shall be well-rewarded for your aid in this trade, no matter how much you may continue to look upon it with disdain in your eyes."

As soon as Mathghamhain saw that the carts were moving, he gestured to the warriors who were accompanying him and Donnchad to be prepared to head out. The Educators Guild Reeve had stayed entirely silent throughout everything, although when he had questioned the man about it, Donnchad had indicated he simply was watching it all as a learning exercise since he had never been out on a hunt before. They would hang back behind the carts not much behind where Caderyn walked with two warriors. The other warriors that the southern Warriors Guild Chief had brought with him were at the head of the procession to scout in advance for any trouble ahead. Loegaire was getting increasingly bothered by events, Mathghamhain thought as they moved. With the success of this trade though, things would begin to look up he was certain. Loegaire would come around, he always did. He had to.

It was a silent procession. Once the border was within sight, Mathghamhain clasped hands with Caderyn once again and wished him good speed in his return journey. At that point, he reached down and assisted Donnchad in climbing up onto the back of the horse with him. The Educator Reeve had already walked plenty. Caderyn and his men seemed a good sort and having a trading partner, or rather at least one neighbour they did not need to fight, might be handy. It was unfortunate it was too early on in their being even partial allies for him to even consider asking them to aid his lands when the gathering enemy to the north finally decided to renew its push. It would have helped things but would also this early on take a heavy toll on how to negotiate such help. No, he had to focus on getting his own people strengthened and prepared.

CHAPTER 30

"You did say, my courageous wife, that Loegaire and an extremely large delegation that has gathered from across all guilds, except the Warriors, are outside Meadhan's walls? Could this be it? Loegaire, friend, mentor, and reeve has chosen to air his concerns openly instead of in my private ear?" Mathghamhain said not at all pleased. Only slightly longer than a week after the Great Hunt and this news was the first thing to greet him upon being delayed returning from their mid-day repast, due to stopping to consult with Donnchad. How had Loegaire organized such a group so quickly?

"Indeed. It could be that or simply that he was chosen since he is the oldest remaining Guild Reeve from before the expansion. That they see him, due to his long-time closeness to you, as the natural person to be chosen to lead a delegation to speak to us," Cacht spoke not nearly as bothered as he was but concerned nonetheless.

"Well then, let us see what he has to say," Mathghamhain added quietly, turning to head back to the doorway, stepping through it enough to look at the warrior who served as a guard to the room this week. "Seisyll, we are ready to receive the delegation now. Please send them in. Then send word to your Reeve, Caiside, that I may have need of him and other warriors shortly."

Re-entering the room, he headed for his seat. If Loegaire had a grievance to air as suspected and had brought others with him, there could be trouble that would require more than reassuring them all by word.

"Brave and wise Mathghamhain, courageous and wise Cacht, you who are Chieftains over all of Cridhe Aonaichte, there are grievous concerns that must be heard that affect all of our people. Will you hear us out?" Loegaire asked once everyone had entered the room.

If there was one thing that Mathghamhain disliked about being in charge, it was that people he had known for years suddenly talked more formally at meetings like this. Even after all this time as chieftain, it still bothered him, especially from a man who had essentially raised him. As for the delegation Loegaire was leading, there were nearly as many present as had once occupied the entire village of Meadhan, and he only recognized a small handful of them. They were not simply from across multiple guilds but multiple villages, as well. That Loegaire could bring a vast assortment of people together with how far the borders of Cridhe Aonaichte stretched was worrisome. He and Cacht should have been the only ones able to bring that about.

"You will be heard, brave and wise Loegaire. What is the concern of this delegation?" he responded looking best he could to catch each individual one of them in the eye. That was important when anyone came to see them but with such a large group it was somewhat difficult, but still necessary if he was to contain this. Cacht, based on the look she had on her face had also noted the variety in the delegation.

"As you, no doubt, are aware after so many years my Chieftains, this is long past the time of year in which the Priest Drust does visit our villages and yet he has not even reached Crioch, the village he would visit earliest in his route. There is concern this is because of the unnecessary battle to the north, that saw the enemy butchered and put on display. That was followed by us having to use the crops to survive the winter that we normally put aside for the Priesthood, and then as soon as the weather was warm again, inviting neighbours to the south to hunt on our lands, and possibly eradicate the last of the bears in our lands. It is our fear that all of these actions have been noticed

by the Priesthood and that such actions are against the wishes of the land and so now we are no longer to be blessed," Loegaire said watching them both carefully.

Ah, Mathghamhain thought, so that was it. This was about the Priesthood, a situation he had let continuously lapse after he was unable to get Fedelmid's attention. Was she truly against his actions as of late and punishing all of Cridhe Aonaichte for them? He had argued in the past with Loegaire that that was not how the Priesthood felt about the situation. He had felt good in those previous rebuttals, considering what the priestess had stated about his actions in the past being welcomed and him being an agent of change that the land was utilizing. Even the old priest, Drust, before he had died, had blessed the idea. Now, of course, as if the situation with Loegaire could not be made worse, the air had chilled.

"He is questioning your rule of the land. Your ability to lead and he has clearly been gathering a case against you, all while professing to be loyal and working by your side. Can you not see, Mathghamhain? Loegaire is no friend to us. He seeks to overthrow you, to perhaps even take Cacht for himself by force? He has ceased biding his time, now that the Priesthood is long overdue in making their visit, and with what he sees as sufficient evidence against you, he is able to rally more people to his side. Soon more will take up his cause. You do face mutiny from your closest friend. Remember, he was initially tied with you in votes for the role of Chieftain," the spirit said in Mathghamhain's ear in a calm yet deeply concerned tone. Not one he could recall hearing from it before.

That alone added weight to the words of the spirit no matter how much he wanted to ignore them.

"You would suggest the choices of your Chieftains are at fault, Loegaire…our people…?" Cacht spoke sharply as she looked at the Reeve and then the people he had brought with him.

"As my wife and fellow Chieftain is saying, perhaps you are too quick to believe that it is our decisions which are at fault but it is possible that you have not considered all possibilities. Let me tell you all a tale which we did not believe was our place to tell but the Priesthood's," Mathghamhain said following Cacht's lead as he rose from his seat as calmly as he could. Drawing his sword slowly to reduce how much he alarmed them all, he needed the spirit to be quiet right now more so than ever. Walking over towards Cacht, he turned it in his hand so the hilt was facing her. "As a gesture that we are listening to your concern, note that I am coming to walk away from my seat and unarmed, not as your Chieftain but as one of you, another villager."

Once Cacht had taken the sword from Mathghamhain, he turned slowly back to the crowd. "I am a man, born and raised in this village. Once a hunter like Loegaire, the reeve you look to in leading this delegation to be your voice in airing your concerns. I am a man who then became a warrior and did work his way through the ranks, that brought guilds together in unity that we might all be stronger. I am a man who has protected these lands. When times were recently tough, we did negotiate a trade to provide food and more farmers to these lands that we might

survive. There is a gathering force of warriors to the north that we do whatever we can to keep in check lest they move into our lands and overrun us all, harming these lands. Harming all of you. That is who I am and I tell you that you are coming here today with a concern that you believe we be responsible for, instead of simply asking if we might know why the Priesthood has not yet come to visit."

Having been walking as he spoke, Mathghamhain paused directly in front of Loegaire and fixed him with a cold hard stare before working his way through the delegation looking them all in the eye up close now. Mostly men but with a vast array of ages. Some were clearly farmers, a few looked to be metal workers, there were a handful of women, and at least two members of the Educators Guild that he did not recognize. They were likely from more remote villages, as were the handful of hunters he did not recognize. It hurt to see such a gathering, full of doubt, gathered against him but even more so because it was Loegaire who led it.

"Perhaps then, brave and wise Mathghamhain, our Chieftain, you and wise Cacht can explain what it is you think we do not need to know with regards to the Priesthood not visiting that absolves you of the blame for this," Loegaire said his voice taking on an edge in its tone, not one Mathghamhain could ever recall hearing from him in all the years he had known him. To hear it from his mentor stung.

"You do forget yourself, Loegaire. You would do well to remember who you are addressing here," Cacht said joining in the conversation. Looking back at his wife, Mathghamhain saw her tensed, her eyes filled with anger, a look that he recalled last seeing before she killed Dubhthach. "Remember that to place blame and lead an uprising against us is an act of betrayal so great that history has decreed another name for it as those members of the Educators Guild who be here present do know. Treason."

At his wife's words, Mathghamhain noticed how her choice in them had caused murmuring amongst several of those in the delegation and that they were slowly working their way to the back of the crowd and closer to the door. He was pleased by that. It meant not everyone present was completely on board with defying him and Cacht. It was as if they had not previously considered how their actions might be perceived and were now worried. He understood how that could be, he only wished everyone gathered had done so.

"Indeed. Treason. Now that is a heavy word to bandy about when what we really have here is a display of a lack of knowledge," Mathghamhain began wanting to try and calm the situation still if possible. It was possible he could still get through to Loegaire at least. If he could do that, perhaps more of the delegation would re-think their position as well. "I do hope that, when you hear what I have to say about the Priesthood, you do all think long and hard about whether you still wish to assign blame here. I did visit, after much work to locate it, the temple of the Priesthood…"

At his words, Mathghamhain noticed a stark increase in murmuring in the crowd. No one ever went to the Priesthood, they always came to them.

"I toured its halls, I marvelled at its work and saw for myself the loneliness they do reside in. They make a great sacrifice to their calling, to the Priesthood, and they give up everything. Then once a year they but ask for a tribute so that they might not die in seclusion. They are cut off from any family, any friends, and we do oblige them for they do speak for the lands on which we live, from which we draw food. It was on this trip that I did learn a hard truth. The Priest Drust who has long visited our villages had, in the past year, succumbed to that greatest of fates and had left this world. His spirit now residing in the afterlife," he added as he moved away from them back to his seat but not reclaiming his blade from Cacht. While he had stated it was a gesture, it also kept it out of his hand where he might use it in anger and also by being drawn, keeping the spirit from whispering to him. He did not need it to fuel his concerns further.

"The priest is dead, and you did locate their temple, a place no one has ever found. How do we know you did not kill the priest yourself in an attempt to enforce your rule?" Loegaire shouted angrier than before, causing the ache in Mathghamhain's heart to grow. "How exactly did you locate the temple at all? Do not speak to us of treason, wise Chieftains! If you have endangered us all then it is you who have committed treason against your people!"

"Loegaire, despite your years of service, you do not prove wise in such an angry accusation..." Cacht snapped back, moving to leave her seat. It was clear from the reactions of others present that seeing her angry was not a thing that sat well with any of them. This situation was growing difficult and Mathgham-hain knew, as much as he wished otherwise, he had been right to send for Caiside. He might be needed to stop him from killing Loegaire right now on the spot with his bare hands.

"At ease my fellow Chieftain. Loegaire, like every-one here today, is merely full of questions and seeks to understand. Let us be clear, Loegaire, everyone here, I did not know the priest had passed from this plane until his successor did show me the marker for his grave," he began, again wanting to try and calm the situation but every time Loegaire spoke it was making it more difficult not to lash out in anger at his old friend. Given the way the crowd was reacting, in general, suggested to Mathghamhain that they had hoped Loegaire's presence would make things go more smoothly, not make it worse. Mathghamhain knew how they felt. The old hunter's presence should have been a welcome one for him, not the dread and concern it had become as of late.

"It is not a site I can find again without much diffi-culty," he added hoping it would stop any questions about such a thing. He needed this to be over. "It was in searching for the well-hidden temple of the Priest-hood in these lands that I did only find it when his successor appeared as if from the air itself and did bring me inside to discuss the concerns that had brought me there."

A few members of the delegation could be heard gasping audibly at his words about people appearing out of thin air. He understood that: They were all

raised to know that members of the Priesthood had access to certain abilities due to their connection to the land. To learn precisely how different they were from everyone else, it would be harder to try and accept.

"Before any of you ask, I had sought the Priesthood out for help in finding a way to protect all of you. Their temple is hidden within the confines of the land itself and is not visible. Only the Priesthood, it seems, with their connection to the land, can open its doors," Mathghamhain continued. This was proving harder to explain then he had hoped it would be. "The priest's death was unexpected, I would suggest, as his successor is still young and has been in her role a short time within the borders of Cridhe Aonaichte. No doubt this is why she has not yet visited rather than because, as you all seem to feel, we have in our decision to protect and serve the well-being of all of you offended the land itself and the Priesthood."

Mathghamhain let those words hang in the air for a moment, letting them talk amongst themselves. It was not because he had wanted to pause there though. Rather it was because he was being signalled from the doorway by Seisyll, that Caiside and others had arrived.

"She? Our new priest is a woman then?" Loegaire responded, bringing him back to the discussion at hand. The reeve's eyes were narrowed and the earlier anger had slipped from his voice. Perhaps this could, indeed, be resolved peacefully. "Your story does grow with how incredulous it sounds, my Chieftain and old friend."

"You would suggest, Loegaire, that a woman

cannot be of the Priesthood when you know as well as anyone that young women do get called to it on occasion?" Cacht interjected angrily, having fully risen from her seat now. Mathghamhain squeezed his eyes shut wishing none of this was actually happening. When he opened them again it was in time to see she had put the tip of his sword to Loegaire's throat. He needed to quickly take back control of the situation.

"Do you believe that a woman cannot be as connected to the land as much as any man?" Cacht continued, still seething with anger. "Do we not nurture the future, give life to new members of the villages, create as much as the land itself does? Is this what you would suggest Loegaire? Choose your words carefully. Unlike my brave and wise husband, I did not spend much of my life calling you a friend and mentor, looking to you for guidance and wisdom."

"I..." Loegaire began before Mathghamhain stepped forward to intervene.

"Loegaire merely voices his surprise at the news in general, not that a woman cannot be a member of the Priesthood," Mathghamhain said as calmly as he could manage right now, moving as he did so to take his sword from his wife's hand before she killed Loegaire in a fit of anger. Mathghamhain was grateful when she let it slip into his hand without any further prompting. "He knows well that to question a woman's capability is folly, but then again he does seem to be full of such acts of folly this day so perhaps it would not be all that surprising. Cacht, if you would have a word with those waiting outside to come in, I will finish bringing this gathered delegation up to speed on events sur-

rounding the Priesthood."

The murmurs started up again at his words. As much as he wanted to keep this situation under control, at this point it did mean having to take actions he wished could have been avoided. Loegaire had insisted on pushing and making things worse. What was about to happen needed to be done before things spiralled further, no matter how much it hurt him to go through with it. Cacht, for her part, looked at him in slight puzzlement for a moment before turning to go.

"Yes, the new representative from the Priesthood is, in fact, a woman. A priestess as they are called." Mathghamhain continued. "Her name is Fedelmid and she had much to say about the choices made under our leadership. That we are agents of change and that the land is acting through us. The late priest Drust had said much the same in the past, nothing has changed there. Therefore, I do assure you all that it is merely a matter of unfamiliarity with travelling these lands that has delayed the Priesthood's yearly visit."

"The Hunters Guild of each village knows these lands well and there are no temples, but if they are hidden by the will of the land itself then, indeed, we would never find them," Loegaire said quietly, rubbing his throat. "This is information—that a new member of the Priesthood would be doing the visits and, therefore, be delayed, possibly due to unfamiliarity—that could have saved trouble and concern."

"It was not our place to say but I have now told you all because it is important you know how unfounded your concerns are," Mathghamhain responded, knowing he had to do what came next. His heart ached at that knowledge but Loegaire had left him no choice. "Far easier was it not, to believe that your Chieftains were at fault and to blame. To accuse us of such, to question our leadership? For all of you to accuse us of not looking out for our people's best interests, that you have met in secret in order to come this day with your accusations? How can you think that after this we would ever be able to look any of you in the eye again without seeing a lack of trust? Of loyalty? Of efforts to bring us down, thereby leaving the lands in turmoil and without a unified leadership? It was far easier, was it not, to come this day with treason on your minds."

"I will mourn and I will miss you," he continued, his voice as calm as it had ever been as he clasped his free hand on Loegaire's shoulder. "But you are a traitor to these lands, Loegaire. Everyone gathered here will be held accountable for this, although not all of you will necessarily face trial. It shall depend on each person's complicity."

Pulling his hand away, Mathghamhain dejectedly returned to his seat, sinking into it. The last thing he had seen before turning had been the sight of Loegaire's eyes growing wide and looking back to the doorway. That view was fairly obstructed, Mathghamhain thought. Everyone in the delegation, save for those who had left earlier, were murmuring loudly and starting to scramble. By his estimation, nearly a third of the original group had left after re-considering the situation. The weight of his last words to Loegaire hung heavily on his mind even more as a contingent of fully armoured warriors filed into the room. Cacht was holding the door open for them, with Caiside and Nuallan striding in behind the warriors. Mathghamhain had not expected so many warriors to be so close by when he had sent for them, let alone both his reeve and loyal Nuallan.

Nuallan stopped partway in and stayed by the door so that Cacht could head back to her seat accompanied by Caiside. Once she had reached her seat, the Warriors Guild Reeve dropped to one knee and looked up at them both. There were enough warriors to fully surround the delegation and prevent any from leaving.

"Mathghamhain, you cannot be serious! Have you lost your mind old friend?" Loegaire shouted over the noise towards him and looking quite alarmed as were the others. He ignored it, focussing his attention on Caiside. He needed to.

"We thank you, Caiside, for your prompt response and arrival. We did not expect you to bring so many warriors with you when we did suspect we might need to contain a crowd if things boiled out of control here today. Instead, it is good and wise that you did so," Mathghamhain said looking from Caiside to his wife and then back again to Caiside, watching as the Warriors Guild Reeve remained on bent knee.

"We feared perhaps that you were under attack and so we did gather all we could do so quickly and come here at great speed. Courageous and wise Cacht did say before we entered that there be treason afoot?" Caiside's words came in response but there was a growing anger in his voice.

"Indeed. We have been accused unjustly of current

circumstances in these lands being the fault of our leadership and that we are wholly to blame," Mathghamhain began keeping one eye on the delegation and another on Caiside best he could while trying to keep his voice from cracking. "That we do lie to the populace and did even seek to suggest we can somehow control the movements of the Priesthood. To that end, at one point we were even accused of killing a member of it. This delegation here did choose the Hunters Guild Reeve, Loegaire, here as their speaker and it is he who even went so far as to question a woman's ability to be a member of the Priesthood. We would ask that these men and women gathered here today be held prisoner until the morning. Upon which, if they are found to be fully complicit, they will stand trial for the crime of treason and be judged accordingly for all those who come to bear witness to see."

"Loegaire is lucky that I am capable of restraint! If I were the type of leader he has accused us of being, he surely would have already tasted the edge of a blade at my hand," Cacht spat angrily.

Even though Cacht was the one who might try to convince him to find a different solution to this situation, it had spun in a direction Mathghamhain could not avoid. Loegaire had been slipping comments in here and there the past few months putting an increased strain on their long friendship. To ignore that he was not a friend any longer was never more difficult than this day. Mathghamhain had meant what he had said to him. He would mourn and miss Loegaire but, in truth, ignoring his act of treason this day would be difficult and threatened to overwhelm the good memories of their friendship. It was already coming dangerously close to doing so.

"Treason indeed!" Caiside roared rising to his feet and turning sharp angry eyes on Loegaire and the others gathered, before looking back to Loegaire. The reeve was quickly moving close enough to his fellow guild reeve to be nose-to-nose with Loegaire.

"To think I did believe all these years you to be a man of honour, worthy of friendship and counsel. You are naught but a snake in the grass that did bide its time to choose when to strike. This is not how a friend or one truly concerned does come to our Chieftain with a personal concern. This was an attempt at a coup," the Warrior Reeve added before turning to face Mathghamhain and Cacht again. "By your leave, my honoured Chieftains, these traitors will be held in sequester while it is determined who among them is fully at fault, and isolated from all others until the trial tomorrow."

"By your honoured leave, brave Caiside. We thank you for your swift response," Cacht said slightly calmer now.

"Take care, Caiside. Be sure that, as Loegaire is still, in fact, Reeve of the Hunters Guild, that he is kept not only isolated but well-guarded. We will need to address his Guild before they can get word of this treasonous act and be coerced by him as their Reeve to turn traitor as well," Mathghamhain said giving one last look to the delegation but not at Loegaire himself, as they were marched from the room with Caiside leading them. Finally, of the warriors who had arrived, only Nuallan remained in the room to bring up the rear again.

"I will see to it that his second-in-command, Corraidhin, is sent for immediately to meet with yourselves as soon as we have these traitors contained. My lieges," Nuallan said bowing sharply before turning to follow the rest of his Guild out. The concern in his voice was impossible to miss.

"We thank you, courageous and loyal Nuallan. You who are our friend and most faithful servant," Cacht stated before the warrior could leave and then turning to Mathghamhain. "That could have gone significantly better. However, it is in a sense a relief to know precisely where Loegaire stands in his thoughts on your actions. It is still discomforting that so many were convinced of his views and the potential loss of life to Cridhe Aonaichte after the recent negotiations is hard to bear. You are right in your words I did overhear from the doorway while directing our warriors. We can scarcely afford to let them go with but a warning as we would never be able to trust them again after this day. We will work hard to determine precisely how closely adhered everybody was to Loegaire's thinking and perhaps some shall yet live. As for the rest, traitors are what they have become whether they realized such would be the case or not, and so they will be dealt with as all traitors must be."

Mathghamhain had been about to respond when he noted she had closed her eyes. They were closed for such a long moment that he suspected she had fallen asleep sitting up. With that in mind, he was about to dismiss Nuallan when his wife opened her eyes and looked at him. She looked weary and he was as well.

"I do think that is all the official business we can deal with today, at least not without a substantial break, one that involves the finest brew we have available to us to dull the pain of this day's events and the decisions we were forced into making," she stated.

"Agreed. Nuallan, it is a shame we do not get to talk much these past years but we thank you for your continued service and we wish you safe travel as you rejoin the rest of your guild. When things have settled down, we will have to make time to sit down, relax, and talk as friends as in the past," Mathghamhain spoke, sheathing his sword before giving the man's hand a firm shake. As soon as he had done so, Nuallan strode quickly from the room to catch up with the other warriors. As the door closed, Mathghamhain looked back to his wife before he continued speaking, sighing heavily as he did so. "Cacht, let us see what we can find to drink."

Encircling her hand in his own, he moved to depart the room. Seisyll would ensure no one entered it until they returned and commanded him to allow it. Mathghamhain was positive this drink with Cacht would be the last break he got for the next while, until long after the ramifications of the meeting with the delegation were done with. The idea that Loegaire, out of everyone he had ever known had so completely turned against him left an ache inside of him that he was not convinced would ever leave.

CHAPTER 31
Caiside

It was as bleak a day as Caiside could expect considering the event taking place. Its location had been changed to west of the more centrally located village of Thabhairt, and the trial delayed several days so that anyone from across Cridhe Aonaichte could attend it should they wish. It had also allowed time for word to spread of a trial, the size of which had never before been seen. The additional time had granted his Chieftains, Mathghamhain and Cacht, more opportunity to be sure exactly how many of the prisoners were, indeed, guilty, and who amongst them had been mostly coerced into being part of the delegation with no real prior knowledge of what was to come.

The rain was holding off, Caiside thought, but the dark clouds that had rolled in with the addition of the fog that lingered from the morning still added to a rather dismal atmosphere. He had already heard rumblings amongst those gathered that it was a portent regarding whether the lands favoured this trial. The Educators Guild Reeve, Donnchad, had gone to great lengths to prove it was always going to be as such outside, whether it be this day or the next: that the clouds had been slowly working their way towards them for a few days now. That Donnchad had done so without being asked made Caiside wonder if, perhaps with how quickly Loegaire had fallen out of favour, the man was doing his best to show he was loyal. If such was the case, then fear was playing a bigger part in their everyday lives than he was comfortable with. No, Caiside thought, it was nervousness. That was what truly gripped everyone assembled.

Rightfully so that they were nervous. Glancing around, he recalled what Cynwrig had taught him many years ago—that nervous people were people on alert. With the minor slash to the overall population this day would certainly bring, everyone needed to be on alert and be prepared to face harder times.

Half of his Warriors Guild was currently stationed on either side of the benches that had been set up for anyone who came to watch. Long logs had also been brought from the nearby woods for additional seating. Where he was standing facing that audience, there were two sides. To his right was where the Chieftains had been set up in proper chairs, and to his left was where the other half of his Warriors Guild surrounded those who still remained accused.

Those who had been found to have been coerced were not amongst them but remained prisoners in-definitely until a better solution was found. His second-in-command, faithful Nuallan was stationed at the back behind the audience, in order to help command the warriors if necessary.

As for himself, he had balked when Mathghamhain and Donnchad had insisted on him leading this trial. It was not so much because of the weight of extra re-sponsibility it brought but because they had insisted on him wearing highly polished armour and a cloak.

When he had first started out as a warrior, Caiside had never considered a leadership role. As warriors had joined over the years since then, he had been all too happy to let them take on such roles. That had changed in the past several years where, despite his age, he had suddenly been thrust into being a second-in-command, and then more recently that of Warriors Guild Reeve. Now, he was being asked to take on even more responsibility by conducting today's trial. If he did not know it to be impossible, he would suspect Mathghamhain of somehow manipulating events to put him in such roles. As if he were to be the chieftains' successor one day. That was not only impossible but highly unlikely. He was significantly older than they were and the chieftains still had plenty of time to have children: Any child of theirs would surely be the lead candidate when it came time eventually for a new chieftain.

Looking over at where the accused were held, he sighed, wishing the trial would start. The Metal Workers Guild, based out of Nabaidh, had brought several chains to form a containment area which, with the addition of the warriors around them, kept the accused secured in one place, so that was one less concern. Still, Caiside already did not want to be standing here doing this but everything being set up was taking far too long for his liking. Seeing a signal from Nuallan that everything was set, he swallowed hard and cleared his throat. Finally.

"We are gathered here today all of you to see to the trial and judgement of individuals who do stand accused of one of the most heinous actions there can be amongst our people," Caiside began. "I have been designated by our Chieftains to conduct this trial in

their stead so that they may focus on their own role within it. Those who we hold here on trial did seek to accuse our beloved Chieftains of being the root of current problems we face. From a shortage of food to the struggle to defend our lands. In the next while, we will let you hear for yourselves why their accusations were made in error and how it has led to this trial today."

Caiside spotted Mathghamhain nodding at him out of the corner of his eye as a murmur went through the crowd. Sure, everyone there had already known this was the accusation that had brought about such a trial. Several craned their necks to try and see who all they recognized in the accused, as others had done before the trial began, and others shouted insults of questionable nature at them. He sincerely wished it was Donnchad up here right now instead of him. Occasions that required such formality and careful wording should have been the Educators Guild Reeve's responsibility. Donnchad had sided with the Chieftains though in insisting that he run things instead. When this was all over, that man and he were going to have to have a long talk about why.

"Our Chieftain, brave and wise Mathghamhain, if you would, please begin by telling those gathered here today what exactly did occur on the day in question," Caiside said resuming the trial and turning to regard his chieftains before stepping to one side. Mathghamhain had already stood, and begun walking somewhat to properly address everyone and answer the question.

"Our people. As your duly chosen leaders, we did admit a delegation that had been gathered to express a concern that needed our help and our thoughts. We have done so often in the past and, indeed, often such visits make up most of our day," Mathghamhain began, pacing as he spoke, continuing on to explain exactly what Loegaire, speaking on behalf of the delegation, had accused himself and Cacht of. There were moments where it was obvious to Caiside that Loegaire's actions hurt deeply. Indeed, it was never more obvious than any time the Chieftain said Loegaire's name. The pain and sadness in his voice all too clear. It hurt Caiside to hear that pain, to know that someone so experienced and so close to Mathghamhain could cause it.

"We thank you, Chieftain Mathghamhain, you can return to your seat now," Caiside uttered moving back to the centre before looking to the crowd again. "We all know our Chieftain's history of service. That the accused would outright accuse him of causing current troubles rather than asking him if he knew the cause, yet expecting him not to react swiftly in anger with the background he has is pure folly on their part and the accused's state of mind must be called into question there. Furthermore, as you will hear next, they added to their words when they called into question openly the capability of our Chieftain, the wise and courageous Cacht. My Chieftain, if you would please speak to what happened."

"Our people. My husband, hearing what he was accused of, did know holding himself in check would prove difficult and so before he did approach them to respond to their baseless accusations did draw his sword and hand it to me to hold," Cacht began before

     DARYL J BALL

going into detail about how Loegaire had insulted her, her final words coming across more angrily than the rest had. The result was a chorus of shouts from those in attendance. Shouts that had been long expected. Women served as the backbone of their society and to doubt their capabilities was an extreme folly.

Pandemonium was on the brink of breaking out, with shouts at the accused by those in attendance. His warriors, with Nuallan assisting on co-ordinating them, moved swiftly to contain the situation with as little force used as necessary. It took a lot longer than Caiside would have liked.

"While everybody settles back down, we would ask that our people do look to the field over to our left where fresh food and drink awaits. Let us take a brief recess from this trial so that frayed nerves can better be settled," Mathghamhain said looking to him for confirmation. Caiside stared back for a moment before nodding in response. He had been confused initially by his chieftain needing him to confirm it but had realized it fell under his responsibilities today. Just one more thing.

"Indeed, let us adjourn and we warriors will take turns so that the accused are not left unsupervised," Caiside added to Mathghamhain's words. "This is a thank-you to all of you for taking time away from your busy days to bear witness to this trial and its judgement."

It was a good while later that Caiside was able to call the trial back to order. He stood where he had before, hands templed in front of him to look out at the audience. He was waiting until he had everyone's focus on him before he spoke. The dark clouds remained but that was to be expected, although the fog which should have dissipated this late in the day still lingered, although no longer as thick.

"We would ask now that our second-in-command, wise and courageous Nuallan, come forward to relay the events as we warriors heard them that led to our presence in containing the accused on the day in question," Caiside said finally. He did not move from his spot until Nuallan had made his way to the front and clasped hands with him.

"I do thank you, my courageous and wise Reeve. Like many of you, I did grow up and was raised in a different village than our Chieftains are from," Nuallan spoke. "On the day in question, a messenger did quickly reach my Reeve's side at the training grounds outside Meadhan. Several of us were training there and I had been about to head out to check on other warriors patrolling our eastern border. The messenger did state that our Chieftain Mathghamhain had requested a few warriors to come quickly as they might be needed. Now, while brave Caiside did not know why such a request was made, he did know that an extremely large delegation had been heading to speak with the Chieftains. The number involved and the fact that there was enough concern to send for a few warriors did quickly get his attention. As he did not know the full scope of what was underway, he gathered all available warriors and did send me to gather all those patrolling nearby to make haste as well. I did immediately set out on fleet foot as concerns mounted in my mind. I then did race there with the warriors I had gathered and we did bring up the rear to the warriors Caiside had brought."

As Nuallan was speaking, those who were held accused could be seen growing agitated. With a glance to the warriors to Caiside's left, they were warned to settle down. Turning his attention back to the trial itself, Caiside waited for Nuallan to finish speaking while he watched the audience. He was not looking forward to what might occur with the next speaker.

"We were all gathering outside the room when our Chieftain Cacht did come to the doorway to usher us in, giving us a quick word about what was unfolding inside. That she and her fellow Chieftain were accused of many things and even mentioned as she did this day here the accusations that had been specifically directed her way," Nuallan continued. At no time, Caiside noticed, did the man's eyes ever leave the audience to look at the accused, pausing long enough to take a breath. "I do tell you all who are gathered here today that I have seen both our Chieftains wield blades and Cacht is as fierce as any other warrior I have served alongside."

"Thank you for your testimony, Nuallan," Caiside said coming over to clasp his second-in-command's hand once more as the man returned to the back of the audience to manage the warriors from there. "Now you have already heard from our Chieftains and gotten the perspective of what we in the Warriors Guild knew but now we will ask the accused to speak."

Caiside turned slowly to the accused who had now

been held prisoner for several days. A consequence he doubted any of them had expected at the time when they had approached Mathghamhain and Cacht with their concerns and accusations. He still could not really wrap his mind around what had transpired either. "Which of you will speak first as we will be fair and offer a few of you a chance to speak as there are many of you who are here and do stand accused."

"As the Hunters Guild Reeve, I will speak first as I did on the day in question, brave Caiside," Loegaire said moving to the edge of the contained group where a warrior helped him bypass the chain and proceeded to hold him at sword point. Glaring at him, Caiside stepped away while Loegaire spoke, making it clear to anyone watching closely how he felt about this. He would not be clasping hands with the man. The lack of respect to a fellow reeve shown by his actions caused everyone to go unnaturally quiet.

"We are not traitors. We were but a delegation of concerned residents of Cridhe Aonaichte and had observed the events around us which did point to our Chieftain Mathghamhain being at fault when the Priesthood had not shown despite it being more than a few months now into when they are scheduled to start arriving at our villages. It was with the concerns of all of you in mind that we did approach the Chieftains on the day in question and made plain these concerns. It was only after we had done so that he," Loegaire said, pointing to Mathghamhain, "did feel it necessary to tell us that part of the reason might, in fact, be that the priest, Drust, who we are all familiar with had died. That a new one had taken his place who might not yet

     DARYL J BALL

be familiar with routes. He did claim that he had not informed any of us of this change as it was not his place to do so, as he put it, and had left it for the Priesthood to explain."

Caiside was not sure how others were feeling, given how quiet everyone was, but he refused to look at the man speaking save to see why he had paused. The moment he had looked, Loegaire had, of course, resumed.

"What you did not hear in Chieftain Cacht's words earlier is what led to my words that she says questioned her capability as a woman," Loegaire continued as the crowd's silence came to an end. Hearing Loegaire admit that what he had said about Cacht was true had stirred everyone up again. Caiside knew he was more than ready to hit the old hunter himself but knew better than to give in to that urge. For now. "I do freely admit they were said in the heat of the moment following on the heels of the revelation that our new priest was a woman. An aspect I had not before considered a likely scenario, that of a woman putting aside providing for a family, to live in seclusion as a member of the Priesthood. This was despite knowing full well they have been called at a young age to learn alongside the Priesthood."

At Loegaire's words about the Priesthood, more shouts from the crowd broke out with rocks being successfully hurled in his direction. When had they armed themselves, Caiside thought, as the warriors moved quickly to shield Loegaire. Those in the crowd who were throwing them were pulled from the crowd and admonished before being escorted back to their seats while order was restored.

A woman's voice came from a slight distance back. "I had been out wandering and wondering why there were fewer people than I had been led to expect present to visit. Then I did hear shouts from afar and now more shouts have led me to investigate. Now here I do find the reason, for the missing people as you have all gathered away from your villages…out here in the midst of the field."

Before Caiside could see who it was, he already knew.

CHAPTER 32

The identity of the newcomer had been made all too obvious when Nuallan had quickly dropped to one knee, bowing his head. Mathghamhain and everyone else had also looked and quickly figured out who she was as they all immediately dropped their heads low, rising to their feet, hands folded in front of them. As Nuallan, his chieftains, and Donnchad had done though, Caiside went the extra step of dropping to one knee instead. He did not have to have ever met her to know who she was. He did not know her name but she was clad in full Priesthood regalia. Her hair loosely braided and blue robes shimmering despite the dark clouds and fog making the landscape seem so dim. It was the contrast compared to her that made her radiate outwards, her movements giving off the impression of gliding along the ground.

Caiside stole a quick glance while keeping his head down to his left. The accused had hung their heads as well. It also caused him to notice that Loegaire had adhered to custom and gone down to one knee. It was a sign of respect those in the roles of leadership gave to the Priesthood. When a representative was present, they deferred to them.

"Now, now, while it is quite kind of you to show such a sign of respect, I am no great leader, simply one who speaks for the lands that we live off of each day. Please be as you were. You seem to be holding a trial of sorts and one that sounds hostile at that," Fedelmid said moving towards the front where Loegaire was. Caiside watched the others best as he could as he slowly rose to his feet. The audience had begun to stir, unsure if they really should follow her words or not. "May I observe while I wait?"

She seemed as humble as a priest would be expected to be under the circumstances, Caiside thought, watching as she tilted her head to regard both Mathghamhain and Cacht.

"Chieftain Mathghamhain, it is so good to see you again. The actions of your rule ripple through the lands with a ferocity that cannot be ignored. You do remain as ever an agent of these lands and one of great change," the priestess continued, smiling at the chieftain warmly before looking to Cacht. "And you would be the woman who but tamed the man. She who serves to provide balance to him and him to you. The courageous voice of women in these lands, Cacht. It is a pleasure to finally meet you. My predecessor, Drust, spoke of you quite highly."

"Priestess Fedelmid, we bid you welcome to observe," Mathghamhain answered while beckoning to Caiside. Wanting to make sure the priestess had a seat, Caiside had been about to speak to one of his warriors but instead gestured to Nuallan what he wanted so he could attend to his chieftain. Hopefully, his request to Nuallan would not take too long to fulfill. If anyone was considered the equal or above of the chieftains, and deserving of a good seat, it was the priestess, or more accurately any member of the Priesthood. While he moved to his chieftains' side to see what they wanted, Mathghamhain had continued speaking. "We do, indeed, have a trial occurring here, one that unfortunately came about due to your delay in visits to our villages."

Already, in the distance a bit, Caiside could see a few of the warriors trying to quickly construct a makeshift chair. Loegaire, on the other hand, had by now moved back to his feet but appeared to be in a state of abject panic.

"Really, there is no need for such a seat. The land itself is more comfortable than one might think but I thank you nonetheless," the priestess, named Fedelmid, based on Mathghamhain's words, said bowing her head slightly at the warriors who were now heading towards the front with the hastily made seat. Caiside smiled when he noted that she had moved to make use of the offered chair, no matter how poorly and quickly it had been made. Mathghamhain still had not told him why he had called him over though. As such, he remained standing beside his chieftain while the seat for the priestess was set next to Cacht. "Please do resume your trial. I am merely here to observe."

"As you were, Loegaire. You were in the middle of defending yourself and your compatriots against the accusations you do face of treason," Caiside said waiting until the warriors were all back in formation and moving to gesture for everyone to be calm.

"I…" Loegaire began before glancing at the priestess. "Wise and honoured Priestess of the lands, I…we believed you were not coming. We suspected that our Chieftain Mathghamhain had done something to offend you and the lands. That you were, in turn, punishing us all. We did not…we did not truly seek to question his leadership but we were concerned that he and the Chieftain Cacht had brought misfortune upon us by offending these lands. From displaying the dead of our enemy, and allowing our neighbours in Caidreach to be afforded free reign on these lands, and then to let them kill what may have been the last great bear of these lands…"

Caiside sighed, shaking his head. Loegaire was rambling, having lost his composure and it was hard to see a once-great man fall apart.

"Loegaire, you are to be speaking to all of us. While the priestess is an honoured guest, she is not the one against whom you are on trial," Caiside said stepping forward away from the chieftains finally. He needed to get this trial focussed again. "My apologies, Priestess Fedelmid, as I heard our Chieftain call you. I hope I am free to address you as such as well. Your presence seems to have caused more of a stir than we did first believe, as it is now affecting testimony, I do suspect it is in part due to how much of the accusations that were levelled against our Chieftains were based on your absence. Yet here you are. If you would not mind, priestess, since you are here, giving your viewpoint so that we can understand the situation from your perspective. If you do wish to, that is."

Even as he spoke, Caiside realized he was as thrown off as Loegaire was. Even when the Priesthood's representative was as much an unknown to people as this newcomer Fedelmid was, still the effect that guild had on people was astounding.

"I would be delighted to share my thoughts on this. I thank you, and yes you may address me as the Priestess Fedelmid. That goes for everyone present as well," Fedelmid said, rising from her seat. The effect was instantaneous as everyone, himself included, quickly bowed their heads again. "It is all right, all of you, do not shield your eyes. I am but a humble servant of the lands we all reside upon and care for."

Loegaire was hastily taken back to the holding area while the priestess moved to the centre area. Caiside looked over at the chieftains and noticed that Mathghamhain was certainly observing her intently. As near as Caiside could tell, everyone else was as well and generally showing Fedelmid greater respect than he could recall them ever showing the Priest Drust.

"As you good people have already heard, I am the new representative of the Priesthood in these lands," Fedelmid began. "As you can possibly also tell, I bear physical traits more commonly found in the north. I assure you that I bid no ill will to these lands or its people. My predecessor, Drust, who you have known for many a year, did pass several months ago, and I

was sent to carry on his great work here. I was already aware of the great changes that had taken place here through your Chieftain Mathghamhain, as he has been chosen by the lands as an agent of change. I had barely settled in our temple when he did come to visit me. A rare event, for it is more often than naught the Priesthood that does the visiting."

She offered the accused a slight smile, Caiside noticed, before she turned her attention back to the audience. She was certainly different from Drust: in addition to being a woman, she was also young, and more easy-going. She radiated hope and brightness. He was not quite sure how else to describe what he felt being in her presence. "We did discuss what he had done by then and what he might do in the future. We talked of his dreams for you, his people, and what he can do to better serve you all. His mind was ever on these lands, these people and what is best for both. You have fears about displaying the dead of your enemy. While gruesome in appearance, does anyone doubt it serves as a message and causes your enemy to be wary of attacking too soon? Does that not grant you all more time to prepare for the battle that is to come? Does it not serve to show that a village of people that only a generation ago was nearly wiped out by others can rise back up and rebuild, to prosper? How about the fact that letting neighbours to the south come here to hunt and kill for so little time that it barely makes a dent..."

At those particular words, Caiside noticed she paused to look directly in Loegaire's direction. She was no longer smiling.

"Would you truly believe that the lands would let such a great beast fall to those not from it unless it was meant to be so? That it served a greater purpose in aiding many in these lands and to the south than it ever could while it lived? Would you question the will of the lands themselves?" Fedelmid continued, her tone growing harsher. It surprised Caiside how vehement she seemed to be about Loegaire questioning the Great Hunt and the Priesthoods' absence as of late. "I also did hear a bit of what was yelled before I arrived."

She had paused again, this time to look at the audience and the chieftains before gliding again over as close to the prisoners as she could and fixing the warrior in front of her with as hard a stare as could possibly exist, Caiside thought. Moving quickly, he prepared himself to intervene if necessary. What had he been thinking about her radiating hope and brightness? Right now, Caiside was afraid of her more than anything. Considering how quickly the warrior nervously moved aside allowing her to approach the prisoners directly, he was certain he was not the only one who was suddenly afraid of this priestess. Caiside knew why he was angry at the prisoners but he could not recall her predecessor, Drust, ever getting angry about anything. Was there more at work here? Was it simply her youthfulness? A predisposition towards anger due to her obvious northern heritage? He had to wonder.

Watching again, Caiside tensed as a resounding sound like a tree branch colliding hard with a boulder to snap in two was heard. She shook her hand lightly afterwards and returned to where she had been speak-

ing from as Loegaire rubbed his cheek gingerly and struggled to stand up again. The impact of the slap she had delivered had been hard enough to upset the reeve's balance. The lingering red mark on Loegaire's face would certainly leave a lasting impression. Caiside made a quick mental note, adding toughness to his assessment of how the priestess differed from her predecessor. He was positive that few could slap Loegaire harder than she had.

"That is for daring to question a woman's ability, especially that of not only your Chieftain but also one who was chosen by the land itself to serve it as a priestess. Now then, as I have addressed the points being debated here today, let us get to why you are all only meeting me now," Fedelmid continued as if she had not nearly broken a man's jaw.

Caiside was still tensed up but was also fascinated. Fedelmid was doing more speaking than the rest of them had but was also using it as a means to cement herself as worthy of her position and introducing herself at the same time. To think, one who looked so slim and unassuming was capable of staggering a renowned hunter such as Loegaire with a single slap to the face. He wondered now what Mathghamhain's initial impression of her had been. A glance in the Chieftain's direction suggested the man was not paying much attention right now. Mathghamhain had that far away look on his face, like when the chieftain was talking to the spirit that the man had sometimes consulted on the field of battle.

"I had no intention of heading out until I was reasonably certain that I did have the temple set to receive what I brought back," Fedelmid was meanwhile saying. "My way of organizing is not necessarily the same as my predecessor, nor should anyone ever expect two people to do things the exact same way in such matters. I was not quite arranged but did not want to tarry too much longer as I knew everyone in the land would be quite anxious. It has already been several months after all. As I am new to all of you, there was also the awareness that each visit to your villages might take longer than might be normal for a member of the Priesthood. I would need to tell you the exact things I tell you now and allow you to know with whom you are dealing. I will say this in closing, I still look forward to doing just that, to taking extra time to meet all of you in your respective villages, so that a long-lasting relationship is forged once more, as it was with my predecessor. It is such a shame we had to first meet under conditions in which so many must be put to death."

The murmur amongst the audience and the accused was unmistakable. Yes, Caiside was certain, everyone there had more or less known that was the outcome but for a member of the Priesthood to state it so openly, let alone be all right with such an action did seem to overrule their natural tendency to stay silent in respect of her position. It was not a fact lost on the priestess either.

"Oh, I see, I see. We were pretending their fates had not yet been decided," Fedelmid continued. "Very well then, let me add that, as evidenced by the way your Chieftain Mathghamhain gained his name, he was appointed by the land itself to lead. To question him in regards to how he serves the land, that to me is to question the lands themselves. As such, why should the lands want to continue to nurture those who would oppose it? A question to consider since a decision has not been openly made regarding the accused's' fate."

Having finished, Caiside saw that she had bowed her head to both Mathghamhain and Cacht before gesturing to him to resume leading the trial. Composing himself as best he could, Caiside hesitatingly headed to where she had been standing while she glided back to her seat.

"Yes…umm thank you, wise and honoured Priestess Fedelmid. Again, it is a great honour to finally meet you," he said before clasping his hands in front of him and bowing his head. "While we did intend to let many of the prisoners speak, it would seem that with the addition of the thoughts brought us by the representative of the lands themselves in the form of the priestess here before us, I would say that, as she suggested, the outcome of this trial can be but one."

Caiside was not overly pleased about the situation, even if he had known this was where it would lead. Fedelmid's presence was certainly throwing everyone off. Taking a deep breath to compose himself, he focussed on what Donnchad had taught him was the proper format for such things. Opening his arms wide, he turned so that they both were gesturing toward the accused. "How do you, our Chieftains, find these accused?"

"As my husband and I are in agreement, I will speak for us both. We find the prisoners guilty of treason.

Against their appointed leaders, against their villages, and against the lands themselves," Cacht said rising to her feet and speaking in a tone that suggested to Caiside that she was struggling to stay calm. "Furthermore, Loegaire should be stripped of his rank immediately and his second-in-command, Corraidhin, be temporarily elevated to the role of Hunters Guild Reeve before we proceed further. That way, the healing process within that guild can begin and the memories of their disgraced Reeve sooner wiped away."

For his part, Caiside thought as Cacht resumed her seat, Mathghamhain had nodded his head at everyone to show he was in agreement. Finally, and thankfully Caiside thought, this trial was ending.

"As only one of greater rank can call for such a decision, and you as our Chieftain have made the case for it, please note that as of this moment, Loegaire, you are now no longer the Hunters Guild Reeve and remain a prisoner," Caiside said narrowing his eyes at the man in question. Then he held his arms up, much as Cynwrig had done in the past to call for actions, in this case for silence, before a ripple of reaction could be heard. Two warriors quickly moved to restrain Loegaire further and clamp a hand over the disgraced former reeve's mouth tightly before he could speak out in anger at the decision. "You who represent the people of Cridhe Aonaichte, what is your decision?"

The overwhelmingly loud shouts of people saying things such as that the accused were guilty, to kill them, and death to traitors were unmistakable. Caiside lowered his eyes while glancing anywhere but at the

crowd. It was too upsetting to hear such things—the call for people who had been their neighbours, their families, and friends, to be put to death.

"Well then, as both the people of Cridhe Aonaichte and its leaders have passed sentence, we do find the prisoners guilty of that most heinous of crimes. Treason against its leadership, its people, and the lands themselves. The sentence for such a crime can only be death. The prisoners are to be taken back into holding and their deaths will come at the cliffs west of Marcairt in four days time following the rising of the sun," Caiside concluded.

Once the warriors had gotten everyone settled back down after the verdict, there were significantly fewer people present in the audience. Some had obviously decided to head back home not wanting to linger there longer than need be. Sentence had been pronounced, the fate of the prisoners decided, but day-to-day life still had to carry on as before and many had left to get back to their homes and their duties to their families and their guilds.

"Well now, Mathghamhain, that was interesting to witness," Fedelmid stated moving towards Cacht and kissing the woman's cheek lightly. For her part, the chieftain did not pull back from it. "Would we had met under more pleasant circumstances Cacht, she who has tamed the bear of Meadhan and with him rules more lands than any before her. I do hope you consider having a child soon, one does need to keep in mind the joy it can bring, not to mention it might serve to further reveal the softer side of your husband. When you were but a Guild Chief, I do understand why such things would have been on hold but now you hold the greatest office in these lands with Mathghamhain, your husband."

Caiside was doing his best not to listen in too much on the conversation while the warriors began to get the prisoners prepared to head out. They would need to be returned to their prison until the long march to their place of execution began in the morning. Still, he was curious about what was being said. Given his recent thoughts, he, too, hoped the chieftains would consider having a child soon.

"As for you, Mathghamhain, as your blade remains sheathed, I will say this," Fedelmid was saying now. "Be wise and follow what you know to be the truth, that to give strength to your enemy is to weaken yourself as well. The reverse is also true. I will look forward to commiserating again with both of you when I do reach Meadhan, that village from which you do oversee these lands, agent of change."

What had been that part about Mathghamhain's blade being sheathed? Why would that make a difference in what the priestess said, Caiside wondered. That was when he noticed she had begun walking toward him and the warriors who had gathered up the prisoners. He was wary of what she wanted considering what had occurred last time she had gotten close to them.

"Chieftains Mathghamhain and Cacht, although I am not staying, I would pass my own sentence on behalf of the Priesthood and these lands upon the prisoners."

Caiside tensed again. With their connection to the

land and the powers the Priesthood were rumoured to have as a result, he dreaded what such a sentence could entail. He quickly moved his hand to where his sword was sheathed, just in case. The chieftains for their part simply looked curious about what she would say. He watched anxiously as she spread her arms wide. Not wanting to accidentally cause trouble, he had his warriors stop in their movements and keep the prisoners still.

"You have falsely accused the agent of change of these lands. You have brought shame upon your name and families. You have brought shame upon your guilds and your children will never truly know their parents. What they do know will be that of people who did betray these lands," the priestess began. Once again, Caiside thought, she had gone from being a beacon of hope and brightness to a person to fear, by her words alone. "Know that while your Chieftains do seek one penalty for your crimes, I, on behalf of the Priesthood, do pass an even harsher sentence this day."

The prisoners looked even more bothered by her words than he was. What could she possibly do besides outright kill them on the spot that would be worse than their upcoming execution? Fedelmid, for all that she commanded instant respect from the populace, remained a relative unknown to them all.

"You did live off these lands and did thrive. For a time, the lands repaid you but now you have repaid that with going against its will and that of they who would see to the lands and its people's protection and well-being," Fedelmid continued. "An enemy from within is far greater than an enemy you can see coming from beyond your borders. When you were each born, the Priesthood did bless you, signifying your eternal connection to these lands. On this day, I say to you all, that blessing will be removed from all of you. The land rejects you, you are but poorly animated constructs no longer truly alive as your spirits lose all that is good in them and rejected by the lands. Your last days walking this world will be those of torment. The air will taste different, the food will not sate you, everything the lands protected you from in the past will now have free reign to make your final hours horrible and torturous. You deserve no less. Your bodies will be destroyed by human hand but your spirits will have no afterlife and they will be condemned to wander these lands, forever unable to be at peace."

Oh, Caiside thought, she could become truly frightening with her words. He felt a fresh chill run down his back with each statement she made about what the prisoners would suffer during their last days. To lose the blessing of the land was the worst punishment he could imagine—to be denied peace in the afterlife. The Priesthood were dangerous indeed in what they could do.

Caiside let go of his sword as he watched her. The last thing he wanted after hearing her words was to give her reason to turn them on him as well. She was bringing her arms up higher and higher to reach for the sky above as she spoke words he did not recognize, the dark clouds growing even darker as she did so. It was a coincidence, Caiside thought, there was no way the Priesthood could command such power. Yet that was precisely how it looked to be what she was doing. The horror on the prisoners faces signalling how much her words terrified them was only rivalled by the greater look of fear on Mathghamhain's. Caiside was not sure he wanted to know why that was.

"Priestess, you cannot..." Loegaire cried out. The former reeve's words were cut short when Fedelmid's arms had extended skyward as much as possible, the fading fog starting to roll in again and much quicker. Rain erupted from the clouds, a trickle at first. It was enough for anyone still lingering in the area other than the prisoners and warriors to head towards Thabhairt as quickly as they could. Right now, Caiside envied the fact that they were free to do so. The trickle was already turning into a steady down-pour. Even the chieftains looked to be preparing to head for shelter. He could not blame them at all. Their safety was paramount and the priestess did not seem to be taking into account the danger her actions were having on everyone else.

"My wife, I would think the land itself is consider-ably angry and we should leave courageous and wise Caiside to see to getting the prisoners to holding until dawn," Mathghamhain could be barely heard over the noise of the rain. Caiside needed them to be safe, quickly gesturing to the chieftains to leave. Ever in charge, he was not surprised that the chieftain ignored him for a moment in order to address the Priestess Fedelmid as well. "Priestess! We must take our leave in these heavy rains. We thank you for your attendance this day and look forward to when next we meet."

Rather than depart after those words, the Chieftains

lingered still. That was what it looked like to Caiside. The reason why was made clear when Mathghamhain approached him and extended a hand to clasp his.

"Keep them moving. To stay here until she has finished is to make any movement nigh impossible as the land will be too wet to walk upon," Mathghamhain said loud enough that Caiside could hear him before the chieftain turned, heading off with Cacht for their steeds, the chieftain holding his cloak over her as they did so. Good, the chieftains would be somewhere safe soon, Caiside thought, as he turned his attention to getting the prisoners and warriors indoors as well.

"Come traitors. Keep it moving, your heads bowed, step lively now," Caiside said watching as his chieftains rode. His warriors would do their best but Mathghamhain was right about the ground. The longer they delayed moving the worse it was going to get for travelling. Looking to the sky as he spoke, Caiside tried to see how widespread this storm was, that although it had been inevitable it had still sprung up as if on the command of the priestess. His eyes glazed over for a brief second when he looked back to where she was still commanding the sky and fog itself. The downpour of rain against the blue robes that had earlier on shimmered with radiance now made them cling tightly to her body. It revealed more about how the Priesthood or at least its priestess chose to dress than he had ever thought to consider or wished to know.

Quickly averting his eyes, Caiside looked to the prisoners again. With prodding from his warriors, they proceeded to march them at an ever-increasing

pace. The ground was getting muddier by the minute and would make it increasingly difficult to be certain. Hopefully, the priestess called it off soon once she saw them marching onwards. It depended on how much of the storm was her doing and how much was inevitable, Caiside supposed, but it was still a terrifying thing. Especially since, storm or no storm, he was positive she had most definitely caused the fog to increase where it had been nearly diminished. The Priesthood could be terrifying when trifled with, a greater danger than any group of warriors he had ever faced in battle, that was for certain. The question was why she was so angry? Could it really be as simple as her lashing out over the chieftains being questioned? Did the changes they wrought mean so much to the Priesthood?

The sole response Fedelmid seemed to give them was a scream that reverberated across the land for some distance, a shrill pitch of anger and hurt mixed together that seemed to drive the fog higher up and for flashes of lightning to strike across the fully darkened skies.

Caiside did not need to look behind him to know that she was following them. The priestess did not seem to be trying to catch up with them, just walking close enough behind them so that the storm followed.

If she was still speaking though, a wind blowing in strongly made her words impossible to hear when coupled with the thunder, lightning, and the sound of the rain. Never doing anything to have the Priesthood turn against him, was quickly becoming Caiside's top priority in life from this day onward. It had already been fairly high up there but seeing the power they could truly wield had firmly rooted the idea.

They had to persevere, Caiside thought, as he commanded without words best he could to everyone to keep their heads down, not to put any further weight on the ground than absolutely necessary and keep moving. They would get the prisoners to holding one way or the other, no matter how long it took, he thought. They had to. He was no longer even sure if the Priestess Fedelmid was aware that it was not simply the prisoners suffering through this storm.

Chapter 33
Mathghamhain

"What was that all about? I thought she and you both said she was a member of the Priesthood? The Priesthood does not call up storms that powerful. Yes, we all knew the sky was getting dark overhead beforehand such that a storm was already looming, but for it to grow that quickly means she helped it along, I suspect, and the fog. She put our own people at risk out there. That is no way to reassure everyone. Does the Priesthood now intend to maintain our faith through the use of fear?" Cacht asked Mathghamhain when they had gotten to Thabhairt finally. They would be having to rest here for the night since they would be heading out before dawn to make their way gradually to Marcairt in time for the executions. If they were still alive given the storm raging on outside, one that had driven everyone in Thabhairt indoors before the two of them had even arrived.

"She seemed quite cross about the prisoners, correction, the condemned's questioning of the lands will or her own. She is young. It is no excuse though and she can explain her actions when we talk with her next. As for the display of power she showed, perhaps we simply have never seen such power exercised because we have never seen any member of the Priesthood angry before. Drust was always calm and respected and welcomed. We have been taught that the Priesthood have a deep connection to the land that none of us can even seek to fathom. Things are good when they are around because they appear calm, happy, and appreciated. Is it all that surprising that when they are the opposite of that, that the land does respond in kind? I doubt she called the storm itself but possibly caused it to be worse than it was," Mathghamhain said trying to comfort her, wanting to not let it show how unnerved he was as well by Fedelmid's actions. As it was, they were in the process still of getting dried off, in part thanks to guards recognizing them upon their arrival.

"I see. You defend her. You are attracted to her, is that it? Perhaps that is why your future self's spirit is so afraid of her and says she killed him? He tried to court her and she rejected him, which set off a battle between the two? After all, did you not say that version of you and I never wed? Perhaps in your old age you tried to convince a member of the Priesthood to see to your needs for pleasure?" Cacht responded with such a mixture of concern and anger to the point that Mathghamhain was not sure which he should pay attention to more.

"Surely you jest but that is worth questioning it about, although it has gone remarkably silent. The last thing it said was warning me that I was about to see the full scope of the power she was capable of and proof of its claims she was not a priestess at all but something else," he mused. "Not the first time it has claimed as such but I know of no one else who could do as such and she does seem to be the Priesthood's representative here. You do present an interesting theory. Do I still need to fear her killing me when things have been changed so much in our present-day? We are wed, we rule as equals, and with the spirit's guidance, when it was not so bloodthirsty, we did attain a position that did not exist before, and caused great expansion across these lands. It has never been terribly forthcoming about where the differences lie. I had always assumed when enough changed in the present to make that future death not occur, that the spirit would cease to be. I realize that was foolish. I can ask it, and once she has had time to sufficiently calm down, consult with the Priestess Fedelmid about it again as well. It matters not whether there was a relationship in the spirit's time between them. Here and now, you and I, we changed what happens, and you are and always will be my only love, my heart, my all."

Mathghamhain had said those last words as reassuringly as he could, still unsure fully of whether she was truly angry or merely presenting a rather reasonable theory. He suspected it was more about bringing forward an explanation in the wake of the chaos the storm had caused. Surely, Cacht knew that he only had eyes for her.

✳

Despite having a chance to relax the past few nights while travelling, it had been repeatedly in less than familiar settings. Mathghamhain had been further kept awake by the idea of the Priestess Fedelmid being fully responsible for the storm, the utter delight she seemed to take in it, and the damage it wrought following the trial. When he did finally awaken the final morning in Marcairt with Cacht, an hour before dawn, he did so with the faint wonder of whether the Priestess would attend the execution of the traitors as well or if she had said her piece and moved on to visiting each village.

Unless she planned to arrive late, he need not have worried, Mathghamhain thought. The executions, conducted by members of the Warriors Guild and overseen by Caiside, had been well underway for a while now. Those villagers who had come to watch at the beginning had already turned away and left. He supposed they had been family members of those who had been convicted of treason. It had been a noisy and messy affair and not for the faint of heart. He had been doing his best not to show emotion as each grouping had their lives come to an end. He was though caught off guard as he saw Caiside call for an extended break after a grouping of four had been executed and headed over to where he and Cacht were watching from.

"There is an issue Caiside?" Mathghamhain asked once the reeve had stopped walking and was in front of them. "It did seem to me the executions of the traitors was running as smoothly as anyone could possibly have expected, despite the muddy walk getting here, and the numbers involved."

"Yes, so far so good, Mathghamhain, were that what concerned me at the moment. Instead, the events of the trial do cause me to wonder. Although he has been stripped of his rank, Loegaire was still a reeve. I think you or courageous Cacht should do the execution. At least part of it, so that Loegaire is executed by a peer, even though, as a traitor, everyone is now his peer. A thought to consider that I should have brought to you earlier," Caiside concluded. Mathghamhain looked at his reeve for a long moment before settling on a proper answer to the suggestion.

"Your suggestion does have merit, although I despise the thought of it. Very well, Caiside, please resume the executions and I and my wise wife will discuss the matter," Mathghamhain responded. "You will know our decision if one of us comes forth when his grouping is taken to the edge of the cliff."

Having offered his answer, Mathghamhain watched as the older man saluted them both and headed back, once more throwing up his arms to call forth the next grouping. From the looks of things, Loegaire was in one of the last groupings which meant he would definitely have time to discuss the matter with Cacht.

"Caiside does raise a valid point but I know you. Loegaire's treason has wounded you deeply, more than the others," Cacht said giving her opinion, a look of grave concern on her face. "He raised you, was your closest ally, and friend, only eclipsed in that role when we did wed, although he, of course, remained your oldest. To have to be the one to execute him, while appropriate, it would surely tear at you worse than any treason on his part could ever do.”

“Indeed. I cannot be the one to do the deed, no matter how appropriate or how it would look to our people. Perhaps I can do something symbolically and simply be the one to shove him off the cliff,” Mathghamhain mused even as he dismounted. “No, that would not work now would it. He would already be dead by then. Perhaps if I were to…no, I cannot do that as that is the exact thing we are seeking to avoid having me do. I will do what is needed and will not wound my own heart to do so nor will I be his personal executioner. Loegaire does not deserve that. He did turn on me and led others against me that resulted in their deaths. No, dear Cacht, I have something symbolic in mind instead that I can do.”

“If you are sure, husband,” Cacht whispered as Mathghamhain kissed her hand, feeling her tremble at his words. When this was all over, they both needed peace for awhile.

Walking over to where Caiside stood, Mathghamhain whispered to him that he would not be executing Loegaire himself. Instead, he wanted to deliver a personal message to the man and fallen reeve before the warrior who would ultimately kill Loegaire took over and performed the execution. It was not long afterwards that Mathghamhain accompanied the warriors to the cliff with the prisoner grouping Loegaire was in. Caiside, for his part, had mentioned to the warriors that the execution would be delayed while their chieftain had a personal chat with Loegaire. A man who now stood before him. No, not a man anymore. The man Mathghamhain had known had been replaced by a creature that had seen fit to slither around and gather forces against him, to betray him, in the guise of a friend and close ally. Not a friend, not a mentor, not an ally.

"Loegaire, you who were once called brave and wise. You now deserve none of those titles, stripped of you like the rank of reeve," Mathghamhain began slowly as he searched for the words he wanted. "Your betrayal did wound me gravely. There are insufficient words to describe all that you were to me for many a year. You chose to throw everything away on the mistaken belief I was responsible for the Priesthood's delayed movements in visiting. You let your personal feelings about the Great Hunt, a hunt that was made so that our people might live and be defended, affect you. So that none may question the severing of what you and I once were, I say this. As your once friend, your once ally, your once student, and now solely as your Chieftain who holds power over your life and death in my hands, do begin your execution thus."

Pausing, Mathghamhain looked around to be sure he had everyone's attention. It also gave him time to brace himself for what he was about to do to a man who had meant so much to him. Drawing his sword, Mathghamhain raised it high, looking down at Loegaire as he did so. The old hunter looked absolutely miserable. The man who had been his friend for so long looked tired, drained of life already. A man who had no sleep, and already had in all but the physical sense moved on from the world. The execution would

be a release. Closing his eyes tightly, Mathghamhain pushed the hurt he was feeling down deep. When he was certain he was ready, he opened his eyes and swung the blade down cutting through Loegaire's right shoulder severing the man's arm.

The cry of anguish that came from Loegaire's lips was one he had to ignore or he would never be able to finish this. Sheathing his sword, Mathghamhain picked up the arm and held it high.

"Loegaire was a reeve and served at the right hand of myself and my fellow Chieftain Cacht, and who with this very hand did shake my own as a friend, ally, and mentor more than once. I have removed it, that it die first before the rest of his traitorous self is executed, and I do hereby toss it over the cliff to lay with the bodies of the other traitors, soon to be joined by the rest of him. This I do, " Mathghamhain shouted before flinging the arm over the cliff.

He did not dare look at Loegaire, not if he wanted to make it back to his horse without being completely overwhelmed by emotion. Patting his other hand on the shoulder of the warrior who would finish the execution, Mathghamhain then strode back to his steed, not looking back until he heard the bodies being shoved off the cliff. Then and only then did he allow himself to look back as the final executions were prepared.

"That was more dramatic than I was expecting, my brave and mighty husband. Are you sure that you are alright?" Cacht remarked as Mathghamhain took the cloth one of the warriors ran over to him with so he could clean his hands and face of Loegaire's blood. He handed it back to the warrior quickly.

"Burn that, do not wash it. Burn it and throw its ashes over the cliff. I thank you, " he said before mounting his steed again and looking to Cacht. Giving her a nod to indicate he was okay, Mathghamhain did his best to blink away the tears that were falling before resuming his previous steadfast demeanour best he could in the wake of witnessing these executions. In truth, he doubted he would ever truly be okay again but there would be time to come to terms with what he had been forced to do once he was home. In the meantime, he needed to look strong in his convictions with so many warriors present.

CHAPTER 34

"Brave Mathghamhain, and who I can but assume is your wife and fellow Chieftain who you did mention before, the courageous and wise Cacht, I thank you for this audience," Caderyn, the Warriors Guild Chief of Caidreach, said. The man had arrived at Meadhan a short time earlier and been quickly ushered in to see them along with the small cadre of warriors that had accompanied him.

It had been well over two months since the execution of Loegaire and the others and Mathghamhain had spent much of that time reassuring the people that all would still be well. It was made easier by the fact the Priestess Fedelmid was also making her way from village to village. The Priesthood did have a proclivity

for helping people to feel better. The sight of a handful of strongly built and imposing warriors making their way from the southern border to here had likely not helped those who had seen them be re-assured but Mathghamhain would address that once this delegation had departed. For that matter, Fed-elmid was set to reach Meadhan itself within the next week, unless she had completely changed the routes the Priesthood took.

"Of course mighty Caderyn. It is good to see you again, although we are surprised it is so soon after we did part ways," Mathghamhain responded nodding and hoping he was wrong about why the air around him had abruptly chilled. "Cacht is, indeed, the woman to my left and my fellow Chieftain in these lands. What is it that brings you all this way?"

"He is a harbinger. A lure to distract you so the enemy to the north can invade and overrun Cridhe Aonaichte while you spend time trifling with a warrior who claims to be an ally," the spirit hissed in Mathghamhain's ear. "Have you not learned by now, Mathghamhain, that you cannot trust anybody close to you? Allies will betray you, friends already have betrayed you, and no doubt Cacht will betray you."

"Cacht would never betray me!" Mathghamhain shouted leaping to his feet before closing his eyes tightly for a moment and smiling lightly at the baffled warrior delegation and casting apologetic eyes to Cacht. He had done so well to avoid reacting to the spirit verbally when others were around, until now.

"My apologies, mighty Caderyn, my husband has had much on his mind as of late and is understandably on edge. His mind does ruminate on all things and he, it would seem, did come to a conclusion while you were here. Normally he does not do so quite so loudly. It is an honour to finally meet you, Warrior Chief," Cacht responded while she waited for Mathghamhain to retake his seat. While yes, she was aware of the spirit that would voice things to him that only he could hear, she had not previously had to cover for him in public but had managed to do so without hesitation. Could she have had that answer ready as a standby should this day ever come? Seated back down Mathghamhain smiled wryly at Caderyn.

"Indeed, my apologies. We have had trouble as of late involving those who I did once trust and call an ally. As you were mighty, Caderyn. What does bring you this day?" Mathghamhain managed, sighing inwardly and hoping the spirit would stay quiet now.

"Of course, quite understandable. You do both have to rule over much more than anyone else does. We had heard of your troubles as of late. I assume the recent storm, which would seem to align with when you did have them, is connected in some way?" Caderyn replied staying a lot calmer than Mathghamhain would have believed him capable of, following his outburst.

"It was already gathering at the time but its size and ferocity may have been ignited further by the member of the Priesthood, angered at the people who did give us trouble as well and making their anger felt," Mathghamhain said, careful not to divulge more about Fedelmid than necessary.

"Who did know the Priesthood did possess such

power, but I suppose it is not outside the realm of possibility with their connection to the land. I am but a warrior. What would I know of such powerful magic?" Caderyn replied, shrugging. "I do mention it, and am glad you brought up your recent trouble, as we were not the only ones who have heard of it. Many of your northern neighbours did as well and as you are no doubt aware, they do gather against you, hoping to work together to be able to contend against your superior force. This being despite you having shown no interest in further expansion in quite some time."

That worried Mathghamhain, was he about to lose Caidreach as a potential ally? Caderyn was looking at both him and Cacht, hesitant to continue speaking. He would have to try and prompt Caderyn and see if that got the warrior talking again. The spirit's words a few moments ago made Mathghamhain wonder if it might be right. After all, it had repeatedly warned him about Cacht, yet she remained his greatest and most steadfast ally. In her case, Mathghamhain wondered if the spirit disliked her purely because she was aware of him. It would also explain why it also disliked Caiside and Nuallan. As for Fedelmid, he was still unsure about that but did want to question her.

"Yes, we are well aware of the enemy. How would you know that they are aware of my recent troubles in my land? Why precisely are you here, mighty Caderyn?" Mathghamhain finally asked.

"They did send a delegation through your other neighbours, brave Chieftains. I do come today to warn you that it is not simply those to the north who do plot against you. They have also moved to work with your neighbours on all sides, to surround you as much as possible," Caderyn said before straightening himself up to his full imposing height.

"That is, indeed, grave news and we are glad to be made aware of it lest we concentrate too much on defences to the north when we could be attacked from other directions. We do thank you for this information," Cacht said although it was obvious by her tone she was not quite as reassured by it as she wanted it to seem.

"There is more. I did say they had merely moved to work with them. They were not wholly successful in this matter as my fellow Chiefs and I, in Caidreach, do well remember that you are a man of your word and the trade agreement that we did strike and of the bounty it did provide us both in leaner times," Caderyn said gesturing to one of the warriors who had come with him. "I am here today not simply to warn you but to bring to you a question. Caidreach's Chiefs would put forth a request for a formal alliance between us and Cridhe Aonaichte. One that goes beyond mere trade but would make us full allies. We would much prefer to aid those who have aided us, rather than those whom we ourselves must view as potential enemies."

Mathghamhain eyed the Warrior Chief questioningly as the warrior that Caderyn had gestured to stepped forward. Producing a scroll from one of the bags they had brought, the warrior held it out. Extending his arm in curiosity, Mathghamhain accepted it before looking back to Caderyn.

"That is a matter that is worth considering, especially in the wake of what you have said about our other neighbours. We do remember you saying that you did barely manage to gain land that touched our own by however narrow a strip through fighting your neighbours," Mathghamhain said after a short pause "Please, we would ask that you and your brave compatriots tarry a bit while we go over this, so that you can go back with a full answer to your fellow Chiefs. We will provide food and drink for you and your warriors while we consult."

Having concluded his thought on the matter, Mathghamhain passed the scroll to Cacht and stepped down from his seat. Approaching Caderyn, he offered his hand, clasping it firmly with the chief's.

"Indeed, we thank you for your hospitality," Caderyn responded before letting go of Mathghamhain's hand. "We would ask you to entertain the possibility of letting us stay indoors. A precaution you understand."

"Of course. We will all retire to a room we can dine in and have it brought to you. By the time we are done, we will no doubt be toasting to a new alliance," Cacht said. She was already looking over the contents of the scroll briefly before getting down from her seat and moving over toward him. Looking to see why, Mathghamhain's answer came in the form of her handing him the scroll to read. She was pointing at a specific set of lines.

"That would be much appreciated, courageous and wise Chieftain Cacht," Caderyn said nodding his head when she went to show Mathghamhain the scroll.

Listening to Caderyn, Mathghamhain looked down

to see what in the scroll was of concern to his wife. Reading it, he could not help but smirk as he glanced up to regard Caderyn. Considering what he was reading and the look of confusion on the chief's face, Mathghamhain suspected the man had not himself read the scroll. Still, as a chief, he had likely been involved while it was written. Clearly, the part he was reading had been inserted without the chief knowing. It was easy enough to find out for sure though.

"Mighty Caderyn, what is this part about you also hopefully finding a wife for yourself while you are here?" Mathghamhain asked, amused by the fact such a thing had been snuck into a formal declaration of negotiations for an alliance.

"Pardon me, good Chieftains, it does say what?" Caderyn sputtered. It was as Mathghamhain had suspected. The Warrior Chief's warriors were also amused as they seemed to be doing their best to stifle their laughter. "I do assure you, Chieftains, I was unaware of that being mentioned in there, nor did I come with any such intention. I suspect my fellow Chiefs who are all wed have decided that since I am not, I must look outside of Caidreach and so they seek to force the situation by making it part of the agreement. Never would I try to rush such an alliance so that I could have time to look for such a woman and win her heart. Especially not in so short a timeframe," the Warrior Chief said, clearly embarrassed by it.

"It did seem an odd thing to include," Mathghamhain said, grinning at the Warrior Chief in response. The poor man looked to be quite embarrassed by the situation. "Perhaps we should ask dear Cacht that any women who do serve us while we are in negotiations be those who are unwed. That they pay special attention to the brave Warrior Chief so that he might see if there are any he may wish to try courting."

Mathghamhain was doing his best not to laugh at the brave Warrior Chief's discomfort and embarrassment but it was proving difficult. It had served to relax the situation considerably. It was hard to believe the man was single. Caderyn was more than old enough and was an impressive and imposing figure, not to mention a Warrior Chief.

"It is unnecessary I assure you. I will deliver a stern response to my fellow chiefs when I see them about including such a personal matter in negotiations without my knowledge or consent," Caderyn finally said. He sounded annoyed and embarrassed still but Mathghamhain knew the man well-enough from their previous meeting that the chief was simply doing his best at this point to show he was of strong enough resolve to handle it.

"Think nothing of it, mighty Caderyn. I am certain Cacht can even help and suggest those who you would be proud to call wife perhaps one day," he offered, wanting to show he could rise above the mirth of the situation as well. "She did lead the Caretakers Guild at one time and is quite familiar with the women who are in this village, enough to be able to help you. It will not be a priority but since we must wait for food and drink anyway, and send for the Reeve of my Educators Guild to help us go over this proposal, there will be time."

"Oh yes, of course. Is that the one I met during the

hunt? The quiet one?" Caderyn asked as Mathghamhain strode to the doorway.

Poking his head out of the room, Mathghamhain asked Seisyll to dispatch a messenger to have seating, food, and drink brought in for themselves and five honoured guests. He hastily added as well that the guard suggest to Eluned that only women who were of age and looking for a husband be the ones to serve it. Turning after he had done so, he headed back over, putting an arm around Caderyn's shoulders.

"Yes, his name is Donnchad. Now, come relax. Are all the men in Caidreach so broad-shouldered? Even the farmers you did bring with you last time were of powerful frame," Mathghamhain said as he worked to steer the conversation in a way that would keep it relaxed. There would be plenty of time for seriousness once Donnchad was there to look over the scroll.

CHAPTER 35

As you can see here, mighty Chieftain Mathghamhain, this agreement would effectively result in a patrolled border where our two lands meet. The patrol would comprise three warriors from Caidreach and three from Cridhe Aonaichte who would be swapped out as need be to let them have a change of scenery and maintain their training," Donnchad was saying following a short repast of food and drink. Caderyn and his warriors were still being entertained elsewhere while things were discussed.

"In exchange, our farmers could freely cross back and forth with a member of their respective Educators Guild present to negotiate trades for their crops that would benefit their respective lands. Caidreach, as we saw from our earlier trade, is able to grow a few crops we cannot and vice versa," Donnchad continued. "When women want to look into changing villages potentially, or relationships across our borders are cultivated, they would be accompanied by a warrior for needs of protection. The end result would be our respective Hunters Guilds can work hand-in-hand to ensure that, if they want to operate within each other's borders, they must be supervised by hunters from those lands. In addition, we would come to each other's defence if one of our lands was attacked. It is a smart bit of an offer they are proposing and they clearly began working on it in depth, possibly as soon as their hunters and warriors returned home following the last trade. I am positive their Educators Guild Chief drew this up, given the preciseness of the ter-minology and careful phrasing."

"They do appear to have thought this through considerably, do they not? Still, we may need a re-finement to it," Mathghamhain said from his seat, nodding at the Reeve. "While freely trading back and forth does help, we will need to be careful that we do not give away more than we do gain. I suspect having a member of the Educators Guild present each time is meant to ensure this but Caidreach would surely ap-preciate such a clause being specified in writing. One that would also require any marriages that come of this grand alliance to be cleared first by the leader of their respective Caretakers Guild so that we can be certain that neither side suddenly finds themselves seeing more women or more men leave than they do gain in return. Other than it needing to be duly ratified by all of our reeves and then myself and Cacht signing off on it officially, that should finish our part. That and the sole remaining note that was tacked on regarding our visiting Warriors Guild Chief, that is. Perhaps I should check on Caderyn while you do send word for the other reeves to meet here to ratify this deal.”

As Mathghamhain finished speaking, he smiled as he noticed Donnchad had already begun writing the necessary addendum that had been suggested.

“Indeed, he did seem rather taken aback by the attention he was getting and we should try to have him be able to truthfully go back to Caidreach and state he has his eyes and thoughts on possible women here. Ones that he may consider trying to court when time allows, should they be willing,” Donnchad replied, glancing up from the parchment he was writing on, concern on his face. ”Something else bothers you, Mathghamhain?”

“Perhaps. More of a thought, given that the enemy is gathering on all sides rather than simply to the north. We are mighty in number and if we arm the farmers and hunters, we can likely handle whatever they send at us, but I dislike leaving it to chance. Even with our potential new allies to back us up in the south,” Mathghamhain began as he rose from his seat, pacing as he continued. “I am thinking of a potential aid that may yet help if we can do so in time. I must

consult with my fellow Chieftain on it before anything is decided. Let us gather the reeves and our
visitors first though. This other matter can wait for
now or I can talk with her while I wait for the reeves,
depending on how Caderyn's luck is holding with the
women."

It was clear in Mathghamhain's mind right now:
they needed additional horses. Yes, they had the two
armoured ones for himself and Cacht, and perhaps a
dozen unarmoured ones combined in Marcairt and
Thabhairt. The more warriors they could get on
horseback the faster they could move across the land to
aid where needed. A thing that would be necessary if
the enemy forces tried to come in at multiple points.

Nearly a quarter of the day had passed by the time the
reeves were finally all gathered, a fact made possible
solely by sheer luck of proximity. It was the first full
meeting of all of them since Corraidhin had been officially elected as the Hunters Guild Reeve. As
Chieftain, Mathghamhain had excused himself to let
the reeves of his guilds sort details out and they could
fill him in when he returned. At the moment, he was
meeting in private at the Warriors Guild training
grounds with Nuallan and Cacht, after a brief word to
Caiside before the meeting had begun.

"It is a grave risk to these lands, is it not, my lieges?
I do understand the necessity and, in fact, do agree
with the concept in theory. I do not wish to question
your judgement but is this not when we are all needed
most?" Nuallan asked looking at both chieftains. Ever

the faithful servant, Mathghamhain thought, despite having been the second-in-command of the Warriors Guild for the past while and having long ago been accepted by the others. It was among the main reasons Mathghamhain was coming to him with such a request as he was. There was no one else he would.

"Agreed, faithful Nuallan, but as my husband has said, if we can negotiate such a deal it will be most helpful in bolstering defences. Now that we know the situation is graver than we did previously believe it to be, we can scarcely afford not to take such a chance. If it is safety you are concerned for, have no fear I shall protect you," Cacht said grinning as Mathghamhain did his best not to laugh knowing full well it was Cacht's safety Nuallan feared for, not his own. Signs of her late father showing through, certainly. It did not happen often with the way things had been going, but once in a while she would make a comment that did serve as a friendly reminder of precisely whose daughter she was.

"There is no one else I would trust more for such a mission, faithful Nuallan. You know the needs of these lands as well as Cacht does. I remain to rule until she returns," Mathghamhain said nodding. "Our decisions have ever been as one, so I will do so with the utmost confidence, and Caiside must remain to direct forces. You would both be departing with a small contingent to accompany you. One that you would both have a hand in choosing, and leave with the delegation that came with Caderyn. You would pass through Caidreach's land before travelling onwards to find sufficient horses to bring back. You can hopefully pick up additional help in Caidreach to help you in accompanying them as they are our allies now if this alliance is approved. This meeting our reeves hold now is proof of what can be gained from an alliance that started as a trade agreement. A second trade partner for horses would no doubt be helpful and a boon."

Mathghamhain disliked the idea of Cacht being gone. Especially since it would likely be for well over a month, the longest they had ever been apart since they were wed. Still, they both knew such a trade was needed. Some would wonder why he simply did not direct Caiside to lead raids on the north to obtain the needed horses. To that, he would answer that it was due to the risk it took and that it would simply serve to aggravate the enemy further. Such aggravation would likely lead to them attacking sooner, and that was the one thing Mathghamhain did not want. He needed additional time to prepare in order to repel them.

"I suppose, and you will have no need to defend myself, or yourself either, my liege. We will be imposing and direct and give them no reason to draw swords upon us," Nuallan said bowing. "If this is the will of my lieges then it shall be so done. We shall not return until negotiations have been successful and a bounty of horses is on its way here."

"Since we are all in agreement, begin gathering an entourage to accompany us then, faithful Nuallan, as I do suspect we will be departing before nightfall," Cacht said holding out her hand as Nuallan swiftly kissed the back of it, after clasping Mathghamhain's hand in a firm shake.

When Nuallan had departed, Mathghamhain looked at Cacht with a weakened smile.

"Even if you are not able to get as many horses as we might need, my main concern is that you come back to me. Nothing is more important than your safety, my heart," Mathghamhain sighed. He knew this was necessary and that for the negotiations to have even a chance, he or Cacht had to go as they represented all of Cridhe Aonaichte.

"Know that I will, no matter what, find my way back to you, my darling Mathghamhain. I shall be fine. I will have faithful Nuallan with me and a contingent of others as well. I might remind you of the daily lessons I have had these past years in the art of combat as well. We shall be well-prepared," she smiled moving to kiss him softly at first, then more deeply. After a few moments, she paused, looking at him amused.

"We should get back to the Reeves to check on their wrangling of the negotiations and fine-tuning of it. Then check on mighty Caderyn. Possibly tear him away from his new…friends," she grinned before kissing him again. "Trade is good. Less messy than conquering but certainly more time-consuming."

"I know, I merely wish the priestess would visit before then. It would be good to have her blessing, whether she truly is a priestess or not, on your journey," he responded quietly. Mathghamhain half wanted to have Cacht wait and Caderyn's delegation as well but it could prove folly not to move with the utmost expediency in current matters. Fedelmid could be arriving any day now.

"I agree it would be helpful. When she arrives then, dear husband, have her make the blessing to you. We are as one. It will extend, or considering the power she demonstrated, perhaps she will be able to send a message through the land so long as I am still upon it," Cacht responded before Mathghamhain took her into another embrace before they headed inside to check on the negotiations.

CHAPTER 36

It had been a long few days' wait it turned out as one of the non-armoured horses they had stabled further north carried two riders to the border and back again. It had been Donnchad's second-in-command and one of Caderyn's warriors who had carried the message. Now the completed deal had been signed back in Caidreach and the agreement had been brought back to Mathghamhain and Cacht.

Now, Mathghamhain had been awake since long before dawn to accompany the group heading south part of the way. The group, it ended up, comprised the warriors who had accompanied Caderyn, the Warrior Chief himself, Nuallan, two farmers, an additional warrior from his own Warriors Guild, and Cacht. Once they entered into Caidreach's lands, Nuallan and Cacht and the three men accompanying them would have to traverse the full scope of it and then travel east from there. Caderyn had promised to make sure the contingent was accompanied by a few of his warriors until they had reached their eastern border. From there, the Chief had indicated a place to find horses was one additional set of lands further over but to get there would require crossing water.

Mathghamhain had been sitting back in his seat for barely a few moments now after his initial accompaniment. It was a strange thing for him not to have his wife there beside him in her own seat. There had been a debate between the two of them about which of them should stay and which should go to negotiate a deal. Mathghamhain knew her to be far wiser than him at times but also she had a cooler head in rough situations, for the most part. He would have to trust that her ongoing training with the Warriors Guild and the warriors going with her would be enough to keep her safe. As for his own safety, Mathghamhain had decided he would keep his sword drawn at all times while she was gone, save for when he slept. The last thing he wanted while Cacht was away, was his future self's spirit whispering in his ear words to worry, concern, and anger. His sword was laying across his lap while he rubbed his forehead and frowned. He was listening as best he could while Donnchad spoke.

"We have reports that the Priestess Fedelmid had been on her way here but then altered her route as she has already been spotted heading southwest. As you know from the map we did put together, it would be far quicker for her to return home from there. I would propose that she is saving a visit to Meadhan for last. I know not what other reason she might have for skipping us over."

Why would she skip, Mathghamhain wondered,

even if it was a personal issue she had with someone in Meadhan, she was still hurting others here by skipping it. More likely, she was indeed saving it for last. Since he and many of the Reeves were based here, there would be a grand need for the Priesthood's words and blessing to their leadership.

"Nor do I. She was on friendly terms when we did see her last. Well, mostly friendly," Mathghamhain mused with a shudder, recalling the storm. "We will give her a chance but if she does not show before being spotted heading in the direction of the temple, we will move to catch up with her by horseback and ask for an explanation. Until then we have other matters. The Priesthood has always ever served their own choices. They do not answer to any of us, even if their actions do vex us and leave us in dire need of answers."

"Well then, my Chieftain, I would add that her demeanour did seem one that our people were not quite prepared for. She is not quite the same as the Priest Drust was at all and it has people concerned, but that can be discussed when you do finally see her," Donnchad replied. "As for the other matter, now that we know that we face an enemy on our other borders, not just to the north, we have enlisted the Metal Workers Guild to prioritize completing the armouring of the horses we have. As you requested as well, we are having the remainder of the horses at Marcairt moved to the more centrally located Thabhairt. They have already finished one full set of armour for a steed—for brave Caiside to use. You can decide who uses the others as is needed."

"Excellent. About the Metal Workers Guild, not so much the demeanour of our new priestess. It is her first year travelling to these villages, the people are as yet fairly unfamiliar to her and, as such, that may be a contributing factor to how she comes across to them. The lack of familiarity they are so used to is gone. That is what I can but hope is the case," Mathghamhain responded frowning somewhat as he spoke.

The last time he had tried to force an audience with the Priestess Fedelmid it had not gone well but by horseback, he could surely catch her if she did indeed try to skip Meadhan.

"Very well, continue with your work. Send Nechtan's delegation in when you leave please," Mathghamhain continued, watching as Donnchad saluted him and then strode from the room. The door had not even closed all of the way before Nechtan and two other farmers had entered the room. It had left him with barely any time at all to leave his seat to obtain a drink. Sighing, he sank back into his seat while he heard what they had to say.

"Brave and wise Chieftain Mathghamhain, you wanted to hear how well the irrigation idea used by Caidreach for crop yields was working. While it is taking time to fully implement it, we do have an unexpected surprise already," Nechtan began. "So much so that we do hope it is a portent of things to yet come."

"Speak plainly, please. Remember, I am not a farmer myself and have but a rudimentary understanding that I have acquired simply so that I can try to understand most of what you do say in these meetings, our wise Reeve," Mathghamhain responded looking to Nechtan and then the other two farmers with him. He was unsure regarding the reason for their presence at the moment. Any good news was a welcome change these days though and he was glad to hear that another aspect of the trade was bringing desired benefits. Benefits, in this case, that Mathghamhain had expected.

"Of course. If you will allow…" the Reeve responded and gestured to the two men with him who quickly moved to lay out on the floor several sticks in neat rows, not unlike a small design that matched how the farmlands were separated into rows of crops. "This is how we used to do things. With irrigation, we have water pumped from a nearby source continuously through the farmland area to keep the soil properly saturated instead of relying on the rains or buckets of water being brought to water evenly with."

As Mathghamhain watched, the two farmers moved finer sticks and then twigs into place on the floor creating a grid-like pattern. It was interesting but not until he saw it close enough, which had meant leaving his seat to where he now hovered nearby watching them.

"I see, and this helps with the yield. Fewer crops wasted and having water always," Mathghamhain mused. "These twigs which you used to show where the water was directed into the farmland, these are the thin lines of metal piping you had ordered from the Metal Workers' Guild to make great quantities of, despite their flimsy nature? To the point, we had to have two members of the guild moved to each village to make them closer to the site of the farmlands? Not to mention the additional trips for metal to be carted from their mines to the various villages."

"Indeed, my Chieftain! Having farmers who knew how to set it up be amongst those who moved here during the trade was a great decision. I am sorry it is taking so long to get it set up for each village," Nechtan continued excitedly. "However, the massive rainstorm that did come about following the unfortunate trial, well, those rains put a lot of water in the ground in general. While it may not look like it, water still moves through the ground. It did fill the surface of most farmlands in the vicinity of the storm quite heavily without doing enough to damage any crops. It has, however, also proven, with its new supply of water, to reveal where seeds in the past had washed up away from farmlands in recent times as we now see them beginning to grow. We are already taking steps to move all of these surprise crops to actual farmland so they can be nurtured."

The reeve was positively beaming about what the man obviously saw as a stroke of good luck that had befallen them, Mathghamhain thought. It made him wonder to the point that he voiced his suspicion aloud.

"Did you believe the Priestess Fedelmid when she did increase the storm's power on that fateful day was merely acting out of anger against those on trial? Despite the fact that it would possibly harm those who were not her targets? It is more likely is it not that she did so to accomplish things two-fold. To help us in our crop yields as we have to direct greater and greater energy towards defence and preparation for war with

the enemy, and lashing out on the lands behalf against the traitors was secondary?" Mathghamhain said warming to the idea.

He watched as the eyes of the reeve went wide and a smile crossed his lips. It may not have been what Nechtan was thinking initially but he had found a way now to help possibly endear the priestess to those who seemed put off by her so far. Mathghamhain hoped that once he spoke to her again, she would prove to be deserving of his aid and that she was not the enemy the spirit insisted.

"Oh, but of course, the Priesthood did bless our farms while also punishing the guilty!" Nechtan replied motioning for the two farmers with him to pick up the display. "That was why she did something using greater power than we do recall any member of the Priesthood using in the past. It was the best way to accomplish such a feat of granting us a benefit while also punishing those who did betray these lands and you and your lovely wife Cacht, who even now does journey abroad to enrich our lands further."

Mathghamhain smirked at how excited Nechtan was in general. It was refreshing to see a reeve so cheerful these days. He would have to find the time, possibly tomorrow even, to visit the farmlands and see what the irrigation grid actually looked like.

"We thank you for your time, great Chieftain, to better explain our situation and gain your insight," Nechtan added while holding his hand out towards him.

"Yes, but see to it that you do not let word of where my wife is get out. One never does know what our enemy might be up to," Mathghamhain replied as he moved to clasp the reeve's hand and acknowledging the other two farmers with a nod of the head to dismiss them before he continued. "We have already had one group of traitors reveal themselves from within our midst of trusted people. There may yet be others, brave Nechtan, and it would go poorly for us if word were to reach the enemy of what we are up to."

"Really? You do think there might be more? Surely there cannot be," the Reeve of the Farmers Guild said incredulously before standing tall and saluting. "You know you can count on our restraint, brave and wise Mathghamhain. It will be kept a secret. If any of our guild suspect traitors, we will bring word to you immediately."

With those words expressing his loyalty, the man left to catch up with the other two farmers. Waiting until the door had closed all the way afterward, Mathghamhain moved over to pour himself a drink. He quickly downed half of it before heading back to his seat to think over what he had learned. It was truly a shame Loegaire had not had the patience to wait and see precisely how beneficial the trade had truly been.

CHAPTER 37

" I do apologize for the delay, brave Mathghamhain. Would that I had known your wife would be absent, I would have altered plans accordingly but simply because I do serve the land does not mean it always

tells me things and it rarely knows the future. Now then, as I intend to visit each reeve here in Meadhan individually now that I was so warmly greeted upon the moment I set foot inside its walls…" Fedelmid said before pausing. She had arrived not much earlier and a solid three days after Cacht and Nuallan had set out for Caidreach with Caderyn and his warriors.

She looked to be more dressed for general travel compared to the last time Mathghamhain had seen her. That was despite her robes having more embroidery this time. They looked thicker and more durable and she had brought along a staff just as her predecessor had always carried, although he had been tempted to believe at first by the spirit of his future self, before it had gone abruptly silent, that it was the same one. The staff had, upon receiving a closer look, revealed itself to be quite a bit different. It was a thing he might not have picked up on if not for his familiarity with wood from his days as a hunter.

"I do understand, wise and courageous Priestess Fedelmid. Would that speed not be so much of the essence I would have had them tarry here longer in the hopes you would arrive sooner than later. Your movements I do admit had a few here concerned that you had cause to skip us over," Mathghamhain responded.

"Of course. I have no reason not to come here, to the seat of power, to bless the people within its walls, and once more speak with the lands' chosen agent of change. One who as of late now seeks to grow as a person by looking into less violent ways to accomplish the changes he so desires. Desires ever fuelled by the need and want to protect his people, the people of these lands. Tell me, how does the situation with your restless self wage?" she said suddenly changing the subject and revealing why she might have delayed exactly in leaving this visit to last. As Mathghamhain had suggested to Nechtan, she had possibly accomplished two goals the day of the trial but this visit was obviously meant to accomplish several.

"You delayed visiting us here until last out of fear of a situation?" he asked wanting to narrow it down and grateful said spirit was not talking at the moment as well.

"Not fear, brave and wise you may be, in this, you would be mistaken. It is scarcely fear but more of a concern for your continued well-being. It clearly has continued to plague you but I have been unable to find a way to exorcise it from you so that you might be healed. At best, I can enchant something else for you besides your blade but there is little else I can do for you and for that I am truly sorry. It shall remain your burden until it either steals away so much of your life's energy that you wither and die, at which point it takes over your body, or you pass on before it can," she responded, her head hung low.

The sadness in her tone was all too clear. Her words bothering Mathghamhain all the more because he knew the spirit could hear them and react if it chose to.

"There really is no other way, Priestess Fedelmid?" he responded, quietly thinking on her exact words. She knew full well it was always present, she had mentioned as such when they had first met, and it had been barred from entering the temple. That thought leading him to consider something she might not have. "Your temple. There are other temples hidden within the borders of Cridhe Aonaichte from when there were additional members of the Priesthood, correct, as you would not normally have had so many villages to visit? Cacht and I could move our seat of power to one of those, could we not?"

"There is a certain sense in your thought. The temples become sealed off when not in use, and it would require the member of the Priesthood who did seal them off upon deserting them to re-open them or if they have died, for their successor to do so. Again, I am sorry. I can possibly re-open a couple of them but it will by no means be an easy process, so it truly needs to be what you want to do. You would still be vulnerable anytime you left it. Still, it is a possible way to delay it, to grant you more days in which you can know peace that does not require your blade being drawn. You have not asked that which I expected you to," Fedelmid said looking at him suddenly more warmly than she had been. That threw Mathghamhain off but he thought quickly to figure out what she was getting at before his future self started speaking and the fact that it was still quiet.

"He is not bothering me right now even though he definitely hates you. As you may recall, immediately after I did leave your temple that I did ask you to let me in again, that I needed to talk right away, although you refused to answer. That is not what you are getting at. The only time it is wont to leave me alone without an explicit order is when the sword is drawn

or when your temple prevented his presence," Mathghamhain thought aloud.

"Explicit orders? You do believe a malevolent spirit
such as it is would leave you alone unless it was forced
to? My dear, darling agent of change, it is quiet now
as it was robbed of choice by my presence. Such a
creature is not merely unable to enter the temple but
cannot abide by the presence of a member of the
Priesthood should that member be willing to exert the
power necessary to make it so. A private conversation
with you is worth that. You could draw your blade to
accomplish much the same but your heart rate accel-
erates when you do so. You become much more alert
and on edge, you pace, the increased heart rate driving
you to want to find a physical solution to situations.
Your late Warrior Reeve Brennus is evident of that, is
he not?" she said, pausing long enough for him to get
in a word edgewise before she continued. "Do not
think I missed that you referred to the spirit as a he
rather than an it. Giving it such an identifier, however
small you think it is, grants the spirit more strength."

"I will do my best to remember that in the future.
Despite your words though, priestess, he…it does
obey my explicit word to stay silent when I am in my
bedroom. It is forced to recognize it as a sacred place
to my wife and I," Mathghamhain began before
noting she had her hand up already to interrupt, her
head shaking back and forth slowly in disagreement
with his words. It was a signal that bothered him and
made his stomach tense in worry.

"Your bedroom is off-limits not because of your
words brave Chieftain. Although, if the first you

became aware of it being unable to speak there was after you forbade it from doing so, then I can understand why you would believe it showed you such respect. It is a malevolent spirit. No matter if it was once you many years from now, it is no longer that. It is a spirit corrupted more greatly over time the longer it lingers and feeds off of you. The bedroom is off-limits because my predecessor, the Priest Drust, did likely work hard to place an enchantment on its doorway that bars the spirit from getting past it. He was much more experienced than I and had done this many years longer. His methods were more subtle. Less flashy as you have no doubt noticed by now. Since you never told him of its presence…" she said before frowning when she saw he was doing so as well. "Yes?"

"He never came here unless you mean to say it is not the doorway it is attached to but that instead it is attached to myself. Wherever my bedroom be, that is the doorway that stops it?" Mathghamhain said musing aloud.

"Indeed, as I said, he was much more subtle. I had attributed it to the doorway. The enchantment is so faint and subtle yet it is not even evident on your person. As for the spirit's dislike of me and the insistent racket you made before, you do realize I had reason to not answer you? You were not in a listening mood at the time, its words pushing you. Even now, you have doubts with regards to myself because of its constant lies in your ear," the Priestess Fedelmid said before continuing moving so that she might finally sit in the seat the women had so quickly rushed to bring in there for her earlier. "Why do you not tell me then, agent of change, you who are so troubled, what lies has it told you? What causes you such alarm when it comes to my presence?"

"Oh yes, that would make sense. I do apologize for that, Priestess Fedelmid. Upon my exit from the temple, it did see fit to advise me that you were in fact not a priestess at all but something darker, that you were the one that did kill it, myself, in the future, which did cause it to come back to the here and now and seek me out," Mathghamhain said pausing at how hard that was to explain. "It is confusing, I know."

"That would do it, I suspect. I am unknown to you then, and who would you trust more? An unknown person you had just met, who had demonstrated power you did not know the Priesthood to have, or the spirit of your own self? It is a hard thing to bring one's self to do, is it not? To ignore your own thoughts—for that is what you are forced to do. That is why it can feed so easily. It knows you cannot forever ignore it and so it plagues you, eating away slowly, looking for an opening that will give it greater strength," she said pausing. "I give you my word, dear agent of change, these are the lands that you rule, your people. You bring unity and growth. I have no need to wish you harm, nor would any Priesthood member ever kill. Our purpose is to aid and protect, and to make sure your spirit finds peace when your final breath comes."

"So I do see, and yet you might as well have killed the traitors at the end of their trial by your actions, or any other number of bystanders who had been present. How does that not refute what you did claim? Why should I believe you when your own actions do cast doubt on your words?" he asked growing irritated. He knew full well it was not her fault but rather the situation he had been forced into.

"What is it you think I did do to them?" Fedelmid answered. "They not only dared to question the will of the land but also did not trust that, if there was an issue, the Priesthood would not act. It is all well and good for everyone to say they believe and provide tribute so that we can continue to serve but for that to vanish simply because we are not around to hold their hand through everything? No, that tells me they let their belief waver. They lost trust in the Priesthood, in the will of the land. As such, I merely served as a conduit through which the lands took away their connection. Their blessings they did receive shortly after they were born being revoked and, thereby, severing ties to the lands which would ensure their spirits suffered, not simply their bodies upon execution. It does not kill, it merely causes a great deal of difficulty and discomfort. They were to die soon after anyway. I surely made certain their death was not felt only physically by them. That they truly suffered. As for the storm, no one would have died by that who would not have died anyway. The storm was already gathering. The land again simply worked through me to increase its power slightly, not that it needed much. I simply augmented it so that rather than it remaining a longer-lasting, weaker storm, you got a shorter one that was much more severe."

As she finished speaking, Mathghamhain watched

nervously as the priestess rose from her seat and began walking towards him. That she would take such actions over a perceived lack of faith was troubling but he did not dare state as such right now lest she bring the Priesthood's wrath down on him as well. No, it could wait until he and Cacht could decide how to discuss it properly, possibly with more than one member of the Priesthood present. Unnerved, he flinched at first when she drew close to him but forced himself to sit still as her hand came to touch his forehead gently. Her other hand moving to rest over his chest where his heart was. Her lips turned up in a slight smile while her eyes closed. If she were not a priestess and he was not married faithfully to Cacht…but he quickly dismissed the thought from his mind.

"Be at peace, dear agent of change. There is still fight in you. The spirit of your future, the malevolent one who does prey upon you has not yet sapped so much from you that the man you are has begun to erode enough to weaken you to where it can take you over. Be sure in your judgements lest you give it strength unwittingly. I will do what I can to get that temple open for you to seek shelter in so that you may know more moments of peace," Fedelmid concluded before stepping back at an unnatural speed he would not have believed possible had he not witnessed it. Actual magic at work again, Mathghamhain wondered, or simply her having distracted him without his realizing it?

"Yes, I suppose, but it has been quite insistent that you are responsible for his death, *its* death. It insists that you killed it and you have demonstrated the power to do so. I cannot explain how else it would have been able to come back through time as it did…" Mathghamhain said a bit startled, still watching as she took a seat. He was half tempted to call for Donnchad to come in and decipher things but that would require explanations to him that he was not prepared to give any time soon.

"No wonder Cacht loves you so. So easily thrown off guard, yet you quickly recover and assert a level of composure and leadership, no matter how much you might have been fazed," she said. To Mathghamhain it sounded like she was trying her best not to sound like she pitied him "It is those who are quickest to adapt who thrive, dear Mathghamhain. You assume much but it is all right. Spirits are not your dominion of specialty and, in truth, they are not much mine."

When she paused in her words, he saw she had done so to lightly dab at her eyes. Mathghamhain, wanting to help, moved to stand but she waved her hand at him to sit as she resumed speaking.

"Worry not for me, dear Mathghamhain, simply something in the air stinging my eyes. Now then, as I was saying, my predecessor and other long-serving Priesthood members might be able to shed better light on this spirit but it is as such—whenever and whatever caused your death in the time yet to be—it was enough that it was felt through the memory of these lands. The lands have longer memories than us mortals," Fedelmid explained. "A spirit not at peace and seeking footing in lands in which it could not, then latched onto the nearest available place it could, even though it was in the past. Able to do so because it is the same spirit: like calling to like."

He sat there watching as she gestured throughout her explanation. She had not been putting off visiting Meadhan until last because of how important it was. No, it was clear now she had done so because of his situation with the spirit. She knew that talking with him about it was going to leave her emotionally exhausted.

"To make matters worse, Mathghamhain, your future self's spirit has undergone changes that yours has not, which prevents it from fully emerging, but as its malevolent nature grows and feasts on your spirit, your body weakens, as it cannot handle more than one spirit within it without consequences. This malevolent spirit advises you in matters that will weaken your own spirit so it can grow stronger. Some of these efforts are unavoidable as they align with your status as an agent of change," the priestess said wrapping up her explanation with a weary smile. "These are all things you have subconsciously recognized, which is why you have fought its advice at every turn, to try to find routes to the same goal by means that leave you less weakened."

The way the Priestess Fedelmid spoke and her openness about it—it was evident to him that she disliked greatly what he had to go through. The genuine concern was evident in her words, just as in the temple. If she was that way with everyone in Cridhe Aonaichte, he had no doubt she would win them over quickly. Mathghamhain wanted to live to see that day but with what she had said, how could he? To be told

despite whatever route he took, he would die. The only choice he really had was whether he lost everything in the process.

"Oh. I see. It is a hard thing I am afraid, dear priestess, to believe you are yourself the root of troubles and that there are only two ways out." he barely whispered, trying to blink back tears. There had to be another way. There had to be. "How can I be an agent of change for these lands, for my people, if I am left with either the choice of dying or letting an immoral version of myself take over my body? The latter would be in a sense even worse than death, as I would not know peace either if my spirit is destroyed."

"You are an agent of change, Mathghamhain. Look at what you have done already. Alliances. Unifying people. Piecing together the best parts of each village in your lands and making thing stronger and whole," Fedelmid replied softly "Those who oppose you? It is that they fear your way will be seen as better, that the old ways are over. Such changes would not have occurred on their own without a person brave enough, and wise enough, to bring them together, to push through the changes no matter what the cost. Your people are blessed to have you, Mathghamhain. Would that I knew precisely how this malevolent spirit was killed in the future, I could advise you better. Please know that with each decision you make that goes against its wishes, you do change what might be, and so its time might never be. We did discuss this aspect before."

Mathghamhain had been so caught up in the weight of what would happen that he had failed to notice she had left her seat again. She was moving towards him, and as she reached him her hands went to touch either side of his face.

"You have told me that the spirit claims I am responsible for your death," she said, her tone more guarded he thought than before. "I can help you only so much. As you said, there are but two possible outcomes and a day of reckoning is coming soon with this war. You take steps to secure your borders and a victory. Let me do one more thing to aid you."

Her hands pressed close against his cheeks, and they began to feel steadily warmer. Unsure as to what she was doing, he looked her in the eye. She was staring straight ahead, her lips moving as if she were speaking but there were no words he could hear. Everything around them seemed to blur as Mathghamhain blinked repeatedly, hoping it would help. He could not even lift his hands to pull hers away. What was she doing? Had she tricked him? Was this how he would die?

"Priestess...I do not know what, " Mathghamhain finally managed to say. His throat felt hoarse as he did so. Before he could continue, his movement was restored. Blinking again, he noted she was no longer directly in front of him but instead standing by her seat watching him. When had she moved? He felt tired but nothing else seemed to have changed. What had she done?

"It is for me to worry about, dear Mathghamhain, but it is an extra enchantment, as promised, one that connects us. I will sense it the moment you are in need of aid against the spirit. If I am to find a way to open that temple for you and still meet with everyone

　　　　　　　　　　DARYL J BALL

though I should proceed with meeting others…" she began to say slowly, her voice soft. "One more thing, Mathghamhain. No matter what else I said today, do please remember that you have accomplished all that you have by being yourself, not because a spirit directed your hand and not because the lands directed you either. It was because you had the mind, the body, and the spirit to make decisions when all the evidence was in front of you. That your fate—whichever way it goes—is in your hands, no one else's."

Once again she moved to approach him, this time leaning in close to plant a soft kiss on his forehead. Stepping back slightly before he could really react, Mathghamhain was still in somewhat of a daze from a few minutes earlier, when she dipped her head to make eye contact. It was the first time he had ever really looked this closely at them: He had known her eyes to be green before, but had never realized anyone could have them be such a bright shade of it.

"I am glad to have been chosen as the priestess for these lands, to know you and to be part of this great time of change. Be well, dear Mathghamhain," she said before pulling quickly from him.

"I do not fully understand this additional enchantment you have performed to aid me, priestess, but am grateful knowing you will be able to help almost immediately, should I need it. Thank you. I will do my best to bear your words in mind. Be sure to collect your tribute from Meadhan before you leave, I only wish that we had more to offer," Mathghamhain said slowly as Fedelmid moved to leave the room, her head turning as he spoke to look back over her shoulder, a warm smile on her lips again, the pity and concern having faded. There was a genuine warmth there in her smile that served to make him worry all the greater and yet, at the same time, feel reassured.

"I assure you, Mathghamhain. Your people and you have given me more than enough. I will find you when the temple is ready for you. Until then, make your decisions carefully but always remember who you are."

Those last words from her had scarcely left her lips before she turned to face the door and exit through it. Alone with his thoughts for the moment, Mathghamhain quickly pulled himself from his seat to get another drink. He needed to compose himself before his future self struck up the conversation again now that the priestess had gone. He was half-tempted to tell Seisyll to decree no more visitors for a while so that he could retire to the bedroom to rest and clear his head, to prolong the spirit's absence. It was a temptation to be certain, Mathghamhain thought, but he had a responsibility and, with that in mind, he drew his sword. The spirit had not spoken yet and now it would be at bay longer.

FIVE

CHAPTER 38

The fighting was fierce. The enemy had finally moved as one to attack Cridhe Aonaichte, not a thing Mathghamhain had expected them to be able to coordinate with so many different villages involved over such a vast distance, but it had come.

Caiside's advance scouts had done a good job of keeping the Warriors Guild Reeve and he appraised of the enemy's movement, with more warriors dispatched to defend where the greatest number of the enemy would come across their borders. With the enemy attacking them on nearly all sides, it was proving significantly harder to defend against them.

It had been a mere two months after Mathghamhain had met with the Priestess Fedelmid. In addition to preparing defences, it had been a vast and busy time. His future self's spirit had been taking delight in bothering him and calling for blood at every available turn, to the point that he had taken to walking around full time with his sword drawn. Now Mathghamhain had no need to make excuses for having it in his hand, not with the fighting taking place.

Caidreach, primarily through Caderyn's warriors, had moved hastily after their alliance had been formalized to help both of their lands' warriors be as armoured as possible including any horses they had.

In order to centralize the command and protect it, unless he was on the battlefield himself, Mathghamhain had taken to giving orders from the temple, located near Thabhairt, that Fedelmid had finally unlocked for him. He had moved into it merely two days before the fighting had broken out.

"Would that we had that storm from the day of the trial now, it would allow us time to rest while the enemy tried to contend with it. I still cannot get over how busy you have been. This place is magnificent in its architecture," Cacht was saying as she, not for the first time, extolled upon the size of the temple the priestess had acquired for their use at his request. "Would that we had enough time to stock it and fully explore it, we might be able to give our people shelter for a time. Time to train and recover and then arise from the ground to attack the enemy anew."

Cacht and Nuallan had arrived home a week ago, with not only a good number of horses but had brought several warriors with them as well from their newly forged alliance across the sea. They were warriors Mathghamhain did not know and more were said to be on their way but right now they were helping Caderyn in protecting Cridhe Aonaichte's southern border. It allowed Mathghamhain's own warriors to focus on the western border and the much longer northern one.

No, thought Mathghamhain, not merely his warriors. There were also his hunters, his farmers, anyone capable of holding a shield and any sort of weapon. Caidreach had been diligent the past month in in-

struction as the preparation had been made to pass on the knowledge of attacking effectively from a distance using bow and arrow. It was a technique Mathghamhain had not seen used in practice before but knew its advantages and had little doubt his enemies would know it as well. In order to best utilize the people available, Mathghamhain had chosen for it to be the technique learned by the women so they could aid in attacks and defence, while also safeguarding the children.

For their part, the children, those of age anyway, were all too eager to prepare other ranged weaponry with the help of the Educators Guild. To fling projectiles at great speed and height using what Donnchad called a catapult. Defences had been tightened as much as they could ever be. Everyone was armed but whether it would be enough had yet to be seen.

He had to agree with Cacht's words about the temple though. This temple was not quite the same layout as Fedelmid's but there were striking similarities Mathghamhain had noticed, such as the ornate columns and the central atrium. After that, it seemed to differ but he could not be fully certain in what ways, considering he had been down a sole corridor at that other temple.

"We would simply emerge to lands conquered and an enemy waiting for us with only this place left to flee to if we were attacked. The moment they knew where it was, they would attack it to no end. We are underground, as hard as that is to believe at times, and therefore, can be trapped," Mathghamhain said frowning but quickly let out a heavy sigh.

Even with Cacht's reassuring hand close by again, still he paced. This was no mere battle they faced. This time it was as if their way for the future, which had proven so effective, was itself under siege as the enemy pushed harder and harder to advance further inland. All while his warriors, his villagers, did everything they could to contain, reroute, slow the advance, or outright kill the enemy on sight. It was as Fedelmid had called it—it was a war.

The enemy comprised nearly all of the villages near Cridhe Aonaichte's borders and had clearly prepared more warriors than the scouts had made note of and greater than Mathghamhain had even thought possible. It was still several different villages trying to co-ordinate efforts though. He merely had to hold them off until that lack of core leadership proved their undoing. Despite his and Cacht's hope over the years that their decision to cease any further expansion would put the minds of those other villages at ease, that had not proven to be the case and no messages to reassure them had made a difference. Right now, it was a war of holding. An attempt to cling hard to what Mathghamhain knew. Every day of fighting bringing new word of how many had fallen and he did not need to be there to know how red the land was becoming, stained with the blood of those who had fallen on both sides.

"How long since we have received word on how any of the fighting goes?" Mathghamhain asked after far too much time thinking about the current situation. As he did so he stepped behind Cacht, encircling her waist within his arms. He felt her tilt her head back to lay against his shoulder as she looked up at him.

"It has not been more than a few moments, I would wager, since last you asked. You need to stay focused, my brave and wise husband. Pacing and dwelling will not be what wins this day. You must be focussed on devising a strategy besides trying to hold our ground," Cacht said before moving her head enough to kiss his cheek before she broke free of his embrace. "We should start moving children from the more nearby villages down here as able."

"Indeed. The younger ones especially. It will need to be done under the cover of the night with accompaniment on horseback. A village at a time. Maybe move them from one village to the next, rotate them slowly here and alternate which village we move them from here into in order not to make it obvious. Who knows where the enemy does have eyes at this point. I tell you, Cacht, if I ever do learn there were indeed other traitors amongst our people, they will not be given the mercy of a trial," Mathghamhain said growing angry.

"Understandable but that is a thing to consider another time, Mathghamhain. Let us concentrate on surviving this and turning them back, of making this enemy think twice about their attacks, to the point they retreat so that we can rebuild. With enough time, we can overrun them. We simply need the time to rebuild first. We have alliances now. Good strong allies. One to the south and one across the water to the east. We can overcome all adversity as we have shown.

This is what we have spent the past years preparing for, it is this attack from the north and we could not have prepared better. We can and will triumph," Cacht said reassuringly although Mathghamhain had no doubt that she was as worried as he was.

"Yes, we will. Whatever would I do without you, Cacht, to put things in perspective and keep me grounded," Mathghamhain said smiling while moving to the entrance. His ears had caught the faint sound of steps above ground. It was a sound the Priestess Fedelmid had taught him to listen for and to identify so he knew if it were friend or foe, where to stand to hear what was said above the surface best. That had been an arduous first day of her teaching.

"For one, I suspect you would forget to bathe and likely eat and drink more than you should. Those come to my mind first. This past while apart from you was not easy on either of us but you at least had the benefit of staying on land with people you knew. I am unsure about you but travelling over water for more than a day with several horses causing a ruckus is most assuredly not a way to keep one calm when they are apart from their husband and people," Cacht said following him.

"We have word! We have word!" he called to Cacht before he paused and waited until the sounds ceased for a good several minutes. He rotated the last piece of land from below that went to the surface. It was an arranged spot that blended in with the land above but was big enough to put an arm through. Normally it was meant so someone could open the hatch next to it but right now it was used for a drop point. As soon as

the piece of land was moved, Mathghamhain was able to catch the piece of parchment that fell through the opening with his free hand. Holding it carefully, he re-secured the small opening.

"I know," Mathghamhain continued in response to her words a moment earlier as he carefully unrolled the piece of parchment, "and were there had been any other way, many of our people have already told you how difficult I had been to deal with, without you present. As for this report, let us see."

Scanning it, Mathghamhain worked to decipher its short and hastily written words. Oftentimes it was two numbers and an indication of where it referred to. Other times, like this one, it was more than that, with pertinent details included. In this case, it was most definitely not good news. A shiver ran through his body as he passed the paper to Cacht and quickly moved to hold her while she read it.

"So I did hear," Cacht whispered quietly as she was given the parchment herself.

Scanning the contents, she seemed to quickly realize all too well why he had reacted as he had, her body shaking only slightly less than his had. While forces had fought along the border, a contingent of the enemy's warriors had been elsewhere—Crioch had been completely run through. Anyone within its walls had been killed and the village had been all but razed to the ground. Those responsible had been killed in turn when they were caught but it was a devastating loss of people.

"They do not fight fair, Mathghamhain! They seek solely to hurt us as much as possible. This is no war, they seek only to kill. To kill and hurt us. There was no need for them to do that. Why would they do that…" Cacht said as she passed the parchment back to Mathghamhain, her voice shaking.

"Because they are not men, Cacht. They are cowards and know they cannot beat us in proper battle so they strike at our hearts, killing those who are no real threat. They will pay for this, oh they will pay. Quickly, I have need to send a message…" Mathghamhain said, his voice quivering with rage.

"And who would deliver it? We are both needed here," Cacht said in slow response, her eyes still glazed over. He knew it would fade soon enough, replaced by rage at the enemy for this act.

"I will go. We will both go. Our people were needlessly and barbarically killed. My blade hungers for the enemy's blood as much as does yours. They thought to strike at our people through its heart. They have roused a sleeping beast! We will go forth and rally our people, lead by example…" Mathghamhain said as he found the parchment he was looking for and wrote as carefully as he could, the same message several times on different pieces before binding them individually. "We will move from group of warriors to group and deliver this message to each. I will stay to aid them for now while you proceed to the next group. Trained as you are, a battlefield such as this one is not the place to put your lessons to the test. We will circle through each village, no matter how long it takes, on the way back to bolster the spirits and deliver the same message. The enemy will regret their actions."

"Time to break out the full armour then, not just the chest plate, I do take it," Cacht replied nodding her head at him before returning to where they had stored their belongings.

Watching as she departed, Mathghamhain was positive she would fight him over his not wishing her to take part in the battle. He had meant what he had said. She was trained, but in combat such as this, the risk was too great. The full armour would help protect her but she would need to keep moving. Putting the parchment she had prepared to one side, he sighed. They could cover more ground if they went in opposite directions but the thought of doing so? He wished she could stay here where she would be safe. He wished everyone could be safe. They had sought to make a better life for everyone but now the enemy seemed determined to take it all away. He was all but helpless here tucked away but his Reeves had insisted on it as he was needed to survive and lead when this was over. Mathghamhain wanted desperately to be out there in the field of battle, directing it. Caiside and Nuallan were capable leaders but it felt wrong not to be there. Soon, when they rode out there to deliver these messages, he would aid in combat as much as he could at each location, and the enemy would regret the day they had harmed his people.

CHAPTER 39

Mathghamhain looked down at the warrior he had knocked down with his shield. They had been trying to sneak up on him. As they moved to get up, Mathghamhain lashed out quickly, slicing the man in the chin with his metal boot, watching him fall unconscious. Turning his steed around, he drove his blade downwards rapidly through the fallen warrior's neck, ignoring the blood that spurted before he and his steed stepped around them and proceeded further into the battlefield. It was the third such group of their own warriors they had come to, or more accurately, that he had come to. Cacht and he had split off from each other after arriving at the first group with her heading to the nearby village and then making her way through groups along the battle lines until she caught up with him again.

"I had forgotten how much you tended to revel in making sure your foe was dead in battle, my brave and wise Chieftain," Caiside spoke from not far to his left. Ah, so that was whose group he had reached. The older warrior looked like he had seen a great deal of killing already that day, as had most of the warriors Mathghamhain had seen. Not only was the land running red but the armour was becoming so stained with blood, grime, and grass, it was getting hard to tell each other apart. "Dare I ask what brings you all the way out here to the front lines, my Chieftain? I did think you were coordinating from a more central location."

"Indeed I would be, had word not reached us that this enemy did burn down Crioch, after killing everyone inside it. A barbaric act and unnecessary. Mighty they may be as foes but they have proven themselves cowards by their actions," Mathghamhain said turning his steed gradually so he could run through an approaching foe.

"Cowards is, indeed, the word then! I take it you did not come out simply to tell me this news. You are too much a strategist for that to be the case: to put yourself in the place of a messenger when so many in Cridhe Aonaichte need your guidance now," Caiside called after him before Mathghamhain could ride away.

"Indeed. I must get going to the others but am being a messenger as it were, albeit one who has a plan. The enemy are not the only ones who can seek to strike through the heart," Mathghamhain nodded putting himself in a spot where Caiside's position served to shield him while he retrieved one of the prepared messages and handed it to the reeve. "Read it. Pass the word to who needs to know and fight on mighty Caiside. We may yet win this war if our men keep to the formations we have perfected over the years."

Nodding at Caiside as he finished, Mathghamhain pulled away finally. The warriors knew how to improvise. The formations he had spoken of were, in fact, a series they rotated through as a battle progressed, and never in the same order. Catching a sight in the distance, Mathghamhain grinned. It was an easily recognizable one although he had only seen them once before in full armour. Yet there was no mistaking it was a woman who was riding on a steed and cutting a swath through any who got in her way.

"Good, I will see to it we carry out your plan to the letter," Caiside nodded, pocketing the message in his boot. Mathghamhain heard his reeve clearly still, which meant the reeve had moved to catch up with him. Likely because he had stopped again and gone silent. "I am to take it then that your other half is the one making my warriors look like they are slacking with how effortlessly she runs through the foes that have afforded them such trouble? Surely you did find a unique woman when you did marry her, Mathgham-hain. I cannot think there can possibly be a woman more worthy of a warrior such as yourself than one who is equally as deadly as she is wise."

"Indeed, she makes myself look weak by compar-ison. Happy was the day I did learn she could handle a blade were it not that I had been the one on the re-ceiving end of much of her initial practice sessions while she learned to control the weight. I do believe I still have bruises. Still, this is no place for her, she is not used to actual combat, especially in a group," Math-ghamhain sighed ever so lightly before nodding at his reeve and heading to meet up with Cacht. Math-ghamhain needed to be sure she knew he had already visited this group of warriors and they could resume heading south together. The sooner he got her away from this battle the better.

The sudden sight of her horse going down caused time to slow to a crawl. It was falling for what seemed like an eternity Mathghamhain found as he charged forward. His sword swinging while his people fought around him, the air was so still and eerily calm, he thought, as every beat of his steed's hooves on the ground below was a hammer in his brain and matched his heartbeat. He could not even hear himself as he screamed her name.

Upon Cacht's shouting of his name in return, Mathghamhain was able to bring his steed to a stop, dismounting and running to her side, hacking through those who had felled her steed. They had cut at its legs and Mathghamhain showed them no mercy or time to defend themselves. His sword gutting them, anger flashing through his eyes until he had his back to Cacht while she steadied herself. Her sword drawn, face dirty from the fall, blood on her armour from the fighting so far, her shield up as he had taught her from day one, and her blade held at precisely the right height as Caiside and so many other warriors had taught her in countless sparring sessions. She was watching all sides and shifting her weight for wherever her attacks were needed, taught repeatedly to her by Nuallan from the day the man had pledged his allegiance to them both as Chieftains.

"We shall best them, Cacht my love…" Mathghamhain whispered feeling his back press to hers as he directed her by movement to help make her way towards where he had stopped his steed. A horse that, in itself, was protected by his own warriors as of the moment Caiside had registered what was happening and ordered it so. Their efforts toward the enemy doubling in their ferocity. The message all too clear by their actions, they would fight the enemy, but if that enemy tried to kill their Chieftains, they would fight all the harder.

"Indeed we shall, my heart, indeed we shall. Can your steed carry us both?" Cacht hissed over her shoulder at him. Blocking narrowly the warrior who had lunged towards her, Cacht summarily cut their throat deeply with an angry swing of her sword.

"It cannot if we wish to move fast but it will carry you and I will walk until I can borrow another and catch up. You must be kept safe, my love, my other half, always. Without you, I am lost," Mathghamhain said in a quick whisper, his back to her, keeping his words short between breaths. The noise of battle made it impossible to hear as it was without screaming.

"You know I will go nowhere. We are as one," Cacht said in response as they reached his steed, Mathghamhain shifting his weight and position to serve along with those shielding the horse to protect her while she mounted it quickly. Would that he had a spear on him, Mathghamhain thought, when he heard the whistling sound through the air and his eyes moved to try and pinpoint the source. He knew too well the sound from practice this past while.

"Cacht! Get down!" Mathghamhain screamed as he heard more of the sound. The world slowing to a crawl again as he had to move suddenly to defend as a warrior attacked him in his distracted state. Bashing the attacker's face in with his shield and killing him as quickly as possible, Mathghamhain's eyes flashed with anger.

The sharp sound of her body falling behind him caused Mathghamhain to wheel around rapidly and drop to his knees using his armour to shield himself and his wife as his warriors closed ranks to protect them. His steed ducked its head down as well to nip at him and Cacht.

She had been struck, caught by several arrows, most of which had been deflected by armour but a few had pierced her skin quite deeply. Mathghamhain could feel her blood running over his hands as he cradled her in his arms. The tears threatening to overwhelm him despite being in the midst of a battle.

"Cacht...courageous and wise and lovely and sweet...My heart, hang on please...hang on. It will be all right..." Mathghamhain said doing his best not to sob as he laid his head on her chest, nuzzling her head as he held her. It was not right. She was armoured, she was protected. She had been safe, they had been about to get away. They were as one. This could not be real; it was a nightmare in his head. It had to be.

"Mathghamhain...my...Mathghamhain...it hurts to breathe. I cannot...it is so cold. Do not leave me, my love..." Cacht barely managed as her body tensed and relaxed several times as she fought to breathe great gulps of air. He could feel her heartbeat slowing as he knelt there holding her, not sure what to do, how to be, not wanting to move.

"I would never leave you, Cacht. My sweet darling Cacht, I would never...we are as one. Please hang on...I am here. Please, Cacht darling, hold on. I beg of you," Mathghamhain sobbed and by now he was positive he could no longer hear fighting around him.

There was no sound of metal hitting metal, no sound of bodies hitting the blood-stained ground.

Nothing but the slowing rate of Cacht's heart and her fading breath. Cradling her still as he moved to kiss her one last time before closing her eyes for her as gently as he could. He stayed there holding her until she had faded away completely and for a good several moments longer. Nothing mattered anymore.

Caiside

Mathghamhain would likely have stayed there until he died of old age, Caiside thought as he lay a hand on his chieftain's shoulder. The man's horse tried as well to get the chieftain's attention by nipping at him again until finally between the two of them they got Mathghamhain's attention. The chieftain's head slowly lifted to regard him, blinking twice. Now that Caiside had his attention, the reeve signalled with his free hand as his warriors moved in to surround them more closely.

"She is gone, my Chieftain. We killed them all for her, for you. This battle here is over. We can accompany you for protection to bring her body home if you wish, old friend," Caiside's voice trembled as he spoke. She had been the last of his family and his chieftain. To pretend her death was not affecting him as well would be lying to everyone. He had little doubt that, if any of the others present attempted to speak, it would be much the same. Cacht had been their chieftain. The strain on all of their faces was clear, as were the tears.

"Thank you…she and I remain as one. Our hearts are forever bound. While I live, she lives, and we, we desire that you do show these monsters no mercy. You

will send word. The messages we delivered are no longer sufficient. Give word, Caiside. March upon the enemy's lands. Burn them. Condemn them to the blazes for what they have done this day…for every day she has been robbed of! For the children we shall never have now, for every child they killed in their cowardice. For every one of our people they have taken, we will enact a vengeance a hundred times worse. We will show them what it means to take from us our entire world," the Chieftain shouted, his voice overtaken by anger and sorrow.

"I understand and obey, my Chieftain," Caiside said sadly while he moved to command his warriors. Helping Mathghamhain's steed to stay steady on the ground while his Chieftain mounted the horse slowly, one foot over its side and still holding Cacht's lifeless body. His warriors quickly stripped Cacht's fallen steed of its armour and secured it to the back of Caiside's horse. Once all was secure, Caiside mounted his own steed, making sure everything was still secured and took partial reins as he moved to have it walk perfectly alongside Mathghamhain's horse so that the man, the grieving Chieftain who had united villages and lands, could focus on keeping his wife's body still.

Two additional warriors accompanied them on foot for protection as they followed, an extremely slow-moving procession all the way back to Meadhan. Those warriors who remained behind taking their last set of orders to heart and with sorrow and anger over the loss of one of their chieftains, a woman who had proven her equal of any warrior in the guild, tramped forward gathering bush and dry wood and leaves to set ablaze the land on the other side of them and fan those flames so it spread like wildfire. A wind slowly building as they did so, first a breeze, and then a strong enough wind to send the flames washing over the enemy's lands rapidly.

It was unexpected but it definitely helped spread the destruction Mathghamhain had called for, Caiside thought. Considering the nature of it, he could not help but wonder if the Priestess Fedelmid was not already aware somehow of what had happened and had reacted best she could from a distance.

The slow trickle of rain two days later began as Meadhan came into view for the weary procession and the sight of who approached it had those within its walls rushing to open the gates to help them inside. Terror and grief-stricken faces quickly spreading as the gravity of what had happened reached them. Caiside's and Mathghamhain's horses entering the village slowly side by side.

It was still unclear if Mathghamhain himself was even alive at that point, the man had not budged since the procession had started out, not even to eat or drink. Those inside were rushing to help the warriors and Caiside ease their chieftain in disembarking from the horse as the chieftain finally looked around. Every footstep Caiside watched him take: It was as if the man was encumbered by the deepest of mud, the movements were so slow. Heads hung low as the warriors escorted those wanting to reach out and help ease Mathghamhain's burden but it was as if the man could not see them, Caiside thought.

Donnchad's eyes were welling up when he looked at his fellow reeve. The Educators Guild Reeve moved out of the way to open the door of the building that until recently had served as the seat of power for Cridhe Aonaichte until the two chieftains had moved to the temple. Once Mathghamhain had gone inside, Caiside stepped inside with Donnchad accompanying him. The others could wait outside.

Watching quietly, Caiside saw Mathghamhain head for what had once been the chieftain's private bedroom, no doubt to set Cacht's lifeless body down on the bed they had once shared. He and his fellow reeve kept their heads bowed waiting for their chieftain to emerge and speak on what he wanted to do. Caiside knew Mathghamhain wanted them to keep fighting but this death, one so close to the chieftain's heart had already robbed him of all vitality and strength, as if forced to keep going. Finally, after several minutes of silence, the chieftain emerged from the room and slowly looked in their direction.

"We take the fight to them. We leave none of them alive. We kill every single last one of them. They have taken away my heart, my light, my all. They shall pay for it in blood until their lands are so soaked in it that they can never again grow anything and then we will burn it all," Mathghamhain said in an angry roar, before slumping to the floor sobbing again. "We were as one…she cannot be gone, my wise, my courageous, my lovely Cacht…"

Exchanging a glance with Donnchad, Caiside noted his fellow reeve seemed to agree, given the look on his face: the Chieftain's mood was alternating rapidly between unbridled rage against the enemy and paralyzing grief.

"We will see it done, Chieftain. Not merely for her, not merely for you, but for all our people. We will see your word carried out," Caiside whispered looking worriedly at Mathghamhain before moving closer. Holding a hand out, he helped his chieftain to his feet again."Come, let us get food into you. She would want you to take care of yourself. You need to live for both of you now."

"We are as one…we *were* as one. How can I carry on without her, Caiside?" Mathghamhain cried, looking to the older warrior, tears staining his cheeks. "She was the balance, the one who made all things possible, the one who raised me up. My heart, my life, my love, my light, and it has now gone out, there is naught but darkness."

If there was a spirit guiding the Chieftain, Caiside thought, where was it now when surely the man could use advice the most?

CHAPTER 40

"Nuallan!" Caiside shouted over the clanging of sword on armour, "Please tell me this day that you have seen our brave and grieving Chieftain. He is sorely needed to motivate the people if we are to triumph."

A few days had passed since they had burned the surrounding lands where the enemy's land touched theirs and those flames had been put out the night

before by a growing rainstorm in the north. Having witnessed the full wrath of a storm already when fuelled by the rage of a priestess, Caiside would not have put it beyond the realm of possibility that this storm in the north was the work of a member of the Priesthood in the enemy's lands acting to contain the damage that the Priestess Fedelmid may have caused on their side, perhaps several of them. Either way, it had meant the fighting had resumed. This time the enemy was more contained, the fire having kept them from being too spread out.

With the time to gather and marshal their forces themselves, he and Nuallan had worked hard to position everyone they had who could raise a sword to force the enemy to cross in a spot they could fully contain the battle at instead of letting them run rampant. It could be felt in the hearts and minds of many of them that after the last several battles, it was the battle this day, this last thrust of effort by the enemy against their weakened forces, that would decide a victor.

"Alas, I have not yet seen him today," Nuallan answered over the din, "but in truth he has not been seen since two days ago when we did hold a full funeral for our departed Chieftain, a woman to whom I had pledged my life, and yet, I was not present when she was killed by these cowards."

Nuallan's eyes looked far too dark and heavy today, Caiside thought, despite the days they had recently had to rest and regroup. His second-in-command was taking Cacht's death extremely hard. Turning as he was able, Caiside caught the rest of what Nuallan was saying.

"Were I in my Chieftain and liege Mathghamhain's place, I, too, would want to be nowhere near such a man as myself lest I be tempted to blame him for not holding up his promise," his second-in-command was saying. The man was far too hard on himself and Caiside needed Nuallan to focus on the task at hand.

"You cannot blame yourself, Nuallan. You served as her protector when you were needed most, being Mathghamhain's shield when he was not there, as you both did journey far across the water to gather new allies and horses," Caiside responded sharply, trying to help the man put aside the feelings of guilt he was having. Noting movement out of the corner of his eye, Caiside shouted quickly to his second-in-command. "On your left, Nuallan! They have broken through."

"I do see it. This battle yet rages on. I can but hope our allies in Caidreach have been able to hold their own so that we need not worry about that border as well," Nuallan shouted back, turning sharply and chopping low to take out the legs of his approaching foe.

His second-in-command would see that the enemy would pay for everything now that he was focussed again, Caiside realized. It had been years since Nuallan had been brought into the guild from Nabaidh by Mathghamhain. The man had been accepted in time as their own, with personal loyalty to the chieftains as well. Shaking his head, Caiside concentrated on the enemy in front of him. Nuallan's anger over not being present to protect Cacht did not need placating: it would drive the man to take it out on the enemy until there was none left. He understood that guilt and when the time came, he hoped he could get his second-in-command to lower his blade, lest Nuallan become as driven as Brennus had been—unable to stop seeking a fight.

The sky slowly began to rumble the longer the battle continued on, with fighters falling on both sides. Arms growing heavy on all sides, Caiside was certain, in a battle that seemed to have no end, the enemy was putting their all into this just as Mathghamhain and the late Cacht had put into defences. After the way she had been killed, few in Cridhe Aonaichte wanted to carry on using bows and arrows, so adaptations had been made. The women willing to fight had stayed in the villages to defend them, while others who were not quite able to do so fled with the younger children to the safety of the temple near Thabhairt. The temple where, even now, Mathghamhain had sequestered himself away to brood. It had been one of the final decisions the Chieftain and Cacht had made together and it had been carried out under the directions of the other reeves even in the wake of her demise. The only question Caiside still really had was when they would receive further orders from their Chieftain about dealing with an enemy who was determined to destroy everything they had worked to build.

Disarming another foe, Caiside slit their throat quickly. The Priestess Fedelmid had appeared briefly from wherever she was hidden away, to say the words of blessing at Cacht's funeral and to sit with Mathghamhain for many hours in silence both before and afterward. Caiside had stopped by to check on his chieftain, his sole remaining family, only to see the priestess seated silently beside Mathghamhain with her hand placed over his. The man had looked up once in a while, anger flashing in his eyes, sometimes vocalized and directed at her before quickly fading way to sorrow and grief again within a few moments. Others who had stopped by to check on the chieftain had reported seeing much the same and that had lasted until Fedelmid and the reeves had helped get the chieftain back to the temple. A great number of the women and children were now at it or on their way, guarded as they travelled by members of the Educators Guild.

Falling back with his warriors slightly to allow them to form up again, Caiside smiled lightly. Things were looking well but the day was not over yet. As he directed the charge, he thought back to when the Priestess had last been seen. It had been when she had let go of Mathghamhain's hand at the entrance of the temple following his being escorted there. Presumably, she had headed off to her own temple at that point. Like himself, as revealed in overheard conversations, many saw her presence through the initial days of grieving at Mathghamhain's side as a sign that she sought to help his mind be at peace even if the chieftain did seem to be physically still struggling. It had served to endear her in their hearts. She was their priestess, not just a member of the Priesthood; the people of Cridhe Aonaichte had come first. It was a comforting thought despite how dangerous she could be. She had been there to catch the fall of the man who had united them when the Chieftain was in his most dire time of need, doing what none of the rest of

them could do in letting Mathghamhain start to mend.

Even now, Caiside had a lingering hope that with the rain that had come to the enemy's land to put out the fires, she might reappear to counteract it. The thought of two members of the Priesthood, or more, possibly fighting against each other was a hard thing to believe possible and yet there were people right now who he knew sorely wished it would be the case. Their Priestess, that was how Caiside had heard her referred to as of late. The People's Priestess. If they got through this, Caiside had no doubt that was how she would be known forevermore, especially if signs indeed came of Mathghamhain truly having re-covered, even if it was only long enough to take command of their war efforts again.

"He comes!" a shout came from far back in the battle ranks, startling Caiside from his thoughts on the past few days. He had been a warrior for more than half his life, and that experience had kept him alive when his thoughts drifted during battle. Thinking about anything other than fighting steadied him more than it detracted from his ability in battle. Quickly stabbing the foe in front of him, Caiside looked over his shoulder from the back of his horse. So far its armour had kept it from falling but as had been proven already recently, their steeds' legs were still exposed enough so they had to still actively work to protect those. His lips formed into a wide grin as he saw the figure galloping at full speed towards the battlefield from out of the distance. Raising his sword high, Caiside turned back around to signal the rest of the warriors.

"He comes! The Bear! He comes!" he shouted as the rallying shout was taken up by the rest of the warriors and soon afterwards by those who had donned make-shift armour, sword, and shield to fight as well. These amounted to farmers, caretakers, boys who could hold a sword, educators who were able to provide strategy quickly and use shields to defend others, and metal workers so heavily armoured and strong from their work that they could wield their large hammers in battle. All of them noting the rallying cry and taking it up as the efforts of fighting doubled then tripled, a greater push put on to strike down the enemy. Caiside hoped his chieftain realized the inspiration his presence had just brought. It would be now. This would be it.

Mathghamhain had arrived, armoured, and determination in his dark eyes, the Chieftain's sword drawn while riding hard towards them. The man was shouting orders as he drew closer, Caiside noted. A wave of worry and fear could be seen on the enemy's faces, those who were close enough to behold the sight of a man enraged and ready to kill coming at them. Caiside hoped his chieftain was indeed ready to live up to expectations today.

Mathghamhain no longer wore the ceremonial armour but looked to have stripped away the ornate parts of it and made adjustments to make the armour stronger and thicker. It had a less refined look to it, darker in a way for the lack of shine. Mathghamhain had a sword in hand and another could be seen strapped on his back, its hilt visible above the shoulder. His chieftain's shield was lowered and trimmed with

leather hide to give it greater support, heavy gauntlets extending halfway up the forearms, metal protecting the elbows held there by leather straps, it looked like. Mathghamhain's boots were longer than most, going to the knee with leather protecting the knees themselves. The simple helmet that covered much of the chieftain's head gave him a look, when combined with everything else, of much less of a man than it was a metal beast the size of a bear in truth, like his namesake. That thought made Caiside chuckle under his breath. It was likely Mathghamhain had cultivated that look on purpose for this exact effect. Two spears strapped to either side of the chieftain's steed looked to be heavily secured by leather to its armour but in such a way that made the steed itself more of a weapon than usual if it came charging at a foe.

Their chieftain had clearly been busy while grieving. Mathghamhain had no experience as a metal worker, of that Caiside was positive. Still, the man had found time to do all of this. No doubt it had helped to keep his chieftain's anger powerfully focused on what were surely sleepless nights. As Mathghamhain's steed galloped onwards past him, Caiside moved out of the way, watching as the chieftain roared with sword in the air.

"Death to the enemy. For all those they have taken from us, let them know our rage! Let them know our heart, that we will not ever succumb to them. We will not fall, we will not know defeat, that this day is their last!" Mathghamhain's angry words came. There was fury in those eyes. Caiside was certain of it.

Taking in the sight of how the battle had changed

with his chieftain's arrival, he was gladdened. His warriors knew enough to get out of the way. No one would want to risk getting between Mathghamhain and whoever the chieftain's target was at the time. None of the enemy would leave here alive. Not ever again. Not with the mood Mathghamhain was in and certainly not with the rush of renewed determination on their side that the chieftain's presence had brought. Caiside watched as the enemy either stood their ground in the face of the redoubled efforts or did their best to flee, a thing he doubted Mathghamhain would allow.

Caiside could not help but feel encouraged himself by the push Mathghamhain's presence had brought. Truth be told he missed fighting alongside the man. It was unfortunate that the chance to do so had come at such a cost. The chieftain's rage and anger coupled with the imposing appearance were proving itself enough to make many of the enemy wary. All the better, Caiside thought, it meant he and those with him on the battlefield would have an easier time cutting the enemy down. The sooner they killed all of them the better. Mathghamhain no doubt still needed additional time to recover, and seemed not to care for his own well-being.

Taking command back of the situation while his chieftain continued his aggressive assault, Caiside directed those fighting to treat the enemy as the baseless cowards their actions had proven them to be since this war had begun. The end was here.

Chapter 41
Mathghamhain

Mathghamhain had lost track of how many of his people had fallen since he had joined the battle, nor was he really trying to, his focus solely on the enemy being killed. Every last single one of them. He was well aware that he was fuelled by anger and grief solely to keep him alert. It also meant he could not allow himself to grow tired and lose that rage. He could feel it dissipating even now and so began galloping towards the back of the battlefield in order to buy himself time. He needed to give in fully, to let the battle fuel him, not drain him, but to do that meant he needed even more anger to push himself.

As much as Mathghamhain knew it would likely serve as a problem, there was little doubt in his mind that the spirit of his future self calling for blood in his ear would push him to the level he needed now to ensure victory. He had kept it silent for several days now, between having his blade drawn, being at the temple, and it being wise enough to not speak when Cacht had been murdered, followed then by the Priestess Fedelmid's presence keeping it at bay. Now he needed that motivating anger though that com-bined with his rage over Cacht's death and his people being killed out of fear by the enemy. He needed it to push himself hard enough to finish this battle, by himself if necessary. It might prove to be the last battle he ever fought if what he recalled of what Fedelmid had said proved true about it feeding off of his spirit to grow in strength.

To protect his people, to avenge them, to give them peace, it was needed. Taking his usual sword after giving it a quick wipe with his cloak, now tattered from battle, Mathghamhain sheathed it and drew the other one he had strapped to his back. His claymore, with its wider longer blade and heavier weight, when swung properly, could cause damage to all but the heaviest of armour that was present and he would have the strength to do so now. The sudden chill in the air did precisely what he needed it to.

"About time you fool! Did I not tell you that you should not have wed that woman? That she would desert you, that she would cost you dearly? Now, look at where we are. She is gone and your people are in disarray. They fight for their lives and what are you going to do?" the spirit of his future self hissed the second he had switched blades. A conniving grin crossed Mathghamhain's lips when he heard it.

"I am ignoring you. You also said the Priestess Fedelmid would kill us and yet she is not here now, is she? Therefore, we ride forth once again to kill the enemy, knowing we will triumph. For you need me to do so and so you will ensure we do," he growled, not caring who heard him. Let them think him mad in his grief and consumed by battle and bloodlust. Let them know fear, the enemy would all soon be dead. As dead as he felt inside without Cacht.

"You say you ignore me and yet you are the one who did give me the freedom to speak! Do you think I want this? This is not us. We were a hunter! We

sought power to lead, to be more. To guide, to lead! This is a war in which you could die! Everything I helped you build for us, it all stands at risk of being destroyed and now you think you can ignore me? Nuallan has yet to betray you, yet he will. He will steal your rule from you when this is over. Caiside will desert you for he will think you mad and seek to save his people by killing you himself. The priestess is merely biding her time. Mark my words, she will bring death to us," the spirit hissed again as Mathghamhain let its words fuel him. Riding back into battle, he brought his claymore down hard on the first foe he saw, watching them go down in a heap before his steed trampled over the fallen warrior.

His people were steadily starting to drop back tired, worn, and badly injured but still, they were doing their best to press onward. They were following his lead as he proceeded to cut a swath through the enemy, showing no quarter. He was giving up no ground as he and his people helped drive the enemy back closer and closer to the border. He was surprised he could hear Caiside and Nuallan over the noise. Were there fewer combatants left than he believed?

"Our Chieftain arrived with anger, now he fights as though he were a man possessed," Caiside could be heard uttering. That was followed by the clear sound of a sword connecting with a shield. From the sound of it, the reeve was fairly nearby.

"There is a saying you hear further north," Nuallan could be heard responding. "Our priestess can likely confirm…"

"Switch!" Caiside had responded.

"It is the term for when battle fervour takes fully hold," Nuallan continued. Obviously, the two men had needed to switch who they were fighting based on Caiside's comment. Nuallan had obviously said something in between that he had missed, Mathghamhain just had no idea what it could have been.

The exchange made him wonder somewhat as he watched another of the enemy fall. How much had he become like his namesake? The enemy was still trying to escape, he noticed, as he pursued them along with other warriors. This fight would not end, not until the enemy was fully routed and not a moment before. No matter how much he ached.

"They mock you, brave Mathghamhain, do you not hear your own warriors? Your so-called faithful servant Nuallan does call you mad and consumed by the lust for battle and blood. Your reeve Caiside does fear that you be possessed," the spirit said with laughter. He had forgotten the spirit was even present for a moment, caught up in the battle at hand.

"Be silent!!" Mathghamhain hissed back as his sword ran through another of the enemy. He could feel his anger growing still, the spirit was doing precisely what it was meant to by being freed to speak and rile him up. The battle was getting bloody but it was coming to an end.

He would be in trouble the second it ended and he knew it. By giving himself over completely to his future self's words, by giving in to rage so deeply he was putting everyone at risk. Still, Mathghamhain knew there had to be a way to protect his people. He merely had to bring himself to go through with it, to

do what was best for all of Cridhe Aonaichte and its needs, to preserve as much as possible what he and his beloved Cacht had accomplished. He had to get away. To get to where he could deal with what was to come.

"Our Chieftain Mathghamhain…the battle is over. We have won this day, against all odds. You can lower your blade now, Chieftain. All that remains is to make sure they remember not to cross our borders again anytime soon," Caiside shouted.

The words barely reached him but they were enough. Mathghamhain realized he was hacking away at enemies that were already dead. Shaking his head he glanced around, his movements slowing. He could see even now how cautiously Caiside approached him. No, Mathghamhain thought, he had to get away before he risked killing his own men. Turning swiftly on his heel, Mathghamhain knocked flat one of his own warriors as he moved to get away from the battlefield. He had little doubt that Caiside and others would be more convinced than ever that he was possessed by the lust for battle.

"Caiside would gladly take your place, any of your warriors would be glad to see you go, they think you are mad! They will hound you, pray your weaknesses hurt you until you are too weak to stop them," the spirit shouted at him, its' voice more easily heard than usual. It sounded so much like his own now.

"Stay your vengeance fuelled hand, brave Mathghamhain. The time for battle is over, let the cowards be chased down. Be at ease now!" his reeve was cautioning, distracting him for the moment from the spirit. The concern and worry all too evident in the man's voice. "We have won this day, a final great victory over the enemy that has plagued these lands and left us all feeling threatened for well over a year now."

"A victory perhaps, but at what cost? Gather your dead, Caiside. Secure the victory for us. Let our people know of our triumph. I will see you and all who won this day in due time," Mathghamhain shouted back wanting to reassure Caiside that he was not crazed.

He looked to them all as he moved through the dead, blinking slowly. He wanted to see how many had fallen, to know at what cost it had all come, the rush of adrenaline slowing. His heart was still racing, his breathing laboured, as the full impact of the weight of swinging his sword reached him. Mathghamhain realized how weak he felt now that the battle, at last, was over, his legs no longer steady. His words to his Warriors Guild Reeve would have to suffice. He needed to deal with one last enemy to his people, to try to protect them.

As Mathghamhain walked slowly, he moved the claymore to his back once more. Finding his horse safe, he mounted it as quickly as he was able. As soon as he was settled in the saddle, he had the horse turn sharply, galloping away at full speed with him holding on dearly. The shouts of his warriors behind him questioning his leaving. Mathghamhain wanted desperately to celebrate with them this day, this hard-won victory over such a large enemy and still there were the attacks along the southern border. Mathghamhain had to trust his allies there to contend with it and route the enemy until his warriors could get there and aid them. A full victory was all but assured but he was his people's greatest enemy right now.

"You do ride away, Mathghamhain? Fleeing those who would hurt you given the chance, when you are at your weakest and most distraught? Ripe for them to overthrow in the name of aiding you," the spirit said, its voice no longer in his ear but somewhere out in the open. It was so clearly the same as his own voice now that it pained him to realize precisely how strong it had gotten.

The Priestess Fedelmid had told Mathghamhain his two choices but she had also said that he was the master of his own fate. If he died, his future self could not take his body over but no one ever said he could not control when and where he fell and was killed. Part of his rage in battle moments earlier had been in the hopes a foe would get in a lucky blow, that he would be so fatigued he would collapse and die, but he had not. Now there was but one way left if he were to defeat a future self that thirsted for blood, that sought to replace his spirit with its own. A refugee from an unknown future that was so deadly it had been killed by a member of the Priesthood and cast back in time to grow, plot, and needle him for however long it took to wear him down, to make his spirit too weak to resist it.

"You would be wrong. The only foe I need fear is myself. You will not win this day, foul spirit of my future. You did err in your plans. I will forever protect my people at whatever cost it may be," Mathghamhain growled out loud, the horse's hooves thundering hard along the terrain. The cliff they had cast the traitors remains off was starting to become visible in the distance. He simply had to go a bit further to handle this. It was so close he could feel it as the air rushed past him.

"Ah, so you are onto what we would do. The priestess filled you in on that when she did whisper sweet nothings in your ear with your wife not around to steady your hand?" the spirit responded smugly. Its hunger and power was growing even still. "Did she lie to you, did I not say she would kill us? You were a fool to ever trust her. Either of them. One did desert you, letting herself venture into battle where she could be killed, where you could not protect her. You may as well have killed her. The priestess lies, yet at every turn, you do believe her, do you not recall her power? What she showed she can do? Did she not endanger so many of your people you claim to love and adore so much, that you claim you would do anything for? You grow weak, Mathghamhain! You will be able to serve your people better if you let the one who has guided you this far have full control—to wield the command that you have."

"You would be wrong. I would serve my people better than you ever could. Do you think I have never noted your need for me to kill anyone who might possibly ever hurt me? That your bloodlust would not become noticeable?" Mathghamhain growled back. "I know your words about the priestess, that it was you who made Loegaire seem such a foe. That it was you who did drive me to quell the bloodlust of Brennus by slaying him. That you did never approve of Cacht. You lose, spirit of my future. That future can never be,

do you not yet understand that? I would never allow one so vile as you to control the future, or live."

Bringing his horse to a halt, Mathghamhain quickly set about dismounting. He was dragging his body as best he could. Now that the battle lust had worn off he felt every ache and pain in his body. His every footstep felt heavy as if he was slogging through the deepest mud.

"What can you possibly do now, Mathghamhain? Do you intend to fling yourself off a cliff? That is your grand solution? Your body would fight to survive, you are a survivor at heart, Mathghamhain!" the spirit, said its voice growing in intensity of tone. "You would find a way, broken and battered at its base, I would simply win then and heal. Then come back and you would have done it all for nothing. Accept this, Mathghamhain: We are the same person; we want the same things. To lead, to utilize power to make things better...".

"You and I are nothing alike! You thirst for power, for what it can do for you using my position. I can see it now. In your time you craved power, devoid of friends, of anyone who would trust you. Enemies at every turn," Mathghamhain hissed. "You became so content in your own ability to handle it that you were likely little more than you are now—a vile, malevolent *thing*. The sole difference now is you be freed from the physical shackles of a body. You know you cannot do anything you wish without one and so you have sought to take the only body available to you. My own! I will deny you that. For unlike you, I would honour these lands, I would protect them. I will protect my people, whatever the cost may be, and you would be wrong. There is more I can do besides casting myself off a cliff."

He was all but crawling on hand and knee towards the edge of the cliff, removing pieces of armour as he went. It made movement easier, to prepare himself for what he knew he must now do to win against a foe no one else could hear.

"And what is that, Mathghamhain…I can stop any action you take! You are too weakened now, too tired, too beaten down. You are without friends, wife, or ally to aid you," the spirit of his future self said menacingly as Mathghamhain blinked through the sweat, caused by the strain of moving, running down his face. Just a little bit further, Mathghamhain thought. "You are alone in this world, precisely as you were in my time, and we will be again when I do take your body for my own. I will free it from the last of what holds it back—your compassion still for people who have done nothing to earn it."

"You be wrong. I can. They have done everything for me. Placed their well-being in my hands. They have entrusted me with leading them to a better way of life. To bringing families together, to enriching their food, to defending them at all costs. They have supported me at every turn, pledged their lives to me and my dear departed wife. You are wrong. I do have allies and look, one comes even now into view," Mathghamhain said looking over his shoulder, the faint rumble of hoofbeats heard, although their source was too far away to be anything but a speck on the horizon.

It was enough though. Enough to distract the spirit, which did not respond right away after his comment. Time enough for Mathghamhain to push himself to his feet devoid of weapons, armour, and shield. His hand gripped the scabbard of the sword the Priestess Fedelmid had enchanted. The one that would silence the spirit. Drawing it before the spirit could speak again, he sank back to his knees.

"I know you can hear me but you cannot respond. This blade has ever been your undoing. It brings peace of mind but I cannot hold it forever. My strength deserts me even now but you did wait to strike for too long, my future self. You who are naught but a malevolent spirit, a demon come to prey on the innocent, to hurt those I would protect and I defy you," he said softly.

Turning the sword in his hands so the tip pointed inwards, Mathghamhain shut his eyes tight as he steeled himself for what came next. There was no other way, he thought.

With one final effort, he shoved it close, as far into his chest as he could, struggling as his eyes opened. Pulling up on the blade to move it slightly, once he felt the blade was all the way through his chest, Mathghamhain tugged it upward with enough remaining strength to ensure the necessary damage was done. Trying to roll his body over to the edge of the cliff as he fell, it should not be so hard, he thought. He was so close to the edge of it.

The final sight he saw in those moments was that of Nuallan coming into sight with Caiside directly behind him. His world faded to black as he heard the faint traces of their shouts to him.

He had fought his greatest foe. The malevolent spirit would not take over his body and threaten anyone again, ever. He had chosen his fate. If he could not die in battle, he would ensure he could never be taken over. The thought that he would see Cacht again in the afterlife flitting across his mind in his final seconds.

Nuallan

"Mathghamhain! My Chieftain! My liege what have you done!' Nuallan cried out seeing the man almost over the cliff's edge. He was unsure why Mathghamhain had ridden out here at all, it was so far away from everything else. There was no battlefront here to check on. This was the place where the traitors were killed. Why would he come here? His footsteps came to a dead halt as he dropped to his knees and checked with his hands over the chieftain's heart. He called over his shoulder as loudly as he could, his voice wavering in anguish as he did so. "I cannot hear it. I cannot feel it. He is unmoving. His body already grows cold, Caiside, there is so much blood…".

"What did happen here?' Caiside responded approaching him, after stopping to look close to where the chieftain's steed waited.

Casting his eyes towards his reeve, Nuallan finally noted the steady strewn line of armour cast off. He had seen bloodlust grip Mathghamhain before, not even that long ago, but never to this degree. What could have possessed his liege to do this?

"Look at his hands. He thrust the blade. By his own hand, he did run himself through. I know not why. What enemy did he face so great that he saw this as a

way out? That to conquer it, he had to die. This is no way for a warrior, a great man to die…" Nuallan answered finally, growing frantic as he spoke. Why had the spirit not helped, was it gone now too?

"We know not what anguish and grief must have gripped him Nuallan. His wife, Cacht…he did say they were as one on more than one occasion. The loss of half his heart may have been too great that he had to join her," Caiside responded, moving to kneel on the other side of Mathghamhain's body. "What did he have left? He had led us in beating back our greatest enemy, his best friend was tried and executed for treason. So much death. We cannot let others learn of this; it is no way for him to be remembered—as a man who did take his own life. Quick before his body does grow too cold, we must remove the blade."

Nodding slowly in agreement, Nuallan held his chieftain's body still while Caiside gripped the hilt of the blade. The reeve pulled as sharply as he was able after prying Mathghamhain's fingers apart from the blade and cautiously moving his arms to the side. He watched as Caiside heaved, and in one pull that likely used a great deal of the reeve's strength, freed the blade and cast it quickly over the edge of the cliff.

"It is done. We bring him, by his steed, home. He deserves…" Caiside whispered, the strain of what they were dealing with all too obvious.

"He deserves a proper funeral. Many would call him a coward for this but truly he was not one. He did so much in the face of the odds against him, even if we never know what would possess him to do this deed," Nuallan said moving to carry the body with Caiside's help towards the chieftain's steed. The horse already looking to them with large eyes.

They had barely secured the chieftain's body to the worried steed's back, its armour refitted to where possible so it would not cause Mathghamhain's body further harm. They had opted to throw the chieftain's armour off the cliff rather than bring it back. It had been a mutual decision by them both that no one else would ever wear it. It was for Mathghamhain and Mathghamhain alone. The pieces Mathghamhain still wore would be buried with him.

Nuallan knew well that Caiside, Mathghamhain's only real family, would fight for that to be the case and he would support him. The days ahead were going to be difficult in the wake of the loss of both their chieftains in such a short span of time. Cacht and Mathghamhain had unified so many villages and led so well. They had been the ones to forge the alliances, to hold it all together. Who could possibly lead as they had? Had they won a war merely for everything to still come undone?

The slow walk by horse towards Meadhan, because of what had happened, meant a detour and would take several days. They swung by where they had left the rest of the warriors to take care of any of the enemy who still were too close to the borders. It allowed those warriors the opportunity to learn firsthand of their chieftain's passing. Their heads hung low as they joined what became a growing procession behind Caiside and himself. From there they sent messengers on to each village. As they journeyed, those closer by joined the procession, weeping, and shocked to silence

at the chieftain's death so soon after Cacht's. The procession stopped briefly when the Priestess Fedelmid came into view and saw them. Dressed in blue, as she had been when at the trial, she moved to whisper a promise to him and Caiside—a promise that she would catch up with them all at Meadhan—and then wandered off.

It was approaching the fifth night and it was well and truly dark out, well past when many would be asleep, when they finally came within view of Meadhan. It had taken far longer than Nuallan would have liked but the warriors had already been exhausted. By now every village in Cridhe Aonaichte had a messenger on its way to them. The Priestess Fedelmid, true to her word, was there although dressed much more sombrely than before. She had gathered those who had taken up hiding at the temple and brought them with her.

Nuallan had little doubt that, as each village learned of this tragedy, everyone would be coming there. If so, it would easily be the most people they had ever had gathered in one place. Upon their arrival, they had word waiting for them from Caidreach. Word that their allies had routed the enemy back for the time being.

After a discussion with Caiside, it was decided that the warriors, as soon as they had rested, would head south to help ensure it stayed secure. The days ahead would certainly be full of uncertainty, Nuallan knew, but for the moment, laying their fallen chieftain to rest was the height of priority.

SIX

CHAPTER 42
Beathan

Beathan was the mere age of ten and, therefore, too young to be out here yet in the situation he now found himself. If he had been anyone else, that was. He was crouched watching intently from behind the outcropping of rocks he had found. They provided the perfect amount of coverage for the task at hand, namely allowing him to spy on the large brown bear that he, and those hunters who he had accompanied on this day, had caught sight of not all that long ago.

For the hunters, it was a chance to prove themselves in having learned their lessons on their first real outing as a group since coming of age and being assigned to the Hunters Guild. For him? It was more of the same—pressure to show what he could do. The bear had wandered close to where they had been out hunting small creatures of the grasslands, finding food with the rest of them to bring back to the closest village in Cridhe Aonaichte. In truth, he should not have even been allowed out of any village even if it was with hunters. The only reason he was? The guild's second-in-command was personally there to keep an eye on him. There were also a few experienced hunters present, serving as both teachers and aid if anything went wrong that required more experienced hands.

It was why Beathan was there. Everyone wanted to see signs that he had, indeed, inherited the skills of his father and mother. As a whole, the nearest village was overdue for a good reaping from a hunt. It was how the hunters were taught: They would train in each village and then get a practical lesson in hunting in the lands closest to it with their hunt benefiting themselves and that village. After that, the guild's second-in-command would head onto the next village with a new set of experienced hunters accompanying those being trained. On occasion, Beathan was sent along as well. It depended on what was decided he needed exposure to that day.

Despite being a good few years younger than the other boys and being neither the strongest nor the fastest amongst them, Beathan did know his way around a knife and a spear as well as any of the others. The sidelong glances so many people in the villages gave him tended to put him on edge though. He had never noticed it much when he was younger but now that he was a bit older and more aware, the looks became increasingly obvious. They were judging him. Unsure of him.

Why should they not fully trust him? Beathan was the one who lived with Chieftains Nuallan and Eluned. Before that, it had been Caiside, a cousin of his he had been told. That man had died nearly six years ago, finally succumbing to a lifetime of wounds. People everywhere whispered about Beathan. They

said he was the son of the first chieftain, Mathgham-hain—a man who had died in battle before he could recall ever seeing him.

The truth was no two people could seem to agree on when he had been born. It was upsetting at times but Caiside and Nuallan had always done their best to cheer him up. His mother had died before his father but yet people said his father must have died before Beathan was born. It made it extremely confusing but everyone was more or less agreed on his age. Their guesses all kept it to within the same year as everyone else's.

The real problem for some, which Beathan still did not understand, seemed to be an unnatural fixation on his hair and eyes. His hair was brown like nearly everyone else's for the most part. Sure it showed the occasional hint of red when the sun hit it the right way or if he was outside too long in the sun, but why was that weird? As for his eyes, why would people be so stuck on that Beathan had often wondered. Every-one's eyes were different. His just happened to be brighter than most were, a bright green at that.

"Beathan. You need to focus. Big bear…" he heard one of the older boys, Arthmael, whisper in his ear. It rousted him from his thoughts suddenly. How deeply had he been immersed in them not to notice he was being approached. Shaking his head, Beathan turned to look over his shoulder at him apologetically. Arth-mael was right, he was supposed to be paying attention, learning movements while the older boys encircled the bear and killed it. It was a chance for him to watch current strategies and make notes, learn from them, and possibly see if there were areas for improvement. They all wanted to see what he came up with, to test his mind, the Reeves had said.

His father, the great Chieftain Mathghamhain, had been said to be a brilliant strategist in both fighting and hunting, but that hunting had been his first calling. Mathghamhain had used it to move from there to the Warriors Guild, and then to unifying all the Guilds with the creation of the chieftain role and then conquering other villages. The now-massive sprawling lands, named Cridhe Aonaichte, allowed greater diversity and a chance to focus on improvements. Ones that would make life better for all rather than be solely focused on a small patch of land. How was Beathan supposed to even compete with that legacy?

"I remember. It is just…there is so much land to look out over. I began thinking too much," Beathan said by way of apology after a moment's consideration. No sense bringing up his having been distracted by thoughts on how people saw him. That would simply make it worse with these boys, who already tended to be wary of him for the special treatment he got by accompanying them at a younger age.

"Yes, well, Beathan, thinking is why you are here. You are the one who they want to see show if you have any signs of your father's knack for it. Anyway, stay focussed, I need to assist," Arthmael whispered again. Beathan watched as the boy then tried to gracefully leap over the boulder outcropping and failing as far as gracefulness went, landing face-first on the ground instead. Arthmael did seem to recover quickly enough to help the other boys in surrounding the bear from a safe distance though.

The bear was a true test. It could kill any of them with a good swipe, and yet according to what Beathan had been taught by both Caiside and Nuallan, his father had managed to kill one single-handedly as a young man. That was hard to believe and yet there were so many people who claimed it was true over the years, he was positive it had either been embellished or was, in fact, somehow true. It was yet even more added on to an already impossible legacy he had to try and live up to. It was not a thing Beathan could ever see himself capable of doing, not even when he was a bit older like the boys were.

It took a while longer, with the boys keeping the bear off guard as they circled and occasionally stabbed a spear in its legs before jumping back, sometimes falling and running back as well before the bear could strike and potentially kill them, before it got close to being frustrated. That had been when the older hunters had gotten involved and with what seemed like it had been rehearsed many times, having the boys move to an even safer distance and drawing knives to swipe at the bear if it moved too close to them, while they struck at its throat and stomach, finally bringing it down.

This was the part now where Beathan knew he was expected to take an active part. The thanking of the bear for presenting itself and allowing itself to die for the people of Cridhe Aonaichte. Several of the boys, well most of them, just went through the motions of staying silent while the Hunters Guild second-in-command said the words, their restlessness and likely lack of belief in this part being clear to him. For Beathan, the words were hypnotic, drawing him in as he stood with the other two experienced hunters, easily picking up what was said and saying the words along with them. It was as if there was a built-in innate knowledge of how important it was to honour the bear's spirit as it moved on to the afterlife, to thank the land for having this bear live on it so long and then allowing itself to be found on this day. The sudden chill of the air around him was new though.

"Beathan. Beathan. Ah, that is you, is it not? My younger self, they do not understand you, do they? I will guide you and you will become everything that your teachers hope for, to be as great as your father was. To be a true chieftain to these lands, not a mere placeholder while they wait for you to take up the mantle like Caiside and Nuallan have been. Show them the true way to be. Your father's son in all ways," a sudden hiss of a voice came from beside him. Not a voice Beathan could ever recall hearing and it was definitely at the same height as he was but older, easily from an adult, he thought. Blinking, he did his best not to look around.

He recalled overhearing the occasional whisper over the years that, in his final days, his father had gone mad. Was this what the voice he could not place referred to? Was he, like his father, meant to go mad but at an even younger age? Had he, instead of inheriting the gift for strategies and rule and everything else the people of Cridhe Aonaichte hoped for from him, that it was the madness he had really inherited? No, he could not think that way. Disembodied voice or no

disembodied voice. Beathan might have been his father's son, his mother's son, but neither was here to guide him, were they? That meant whatever he accomplished in life had to be his and his alone, not to be in his parent's shadow, but to be more than that.

A spirit. He was being talked to by a spirit that claimed to be him from the future, Beathan thought, as the full weight of the voice's words finally hit him.

Beathan looked around realizing he was being stared at. The ceremony had ended and the bear was being prepared to be carried to the nearest village. Murmurs that he had spaced out again and was daydreaming could be heard from a few of the boys as they were put to work by the two experienced hunters. The Hunters Guild's second-in-command, though, had knelt in front of him, staring with concern.

"Everything okay, Beathan? You looked a little dead there for a moment. It is over now, we are heading back to the village. You can rest there and we will send word of the hunt's success to brave and wise Chieftain Nuallan that you continue to fare well in these outings. Is it that you do not feel helpful right now? I assure you, I knew your father. He was a good man. A powerful man as I have told you before, but he also had a great deal to contend with. He, and your mother. Do not worry if you feel too pressured, you have so many years ahead of you," the second-in-command said reassuringly as Beathan blinked at him

"I am well. Just thought I heard something is all when the ceremony of thankfulness was being conducted. A whisper on the wind, but that is all it was. I just need to rest maybe. There is so much out here to take in. I just get overwhelmed, I think that is the right word," Beathan responded as he shook his head, putting the voice out of his mind, and made to follow them all to the village.

"Oh. Well, it is when we do these ceremonies that we are most in touch with the world of the spirits that are in all things the most. The whisper may have been just that—the last whisper of the bear's spirit. Caught only by you because we focussed on the ceremony itself and your peers, well, they were mostly just trying to behave and stand still. If only they had your ability to be at peace when the right time comes, and learn there is a time for action and a time for words. For you, so new to it all, not knowing what fully to expect? Your mind and senses may have been more captive to hearing those whispers. Just the last whispers of the dead, Beathan. Of that, I assure you. If you think it more, the best one to talk to is the Priestess Fedelmid. She is due to visit with Chieftain Nuallan in Meadhan soon, and we are but two villages away from there right now. One, if you want to be escorted straight there," the second-in-command said smiling lightly. The words did a little to put Beathan's mind at ease but he still remained somewhat unsure.

"Yes, I am sure you are correct," Beathan said smiling back at the second-in-command. As reassuring as the words had been, that was no whisper of a dying bear's spirit, not from what it had said. He knew who the Priestess Fedelmid was. More than that, she was said to have known his parents quite well. That and, more so than any other known member of the

Priesthood, she had been actively visiting more often than the traditional once a year. She would often provide refuge if the rains threatened to come down too hard for villagers too far afield to get home in time. She made sure no one was wed without her presence to bless it rather than scheduling all of them around an annual visit. She was lovely, with bright shimmering blond hair and green eyes, signs of those from the far north, Beathan had been taught. Everyone in Cridhe Aonaichte knew who she was. She was a priestess of the people. Yes, he might just have to ask for a private audience from her, she would surely know what to do about this voice he had heard. Surely, despite his age, he could get an audience with her as Mathghamhain's son, right?

"You cannot go to her, she only claims to be a priestess. But a priestess merely speaks for the land, does she not? Delivers blessings, serves to honour those who have just been born. She would not understand what we are. You are here by yourself from a future where we have died because others never learned to accept us. One where they were always wary of us, looking at us. Those boys back on the hunt? Do you think they will ever see you as a leader? As a person to follow when all they see so far is that you are treated differently, getting special treatment from the adults? I can teach you things you will learn in time but before you normally would. They will see how grand you can be and they will be all too happy to follow you," the voice of himself, as the spirit claimed to be, said in

Beathan's ear as he sat there in his room for the night.

Earlier, the bear had been cut up and prepared. Some of it had been eaten with dinner, the rest put aside to cure. Talk of the bear being successfully killed had been the talk of dinner in the village. The occasional glance had been sent his way. There had been words Beathan had overheard, that his mere presence as the son of Mathghamhain had been what had allowed such a grand kill. Others had dismissed it as pure coincidence or else bears would be killed at each village while Beathan was accompanying the hunters who had recently come of age.

"She is the perfect person to talk to. You could be lying. You just told me not to trust the one person who is pretty much the expert on these things. If you died and then came back to talk to me now, why would I believe anything you said would not result in the same outcome? I am better off ignoring you and doing things the way I decide to do them instead of trusting the guidance of someone who failed at being me!" Beathan growled back as menacingly as he could in response to the spirit.

He would have said more if not for the faint knocking at his door and a woman's voice Beathan was surprised he even recognized, considering this was not a village he had stayed in much. He had not stayed for long in any of the villages really. He mostly had alternated between the temple his parents had stayed in shortly before they died and Meadhan where first Caiside, and then Nuallan, with his wife Eluned, had ruled from while Beathan grew up. Moving from sitting on his bed, Beathan opened the door cautiously

and blinked. "Priestess Fedelmid! You are here. I did not expect…" he stammered.

"I saw the procession of hunters carrying the bear earlier and knowing the place bears, in particular, have in your father's history and knowing you would be with them, I was curious if anything interesting happened. The lands have led me to believe over the years, as did your father, that, well, let us sit and talk in private a moment, young Beathan. There are things you need to know despite your young age about the man who did sire you," Fedelmid said. It was soft and it sounded to him like there was sadness in her words. He was not sure he had caught any of the previous times he had seen her when she had visited with Nuallan. He was reasonably certain that she most definitely did not normally visit people in their private quarters. At least Beathan was pretty sure she did not.

"Of course, you are always welcome, Priestess Fedelmid, wise and courageous as you are…" Beathan began before pausing. "Sorry. I am not used to having to do formal greetings. Did I do it right?" he asked motioning for her to come in and looking to see if there was a chair anywhere. "What is this about my parents?"

"You did quite well, young Beathan, quite well indeed. It will become more natural in time. As for your parents," Fedelmid began, motioning for him to sit down as she entered the room. Before Beathan could locate a place for her to sit, she had taken up a seat on the floor, gathering her robes about her as she carefully did so.

"I overheard part of what you were saying aloud in

the privacy of your bedroom before I knocked and you have it right. You did dismiss a spirit, one that would have proven most malevolent. Your father had a similar situation but he chose not to say anything about it until it had deeply rooted itself in his life," the priestess said slowly. His eyes went wide at her words.

"What? So I have gone mad just as he was rumoured to have, as I did fear, is that what you did come to tell me, Priestess Fedelmid?" he asked as he sat upright to the point of leaning forward. Doing so soon after just dropping himself onto his bed after she had come in and sat on the floor was dizzying.

"You note it is no longer speaking to you? It cannot abide the presence of a member of the Priesthood if that member so wishes. As for going mad, neither you nor your father are going nor went mad. A spirit, said to be of his future self, came back and slowly corrupted him, urging him onwards in seeking blood, and dismantling the trust he had in people. Your father was, at his core, a good man, Beathan, and at least on some level always recognized that the spirit guiding him was not entirely looking out for his best interests but rather its own," Fedelmid said still watching him.

"Huh, yes, you are right, it stopped talking, and that does sound like what I was hearing from it. So I did the right thing telling it I had no interest? Will that be enough? It is just you said it had gotten too attached to my father," Beathan asked worriedly. This was stuff he had never even heard rumours of and it was fascinating to hear. Right now the priestess had become a thousand times more interesting to him than any other adult he knew just by the fact she felt he was old enough to know this stuff. Not to mention the fact that she spoke to him like he was just another adult.

"It is a good beginning not letting it get a chance to take root, but before I leave I will do what I can to protect you. I was unable to do much for your father because I learned of it too late. I could merely help him keep it at bay for short amounts of time. In the end, …you have to promise never to tell anyone else you know, okay?" the priestess replied, her voice becoming a hushed whisper as she slid slowly along the floor closer to him, her eyes making contact with his to the point that he could not bring himself to look away.

"I promise. Whatever it is you need to tell me about my father and this thing I will not tell another. You have my word as his son and as a servant of these lands and as its future chieftain." Beathan said his voice growing in confidence of tone as he spoke. He noticed it was causing her to smile.

"You did that quite well. You will make a fine Chieftain one day, Beathan. Your father, he knew he was losing against it. The war that ended shortly before you were born had claimed too much of him. It had taken his wife and fellow Chieftain Cacht away. Lost in grief and anger, he used it to help lead the people of Cridhe Aonaichte to victory finally. In so doing, he had to let the spirit drive him into a greater sense of bloodlust. As such, when the battle was won he did race away by horse as far as he could from people. He then did the only thing he could do, because as much as he had given in to what the spirit was saying, it was on the verge of taking him over and replacing the spirit of his own self with this corrupt malevolent one," the Priestess Fedelmid said pausing again as she moved to hold his face in her hands gently, still maintaining eye contact. "He took his own life, Beathan, so that he would not be corrupted and become a threat to the people he loved and had pledged to protect."

"He…killed himself…he…that…but everyone says he…" Beathan said his eyes filling with tears. He had been taught to believe his parents were great people, but his mother had died in a battle, and his father, as he had just heard, killed himself to stop from becoming an enemy to everyone. It was too much to take but the priestess was still holding him steady, so Beathan did his best to compose himself. She would not have told him if he could not handle it. She had said that. She believed him to be old enough to handle this news. He was not about to prove her wrong. It was just going to take time.

"Yes, it was known to just Caiside, Nuallan, and myself. Although neither of those two men knows what led him to it, as far as I know. That is a secret between just the two of us. I told them I would tell you when I felt you were ready, spinning it to them that as a member of the Priesthood and a woman I was better equipped to handle it. They seemed to accept that argument. Your father was a great man, Beathan, and he meant a great deal to these lands. Mathgham-hain and Cacht helped unite many villages, to do things no one else had ever attempted and they saw it through, while not losing sight of what had gone before. An uphill battle the whole way," she said before smiling. "Do not let the how of his death take away from the things he did with his life or from what you can do with yours. The fact a spirit wants to corrupt you as it did him suggests that one day you will be in a position of power it could not handle. That it wants to change things and hurt those you care about to get there. These malevolent spirits do that, they tear your life apart until you have no one left to help you, and then when you are at your weakest they take you over and cast your spirit out, taking your body for their own. You and I both already know they will fail to do that with you, do we not?"

"Oh, so does that mean Chieftain Nuallan and I can talk freely a bit more with each other now that I know how my father died? Wait! As a priestess, you can protect me and I get that and I kind of get what you are saying about all this stuff but I am going to have more questions. You will answer them, right, if I have them? Because I have always wondered…" Beathan asked noting she had let go of his face and was sitting back further while he talked.

"Yes, that is absolutely what it means. I will always be available best I can be to answer questions about the matters of spirits and in particular yours and your father's cases. What is it that you have been wondering about?" she asked quietly.

"I always hear people talking about trying to place my actual day of birth and trying to figure out when my mother would have been pregnant with me and everything. If I were to put all the different dates together, the claims of everyone would place my birth after both my parents had been killed. And I am choosing to say that is how my father died still because he was killed and it was while in a battle. That time of birth is not possible so, what I want to know is, do you know? When I was born?" Beathan asked quietly because, despite everything else the priestess had told him and as hard to really understand as it was, this was a question he had been dealing with for ages. Even if he never told anyone the answer, he would know for himself.

"Oh. Yes, I do suppose that would be a question one would have considering your upbringing. I will make you a deal, young Beathan. You have already learned so much about yourself and your parents tonight. Let us wait until tomorrow to address the answer to this one in depth. Because I do, in fact, have those answers but it is better to hear it all after you have slept. Digest what you have learned, plus I still need to weave that blessing over you to protect you more from future problems with malevolent spirits," Fedelmid said moving to her feet. "You lay down and I will get to work on that."

"I guess…" Beathan said reluctantly after a pause. He was tired and it had been a lot to take in already. Moving to lay down, he began pulling the blanket over himself as he closed his eyes "Priestess Fedelmid, thank you for treating me like I am not a child. It is good to know the truth."

"Indeed it is, young Beathan, indeed it is," the priestess smiled just barely as she began to gesture and speak under her breath. He did not hear what she said as sleep claimed him far quicker than expected, he just knew that she believed in him.

She had waited in the guest room Beathan was using until she was positive he was asleep. Years of preparation to protect him and still the boy had inherited his father's problems. Sighing softly, she exited the room slowly. There would be even greater work in the days ahead than she had told him. She had not wanted to worry him too much, Beathan just needed to be aware of the danger. If he was aware of it, perhaps since it had been caught so early on, perhaps this time it would make a difference.

She had studied with others of the Priesthood since before Mathghamhain had died, digging with them deep into what they knew. Seeking any possible answers to help the chieftain but it had not been enough. Now? Now there had been an additional ten years to study so she would be ready. She just had not expected Beathan to be affected so soon. He was so much younger than Mathghamhain had been.

Shaking her head, she turned and stared at the door. She had already made plenty of blessings directly over Beathan in the past, but additional ones would not hurt. No one else would be around right now, she thought, as she took a seat on the floor and closed her eyes. She called on the lands to bless the boy and shield him fully, to steel his mind and heart against the intrusion of malevolent spirits. To keep him strong in the face of such danger, to protect him always. To be safe from the troubles of the mind and restless thoughts.

She and her predecessor had been wrong to a

degree. The day the bear had been killed by Mathghamhain and he had given thanks, it had put his mind in touch with something else, a spirit that claimed it was him from the future. The truth Fedelmid had learned was much worse. It had burrowed deep into the mind, giving voice to all of Mathghamhain's fears, clouding his thoughts, obscuring the light of moments he would experience, skewing his memories. A disease of the mind, given a voice, one in which all the doubts that plagued him deep down became stronger and feasted upon him until he could no longer see a way to escape the darkness. Had Mathghamhain survived, she had little doubt that the man would be the same as he had been—consumed by anger and darkness, truly a threat to everything he had built. She had not been wrong. On some level, she knew Mathghamhain had been well aware of what was truly happening to him. Mathghamhain had been brave and strong and trying to fight back. He had known he did not want to become the person he would have, and it had shown in how he regarded the spirit.

The sword and the room, much like Beathan's now, had been blessed and shielded to bring contentment and ease the burdens of the mind. It had been to help Mathghamhain cope, whether the spirit was a separate thing from him or not. Being consumed by dark thoughts when trying to sleep or unwind would have made everything worse so much more quickly. She had been too late to save him, too young to realize what was going on. Now that the Priesthood as a whole was aware that such troubles could exist? They would be on guard for it in the people they looked over. Even in his suffering, Mathghamhain had brought change that would benefit so many for years to come.

Fedelmid especially would keep Beathan safe, even at the risk of losing any goodwill from the people of Cridhe Aonaichte. She would not let him suffer, no matter what it took, she would help find a way to beat this thing that plagued him. Beathan would know joy and happiness, he would find fulfillment and smile. She would do whatever it took, go wherever she had to in order to study how to achieve it.

As for Beathan's final question to her, before he had gone to sleep, she thought, well he would know the truth in full soon enough. She merely hoped he still trusted her once he learned the answer to his final question of the night.

She would be as honest as she could be with him at all times, it was the sole way she would have a true chance of helping him through the hard times ahead. She smiled but with tears in her eyes as she rose to her feet and headed to leave. She had adjusted her duties as much as she could over the years so that she was around far more throughout each year than was standard practice for her guild. It was all she could do at the time.

To everyone who met him, Beathan was the lost infant son of Mathghamhain and Cacht that the Priestess had delivered to Meadhan so that he could be raised properly. Beathan, the little bear, a gift of life, a final act of change for the lands by Mathghamhain for his people.

Through her, not only would she help protect the future ruler, but she would help him to continue to change the lands for the better—and carry on all the best parts of Mathghamhain's legacy.

Author's Note

As we learn by the end of the book, Mathghamhain dealt with his own form of mental illness. It was one that ultimately led him to believe there was no choice but to end it all. Speaking from my own experience with depression, I would urge anyone who feels suicide is the answer to please talk to a doctor. For more immediate help, please check the following link to find the national suicide hotline for your country:

    ibpf.org/resource/list-inter-
    national-suicide-hotlines

No matter how dark it might seem, there are people out there who can help. You are not alone.

Character Names

While I do use Celtic names for many of the characters, it must be acknowledged they are not based on anyone who historically had these names. In some cases, I have altered the names slightly but primarily they were chosen purposefully to reflect the nature of the characters in this book. I am by no means an expert in the Gaelic languages, despite my roots, and apologize for any errors I have made in using it.

Acknowledgements

To Michelle Dunbar at Michelle Dunbar Editing Services and Van D Vicious, you both helped immensely by providing your insights and helping me develop this book into something I could be proud of.

To Jane Barfoot and Lia Rees, my proofreader and formatter respectively. Thank you for all of your hard work and making this experience enjoyable.

To my editor Catherine Muss, you put in countless hours helping me refine this book, sharing your knowledge, and encouraging me every step of the way in making this book shine. I can not praise you enough.

To Anika Willmanns at Ravenborn Covers, your work as a cover designer never ceases to impress me. Thank you for being so awesome to work with. You are amazing.

Kelly Blanchard and Tenley Ramirez, you both deserve more than a dedication. Kelly, you have encouraged me from the very beginning as an author, refusing to let me give in to self-doubt. Tenley, I was content to let this be a book I wrote and set aside after the first draft. You pushed me to see it all the way through, to become a book that others could read.

About the Author

Born in Ontario, Canada in 1977, Daryl J Ball has spent many of his years with one feline pal or another. He developed a love for reading at a young age especially in regards to Science Fiction and Fantasy.

You can subscribe to his mailing list at eepurl.com/cPzqqr

You can also connect with him online at:

facebook.com/AuthorDarylJBall
twitter.com/DarylBallTM